SURVIVORS

SURVIVORS

CHRISTOPHER
MEYER

First published in 2023 by
Christopher Meyer, in partnership with Whitefox Publishing

www.wearewhitefox.com

Copyright © Christopher Meyer, 2023

ISBN 9781915635211
Also available as an eBook
ISBN 9781915635228

Christopher Meyer asserts the moral right to be
identified as the author of this work.

Map illustrations © Jamie Whyte, 2023

Designed and typeset by Typo•glyphix
Cover design by Simon Levy
Project management by Whitefox

To Olga and Catherine.

Author's Note

Survivors is a novel which draws its inspiration from a number of sources: my late Russian mother-in-law, Olga Iossofovna Ilyina, who, born of an aristocratic family in St Petersburg on the eve of the Russian Revolution, died at the age of 100 in 2017; her father, a Tsarist artillery officer, who, after the Revolution, fought for the Whites in the Russian Civil War and led his family into Manchurian exile; and my wife's memories of visiting Russia as a child and young woman. I have injected into the narrative some of my own experiences as a diplomat in Moscow in the 1960s and 1980s.

Christopher Meyer, 2022

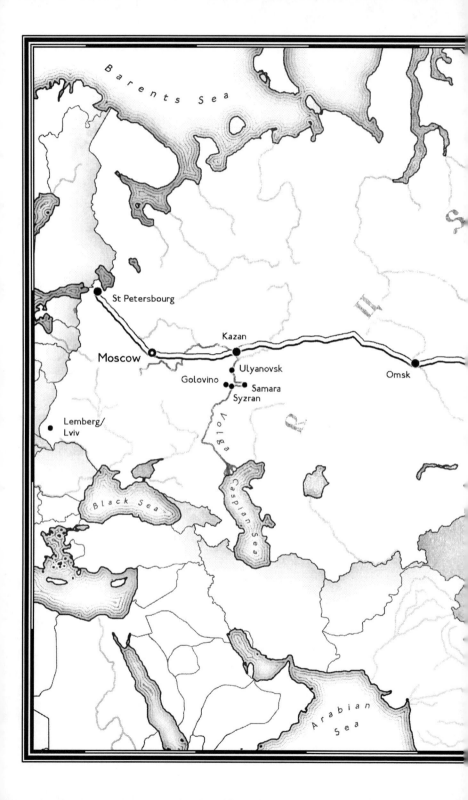

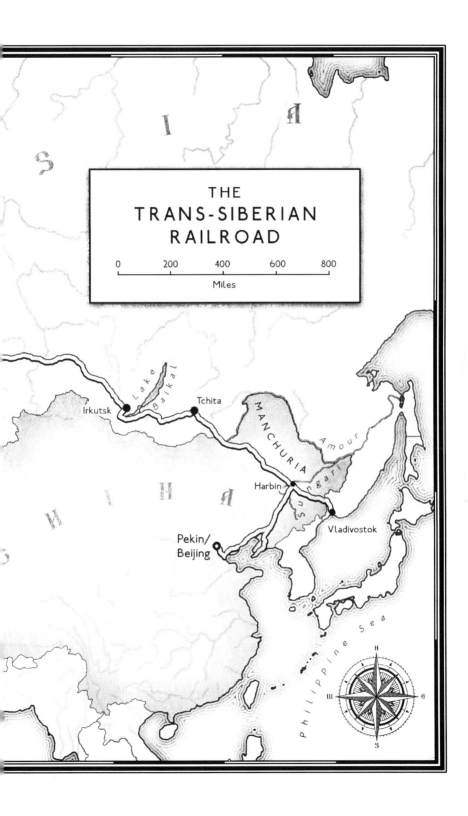

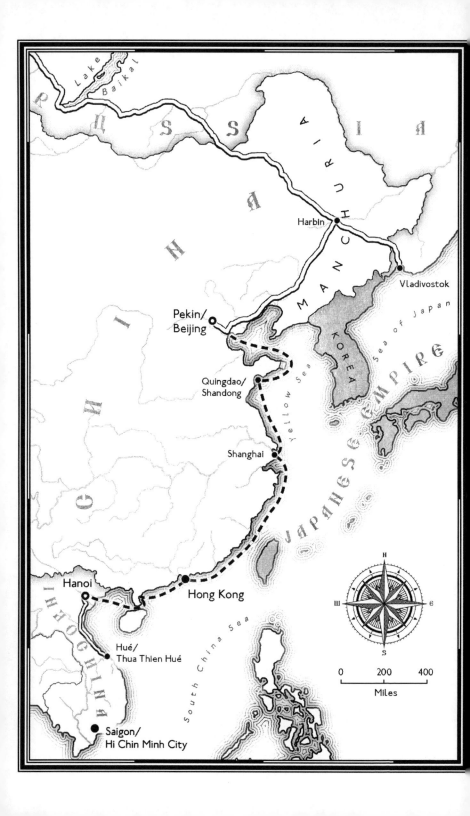

Part I

RUSSIA

Chapter I

As the Countess Ekaterina Alexandrovna Polkonina went into labour, she could hear the turmoil in the street. The maids clucked in alarm as they peered through the curtains covering the great windows, almost as tall as the room itself. With her hands clasped to her mouth, one of them kept crying out *'Gospodi! Gospodi!* My God! My God!' as the crowd surged past, heading for Palace Square in the centre of St Petersburg. Even the old wrinkly-faced midwife seemed distracted.

The air was fetid inside the bedroom of the Alexandrov palace beside the Fontanka Canal. It was where for almost two centuries Alexandrov women had given birth. Perish the thought that fresh air should be allowed into the room. The midwife, who had delivered Alexandrov babies for a good thirty years – and buried not a few – considered open windows and winter air fatal to mother and baby alike.

It was early March and spring was not far away, but St Petersburg was still in the grip of winter. The curtains were closed to keep in the warmth from the tall, ornate porcelain stove standing in one corner of the room. There was no electric light, though the family had installed the new invention on the ground floor, where the reception rooms were to be found. Candles flickered, throwing monstrous shadows on the ornate blue walls, where cornices, picked out in gold, shone and sparkled with every leap of the flames. Count Pyotr Nikolaevich Alexandrov had built the palace after the great St Petersburg fire of 1736, when the Baroque style was all the rage. The story went that Rastrelli, the Italian master himself, had designed the Alexandrov palace.

Katya was filled with dread. Facing hours of labour after a difficult pregnancy was bad enough, but to do so with the sound of revolution in her ears was almost unbearable. Fear of the world that would greet her newborn child only sharpened the pain.

She begged the midwife for more laudanum. As it began to take effect, fearful, formless hallucinations appeared before her. She drifted in and out of consciousness. Then, with a shocking suddenness, the piercing pains began again, forcing her to sit up in a violent spasm, back arched in agony. The midwife and maids rushed to help her, but none of them, not even Katya herself, was so distracted as to miss the sound of distant shooting.

*

Since the turn of the year the Polkonin family, comfortably ensconced in their elegant apartment within the palace, had smelled the city's rising discontent. It was as acrid as the smoke from the multitude of wood-burning stoves which hung in the freezing stillness of the winter's air. It took Katya back to her childhood and the frightening year of 1905, when riots and mutinies against the Tsar had swept the city. This time the menace seemed even darker. Officers from the garrison, friends of her husband Andrey, warned them to stay indoors as much as possible and never, ever, to step outside after dark. As food shortages became desperate, so did the people of St Petersburg.

The Polkonins became prisoners in their own home. Katya had yearned for the tranquillity of the family's country estate at Golovino. She had longed to spend the rest of her confinement in the winter calmness of its birch and fir trees, from which great sheets of snow would silently fall. For a few especially tense days, when there was disorder almost every night, she thought of making a mad dash to Golovino on the new railway. But it was too late. The journey was much too long and arduous for a woman of delicate health at her advanced stage of pregnancy. If the birth proved difficult, as was likely, there was a not a doctor to be had within a day's ride of Golovino. A letter arrived from her anxious husband at the Galician Front, telling her in his habitually autocratic manner to stop fretting and to stay put.

The eruption of disorder in the streets of St Petersburg early in 1917 had been a long time brewing. Almost from its outbreak three years earlier, the Great War had become an unending chronicle of military defeats at the hands of the Germans. The calamities that had befallen the Imperial Army were colossal, the casualties prodigious. With the passing of the years, the tales the servants brought back from the markets became more and more disaffected. It seemed that everyone had a son, a father, an uncle or a nephew serving on the Eastern Front. So many had perished or just disappeared. Stories of military incompetence were rife. Reports of unrest, even in the most illustrious regiments, began to circulate.

Things had only got worse when, the previous year, the Tsar himself left St Petersburg to take command of the army. He became tainted by defeat. His wife, the German-born Tsarina Alexandra Feodorovna, was suspected of either working for the enemy or engaging in an unhealthy relationship with the sinister monk Rasputin – or both.

In the absence of Andrey, while things seemed to be going well on his part of the front Katya shut out the world of military bulletins by devoting herself to literature. She read voraciously in several languages, with a special liking for novels and poetry and a weakness for the romantic idea of 'the Poet'.

Winter life with its short days and long nights was built around literary salons; they became quite the fashion in wartime St Petersburg. Women from the aristocracy and rich bourgeoisie were expected to pass their time in the cultivation of mind and soul, the latter requited by spiritualist gatherings presided over by dubious preachers in the image of Rasputin. Katya had no time for these charlatans and their séances, where inconsolable mothers and widows sought to make contact with loved ones lost in battle. Later, as the war went on and on and the casualties mounted, ladies of good breeding abandoned these pastimes and flocked to volunteer in the military hospitals that sprung up around the city like mushrooms.

Katya opened a salon of her own, attended by close friends and relatives, all women, in the Alexandrov palace's grand drawing room.

With its chandeliers lit by the novelty of electric lighting, her salon acquired sufficient reputation to attract the occasional attendance of members of the Imperial court. Once even the Grand Duchess Olga Nikolaevna, the Tsar's handsome oldest daughter, made an appearance. She was lively and talkative and seemed to relish the chance to discuss literature and poetry. But she never returned. The Tsarina, rarely seen in the Winter Palace, preferred her four daughters to stay safe with her in Tsarskoe Selo.

But Katya and her friends would continue to gather once a week, usually to meet some Russian disciple of the French Romantic poets. To add authenticity to the occasion the ladies would converse in French, a language that all members of their class were expected to speak fluently. This was no problem for Katya, who had a natural gift for languages and was perfectly comfortable in German and English as well. The poet would be invited to declaim his ersatz verses. If he was passionate and good-looking, which was sometimes the case, he would find before him a crescent of rapturous, blushing faces, who emitted discreet sighs of approval. Indeed, some of the poets offered, in whispered asides, to give private readings, from which, it was said, the occasional liaison blossomed.

Alissa, the family matriarch, did not really approve of her daughter's salon with its subversively erotic undercurrent. Since being widowed early in her marriage she had become a woman of unbending sternness. She had her own spartan living quarters in the palace from which she would emerge twice a day, for tea and supper. As far as she was concerned, the poets who appeared at Katya's salon were cowards and shirkers, who had declared themselves unfit for military service.

But mother and daughter were at one in adoring the poet Lunkov, a man of prodigious girth with a voice to match, who, riding the patriotic mood, enjoyed a *succès d'estime* in the salons of St Petersburg and Moscow. He was far too fat to be called to the colours so instead, he composed poems with a stirring martial theme. He declaimed these in a booming voice, and with much banging of his fist on an ornate eighteenth-century dresser, while perspiration streamed down his wobbling jowls. His noisy stanzas, which always included a rousing climax, set off the house dogs, retired hounds from the country estate, which would bark and howl hysterically.

Lunkov met a grotesque end. One evening, at Katya's salon, he was declaiming before an unusually large group of women a heroic poem of his own composition about the Battle of Borodino. He arrived at its stentorian climax, arms flailing and huge stomach heaving, his booming voice filling the room like the cannon fire he was describing. As he sought to render with histrionic flamboyance the mortally wounded Prince Pyotr Ivanovich Bagration, the exertion became more than his overworked heart could bear and he fell lifeless to the floor, mid-stanza. The ladies of the salon clapped vigorously for a full minute before realising in stupefied horror that they were applauding a corpse.

That was the end of Katya's salon. But in any case the city's mood was changing. After the early success of the grand offensive in 1916, the familiar pattern of disasters and defeats had set in. The gloom and pessimism were the greater for the unrealistic optimism of earlier in the year.

*

Confined to bed after giving birth, Katya dreamed of Golovino. It lay some fifteen hundred kilometres to the south-east of St Petersburg in the province of Simbirsk, not far from the Volga river, in rich, flat agricultural land. It had been in the Alexandrov family for centuries. They had a document from the time of Ivan the Terrible in the sixteenth century, confirming their ownership of the estate, including a house, the land, the village and the church within it. Alexandrov family tradition had it that they had belonged to the landed nobility for far longer, and that in the thirteenth century an ancestor had fought beside Alexander Nevsky against the Teutonic Knights in the great victory on the frozen Lake Peipus. Golovino had been his reward.

The house was now a large, rambling structure on three floors, architecturally undistinguished, an assemblage of different styles and periods, but not unpleasing to the eye. There were outhouses scattered around untidily, including stables for the dozen or so horses kept for both hunting and recreation. The house itself was comfortable and welcoming, if a little shabby and cluttered. Paintings seemed to cover every inch of wall space, hung without visible rhyme or reason. Along the entire front elevation of the house stretched a veranda, interrupted only by the imposing front door.

A long driveway led from the road to the village, ending in a spacious, circular area for carriages. There were apple, apricot and cherry orchards to the rear, a large vegetable garden to one side next to the kitchen and an attempt to create, without any apparent enthusiasm, a formal garden, with the odd statue here and there. The Alexandrovs, though they considered it unthinkable not to be able to speak French and send their finer laundry from St Petersburg to be washed and pressed in London, were no lovers of the English or French fashion for formal parks. They preferred a rougher, somewhat unkempt style, more in keeping with the authentic Russian soul.

And so, as soon as she was strong enough to leave her bed, Katya packed her bags, put her new baby Olga in a travel cot, shut up the palace and, with her older daughter Svyetlana and the household servants, set off for what she thought was the safety and peace of Golovino.

Chapter 2

German shelling was bracketing the Russians with its usual deadly efficiency, two hundred metres behind, two hundred in front. The next salvo would be in among them, blowing guns, men and horses to pieces. Andrey Andreyevich Polkonin gave the order to pull back. With practised speed, his men attached the guns to their carriages and whipped the horses to the rear. Just in time. Minutes later the shells came crashing down, canister shot designed to kill and maim.

His unit, an exhausted and bedraggled remnant of the Life Guards Second Artillery Brigade, had been retreating from the German offensive for days. Their lorries had long since given up the ghost. Even if they had been in working order, there was no fuel. It was back to horse-drawn gun carriages, as it had been for centuries. But the nags, short of feed, were in a pitiful state.

His field guns were good – 107mm and 76mm – stalwarts of the Imperial Russian Army. But German artillery was better. Throughout the war the Germans had continuously improved their field guns and howitzers. The Ministry of War in St Petersburg seemed incapable of doing the same. In the beginning Polkonin and his men could match the Germans cannonade for cannonade, sometimes even outrange them. Now, each time the army tried to make a stand, the German guns simply sat back out of range and ravaged their ranks.

He and his gunners were being steadily pushed back along the road from Sambir to Lemberg. The going was easy enough. The road, which ran through the Galician countryside, was good. It passed through frequent woods – fine for cover from German reconnaissance aircraft – and was largely flat. Occasionally they came across areas of gently rolling hills, which provided them with firing points out of sight of the enemy. But if they could not make a stand at Lemberg and the retreat continued, it would not be long before they crossed the frontier into Russia. It would then be a matter of defending the sacred soil of Holy Rus against the foreign invader.

It seemed an age since, three years before, coming from the other direction, Andrey had ridden proudly into Lemberg at the head of his regiment. Even last year, General Brusilov's great offensive had taken them deep into enemy territory and smashed the Austrian army. Then the Germans had come to the aid of the Austrians. With their better organisation and equipment, they had stopped the Russian army in its tracks.

Now it had become more like a rout. With increasing despair he had watched the disorder grow around him. But something more insidious had been draining the army's strength. Its spirit had begun to break. It was rotting from within.

Morale had always been good in the brigade. There had been a fierce pride in its battle honours which dated back to the time of Peter the Great. But the half-trained recruits sent to replace fallen veterans knew little of this. They were rapidly demoralised by the casualties, the endless retreat and the fitful supplies of food and ammunition. Even worse was the growing disaffection of the infantry, who were like an infectious swamp around them.

And then there was collapse at home. Nothing more undermines an army in the field. Thanks to the wonders of the new-fangled electric telegraph, news of disorder in St Petersburg reached the front immediately.

Andrey had learned to his dismay that women workers in the munitions factories had gone on strike, including at the Putilovsky works, where his very own artillery pieces were manufactured and repaired. Soon the women had been joined by thousands of other workers – the demonstrators Katya had described passing beneath the palace windows as she gave birth.

The police and the St Petersburg garrison had been unable to quell the disorder. Even the Preobrazhensky Regiment had mutinied. This had been utterly shocking to Andrey, worse than the abdication of that weakling the Tsar, under the thumb of his German wife. The regiment was steeped in the military traditions of Imperial Russia. There was none more illustrious than the Preobrazhensky, the equivalent of the British army's Grenadier Guards or Napoleon's Imperial Guard. The entire Russian army would be tainted by their insubordination.

They had to answer now to a so-called provisional government. Any fool could see that the army was in no state to go to war. Yet this cursed collection of crooks, chancers and anarchists under that cad Kerensky had ordered another offensive against the Austrians. Like a mortally wounded beast in its death throes, the Russian army had moved into action one last time. For a few days there was a spark of hope, an illusion of success, as the Austrians, even more ground down than the Russians, had rapidly abandoned their positions and vanished into the surrounding countryside. Then the Russian army had run into the Germans and that was that.

Anarchy was erupting everywhere. Some units were turning on their officers and shooting them. Strange figures from St Petersburg and Moscow had begun to appear among the ranks, inciting mutiny and revolution. There was an order from headquarters to shoot on sight a notorious Jewish agitator by the name of Lev Bronstein, otherwise known as Leon Trotsky. This order, like others to detain agitators, was ignored.

Andrey's own artillery brigade had continued to the bitter end to respect the old order, because the officers, like him, were tough and knew their business. But things were starting to fray around the edges. How could they not? The authority of superior officers was no longer officially recognised. The insignia of rank had been scrapped. Worst of all in wartime, the death penalty for desertion had been abolished. How could you stop men deserting without the threat of summary execution? Even with it, demoralisation had gone so deep it would have been the devil's own job to hold the men in line.

And so it proved. At first it had been only a handful of deserters a week. Now it was a steady stream. As a lieutenant-colonel, the second-in-command of his brigade, and with a reputation as a fierce disciplinarian to protect, he had no choice. Damn it, he would personally shoot any man who tried to run from the battlefield! He made sure the message reached every single soldier under his command.

But then something occurred that shook even Andrey's resolve. Just after dawn one morning, as they were resting in the cover of a thick wood, a squadron of Cossack cavalry had brought in one of his most trusted sergeants.

With the Tsar gone and their fealty to the Romanovs dissolved, most of the Cossack units had disappeared, heaven knew where – just when their horsemanship, tactical brilliance and savagery were needed. But a few units remained, screening the brigade's rear and scouting the line of retreat to ensure the Germans did not get in behind them. They had caught the sergeant and half a dozen infantrymen driving a cart eastwards on the road to Russia. The Cossacks had cut down everyone but the sergeant, because of his rank.

Sergeant Vlasov was a man he would have trusted with his life. They had fought together in every campaign since 1914. Vlasov was a leader of exemplary courage, respected by the men.

Andrey stepped out of his tent. The sergeant was standing with his captors. He looked at the familiar grizzled face with its livid scar running down one cheek, a wound received from a sabre slash in '15, when the sergeant's steady courage and leadership had saved them from the Hungarian cavalry.

They stood facing each other. The tents flapped in the brisk summer breeze. Birdsong rose from the trees. Clouds raced each other dementedly across a brilliant blue sky. Andrey registered every detail. I will not forget this day, he thought grimly.

'Untie his hands,' he ordered. 'Return to him his cap and belt.' Give the man some dignity, for pity's sake. 'Valery, in heaven's name what has got into you?' asked Andrey, overwhelmed by despair.

'Andrey Andreyevich, it is the end of our world.' The two men had campaigned together for so long that they no longer bothered with each other's ranks. There was no other non-commissioned officer in the entire army from whom he would have tolerated such familiarity.

'Our commanders are idiots and the army is bleeding to death. There is no food for the troops and, unless supplies arrive today, we will run out of ammunition tomorrow. At home our families are starving. Last month my wife buried our newborn infant, a son I have never seen. The government is rotten to the core. It's time to clean out the whole stinking shithole. I just wanted to be there when the moment came.'

The sergeant paused to calm his fury. 'It has been an honour to have served with you, Andrey Andreyevich,' he continued. 'If the generals had been like you, we would have been in Vienna by now, our boots on the throat of the Austrian Emperor. But everything we have done together, all the hardships we have endured, have been for . . . nothing.'

The sergeant's voice trailed away. His agitation was replaced by a calm detachment, almost a smile, as he looked up at a kestrel perched on a high branch.

There was a long silence between the two men. Each knew what had to happen. Andrey sighed deeply.

'Valery, you know the punishment for desertion.'

'Do what you have to do, my Colonel!' exclaimed the sergeant, now looking Andrey in the eye, erect and unblinking. For a few seconds they held each other's gaze. Then Andrey said a brief prayer. Some of the Cossacks, in their black blouses and bandoliers, crossed themselves in the Orthodox fashion. Two of them fell to their knees, their lips silently moving.

Andrey took two steps back. He removed his pistol from its holster. He stretched out his arm to its full extent. He pointed the gun at Valery's head and shot him between the eyes. The sergeant was dead before he hit the ground, flat on his back, his arms flung outwards, his knees bent. His cap rolled down the grassy slope.

'Bury him there in the sunlight and find some wood to put a cross on the grave. Then bring me his identification tag,' Andrey ordered the Cossacks.

Behind him a voice said, 'No, we will do that, Colonel.'

He turned to see four of his gunners, shovels in hand. Behind them stood his entire troop. They had seen everything, as he had intended they should. Now they looked at him, eyes filled with reproach and anger.

'Very good. Carry on. We move out within the hour,' he ordered, his voice harsh and cutting to conceal the rising emotion.

He hurried back to his tent, lay down on the canvas groundsheet and, for the first time since childhood, wept uncontrollably.

*

Andrey lay in his tent, trying to collect himself. He began to talk out loud, as one part of his soul wrestled with the other.

What else could he have done? He could not have spared the man's life. The punishment for desertion had always been death. It was the worst of military crimes. Show weakness and the whole edifice of brigades, regiments and battalions would crumble. How else could you steel men to charge the machine guns that would scythe them down like corn? He had never hesitated to shoot deserters. His stern belief in discipline and order was legendary among his men. If ever there were a moment to maintain standards, it was now, with the army on the cusp of disintegration.

But, said the other side of his soul, something had been wrong, even dishonourable about what he had done. How was he different from Sergeant Vlasov, except in having the power of life and death? He had murdered a good man, a man who had been enraged that he would never see his infant son. He thought of little Olga, as he always did at times of extreme danger and stress.

Olga – nicknamed Gulya – had been the fruit of a surprising passion. It endeared her beyond reason to his harsh, acerbic soul. He had to be honest, he had not married for love – who did these days? He needed money to restore the family estates. He wanted at least a couple of sons, of whom, God willing, one would be sufficiently talented and interested to manage the property. His family had never recovered financially from the idiotic freeing of the serfs. Their estates had fallen under a mountain of debt. He hated the idea that he, a Russian noble who could trace his line back over a thousand years, should be in thrall to Jewish bankers.

Katya's dowry had, thank the Lord, relieved the situation. Once the war was over, he would be able to dedicate himself to the restoration of his estate. Her parents had been well aware of what he was up to. There was nothing unusual about marrying for money, but they did not like him because of his harshness and his cutting tongue.

To the frustration of his autocratic soul, Katya had kept him at bay for years, although he knew she liked him. She had apparently been less bothered by his manners or poverty than by their being second cousins. He simply did not understand. It was no bar to marriage in high society: cousin was always marrying cousin. It was a positive advantage, for heaven's sake! It strengthened the ties of kinship and kept property in the family. But Katya, who always had her nose in a book, had come across some article in a learned German journal that warned of deformities in the offspring of close cousins. Stuff and nonsense!

As for his manners, he knew that she was attracted by his domineering brusqueness. He had been like that as a little boy and it had never put her off. It was a damned sight better than those spindly weeds who chased her with their effeminate poetry. Katya had made him laugh with her descriptions of hopeless suitors, whose pitiful obsequiousness made her sick to her stomach.

Once, after Katya had finally accepted his offer of marriage, they had sat down together and listed what each found the most admirable in the other. To his surprise she had said that she liked his mind. He was, she said, an unusual officer. In her experience soldiers were brainless nincompoops, who had secured entry into prestigious regiments by paying for their commissions – true enough. The closer to the court of the Tsar and Tsarina, the more brainless they seemed to be – true again.

He did think deeply about politics and the science of war. She liked it when he came round to the St Petersburg palace with a couple of his fellow officers and they would debate far into the night. These were not, she confessed, the subjects that interested her the most. She leaned towards literature and philosophy. But it was interesting to listen to the cut and thrust of enthusiastic minds.

His own list was less original. Among her attributes he included knowing her since childhood. They were comfortable in each other's presence, which boded well for the future. She was a damned fine horsewoman, almost as good as he. She was exceptionally well educated, could recite Latin poetry and spoke goodness knows how many languages. She was tall and handsome, with the broad cheekbones of a typical Slav. This had made her blush, but it pleased her to hear it. In truth she was no great beauty. But passion and sex were for the women of the demi-monde in St Petersburg, like his mistress, Tanya. Sex with a wife was more duty than pleasure, usually with the express purpose of producing an heir.

So it had been with Svyet, who had been born just before the war while he was on garrison duty outside Novgorod in northern Russia. Katya had been more enthusiastic in bed than he had expected, but she was hardly Tanya in St Petersburg.

There had been something different about little Gulya's conception, something that he had never experienced before with Katya. She had been conceived in the late summer of '16, while he was convalescing at Golovino. He would never admit it to anyone, but he had been deeply shaken by being wounded in battle. For the first time in his life he had felt afraid. His leg pained him for months. He was unable to ride. But in Golovino he felt protected and comforted, especially in the company of his wife. Katya sensed his vulnerability and responded accordingly, treating him with a tenderness that, he had to admit, moved him.

From this, Gulya had been produced, a true love child. He now felt a powerful yearning to see her. Like Sergeant Vlasov, he had to get home.

His reverie – or was it sleep? – was interrupted by shouting. He shook himself like a dog emerging from water. The time had come to move on. There was a place just to the west of Lemberg, well protected from aerial observation, where the guns could be placed and, with luck, catch the Germans by surprise. It was only two hours' ride away.

Suddenly the flap on his tent was thrown back to reveal the face of Commander Mikhail 'Misha' Dimitrovich Chazov, his second-in-command and an old friend.

'Andryusha, come quickly. We have a mutiny on our hands. The men refuse to take the guns any further and demand to go home. They say that if we try to stop them, they will shoot us.'

Chapter 3

Misha, as he was known to family and friends, was a naval commander and gunner. He and Andrey had known each other since they were teenagers, when Andrey was thinking of joining the navy and had become a naval cadet for a time.

Misha was small of stature and slight of build. His long, thin nose might have given him a slightly rattish look had his features not been redeemed by permanently twinkling eyes. He had been the gunnery officer on the cruiser *Aurora*, which was moored at the naval yard in St Petersburg when the troubles broke out. The ship's crew had mutinied, all too easily infected by a revolution which decreed that there should be no class distinction between officers and men. When the captain tried to put down the mutiny, they killed him and several other officers.

Misha had managed to jump ship disguised as an ordinary seaman and reach his uncle's estate outside St Petersburg. He found it in turmoil. The peasants, led by a local Bolshevik agitator, had seized much good farming land and had confiscated livestock and horses while his uncle, a general, was away on the Eastern Front, commanding a division. The steward, who was supposed to be looking after the estate, had thrown in his lot with the peasants.

Misha was enraged at the steward's cowardice.

'But, if I had got in their way, my lord, they would have killed me. Tell your aunt and cousins to stay put in St Petersburg. It's just too dangerous here.'

'It's no better there,' muttered Misha, almost to himself. Then more loudly, in his officer's voice, 'I need horses, two, three, if you have them. I'll pay.'

'The villagers have left us with only a few ponies,' replied the steward. 'But they are strong and fast. I should be able to find you three.'

Misha believed he had a good plan. It would take weeks, but he would try to reach the Black Sea Fleet in the Crimean port of Sevastopol. Then he had another thought. What if the fleet there was in the same state of disaffection and mutiny as the Baltic Fleet in St Petersburg and Kronstadt? His services as a gunner would be useless. More likely he would end up before a firing squad.

His mind turned to his old friend Andrey Andreyevich Polkonin. Andryusha, as Misha called him, was somewhere down on the Galician Front with his artillery brigade. He'd heard that things had not been going too well since the Germans had joined the fight. Andryusha could probably do with another gunnery officer, even from the navy. That was where he would go.

The ponies were as strong and fast as the steward had promised. After a week of hard riding to the south, in which one of the animals went lame, Misha came upon a troop train taking on water at a small junction. Three of the wagons were carrying horses for the cavalry in Galicia. With a little persuasion and a few silver roubles, he was allowed to jump aboard with his ponies.

The train stopped at the terminal in Lemberg, the last staging point before the Galician Front. Misha disembarked into a city of chaos. The roads were choked with lorries and wagons taking supplies to the front. At the same time troops were straggling in from the opposite direction, from the west, under no obvious command. Many of them were drunk. Deserters, Misha assumed, which meant things weren't going well.

He could not see an officer anywhere. There was an angry, dangerous atmosphere. His naval dress began to attract attention, much of it not entirely friendly.

'What's the navy doing here? The sea's a thousand versts away! You don't need those ponies!' A group of soldiers barred his way on the road out of Lemberg, suspicious, drunk, ready to shoot at the drop of a hat. Misha had already grasped that he was in very great danger, having finally come across the body of an officer, hanging from a lamppost.

With an ingenuity brought on by desperation, Misha replied, 'Comrades, do not delay me for a moment. I carry messages from the Soviet of Workers, Soldiers and Sailors in St Petersburg to our comrades at the front. I bring you the glorious news that the sailors of the Baltic Fleet have mutinied, overthrown their officers and taken control of the ships. Long live the Revolution!'

At this the soldiers cheered, lowered their rifles and let Misha go on his way. He was about to lash his ponies into life, when a hand gripped his reins and a pale, sardonic face, utterly sober, looked up at him.

'That was a fine speech, Comrade, though I must say that you sounded more like an officer than, shall we say, a stoker. I am Commissar Lebedev. Let me see your papers and these messages you claim to be carrying. Then we can send you on your way. Please dismount.'

The man was dressed in a grey civilian tunic, with trousers tucked into knee-high black boots. He wore a flat cap, with a red star pinned to its front. He carried a large military revolver on a belt at his waist. His hand rested on its butt. He was young, clean-shaven, cruel.

'Of course, Comrade Commissar.' Misha smiled one of his charming, carefree smiles and started to dismount. Halfway through the manoeuvre, he pulled the pony's mane violently with his left hand and kicked it hard in the flank, while his right hand clutched the reins of the other animal. Then, bent low and clinging one-handed to his own pony's neck, he sped off as fast he could. He heard the crackle of rifle fire, but the aim was so poor that no bullet came near him. Then he heard a pistol shot and simultaneously felt a huge weight on his right arm that almost pulled him from the saddle. His other pony had been hit and was falling. He let it go. Then something hit him hard in the heel of his right boot and again he heard the sound of a pistol. He stole a glance behind him. He was out of range and almost out of sight.

He rode fast until his pony began to tire. He must have put several versts between himself and the pale-faced commissar before he dismounted so that the beast could get its wind back and drink from a roadside stream. Putting his ear to the ground, he listened intently: there was no sound of approaching hooves or mechanised wheels. He stood up and again listened carefully. No evidence of pursuit. Then he examined his boot. The bullet had knocked a piece off his heel. His foot was sore and bruised, but no more than that. His heart was beating wildly. That had been too close a call. He lay down to calm himself on the grassy verge, while the pony grazed contentedly a few yards away. He slept a little. Then, waking with a start, he remounted and continued westwards.

Misha followed the sound of the guns. He passed ambulances and carts, travelling in the opposite direction, packed with wounded. Groups of deserters, sometimes on horseback, but mostly on foot, called out to him to turn round because all was lost. Once or twice he had to pull off the road to allow a rare column of ammunition lorries to pass, heading for the front.

The sound of artillery became louder and now an unbroken stream of wounded men and deserters clogged the road. Misha made his way with difficulty. Some tried forcibly to make him turn round and join the retreat. Then an artillery salvo seemed to go off in his ear, rattling his pony and making his head ring. He rounded a bend in the road, and there he found Andryusha in a clearing in the woods, four of his field guns blazing away at the enemy.

Misha dismounted and walked towards the guns. It was a boiling hot day and the gunners were stripped to the waist as they carried the heavy ammunition boxes from the wagons, each with six shells, and then went through the almost robotic motion of loading and firing. In the windless air a thick pall of acrid smoke hung over the little artillery park, making the men cough and choke. Many had tied pieces of cloth around their mouths and noses. Misha did the same as the smoke started to claw and scratch at his throat.

He peered through the smoke to see the guns' target. On the other side of a shallow valley, lines of grey-uniformed German soldiers were streaming down a hill. Through his binoculars he saw bodies on the ground. He heard the rattle of machine-gun fire from a Russian defensive position somewhere out of sight below the guns. Then there was the boom of German artillery fire from somewhere behind the opposite hill. Misha instinctively ducked, but the shells were aimed at the Russian lines below. Just as he raised his head again, Andryusha's guns fired a salvo at the approaching Germans. The fire was accurate and deadly, except for one gun which was firing too far to the right. Its gunners did not appear to notice or even to care.

As a skilled gunnery officer, Misha could not allow this to continue. With the elegant athleticism of a Mariinsky dancer, he ran, almost skipped, to the erratic gun. The sweating gunners were stunned to see in their midst this apparition in naval fatigues, who, with astonishing strength for his build, pushed the wheel round a turn or two and reset the sights. Their next shot landed plumb in the German lines. After that the gunners treated Misha as if he had shared their tents from the beginning of time. That evening he would seal the new friendship with two bottles of vodka from his saddlebag.

Meanwhile, Andrey had been storming along the line of guns, encouraging, chastising and instructing the crews in equal measure. When he reached Misha's gun, he started to roar, 'About time you layabouts got your range, you—'

He stopped abruptly, espying through the smoke the now grimy face and ever-twinkling eyes of his dear old friend.

They stood on that dusty patch in the woods, in a warm embrace, tears in their eyes, lost for words. Then Misha recovered sufficiently to blurt out, 'Reporting for duty, sir. The navy's here to save your bacon.'

With that they both laughed uproariously. The bemused gunners looked on with baffled smiles, while those close enough to hear the exchange joined the laughter till the entire unit was swept with a kind of hysteria that released their fear and tension like air from a balloon.

'How on earth did you get here? Why are you here? But thank God you are. I have hardly a gun that can shoot straight. These are good men, but they're learning on the job and that's not ideal against the finest artillery in Europe. I don't mind telling you, we're in a pretty pickle. That position beneath us won't hold. We need to move out soon before the German guns find us.'

As if on cue, a shell exploded somewhere nearby in the woods and they were showered with leaves and branches.

*

That night in the Galician woods Misha recounted his adventures. He concluded gloomily, 'Andryusha, I have no good news to bring from home. It's going from bad to worse in St Petersburg and I hear that things are no better in Moscow. It's anarchy. Dark forces are behind the disorder. I have no idea where it will all end.'

Andrey grunted. He should have been depressed, but his overwhelming emotion had been relief, bordering on joy, that he had his friend Misha – and a gunner to boot – by his side.

They sat in silence around the paraffin lamp inside Andrey's tent, drinking vodka and drawing on cigars that Misha had secreted in a saddlebag. Bugs, flies and moths, attracted by the light, died instantly on the lamp's hot glass. Finally, Andrey spoke.

'Misha, you will find those self-same dark forces at work here on the very front line. You say you don't know how this cursed revolution will end. I say I don't know how long my unit will hold together. All I do know is that if you'd agree to be my second-in-command, we may stand a chance.'

'It would be an honour, Andryusha, to be sandwiched between you, the toughest disciplinarian in the army, and a rabble of wayward gunners on the edge of mutiny,' Misha had said, laughing uproariously. 'Will the men accept a naval officer?'

'They will accept a good gunner, which you have already shown yourself to be. And perhaps together we might put off the day of reckoning.'

Chapter 4

Two weeks later, that day of reckoning had arrived. Andrey's execution of Sergeant Vlasov snapped the last remaining bonds that bound his unit together. They ignored Misha's increasingly strident order to desist and prepare to move on. He could have shot a couple of them to encourage the others, but he knew how that would have ended. There was nothing left to do but inform Andryusha.

Andrey got to his feet, drew his pistol and walked once again into the bright sunlight. Though his execution of Sergeant Vlasov would haunt him for the rest of his days, talk of mutiny had brought him sharply to his senses.

Andrey was a powerful, stocky man with a hard face, softened only by his large, luminous eyes. He affected a big moustache and a shaved head. He found it easy to intimidate. When he reached the little artillery park, the men were drawn up in a loose semi-circle in front of the guns, while several of their number were hard at work disabling them. Some of the men were sitting on the horses whose job it had been to pull the guns.

'Does anyone here have a problem with obeying an order?' Andrey asked menacingly.

His mere presence had already started to weaken the resolve of some of the men. There was a shuffling of feet. Many of them were studying their boots with unusual attention. They were a shabby, dishevelled lot, their uniforms stained and torn. Everybody was filthy with mud, their faces drawn with fatigue. Andrey knew that he did not look much better himself.

There appeared to be no leader or spokesman. Finally, one of his last remaining veterans – a close friend of Sergeant Vlasov – spoke up.

'We are sorry, Andrey Andreyevich, but this is the end of the road. We are going home. We have had enough of this bloody war. There is work to be done in Mother Russia.' There was much nodding and murmuring of assent among the men.

Something snapped inside Andrey. He, too, had reached the end of the road.

'Work? Work?' he shouted, now scarlet with rage. 'The only work to be done is to defend Mother Russia from the German armies. If we leave our posts, what stands between the Teutonic Knights and Russia's sacred soil?'

Andrey's invocation of this bloody but glorious chapter in Russian history produced more shuffling of feet and staring at the ground.

'Then let them come and suffer the fate of the Teutonic Knights,' said another mutineer, fiercely. 'We have always respected you as our commander, Andrey Andreyevich, but if you stand in our way, we will shoot you as surely as you shot Sergeant Vlasov.'

The mention of the popular sergeant stiffened the mutineers' resolve. Faces hardened. Rifles were raised and pointed at Andrey and Misha. They in turn cocked their pistols and aimed them at the mutineers. For what seemed an eternity this tableau of figures stood immobile and silent, the only sound distant flocks of geese honking their way to the nearest stretch of water.

Misha whispered, 'It's over, Andryusha. Let's face it.'

'Very well,' said Andrey loudly.

He slowly lowered his weapon, Misha likewise. So did the mutineers. The tension evaporated in an instant. A soldier stepped out of the ranks and shook Andrey's hand, wishing him God's blessing. A few others did likewise. It was all Andrey could do to maintain his dignity as tides of emotion swept through him.

Andrey and Misha, standing forlornly together, watched as the men finished spiking the guns and saddled up the horses. As they galloped away, one turned his head and shouted, 'You had better get rid of those officers' insignia. There are infantry units not far behind. They're shooting officers on sight!'

The dust thrown up by the soldiers' horses gently subsided in whorls and small clouds, thrown into sharp relief by the early morning sunlight. There was birdsong and the smell of trees and summer flowers. Butterflies and bees settled on the abandoned tents. Misha's pony and a couple of nags, which the deserters had at least left, munched happily on the grass, from time to time shaking their heads to throw off the flies around their muzzles. Could there have been a more peaceful, bucolic sight? No sooner had the thought struck Andrey than he heard the crack of a rifle shot from some way off. Had it been preceded by the whizz of a bullet? It was hard to tell with all the buzzing, flying creatures.

Misha broke their silence. 'I think that was directed at us. It came from the little hill opposite. We are very exposed here. Anyone with binoculars can see you are an officer. We should get going. Let's take the nags.'

Andrey did not resist. He had to get home to see little Gulya. He must survive to pick up and hug his baby girl.

After riding a few miles, they stopped at a stream, let the horses drink their fill and topped up their water bottles. They made a plan.

'You realise what we are. We are deserters,' said Andrey with a sardonic laugh. 'We are friendless. If the Cossacks don't get us, the Germans or the mutineers will.'

'Actually, I don't think we need worry about the Germans, so long as we don't delay too much,' said Misha, his brow furrowed in concentration. 'Now that they have broken our back, they will want to move their divisions to the Western Front. The last thing they want to do is cross the border into Russia. It would take more divisions than they have. So . . . I don't think they will advance much further than Lemberg.

'I agree,' Misha continued, 'that we might run into Cossacks. But I doubt that a proper chain of command exists any more. From what exactly are we supposed to be deserting? An army that has dissolved? I have enough silver roubles in my saddlebag to pay them off.'

'Knowing the Cossacks, they will take your money and still kill us!' Andrey interrupted, again with his sardonic chuckle. 'Better be sure our rifles and pistols are loaded and visible. I've also got a bayonet in my belt.'

'Actually, the people who worry me most are our own men,' said Misha. 'Don't forget that shot came from one of our rifles behind us. It's not just because they are deserters, it's because so many of them have been infected by this nihilism, this so-called Bolshevism. They see people like us as the enemy, to be shot on sight. You need, as our friendly mutineer told us, to get rid of all those officer insignia – cap badge, epaulettes and the like. You need to stop shaving. You need to look like a deserter. Wherever we decide to go now, we will find ourselves in the company of mutineers and revolutionaries!'

Andrey needed no persuading, though it was deeply distasteful to him to have to mutilate his uniform in this way.

'I'll take the identity of the sergeant I had to shoot for desertion. I have his tag in my pocket.' He paused. 'Do we avoid Lemberg or try to go through it? You say it's a dangerous place?'

'It is extremely dangerous,' agreed Misha, 'and almost certainly under some kind of revolutionary control. I would rather not run into that sinister, pale-faced commissar I told you about. He has a score to settle with me. But there's no avoiding Lemberg as this is where we can find a train. All horses are being requisitioned for the cavalry. They're not going to let deserters like us walk off with two nags.'

Misha stopped to think again.

'I don't know where you're going, but I need to get back to St Petersburg, to my family and our properties. I know trains run from Lemberg to Samara, and in Samara I can find a train to the north. And if I can't, I can always hitch a ride on a barge going up the Volga.'

'Then,' cried Andrey, 'we shall travel together.'

Before the war, Samara had grown into a great trading centre and regional capital on the Volga River. With its large rail junction, it had become the main staging post for the transportation of troops and their supplies to Lemberg and the Galician Front.

'From Samara it's two weeks by horse to our family estate at Golovino, where Katya and my daughters should now be. Better still, if I can find a train to Syzran, I can probably walk home in a few days.'

Andrey's mood suddenly went from one extreme to another. They had just escaped death by a whisker. He was exhilarated at the idea of going home. I am, he thought, emerging from the Slough of Despond. This was almost like an adventure. He looked at Misha, whose eyes were twinkling with a similar excitement at the thrills and spills that lay ahead.

*

Several hours later, as the sun was setting behind them, they espied the great fortress of Lemberg. It had been a tough journey, partly on horseback, partly on foot to give the horses some relief. Their euphoria had long since settled into the kind of nervous anticipation that each had always felt before a battle. In the company now of a motley collection of trudging deserters, they entered the city's suburbs along the very road where Brusilov's Eighth Army, Andrey included, had chased the Austrians out of Lemberg.

It was, thank goodness, twilight. They were stopped on a couple of occasions by patrols, which seemed interested more in discovering whether they were officers than German spies. In the dusk they passed inspection easily enough. Both Andrey and Misha coarsened their accents. They explained that they were gunners ordered to the northern front. They were told to take their exhausted, lame horses to the cavalry depot and then to report to the inspection post at the railway station.

They slept that night in a looted furniture store in a side street. They had found inside it a couple of undamaged divans. They tied up the horses outside. Both animals were now exhausted and in a pitiful state, but neither man was prepared to dispense with a mount, whatever its condition, until the last possible moment.

They awoke before dawn. They drank from a water tap in the store and chewed on stale bread that they found in a cupboard then decided to go straight to the horse depot and make for the station. With any luck the guards would not be early risers. As they led the horses through Lemberg's quiet streets, they had the impression that it was populated exclusively by snoring Russian troops, scattered on benches, pavements and in doorways, sleeping off the drink that they had doubtless consumed in vast quantities the night before.

The depot was in what had been an elegant park in the city centre. An enclosure had been set up to corral a large collection of horses and ponies of all sizes and conditions.

'God, what a bunch of broken nags,' Andrey remarked to the young corporal who had taken their horses.

'Too right, comrade,' he replied. 'But we need anything with four legs we can lay our hands on. Cavalry's no good without horses. The ones that don't recover we slaughter for meat.' The corporal, scrawny, spotty and toothless, grinned. 'Yours will fill the bellies of a platoon for a day or two.' He laughed out loud. Then, with a sharp change of expression, he looked them over in knowing fashion.

'You're off to the station, are you, like everyone else? It's no business of mine, but you'd better be careful. You can't just go in and get a ticket. Commissar Lebedev has set up his inspection post there. He's a tough 'un. He shoots anyone without the right papers. They say he has a sixth sense for officers in disguise. He shoots them as well. So your story had better be good.'

Andrey and Misha bade farewell to the corporal. A few yards on they stopped and looked at each other. Mention of Lebedev had chilled them both. Might it be better to try to find a ride on a lorry going east? Maybe they could steal fresh horses from the corral at night? Or just start walking in the hope that something would turn up? But each felt impelled by the urge to get home without delay. A train was essential. So, with rifles strapped to their shoulders and pistols prominently at their belts, they started walking towards Lemberg railway station.

Chapter 5

Another pile of blood-soaked bandages came in to be washed. Ekaterina Alexandrovna Polkonina looked at her hands. They were rough, red and swollen, despite the cotton gloves she wore for protection from the bleach and hot water. She could hardly get her rings on now.

Not that there was anyone who would really notice. Andryusha would, of course. And he would probably say something unintentionally hurtful about the state of her hands.

Where was Andryusha? Every day she expected him to turn up, wounded and broken, at their hospital in Golovino's grounds. It had started as a convalescence home for officers when the government, overwhelmed by casualties from the war, had pleaded for landowners to help. But the Revolution had swept all that away, as an endless tide of casualties turned their converted barns into a true hospital for wounds, burns and broken bones.

Men died every day. The village cemetery was filled with the graves of strangers, some with no names. Keeping the hospital clean and disinfected was a daily battle with patients, who, at the best of times, had no notion of hygiene.

The peace and safety Katya had hoped to find at Golovino had proved a mirage. It was impossible to block out news of the chaos of revolution. The hospital was a constant reminder of a war that Russia was losing badly.

But what really disturbed her were the local villagers. From time immemorial it had been a tradition that each newborn child of the landlord should be brought to the village for baptism and to be shown to the peasants. The entire village would cram into the tiny wooden church with its rough-hewn stone font. So, a few days after arriving from St Petersburg, she had taken the pony and trap and, putting Svyet and Gulya in the back, along with Madame Boujert, the French nanny, drove to the village as custom demanded.

Katya came from an aristocratic tradition that viewed the local peasantry as part of an extended family, almost as children that should be guided, nurtured and, where necessary, chastised for their sins. The senior male Alexandrov had for centuries played the role of magistrate. With the local priest, when he was sober, an Alexandrov had always guaranteed the good order and welfare of the village community.

Katya remembered playing with the village children in her summer holidays at Golovino. Once a year, after the harvest, the Alexandrovs would give a great *déjeuner sur l'herbe* for her village friends and their parents. It meant that the entire village turned up.

For Katya it had been the very best day of the year, with all kinds of races and games for the children. Everyone was in good spirits. The villagers brought gifts of cheese, bread and cured meats.

She had tried to maintain her childhood friendships into her teenage years and was always warmly welcomed in the village. Her old playmates liked to hear tales of St Petersburg – its stores, fashions and palaces – and what the Tsar and Tsarina were really like. But they were already burdened by the crushing routine of adult life. When Katya was fifteen she had noticed for the first time how hard they worked and how poor they were. Some of the older boys, with whom she used to have swimming races in the lake, were now husbands and fathers, who were regularly drunk and always fighting. The girls seemed permanently pregnant, losing one child after another to disease and the superstitions of the village midwife.

It didn't seem right, but it was, she supposed, God's will. It saddened her enormously. She realised that as an adult it would be impossible for her to bridge the gap between her own position and the abject poverty of the village.

It was a Sunday morning when she drove into Golovino. It was a typical Russian village, a modest collection of wooden huts – or *izbas*

– with little fences around them, and the odd barn. To her surprise the place seemed deserted. Could the villagers already be in the church? They must have known she was coming because she had told the household staff. Then she saw doors opening and people peering at her from inside. No one came out to greet her, as they always had in the past. She spotted her oldest friend, Maria, and called out to her. Maria gave her a little wave and then quickly closed the door to her *izba*. What was going on?

She reached the little church with its green onion dome, and went in with Gulya, leaving Madame Boujert and Svyet with the pony and cart. It was empty, except for the priest, Father Nikolai, who greeted her with a sombre, anxious face.

'We must conduct the ceremony quickly and then you must leave. It is only because you used to have friends in the village that we have been given a few minutes to baptise your child,' said the priest.

'*Used* to have friends? I still have. What in heaven is happening?'

'You no longer have anyone in the village you can count as a friend. Many have been turned against you and your family, others are afraid to be seen with you.'

She thought of Maria's look of fear.

'Even my own position is perilous,' Father Nikolai continued nervously. 'These agitators from Simbirsk believe in nothing, certainly not the church. Have you not heard about them, my lady? They preach hatred, violence and the overthrow of the established order. Three of them were here only last week, exhorting the villagers to throw off the yoke of tyranny imposed for centuries by people like your family. They encouraged the peasants to seize your land and your animals. They told them that they had as much right to these things as do you.'

The priest paused, breathing hard. Then he went on.

'At first the villagers were dubious. But then Afanasyev, the village elder, and his two brothers – drunken scoundrels of the worst kind – got up and spoke in support of these anarchists. The agitators said there would be no reprisals if the villagers seized your estate. This started to sway a lot of people.'

The priest was now sweating with the effort of telling his story. Katya was shocked by his unconcealed fear. They went quickly to the plain stone font. In accordance with the Orthodox rite, Father Nikolai took Gulya from Katya's arms and quickly immersed her, naked, in the water of the font. He muttered a few prayers, crossed himself and it was all over.

Outside, Katya found a small group of villagers had surrounded the pony and trap. Madame Boujert was shouting at them in heavily accented Russian to go away. Svyet had begun to cry. The pony, usually the most placid of beasts, was getting restless.

Afanasyev, a giant of a man, took the pony's reins in one of his enormous hands. He was dressed like a typical village elder of the Volga region, in a long, buttoned tunic which reached below his knees. He wore long, creased boots and a wide leather belt which carried a sheathed knife on one side and on the other an ugly-looking billhook. His hair was long, lank and greasy, parted in the middle.

She could smell that he and the other men had already started drinking. There were women in the group as well, white scarves over their heads, arms akimbo, eyes hard. Two of them had been maids in the big house! This, more than the foul-smelling men, almost unnerved Katya. But with her head held high, she greeted Afanasyev with the formal respect due to the village elder, passed Gulya to the nanny, whom she told in French to calm down and show some dignity, and took the reins from Afanasyev, while looking straight up into the baleful, bloodshot eyes above his bulbous, red-veined nose. Goodness knows what mischief he had intended. But some ancient reflex of subservience took control of him and he let the pony and trap go.

From then on, all communication between the house and village ceased. The maids, stable boys and ground staff, who lived in the village, stopped coming to work. She found out later that they had been threatened with death by the agitators. Her steward reported that the peasants had begun grazing their animals without permission on pastures that belonged to the house. Then some of their own animals began to disappear. At first it was just a few chickens and goats. Later most of a herd of milk cows disappeared and were eventually found on the other side of the village.

Katya wished she were back in St Petersburg. The countryside she had once so loved had become a place of brooding menace. Every evening she sat on her veranda and looked at the thick woods surrounding the house. She imagined a group of peasants, led by Afanasyev, emerging from the trees, scythes and axes in hand. She had heard stories of landowners being slaughtered by the peasants they had once trusted.

She tried hard to conceal her fears, flinging herself into her work at the hospital. This was the only place where she met some of her old friends from the village. She had hired them as orderlies – trained a couple of the women as nurses – and they were grateful for the modest pay. One of the women whispered to her outside the main ward that she and her family should save themselves and leave. There would be an attack on the house, but she didn't know when.

Katya's two sisters, Anna from St Petersburg and Lily from Moscow, and their respective husbands, Sasha and Volodya, were staying in the house and helping in the hospital. Sasha was an entomologist, tall and spindly like one of his insects, Volodya a stocky professor of medicine and anatomy.

They always gathered for dinner in the grand dining room, with its walls covered in family portraits, interspersed with the horns and heads of beasts hunted on the estate over the years. For old times' sake, Katya insisted on the best plate, crystal and silver and that everyone should dress properly. Dinner was served by the few elderly retainers remaining in the house.

For a while these had been agreeable occasions. Katya got on well with her sisters. Sasha was surprisingly interesting about his insects and their mating habits and Volodya made them laugh with stories of strange patients and their even stranger afflictions. He had proved invaluable in advising her how she should run her little hospital. But things changed for the worse as the news from the outside world grew ever darker. The agreeable dinners became an occasion for sharp disagreement. It was always the same thing. Was it more dangerous to stay or to return to St Petersburg? As time passed the debate became rancorous. Soon they were shouting at each other. Katya's response was always the same.

'Let's wait for Andryusha to return. He's a soldier, he'll know what to do.'

One day it reached an ugly climax. Sasha had just returned from a week spent with a scientist friend in some small town to the south of Golovino. The place had been in chaos, overrun with mutinous deserters. Sasha was terrified. Now convinced that the retreating army, led by murderous revolutionaries, would reach Golovino, bringing pillage and massacre in its wake, he insisted they leave immediately.

'But that's eight hundred versts away,' replied Katya. 'We don't know for sure that they're coming our way. Besides, this is a decision I refuse to take without Andryusha. I am not abandoning this house without him.'

'For God's sake, woman, can't you see? Andryusha is dead!' Sasha screamed hysterically, voicing the thought that none had dared utter. 'When did you last hear from him? Months ago. We can't risk our lives because you are clinging to a forlorn hope that he might have survived.'

Volodya quietly agreed with the panicking Sasha.

'I am sorry, Katya, but Sasha is right. Had Andryusha survived, he would have got a message to you by now. It's time for us all to leave. Even if the troops are hundreds of versts away, the villagers are just down the road and you yourself said that they may attack the house.'

'So be it if I'm ravished by soldiers or scythed by peasants. I have my duties at the hospital – as have you.' The guilty, fearful faces in front of her looked demonic in the dancing candlelight. 'As long as there's the slightest hope that Andryusha may be alive, I am staying here.' She banged her small fist so hard upon the table that the silver rattled and the glasses sang.

But it was to no avail. The house guests left two days later in the horse-drawn buggy, heading for the small town of Syzran where they could take the daily train to Samara. There they would find, they hoped, expresses to Moscow and St Petersburg. They were joined by Madame Boujert, who had had quite enough of these savage Slavs.

The villagers noticed their departure, and that Katya was now alone in the house with two babies and only a few old servants.

Chapter 6

At the very moment that Katya was bidding a tearful farewell at Syzran station to her sisters, their husbands and Madame Boujert, Andrey and Misha were looking out of the window of a train travelling from Lemberg to Voronezh in western Russia. It was slowing down as it approached its destination. There they hoped to catch a connection to Samara.

They had escaped Lemberg by the skin of their teeth. Deciding that boldness was the best strategy, they had presented themselves at the inspection point as the most desperate of mutineers, eager to serve the Revolution.

They certainly looked the part. They gambled on Commissar Lebedev not recognising Misha, who now sported an unkempt beard and straggly hair. He had long since swapped his naval fatigues for a gunner's khaki tunic. With his unshaven face Andrey gave off an air of menace, enhanced by the scowl which Misha had encouraged him to affect. They were filthy and stank to high heaven. They felt confident of their disguise as they were stopped by guards at the entrance to the enormous station, recently built in the Art Nouveau style.

'Hand in your weapons,' ordered one of the guards, who, like his companions, was probably local militia hastily recruited to maintain order. They were an unimpressive-looking bunch. Andrey fixed him with a harsh, intimidating stare.

'Try to disarm us and I'll slice your belly open. Get out of our way, you fool. We have a meeting with Commissar Lebedev.' At the mention of the name, the guards sullenly stepped aside and pointed to the station waiting room.

They pushed their way in. Even at this early hour it was packed with a snaking line of soldiers that spilled out onto the station courtyard. A large table had been placed against one of the long walls. Behind it sat a man in grey military uniform, wearing a cap with a red star. Behind him were a dozen guards with rifles, on which the traditional long bayonet of the Russian army had been fixed. Unlike the amateur bunch outside, these were seasoned soldiers. The whole tableau projected threat and menace, as no doubt it was intended to do. Andrey and Misha forced their way closer to the front of the queue, ignoring the protests of those in line.

The soldier at the head of the queue had just stepped forward, saluted not very smartly and placed his identification tag on the table. The fleshy interrogator barked, 'Name, rank, unit and destination!'

He took careful note of the answers on a piece of paper, then wrapped it around the tag and gave it to one of the guards, who took it through a frosted-glass door behind the table into what had been the women's waiting room. Voices could be heard from within. After a few minutes the guard emerged, carrying the identification tag. He whispered to the interrogator, who then returned the tag to the soldier and told him to carry on and get his ticket.

'You're one of the lucky ones,' the interrogator said with an unpleasant laugh. 'We've shot two traitors already today.' He spoke loudly so that all in the room could hear.

The next soldier, right in front of Andrey and Misha, could not keep the tremor out of his voice.

'I have lost my identification tag.'

'How come, comrade?' asked the interrogator, a disagreeable smirk on his face.

'Somewhere in the Bogdan forest, comrade,' replied the soldier, repeatedly clearing his throat. 'We were bayonet to bayonet with the Saxons and, after we withdrew, I found my tag was gone.'

'How do we know you're not a traitor – or even an officer? You have soft hands, unbroken nails and it looks like you shaved this morning. And now you tell us that you ran away from the enemy, you snivelling dog!'

'No, no,' said the soldier in desperation. 'Our officers told us to retreat. We were heavily outnumbered by the Saxons. But I skewered a couple of them with my *shtyk*. All I want to do now is to get back to my unit. Just tell me where to report. If I were a traitor, I wouldn't be here.'

The soldier turned as if to seek support from those behind him, his eyes wild with despair. Andrey noticed how young he was, sixteen at most, probably an officer cadet from one of the academies.

The interrogator prolonged the young soldier's agony by contemplating him for several moments, still smirking. The queue in the waiting room was now even longer, extending far into the courtyard where a large crowd of soldiers had gathered, faces pressed against the waiting-room window.

Suddenly the interrogator began to scribble on his piece of paper. When he finished, he once again gave it to a guard, who took it into the room behind the frosted-glass door. A few minutes later, the door was flung open and Lebedev himself strode into the waiting room. The interrogator leapt to his feet and the guards snapped to attention. The soldiers in the queue fell silent. Lebedev surveyed the room with a glacial eye and an expressionless face. Misha could not avoid an intake of breath. He and Lebedev locked eyes for a second, but Lebedev betrayed no trace of recognition.

The young soldier was shaking with fear. Lebedev addressed him in a calm, soft voice. He sounded almost friendly.

'Calm yourself. You are a soldier. Be a man. Let me ask you this. Would you do anything to serve the cause of the Revolution?'

'Anything, Comrade Commissar,' the young soldier whispered, with a flicker of hope. 'That is why I am here.'

'Then you must know that to defeat our enemies only the harshest and most implacable measures will suffice. This is no country for the weak or faint-hearted. Are you weak or faint-hearted?' Lebedev stared at the young soldier with one eyebrow slightly raised.

'No, no, Comrade Commissar!' The young soldier's voice rose to a screech.

'Well,' said Lebedev equably, 'I think you are. I smell a young officer on the run. I am never wrong. I have the instincts of a terrier down a rabbit hole.'

At this there was some laughter in the room and a shiver of high expectation.

'But you can still help our glorious cause.'

'I will do anything!' the young soldier cried, that flicker of hope not yet extinguished.

'Very well,' said Lebedev. 'I shall make an example of you to all the men in this room and outside. The feeble and the treacherous must be extinguished. Terror is a holy weapon. Let that message travel to the four corners of the Motherland.'

His voice maintained its calm equanimity. He turned to the guards and said in the same quiet tones, 'Take him out and put him to death by the bayonet.'

The young soldier fainted, crashing heavily to the floor. The interrogator grinned. Two guards dragged the condemned boy by the arms, with a third following. They stopped outside just in front of the waiting-room window. The young soldier had found his voice and was now crying piteously, 'Mama, Mama!' They pushed him to his knees. Stillness fell, in the distance the sound of puffing locomotives and rattling wagons.

Andrey and Misha saw the guards lift their arms and plunge their rifles downwards. Instinctively, they both crossed themselves. 'Make it quick,' Andrey muttered. There came a series of piercing screams, gradually fading into gurgles as the boy choked on his own blood. 'That was slow,' muttered Misha.

'Good,' said Lebedev. He turned on his heel and went back into his office behind the frosted-glass door. The guards returned, wiping their bloodied bayonets. The interrogator was still grinning as Andrey and Misha stepped forward.

They threw their identification tags on the table.

'One at a time, comrades!' the interrogator shouted. At the sight of their shabby menace, the smirk had gone replaced by a wary look.

'You take us together or not at all,' Andrey growled.

'Then you will die together if you don't show more respect. And we will take you with us, squealing like piglets on the end of our bayonets.'

There was commotion and laughter behind them. 'Do you think that after three years of killing Austrians, Hungarians, Czechs, Germans, and heaven knows who else, with our men falling like flies around us, we are afraid of death? We are not like that poor little milksop you just slaughtered.'

As he looked at the now sweating, anxious face of the interrogator, Andrey realised he was genuinely angry.

'Have you ever had six inches of shrapnel in your leg?' he began, now shouting. 'Have you ever faced at six feet a Saxon grenadier or a Hungarian lancer with murder in his eyes? Go fuck your mother!'

The room filled with applause and shouting, the hubbub bringing scores more faces to the window. Others tried to push their way in. The guards hesitated, uncertain. Things looked to be getting out of control. Suddenly the turmoil ceased. A lone pair of hands continued to applaud. They looked up. It was Lebedev. Andrey realised he had the interrogator by the throat and slowly let him go. Misha muttered, 'Calm, calm, play it calm.'

'I haven't heard such a fine speech in years,' said Lebedev, the faintest of smiles playing on his lips. 'Come into my office, if that is not too much to ask. And if you decide to bayonet me, I will not squeal like a piglet. Rather, I will manage to shoot one of you before I die, maybe the other also if you fail to stab me in the heart.'

He looked at the interrogator with contempt. 'Get on with your work. I want the rest of this room processed by the time I decide what to do with these two.'

They went into Lebedev's office. One of the guards moved to go in, too. Lebedev waved him away. He took a seat behind a vast, bare desk, on which he placed his revolver within easy reach.

'You two are good, very good. In another time I could have done with men like you. We might even have become friends.' He looked at Misha. 'What happened to my second shot? Did it hit you?'

Without missing a beat, Misha replied, 'It knocked the heel off my boot but happily missed my foot. Good shooting, though. I was riding fast and you were almost out of range.'

'Good horsemanship, too.'

Lebedev turned to Andrey.

'I would never have taken you for an officer, but for those threads on your shoulders. Shows your uniform once had epaulettes. Who is "Vlasov V.?" Is that really you?'

'No. He was one of my men. I shot him for desertion.'

'Quite right. Were you infantry?'

'No again. I'm a gunner. Life Guards Second Artillery Brigade. And if you had been under my command, I would have shot you, too, and left your corpse to the ravens.'

Lebedev raised an eyebrow and turned again to Misha.

'And you?'

'I'm a naval gunner from the *Aurora*. The mutineers stopped me doing my job. So I decided to make myself useful somewhere else. I was on my way to my friend's aid when you tried to stop me. But when I arrived, I found that there was only so much to be done when the Germans outgun you.'

'I know, I know,' said Lebedev, in a tone that suggested that the conversation had now become one between equals on the relative merits of the Russian and German armies. 'All that will change once we have a grip on things in St Petersburg. I was Preobrazhensky once, two years in the north in the slaughterhouse of the Pripet Marshes. We never recovered from Tannenberg in August '14. There was no better vantage point from which to see into the rotten heart of our system.'

From the start it had been obvious they were dealing with a former Tsarist officer, a lieutenant or a captain. No wonder he was so good at spotting officers among the refugees. It took one to catch one.

'What are you going to do with us? We need a train to Samara.' As Andrey said this, he and Misha unhooked their rifles from their shoulders and placed them in the crooks of their arms. Andrey screwed his bayonet onto his rifle barrel.

'I bet you do,' said Lebedev evenly. 'But I don't think that can happen.' His body flexed almost imperceptibly. He was coiling himself for violent action, to seize his pistol and either shoot them or take them prisoner.

Andrey and Misha, so tuned to combat, responded likewise. But that was as far as it got. Suddenly, several things happened at once. There was a thunderous explosion, the window was blown in and they were all thrown across the room. Lebedev was either dead or unconscious. His desk had been splintered in half, with one piece lying on top of him. Andrey and Misha were conscious, but lacerated by broken glass. Above them they heard the droning of aircraft: the Germans were bombing the station.

'Let's get out of here, Misha,' Andrey shouted. Retrieving their identity tags from the floor and clutching their rifles in bloodied hands, they pushed open the door into the waiting room. They were confronted by a charnel house: men wounded, dead or bleeding to death from flying glass. There was a choir of discordant groaning, interspersed with the screaming of men in agony. Their erstwhile interrogator's neck had been sliced through.

They picked their way through the bodies and ran outside. The bomb had exploded in the courtyard, leaving a crater strewn with corpses. They heard the sound of aircraft again and somewhere a machine gun rattled. Running into the station, they saw a train standing at one of the platforms. A sergeant roared at them to get on immediately. As he dragged them aboard, the train was already picking up speed, its locomotive billowing enormous clouds of smoke and steam. Just in time. Behind them bombs had demolished the station roof, the signal box and some of the track. It was a good day's work for the German *Luftstreitkräfte*.

Andrey thanked the sergeant profusely. He recognised the type. Tough, experienced, steady as a rock. The backbone of the army. Just like poor Vlasov, whom he now bitterly regretted shooting.

For a while Andrey was lost in his memories of war. Then Misha asked, 'Where does this train go?'

'Voronezh,' came the answer from the sergeant as the three of them stook in the rocking train.

'Can we get a connection to Samara?'

As if noticing for the first time their bloodied appearance, the sergeant said, 'You can't go anywhere till you get yourselves patched up. Those wounds look nasty. There's a medical station in Voronezh just across from the station, in an old church. And don't worry about getting to Samara. Trains run every day.'

'Only problem is,' said Misha, 'the commissar was about to give us our *laissez-passer* when the bomb blew everything to smithereens. We have no travel documents, just our identity tags.'

Andrey thanked heaven that Misha's brain was working faster than his. He must be suffering from concussion or something. The sergeant reached into a top pocket on his tunic and pulled out a wad of official-looking forms. 'What a comedown! A month ago, I was a fighting man as I have always been. Now I'm a clerk who gives out railway tickets. Show me your tags.'

Then, propping himself against a window, he laboriously transcribed with a pencil stub each of their ranks and names onto a form.

'Not worth a damn without an official stamp,' he said, disappearing down the corridor and returning five minutes later. He gave them both a stamped form, which authorised travel by train to Samara. It was issued in the name of the governorate of Voronezh district.

As all the compartments were filled to bursting, they lay down on the floor of the carriage corridor and tried to forget their pain. It was not till many hours later, when after innumerable stops their train crossed the frontier into Russia, that they relaxed enough finally to fall asleep.

Chapter 7

Andrey and Misha awoke on the outskirts of Voronezh. The train was slowing and the rhythm of the carriage's rocking had begun to change. It was agony to stand up. They had been badly bruised as well as cut. Though none of their cuts was in itself serious, Andrey knew the wisdom of the sergeant's warning. He had seen too many men with infected wounds.

The train stopped in the station, and a flood of men flowed out of the carriages onto the platform. It looked chaotic at first, but unlike Lemberg, there were military police in large numbers to maintain order and give directions. Men were assembled in groups of fifty and assigned to brigades, which had their rallying points in a fan formation on the station forecourt. There was no way for deserters to break through this curtain of security.

Andrey and Misha bade farewell to the sergeant. They both looked in a more desperate condition than they realised. They were directed across the road to the medical station in the large church. Nobody tried to dispossess them of their rifles, pistols or Misha's saddlebag. Their *laissez-passer* worked like magic.

The church was full of walking wounded. They presented themselves to a tough-looking matron with glasses, salt-and-pepper hair in a bun and a white uniform splashed with blood. They explained what had happened to them. She told them to go behind a screen, remove their clothing and she would herself bathe them in salt water. Andrey looked at her handsome face and well-proportioned body and suddenly, for the first time in months, felt a stirring of desire.

'This will hurt but it will help sterilise the lacerations. You also need to wash – you smell truly horrible,' she said with a ghost of a smile. 'Off you go!'

They found themselves behind a cotton curtain where a canvas pool was filling with cold water from a tap high on the wall. A pair of sweating *babushkyi* were boiling water in a great cauldron on the church stove. Andrey and Misha took off their filthy clothes and boots, shards of glass falling out of their tunics as they did so. They had taken cuts to the torso as well as to face and hands. In their birthday suits they looked a thoroughly miserable pair.

The matron swept back the curtain and turned off the tap. She then helped one of the *babushkyi* carry the cauldron and pour its boiling contents into the canvas pool. She put her arm in the water and nodded. Then she dragged a large pail towards the pool.

'One of you help me pour this into the water,' she said to the two men. 'It's the special salt that will help your wounds.' Andrey lifted the pail and dropped its contents into the water.

'Right,' said the matron briskly, 'in you go. Just sit until I tell you to get out. Try to immerse your faces in the water. If you don't like doing that, keeping splashing them all the time.'

They clambered in, swearing obscenely as the salt burned into their lacerations.

'Mind your language, this is the house of God!' the matron laughed. 'In about ten minutes the pain will reduce and you will find the experience quite pleasant. The salt will not only disinfect you but also clean you.'

As the water's warmth began to soothe him, Andrey drifted into sleep. Before long, the matron's barking broke into a hallucination about hunting boar with his dog in the woods around Golovino.

'Out you get! Please stand over there under the tap and rinse yourselves off. Then we will dry you. We have to do this carefully so as not to make the bleeding worse.'

The matron dried Andrey. 'At least you smell better,' she said, in her pleasing contralto voice. Did he imagine that she gave the towel a light flick around his genitals? He found himself starting to harden and immediately thought of boiled parsnips, the food he hated most in the world.

The *bábushka* brought underwear and the two men dressed, becoming aware that a small queue of soldiers had formed, awaiting the matron's attentions.

'This is where I must leave you,' she said, looking up at the queue. 'Irina and Elena will put iodine on your cuts to complete the disinfection. You then need to rest for an hour on one of the benches in the cemetery behind the church. After that, if you like, you can go down the road to the soup kitchen.'

'Half-naked with our rifles?' asked Misha with a grin.

The matron smiled. God and the saints, she's good-looking, thought Andrey.

'I forgot. Irina and Elena will show you where we have a pile of freshly boiled, clean uniforms. You can't wear your own unless you want gangrene. Good luck and God be with you.'

It did not take them long to find in the huge pile of boiled clothing a uniform that fitted. They chose tunics worn by corporals, a junior rank but not the lowest. They buckled on their belts, pistols still secure in their holsters. They picked up their rifles, bayonets affixed, and, with Misha also clutching his saddlebag and its few remaining silver roubles, they walked out into the warm summer sunshine. At the back of the church, as the matron had suggested, they found a bench in the large, leafy cemetery.

'We need a plan,' said Andrey.

'We do,' said Misha. 'But the situation isn't that complicated. We go and find somewhere to eat. I'm starting to get light-headed with hunger. And, after filling our bellies, we wave our *laissez-passer* and we get on the next train to Samara.'

The same thought occurred to them both. For safekeeping they had each put their precious *laissez-passer* in a buttoned tunic pocket. And the last thing they had seen on leaving the church was the two *babushkyi* throwing their old uniforms into a steaming cauldron of carbolic soap and boiling water.

'Shit!' shouted Andrey.

'No point in trying to retrieve them,' said Misha, 'they'll be pulped to nothing. Fuck, fuck, fuck!'

Exhausted and desperate with frustration, they debated what they should do. They were, in truth, still in shock after the near escape at Lemberg station. They started shouting at each other, violating the calm of the cemetery. Misha kicked a gravestone so hard with his injured leg that it began to bleed again, and he yelped with pain.

Then a calm voice insinuated itself into their seething frustration.

'*Rebyata, rebyata*, boys, boys,' the voice said, 'the Revolution needs that aggression, that fighting spirit. But I would rather you didn't waste it on a stony path, when your bayonet could be put to use against our enemies. What is the problem?'

Andrey looked up. Standing in front of them was a group of five men, in grey tunics like Lebedev's, each with a red star on his cap. It was hard to place them. They were neither soldiers nor civilians. They had no distinguishing rank, but exuded an air of confident authority. Each had a belt and holster with an army service revolver. They looked at Andrey and Misha without hostility, more in quizzical amusement. The man who had spoken was clearly their leader.

This time it was Andrey who was quicker off the mark. He knew the man behind the voice. He looked at the familiar bushy hair, full moustache and goatee beard, covering a dimpled, determined jaw. He had stared at this impressive face for at least a month, on a poster sent by headquarters to all officers in his brigade. *Lev Davidovich Bronstein, sometimes known as Leon Trotsky. To be taken dead or alive.* The poster had described Bronstein as a dangerous Bolshevik revolutionary, intent on inciting mutiny in the army. Though now resident in St Petersburg, he was suspected of being active on the Galician Front, not far from his hometown of Yanovka.

Bronstein wore a pair of spectacles attached to his nose, what the French call *pince-nez*. His piercing eyes twinkled. He was, thought Andrey, the spitting image of his Jewish philosophy professor.

'Comrade,' said Andrey in the rough voice of a common soldier, 'we were under orders to report to military headquarters in Samara, but the *babushkyi* in the first-aid post threw our uniforms into the laundry pot with our passes in them. We have only just realised.'

'Who gave you the *laissez-passer*?' asked Bronstein in his clear, precise voice.

'Commissar Lebedev in Lemberg,' Andrey replied.

'Ah, a good man, a true son of the Revolution! Seriously injured only yesterday in a German bombing raid. He has lost an eye and part of one arm. But he'll be back. The Revolution needs him!' said Bronstein, turning to his entourage, who nodded vigorously and obsequiously. This Bronstein was clearly a man of substance.

'If you survived his inspection, you must be *kosher*. Tell me more about yourselves.'

Misha took up the tale.

'Look, comrade, we have been in every campaign since the Pripet Marshes in '14. Then they switched us to the south on the Galician Front. It was all going well until we ran into the Germans. The army broke. We had no ammunition, no food, no nothing. We were being butchered by the German guns like cows in a slaughterhouse. Our generals ran away. It was every man for himself. A few officers tried to stop us, so we shot them. That's how we got these pistols and belts. Now, all we want is some food in our stomachs and to join this Revolution everyone is talking about.'

Bronstein studied Andrey and Misha. Even in their clean uniforms they must have looked a desperate pair of brigands, unkempt, unshaven, cut about the face.

Bronstein turned to his entourage.

'These are just the kind of men we need for the next stage in Samara. They look menacing enough and can join our bodyguards. They are the perfect model of the proletarian soldier, the kind we need to recruit for the Red Army we will create one day. They are protection and they are propaganda,' he said, as if he were coining a revolutionary slogan.

Again, Bronstein's entourage nodded vigorous assent. Then he turned to Andrey and Misha.

'My name is Lev Bronstein, but you will call me Trotsky. I am here on behalf of the St Petersburg Soviet of Workers, Soldiers and Sailors. You may have heard of us.'

Trotsky ratcheted up his voice by several decibels. He raised his head to look into the distance above Andrey and Misha. He put a hand on one hip, one leg in front of the other. He leaned forward.

'We are the guardians of the sacred flame of Revolution. My mission is to bring the word to the brave soldiers of the Russian army. The time has come to break the yoke of tyranny. It is the moment to sunder the chains of slavery which that fool Nikolai Romanov hung around your neck and which the traitor Kerensky refuses to remove. The Revolution will prevail. But first we must strike down the many counter-revolutionary enemies who would kill or imprison us if they could. The day is nigh when we will put them all to the bayonet.'

Trotsky paused for breath, his face flushed and sweating. It sounded to Andrey like a speech already given many times.

Trotsky turned his attention once more to Andrey and Misha.

'Meanwhile,' he continued, lowering himself into a conversational tone, 'there is much work to be accomplished. Will you do me the honour of accompanying me to Samara as my bodyguards?'

'With pleasure, comrade,' Andrey answered.

'Then report to me at six p.m. on the main station platform. You will receive new identity cards issued in the name of the St Petersburg Soviet and *laissez-passer* for the railway!' With that he turned on his heel and, followed by his entourage, walked out of the cemetery.

The two men looked at each other. The wind had picked up. The trees in the cemetery swayed in the breeze. The wind was a call to action. More than anything, it was the prospect of getting to Samara that made their blood run faster. What luck to have run into this Bronstein, or Trotsky, or whatever he was called! As his bodyguards, who could possibly stand in their way?

'But what then?' asked Misha in his diligent way. 'What if we can't slip away?'

They agreed there was no point in fretting. That was a bridge to cross when they reached Samara. They would trust to God, who so far had not let them down.

*

That evening, after a well-deserved supper at the Golden Dawn café, they found themselves in an armoured railway car speeding towards Samara. As instructed, they had made their rendezvous with Trotsky at Voronezh station. They were not alone. A dozen or so soldiers, also armed with rifles, were present. They were deserters from just about every regiment in the army. Most were privates, illiterate peasants. Some were Turkic Asians from the far-flung provinces of the old empire. Bloodthirsty-looking villains, thought Andrey, whose nanny had terrified him into submission with stories of the Mongol hordes.

One of the soldiers, Kostya, wore a sergeant's stripes and appeared to be in charge. As they were corporals, he immediately made Andrey and Misha his deputies. Kostya, who had clearly been instructed by Trotsky, issued them with new identity cards and *laissez-passer*, emblazoned with a red star. He told them each to pick from a canvas bag a *budyenovka*, the ubiquitous pointed felt hat with earflaps for the winter. These, too, were adorned with a large red star.

They had become Bolsheviks.

Chapter 8

Katya woke with a start. The old chambermaid, frightened to death, was shaking her by the shoulder.

'Wake up, my lady, wake up! There's someone at the door. Can't you hear?'

As she came to her senses, Katya heard a relentless banging at the front door. It was just after two in the morning. It could only be brigands – almost every day news arrived of another estate being plundered. Throwing on a dressing gown, she rushed downstairs to the gun room and took the big Mauser that Andryusha used for hunting boar. She had fired it once and its kick had almost broken her shoulder.

Then she heard Andryusha's hound, Stenka, baying in the hall. He was monstrous, the size of a calf, a mongrel with shaggy grey fur. There were few animals more frightening than Stenka with his fangs bared. He could run down a boar and kill it. The peasants, who were terrified of him, would cross themselves in his presence. They were convinced that at the full moon Stenka was possessed by the devil and would devour their babies if given the chance. But with the family he was gentleness personified.

In her slippers, she raced silently into the hall. From outside a harsh, croaking voice was calling her name. Stenka stopped barking and started to behave in a most curious way. He was on his hind feet, taller than her, pawing at the door and making high-pitched yipping sounds, as he used to do when he was a puppy.

Katya cocked the Mauser and pulled back the cover of the small iron grille in the front door. She pushed the rifle barrel through one of the iron squares and peered into the moonlit night. Outside she could see no mob, just the lone figure of a bearded man with a rifle on his shoulder, still croaking her name. He wore some kind of shabby uniform and a strange hat with a star on it. Was this one of those Bolsheviks who were causing mayhem in the countryside? She thought of shooting him before he could get his rifle off his shoulder. Better still, she would set Stenka on him.

The hound was now beside himself, barking, howling and squealing, scratching ever more furiously at the door with his enormous paws. She threw open the door. Stenka raced out and flung himself at the bearded figure. Man and dog fell to the ground in a heap. To her amazement, the dog set about excitedly licking the man's face, slobbering all over him, barking in a high-pitched squeak, with his front legs on the chest of the prostrate figure.

The man, laughing, cried hoarsely, 'Stenka, Stenka, my dear old faithful friend, how good to see you. Now, will you let me get up?'

Then the man looked up at Katya as she peered intently at him. The great lamp above the entrance came on. Behind her she heard the old major domo, Valentin, awoken by the noise, cry out, 'Dear God, it's the master. He has come back! I knew he would.'

And so did I, thought Katya, as surprise, joy and relief flooded through her. She helped her husband to his feet, took his hand and brought him under the lamp's golden light. The crazed Stenka was now jumping up and down in a curious rocking-horse motion, baying joyfully into the night.

Katya looked up at Andrey and cupped his bearded, scarred face in her hands.

'Yes, it is you, Andryusha, though you've done everything possible to disguise yourself!' She let out a noise that was half-sob, half-laugh. 'Thank the Lord you're back. Oh, you have no idea how much I have prayed for this moment.'

She stared at his exhausted face and could see his lips working in the effort to form words. Suddenly, she shook herself.

'What a silly fool I am! Look at those cuts! Are you hurt? Should we go straightaway to our little hospital?'

Andrey found his voice.

'No, Katyenka, I'm all right. But I could eat a hog and drink a barrel of beer. Then I would like to take a peek at the little ones. Then I want to have a bath and sleep for a week. And after that I'll tell you everything that has happened to me, and you will tell me everything that has happened to you. But first, are you and the children well?'

Stenka, uncontrollably excited, cocked his leg against a suit of armour said to have been used by a Polish ancestor in the Thirty Years' War. The old chambermaid, overcome with emotion, sat down on the stairs, muttering thanks to God. Valentin, grinning from ear to ear and looking ten years younger, proposed supper in the kitchen. Andrey greeted them both warmly. They scuttled off to prepare the food.

*

Sides of ham and beef, with a bowl of radishes, spring onions and lettuce, had appeared on the long wooden kitchen table, along with jugs of beer and *kvass*. Andrey ate and drank prodigiously and at speed. Suddenly, as he began to digest, his head slumped to his chest and he fell asleep in his chair. Katya, helped by Valentin, dragged him to the bedroom and placed him on the bed. There she undressed him, noting the small cuts and scars all over his face and body and how thin he had become.

When she peeled off his tunic, some papers fell to the floor. She peered at them. What could they mean? Who was this Vlasov? And what was this committee or council in St Petersburg? Had he been there? She would find out soon enough. She pulled a sheet over him and climbed into bed. Feeling the safety of his warm body next to hers, she instantly fell asleep.

As usual, she awoke with the dawn, but, unusually, she did not have that gnawing anxiety in the pit of her stomach. Andryusha was back. And now she wanted to hear how he had found his way from the Galician Front to Golovino dressed as a revolutionary soldier and equipped with another man's papers.

Nine hours later, he told her. Katya listened, enthralled. When he got to the part where he was standing guard over Trotsky she exclaimed, 'It's beyond belief that you were with this Trotsky in Samara!'

'There is more to come,' said Andrey, laughing. 'Perhaps we should take a break and ask Valentin to bring us some coffee.'

They settled into the comfortable chairs at the bedroom breakfast table as Valentin brought up a large pot of coffee. Andrey drank two cups before Katya had even taken a first sip.

'Misha Chazov and I . . . ' he continued, only to be immediately interrupted.

'I pray I will meet Misha Chazov one of these days.'

'You will, my love, you will. Anyway . . . ' he continued, irritated by the interruption, 'Misha Chazov and I arrived in Samara without incident along with Trotsky, his staff and the rest of the guards. But as soon as we stepped off the train, we detected something quite different from Lemberg or Voronezh. For a moment we couldn't work out what it was. Then it struck us. The revolutionaries were not in control. No one on the station platform wore a red star. For a moment, I thought I'd been transported back to the time of the Tsar. Samara was still in the hands of Kerensky's Provisional Government.

'When they saw the red stars on our caps, a detail of guards barred our way from the station, pointing rifles at us. Trotsky whispered to Kostya, who ordered us not to respond and to keep our rifles shouldered. Our papers were examined carefully. Then Trotsky really came into his own.'

'You rather admire Trotsky, don't you, Andryusha,' said Katya carefully.

'Up to a point. He knows how to lead.' This was one of the highest compliments Andrey could pay.

'Trotsky insisted to the commanding officer that he be allowed to address the soldiers we could see in the station square. He made play of his influence in St Petersburg and close links to both the Soviet and the Provisional Government, including to Kerensky himself. He was on a vital mission to boost the morale of the troops. He knew what he was talking about, he added, jabbing his finger in the officer's face, because he had just come from the front.'

Andrey rang for more coffee and continued.

'He's a silver-tongued, arrogant swine. But you've got to give it to him. The officer reluctantly gave way, calling him Boss. Trotsky seemed to like that.

'We followed Trotsky out of the station into a large, cobbled square. I tell you, Katyenka, it was quite something. The square is huge. The heat, the smell, the crowd, the brilliant sunlight – it was like walking into another world. It was market day. What a sight it was!'

'Tell me everything, Andryusha.'

'Well, around this huge square was a solid line of market stalls, selling everything under the sun. It was like St Petersburg before the war. The place was packed.

'In the centre of the square, surrounded by rifles stacked upright in little bundles, were a couple of hundred troops, stretched out on the cobbles, trying to take it easy until ordered to move. But they had no shelter, it was desperately hot and, like Misha and me, they were dripping in sweat. Their officers, who should have been sharing the hardships of their men, were lounging around in the shade of a vacant stall.

'Trotsky took all this in in an instant. His staff found a large wooden crate and placed it next to the reclining troops, some of whom were asleep. He jumped with an easy agility onto the crate, so that he was facing the troops. Kostya organised the guards into a semicircle of protection, facing outwards. But he placed Misha and me on either side of Trotsky's makeshift podium, facing the troops. We were all ordered to stand easy but with bayonets fixed.

'Trotsky began to harangue the troops. It was a longer, more florid, more impassioned version of what he had said to us at the cemetery in Voronezh. Slowly the soldiers roused themselves and began to gather round the wooden crate. Trotsky's voice, though pitched a little high, carried easily on the hot summer's air. He denounced the Provisional Government in St Petersburg, exalted the Soviet of Workers, Soldiers and Sailors and called on the troops to throw off their chains and join the Revolution.'

'But they had joined the Revolution,' Katya interjected, 'when they overthrew the Tsar.'

'That was Kerensky's revolution. Trotsky was talking about the Bolshevik revolution, his revolution. He and his ilk are Kerensky's mortal enemies.'

Katya just nodded. Andrey continued.

'By the time Trotsky had finished, most of the troops were cheering and throwing their caps in the air. They pressed forward eagerly. I think they wanted to put Trotsky on their shoulders and carry him round the square. It was only then, Katyenka, that I truly realised how formidable this man and his message was.

'Then things began to get out of control. Trotsky was in seventh heaven, bathing in the adoration of the mob. Soldiers were pulling at his tunic. His staff were starting to panic. The troops' officers came running over, pistols drawn, screaming at the men to get back in formation. Shots were fired in the air. I grabbed Trotsky by one arm, Misha by the other. He was almost reluctant to come with us. Despite the pressing crush, he shook hands with the soldiers, a true politician. He was not in the least afraid. His expression, eyes gleaming behind his glasses, was one of almost mystical exaltation.

'He said to us, "There is no need to panic. Let us return to the station calmly and with dignity."'

'So, he was brave, this Trotsky?' asked Katya.

'As cool as a cucumber.'

'Go on,' said Katya, as she filled his coffee cup from the fresh pot.

'Well, just as we started to go up the station steps, we heard the clattering of horses' hooves and a detachment of Cossack cavalry came galloping into the square. They began riding into the soldiery and subduing them with whips and the flats of their sabres. The shoppers, who had ignored Trotsky, interrupted their purchases to gape open-mouthed at the spectacle. Half a dozen of the Cossacks broke off and rode through the crowd towards us, separating Misha, me and the other guards from Trotsky and his staff. Each of us felt the sting of a Cossack whip on our shoulders. The riders dismounted right in front of us, with swords and pistols drawn. One of them, an officer, ran up the steps and bellowed, "Lev Bronstein, stay where you are! In the name of the Provisional Government, you are under arrest!"

'Kostya, brave but foolish, made to lunge with his bayonet, but was immediately cut down by a Cossack. He fell to the ground, dying instantly. The rest of the guard stood frozen in indecision and fear at the foot of the steps. "Enough!" shouted Trotsky. "No more bloodshed. Do not resist. Let them take me."

'He adopted a heroic pose at the top of the steps, one hand stretched out towards the square, the other placed on a hip. It was as if he were inviting martyrdom. The guards were told to hand over their weapons and disperse immediately, if they did not want to share Kostya's fate. They needed no encouragement. They flung their weapons to the ground and disappeared into the crowd. Then the riders remounted and, walking their horses through a sullen, subdued crowd of soldiers, they ostentatiously pulled Trotsky and his men to their fate.

'Meanwhile, Katyenka, Misha and your husband, from behind the cover of the horses' rumps, had managed to take off our *budyenovkyi* and stuff them into Misha's saddlebag. We rapidly removed our bayonets and sheathed them. We were now almost indistinguishable from the troops in the square.

'And that, dearest Katyenka, concludes the story of Commissar Lev Davidovich Bronstein, Commander Mikhail Dimitrovich Chazov and Colonel Andrey Andreyevich Polkonin and their adventures together.'

*

They sat in silence until dusk's long shadow fell across the house. The telling of the story made Andrey wonder whether it had really happened; or had it been a dream? Katya asked herself whether her husband could go through such experiences and remain the same man.

Andrey was now very tired. He had been talking for hours. But there was more to tell. Feeling the strength draining from him, Andrey was economical as he came to the final episodes of his story.

'As soon as the cavalry with their prisoners had left the square, Misha and I walked back into the station and sat in the waiting room. Once again we decided on boldness. It was packed with soldiers and civilians. The heat was suffocating. A patrol came by under a corporal and demanded to see our papers. We showed the passes that Trotsky had given us. We knew this could lead to our immediate arrest. But as the corporal fingered and stared at the passes, we both realised he was illiterate. He had no idea what a red star signified.

'He asked us where we were going, and Misha told him we were artillery, heading north to fight the Germans. He wished us luck with a sour smile and moved on.

'After a two-hour wait, a train to St Petersburg was announced. I walked with Misha, through the chaotic crowd of soldiers and civilians, who surged towards the train as it pulled into the platform. People fell over and were trampled. Many did not have tickets. We saw the ticket inspectors taking bribes from desperate travellers. But Trotsky's pass worked like magic.

'Misha leaned out of the train window. "Don't know how I'll survive without you, Andryusha," he said. Then he was gone. I returned to the waiting room with a good fifty travellers who had failed to get on the train and would have to wait several hours for the next St Petersburg express. There was supposed to be a train to Syzran within the hour.

'You know, Katya, I didn't have time to be depressed about losing Misha. The damnedest thing happened. I was sitting on this bench, thinking about the extraordinary adventures he and I had had together, when who do I see in front of me: none other than your sister, Lily, and her husband, Volodya. They didn't recognise me, thank God! That would have been the last thing I needed, to have them throwing their arms around my neck. It would have given my game away immediately. They were about to catch the Moscow express. They were talking about you – how worried they were at leaving you alone in the house with the babies. Volodya said you had the courage of ten men! It made me more anxious than you can imagine.'

'Did you never say who you were?' Katya asked.

'I did – at the very end. I could see there would be the same chaos to get on the Moscow train as there had been for St Petersburg. So I followed them to the platform. It was actually worse than the St Petersburg express. I pushed myself in front of them and told them to follow me. They had no idea who I was at first. They were terrified I was going to arrest them. I showed my Trotsky pass to the ticket inspector, telling him I was escorting an extremely important government official who had to catch the express. The inspector waved them through. Lily and Volodya looked at me in complete surprise – you should have seen their faces – and then the penny dropped. "Don't say a word," I told them. "I'm on my way to Golovino." Volodya – now there's a steady fellow – replied as if he were discussing the weather, "Katya was in good heart when we left, but, by God, she needs you." Last thing I saw, they were settling comfortably in a first-class compartment.'

'Heavens, Andryusha, what adventures, what coincidences! The twists and turns of fate! And then what happened?'

'Half an hour later the afternoon train to Syzran was announced,' Andrey continued. 'Since Syzran is a small town, there was no great rush to board. I found a seat in a third-class compartment, which I shared with a family of grain farmers. They looked at me warily at first – hardly surprising really. I must have been a terrible sight and I was armed. But soon we were deep in conversation about crops, soil and the weather. They took me half the way from Syzran to Golovino in their wagon. I walked the rest. It soon became pitch dark. I was on my last legs. I started to hallucinate. I think I slept for a while in a field. I barely had the energy to bang on our door and call your name.'

*

After he had finished his story, and Katya had recounted in great detail, over supper, everything that had happened at Golovino in his absence, they sat awhile on the veranda. The rich and varied scents of the countryside came to them on the light breezes of the night. There was the constant noise of night animals and birds from the bank of trees in the middle distance, now just a dim shape in the darkness. Katya looked at her husband. He was gazing into the night, his eyes hard.

'A penny for your thoughts,' she said.

'I'm thinking of how I shall settle accounts in the village,' he replied. Then he sat back, closed his eyes and was soon snoring.

Chapter 9

There was no doubt about it, thought Katya. He had changed. His bedside manner had always left something to be desired. But now, across the breakfast table, she faced a harsh, unyielding husband, utterly intolerant of her views. It was as if the prolonged dangers and hardships of the last months had burned away some essential part of his humanity.

They were having an argument, a bad one, the worst of their marriage. How could it be, she thought, so soon after his joyous return? Stenka, usually content to doze at their feet, had picked up the quarrelsome tone and was prowling around the table, ears flat to his head.

Without disturbing Katya, Andryusha had risen well before dawn. He had gone down to the stables with Stenka and found that, except for the ponies that pulled the house carts, all the horses had gone, including his black stallion, Molnya. He'd had the horse since it could barely stand. He had bought it at the great horse fair in Syzran, and it had grown into the best hunter he'd ever known. More than one cavalry officer had offered a fortune for him. Andrey had turned them all down. The villagers had immediately christened him 'Molnya', lightning. Now, with Molnya gone, a red mist of rage descended on Andrey.

He had found the stable boy, Goga, asleep on the straw in one of the stalls. He kicked him in the back. The boy opened his eyes, for a second uncomprehending. Then, with a look of horror, he leapt to his feet and tried to run away. Andrey seized him by the seat of his trousers and threw him to the ground.

The boy immediately began to babble. 'Don't whip me again, please!

I'm not hiding anything! There are no more horses to be taken. Only the old ponies are left. You took everything the last time!'

Goga had not recognised him, even though the boy had spent almost all his sixteen years living in the house, the orphan survivor of a typhoid epidemic that had killed half the village, including his parents and six siblings. The boy's shirt had ridden up his torso to reveal the scarlet weals of a harsh whipping.

'Calm yourself, Goga, it is your master, Polkonin. I've just returned from the war. Who took the horses and who gave you the beating?' Andrey softened his voice.

He had always liked Goga. There was something of Misha Chazov in him. Molnya, no easy horse, was like a docile donkey in his hands, but would bite or kick any of the other stable hands who tried to put a saddle on his back. Andrey trusted a man who was trusted by his dog or horse.

Goga peered into Andrey's face and then clutched his leg, weeping tears of relief. Andrey pushed him away and sat on his haunches next to the boy. Stenka's massive bulk came between them as the hound licked Goga's tears and pushed his muzzle under the boy's shirt to tend to his weals.

'What happened, Goga?'

'Master,' said Goga, collecting himself and hugging Stenka, 'they have come three times to steal the horses. Each time they have been bolder. Two days ago they took Molnya. He kicked and reared when they saddled him, so they whipped the poor beast. Then they whipped me because I tried to stop them. I said you would punish them when you came back from the fighting. So they whipped me again. They laughed at me and said you were dead.' Goga looked at the hound. 'Fortunately, Stenka was with the mistress, because he would have attacked them and they would have killed him.'

'Who, who?' interrupted Andrey impatiently.

'It was the Afanasyev brothers with two men I've never seen before. They had red stars on their caps and a strange uniform. They said that next time they would come for the mistress and the babes and that I should scarper before they burned me to death in the stables!'

As Goga, skinny but muscular, told his story, the tears stopped and a hard, angry light entered his eyes. It matched Andrey's own seething rage, glowing and bubbling inside him like molten lava.

'Goga, you did well. Help me hitch the ponies to the cart. Then go to the house and get something on those wounds before they become infected. I'm going to the village to get Molnya back and teach those Afanasyevs something they will never forget.'

Goga, who only then noticed that Andrey was carrying a rifle and the Mauser, cried out, 'Let me come with you, Master! I can shoot. I get the rabbits and partridge for the cooking pot. I never miss. You'll need another pair of eyes anyway!'

Andrey looked down at the boy, eager for the fight. Tough little fellow! Those beatings could have killed a man, let alone a child. The boy should have his revenge. And another pair of eyes would certainly be useful.

'All right, Goga. Get your rabbit gun. We'll go together. You watch my back and shoot anyone who tries to attack us. Don't hesitate. Aim for the face. It's only a peashooter but it can hurt.' Then he surveyed the stable walls and took down one of the larger whips.

They hitched the ponies, hardy little creatures, to the old wooden cart. There was a bench at the front for the driver and another at the back, on which Goga took up position. Stenka leapt aboard and refused all commands to return to the house. It was now getting light. Andrey drove at pace down the drive, the cart rocking from side to side, the axles screeching. He had his Mauser across his knees, his army rifle on his shoulder, his pistol on his belt and the ponies' reins in one hand and the whip in the other. He wore the corporal's uniform he had been given at the first-aid post in Voronezh, and the cap of a Tsarist artillery officer. He had decided to leave his beard unkempt. His face was covered in scabs from the flying glass in Lemberg. He turned to look at Goga.

'Master,' said the now smiling boy, his blond hair blowing in the wind, 'you look like Satan. You would terrify Genghis Khan himself!' Andrey guffawed. Stenka barked in his deep bass.

They clattered down the rutted country road towards the village. They had first to pass through a small wood. The air was still cool, a profusion of birdsong in the trees and the morning was dappled by the sun's early rays. What could be more peaceful? It reminded Andrey of an idyllic dawn in the Galician woods, which had been followed by a day of savage fighting and terrible casualties.

He slowed the cart to a deliberate pace as he entered the shabby hamlet. A few of the villagers were up and about. They looked in alarm at the cart and the two armed figures aboard, one a bearded ruffian in uniform, the other a flaxen-haired boy. They also saw Stenka, the hound from hell, who fed on babies. As Andrey had hoped, somebody ran ahead to warn Afanasyev, the village elder.

The first rays of the sun were touching the village as he brought the cart to a halt in the square between the little church and the Afanasyev compound. As a rich peasant – a *kulak* – and village elder, Afanasyev, with his brothers and their families, lived in a large wooden house surrounded by a high fence. Andrey reached back into the cart for the shotgun and fired both barrels into the air. The thunderous volley woke the entire village. Then, in a voice almost as loud as the shotgun blast, he called out to the village elder.

'Yury Yuryevich Afanasyev! Step out and face your master!'

Accompanied by Stenka, now on a tight leash, he jumped down from the cart, Mauser at the ready. Goga, sitting up on the cart, singing to himself, watched the villagers as they stumbled out of their wooden huts and hovels.

The three Afanasyevs emerged through the gate in the fence surrounding their compound, greasy and dishevelled from sleep, still buttoning their tunics. Behind them were two shaven-headed men, neat and tidy, in uniforms of the kind worn by Trotsky and his entourage. The expressions of all five were a mix of the quizzical and the mildly alarmed. Each man shielded his eyes with a hand as the rising sun flooded their faces. Stenka snarled and bared his teeth.

'Who in hell are you?' growled Afanasyev, his tongue thick from sleep and last night's alcohol, the brew he cooked up with his brothers behind their house.

'I am your Master and Lord, Colonel Andrey Andreyevich Polkonin, returned from the war, unhappily for you. Before the sun goes down you will return all the horses you have stolen from my stable and the herd of milk cows.' A murmur rippled through the gathering crowd. 'But, first, before all else, you will now – immediately – return to me my horse, Molnya.'

Afanasyev came close, eyeing Andrey carefully. Stenka growled and snarled. The village elder stepped back a couple of paces and exclaimed in a rasping baritone, so that the whole village could hear.

'By God, it *is* you, Polkonin. Welcome home! But, be warned, it is not the home you left. While you have been running from the Teutons, things have changed here in Mother Russia. Now it is power to the peasants and the workers, power to all those who have been trampled for centuries by the likes of you. You will not have your pastures back. You will not have your milk herd back. Above all, you will not have your Molnya back. If you are stupid enough to think of using one of those rifles, you will soon face the pitiless force of the law. May I introduce Commissar Rogov and Commissar Kislyak from Simbirsk?' As he said it, Afanasyev turned to the two shaven-headed Bolsheviks behind him, who, thumbs tucked in belts, moved forward to stand either side of Afanasyev.

The trio stood defiantly. Afanasyev, his eyes gleaming, was a good two heads taller than the Bolsheviks. Vile creature though he was, there was no doubting his courage. In contrast, the two other Afanasyev brothers were edging slowly sideways, trying to lose themselves in the crowd.

Afanasyev began to laugh, mocking and contemptuous. The two commissars started to unholster their pistols. Andrey held his Mauser in one hand, Stenka's leash in the other. The dog was straining to attack. At that moment he was not quite sure what he was going to do. The decision was taken for him by a sharp crack from behind. One of the commissars clutched his face, screaming, as the blood seeped through his fingers. Andrey spun round to see Goga reloading his smoking rabbit gun, a broad smile on his face.

'Got him in the eye. Not bad for a peashooter!' said Goga, laughing.

'Take the shotgun instead,' he ordered the boy, 'in case the crowd tries to rush us.' Goga seized the big gun with delight, reloaded it and, standing up in the cart, pointed it at the cowering villagers.

As Andrey turned to face Afanasyev, he saw that the other commissar had removed his revolver from its holster and was taking aim at Goga. Afanasyev had a long knife in his hand. Suddenly, Stenka pulled away from Andrey's grasp and in one ferocious leap knocked the commissar to the ground. In less than a minute it was all over. The man lay lifeless, his throat torn from his neck.

Afanasyev had been caught out by the speed and ferocity of the dog's attack. Now he and Stenka stood facing each other, the hound snarling and baring his bloodied fangs; Afanasyev holding his knife in front of him, ready to parry Stenka's attack. Andrey called the hound to heel. He had another fate in store for Afanasyev and his siblings. He spotted the village elder's two terrified brothers trying to slip away.

'Get back here where I can see you!' he roared. 'Stand either side of your big brother or I'll set the hound on you, too.'

Afanasyev the elder was silent now, staring at Andrey with unadulterated loathing, knife still in hand. He was joined by his brothers. Behind him the wounded commissar was crawling into the compound, leaving a trail of blood in the dust. Stenka was rumbling like a distant thunderstorm.

'Who whipped you, Goga?' Andrey asked loudly, for the benefit of the villagers.

'Afanasyev, the village elder!' shouted Goga, his youthful voice cracking.

'Who threatened to kill my wife and children, Goga?' he asked again.

'Afanasyev, the village elder!' came the reply. The crowd let out a collective gasp. The *barynia* and her babies? Surely not!

'Who, Goga, threatened to burn you to death in the stables?'

'Afanasyev, the village elder!' shouted Goga, with a strange exultation in his voice.

For the first time fear began to creep into Afanasyev's bloodshot eyes, as he sensed the crowd starting to turn against him.

Andrey aimed the Mauser at Afanasyev and shot him in both knees. The village elder let out a howl of agony as he fell to the ground, dropping the knife.

Andrey ordered the brothers to drag the bawling Afanasyev to the fence surrounding their house, strip him of his clothes and tie him with rope to the bars of the fence. This took some time. Afanasyev was a huge, heavy man. Even with his kneecaps smashed beyond repair, and in agonising pain, he fought and struggled against the fate he knew was awaiting him. His brothers, puny and fearful, needed to feel the lash of Andrey's whip to do as they had been ordered. Finally, they managed to fix him in place, his arms outstretched like a reverse Christ on the cross, his feet roped likewise to the fence, his back arched.

Andrey took his whip firmly in his right hand and lashed Afanasyev some fifty times, starting just below the giant man's neck and working down to the heels. Then he began again and again, till his uniform was black with sweat.

'Goga,' he said, panting, rivulets of sweat pouring down his face, 'your turn.'

Afanasyev's howls had long been replaced by a pitiful whimpering, alternating with hoarse cries for mercy. Goga lashed him as hard as he could, each moan and whimper giving him extra strength, till Andrey stayed his arm.

'We don't want him to die, Goga, we want him to suffer.'

Andrey turned to the villagers.

'Mark this day well, all of you. You have witnessed what happens to those who turn against God and his saints. You must choose a new village elder who will respect the natural order and not lead you to stray from the path of righteousness. If you return to me before sunset all that you have stolen, I will close the book on your crimes and we will start anew and bring in the harvest together. But if you fail, I will return tomorrow with a squadron of Cossacks and burn the village down.'

He looked around him. What he saw gave him the greatest satisfaction. Afanasyev was being untied from the fence, a quivering mess of blood. Flies were starting to feed on the dead commissar's ruined neck. The villagers stood mute in collective shock.

Andrey jumped up onto the driver's seat of the cart, taking Stenka with him. A villager broke the silence and called out, 'What do we do with the men from Simbirsk?'

'Bury them in the graveyard behind the hospital among the unknown soldiers,' Andrey replied.

'But one of them is still alive.'

'I don't care what you do with him. But he mustn't be allowed to return to Simbirsk. Perhaps feed him to the pigs,' he said, only half in jest.

'But what if the Red Stars from Simbirsk come to our village in search of them?'

'You tell them Afanasyev killed them and I punished Afanasyev. Did I not tell you? I *am* a Red Star.' With that he pulled from inside his tunic the *budyenovka* with its red star and, taking off his officer's cap, placed it on his head. There were gasps of astonishment. Then he leaned down and showed the villager the travel pass signed by Trotsky. The villager could not read, but understood the meaning of a document stamped with a red star.

Andrey called out to the villagers, 'Don't forget! All the animals to be returned and our pastures cleared by nightfall. And Molnya by noon!'

With the hound beside him and Goga in the back, Andrey lashed the ponies and drove out, leaving the villagers in a cloud of dust. It would be another day of oppressive heat, and he was glad to enter the shelter of the woods. The dawn chorus that had greeted them an hour ago had fallen silent. There was not a breath of wind to disturb the branches. A few shafts of sunlight penetrated the thickly entwined foliage. His racing heart began to calm itself. He slowed the ponies almost to walking pace, breathing in the tranquillising stillness of the silent wood.

'What's that?' Goga suddenly asked, raising his shotgun. 'I can hear hooves. Somebody's coming after us.'

Andrey brought the cart to a halt, pulled the bolt on his Mauser and turned. Stenka rushed barking to the back of the cart. Then, pitch-black and majestic, a riderless Molnya came round the bend in the track at full gallop. The huge horse stopped beside them and reared high into the air, whinnying loudly, nostrils flared. It began to paw the ground. Goga leapt from the cart onto Molnya's unsaddled back. He hugged the horse's neck, talking joyful nonsense into the creature's ears, which he tugged and pulled affectionately. Andrey stood in the cart, stroking and patting Molnya's muzzle. The stallion pushed his head ever deeper into Andrey's embrace, chewing and pulling on his tunic, all the while snorting and grunting. Stenka jumped out of the cart and raced dementedly around Molnya, barking uncontrollably.

'How's his back, Goga?' Andrey asked, thinking of the whipping Afanasyev had given the animal.

'Not too bad, Master,' said Goga. 'I wouldn't put a saddle on him for a few days. But you could ride him without one if you sit a little further forward than you usually do.'

Goga jumped off the horse back into the cart and Andrey gave him the reins. Then he in turn mounted the great stallion, seeing the whip marks. He did as Goga had suggested, riding closer to Molnya's neck, still able to guide the animal by the touch of his boots. Molnya was eager to gallop again, and it was all Andrey could do to restrain the horse by pulling on his mane.

He suddenly laughed out loud. What a sight! A senior artillery officer of the Imperial Army, dressed as a Bolshevik, riding with a teenaged boy driving a cart, both armed to the teeth and at complete ease with each other after successfully completing a dangerous mission. Goga might fill the hole in his life left by Misha Chazov. He thought it important that, after the retribution visited on the Afanasyev clan, the house should see them ride up the drive together.

As for Goga, he was in the highest heaven. He sensed his master's confidence in him. He felt like a man, not the naughty boy with *pirogi* in his pockets who was chased by the maids out of the pantry.

Katya observed the strange sight from the bedroom window. She was not surprised to see Andryusha on Molnya. She'd guessed that he had gone to get him back. But young Goga, driving the cart with the reins in one hand and a huge shotgun in the other? And Andryusha was wearing that Bolshevik uniform again. What on earth had happened?

She raced down the stairs with her light, springy step and through the great front door, out into the courtyard. Valentin and Oksana were there before her.

Andryusha was giving orders.

'Goga, please take the cart back to the stables and feed and water the ponies. Do likewise for Molnya. Take a look at his wounds and, if you think it necessary, put on some of that liniment I got from the cavalry. Keep the shotgun with you in the stables. You never know when it will come in handy. Then hurry to the kitchen and get yourself a decent breakfast.'

'Yes, Master. Thank you, Master. I had better take the whip as well and clean it up,' said Goga in a matter-of-fact voice.

'Good thinking.' Andrey handed him the bloody whip.

Katya was astonished. Here was Colonel Andrey Andreyevich Polkonin, the harsh aristocrat and firm believer in the social hierarchy, talking on almost level terms with a young peasant boy, the lowest in their domestic establishment. Her astonishment was replaced by anxiety when she saw the state of the whip that Andryusha handed Goga. What had happened in the village?

That was the question she immediately put to her husband as they sat down in canvas chairs for breakfast on the veranda.

Andrey had removed his sweat-soaked uniform, bathed, and dressed in the typical summer clothes of a nobleman or *baryn*: collarless white long-sleeved peasant shirt and black trousers tucked into black knee-high boots. Katya wore the customary long-skirted dress of a noblewoman or *barynia*, all in white.

'It was a good morning's work', he replied. 'In Goga I have found a real gem. He is brave and cool-headed beyond his years. I could have done with more like him in Galicia.'

'What do you mean, a good morning's work?' asked Katya in the brief pause that followed.

'I mean this,' said Andrey drily. 'If the house was about to be attacked from the village, I have put a stop to that. You were quite right. It was a combination of the Afanasyevs and the Bolsheviks from Simbirsk at the heart of the conspiracy. Well, the commissars are no more and Afanasyev may never recover from the whipping I gave him this morning. His brothers are cowardly drunks. The villagers are easily led. I had the strong feeling that it was much more fear of Afanasyev than belief in revolution that made them turn their backs on us. From now on we should have some peace and quiet.'

Then he gave a detailed account of the events of the morning, a story he told with a good deal of braggadocio.

Katya listened with growing distress. When he had finished, she remained silent for a while, unsure about what to say to her husband.

'So, what do you think?' he asked to break the silence. Before she could answer, Valentin interrupted them to report that the milk herd was being driven back onto the pasture behind the house.

'There,' said Andrey with a smile of satisfaction, 'what could be better? Firmness always pays.'

'But Andryusha,' she at last replied, 'firmness is one thing, murder and violence are another. You have killed one, maybe two, Bolshevik officials from Simbirsk. You have crippled, perhaps killed, the leader of a large clan whose members are not confined just to our village. The tradition of centuries will impel the Afanasyevs to seek revenge. And goodness knows what these revolutionaries will do when they find out that two of their men have disappeared in Golovino!'

Katya's anxiety got the better of her and her voice rose to a higher pitch than she would have wanted.

Andrey looked at her with baffled irritation.

'What? I have just saved the estate from destruction and ruin. I have just saved you from being raped and murdered. I have just saved our children. I have done all these things in the nick of time at risk to my own life and Goga's – and that is the only thanks I get!' His face was scarlet with rage.

What he really doesn't like, thought Katya, is that I should be criticising his judgement and character – and that I could be right. She thought for an instant of yielding, of apologising, of saying that the stress of recent months had warped her own judgement. In the early years that was exactly what she would have done – bent the knee to the duty of obedience in their marriage vows.

But it was not just Andrey who had changed after months of danger and war. So had she. The threat from the village had been constant for months. Death had been her daily companion at the hospital, and, if not death, the horror of wounds and injuries that were beyond description. Then there had been the endless demands placed on her by the running of the estate. And, if all that had not been enough, there had been the nagging dread that Andryusha would not return from the war, a fear that would, like pus from a boil, burst out into panic attacks in the middle of the night. She would rush in her nightdress to pick up and hug her sleeping babies. Their sweet smell and the soft touch of their skin would slowly calm the racing palpitation of her heart. With her worry lines and near-permanent frown she had, she knew, aged before her time. And with that had come a toughness, of which her husband was wholly unaware.

'Calm yourself, Andryusha,' she said with a sternness that surprised both of them in equal measure. 'We have to think ahead and to think clearly. This is not the Golovino you left behind. It is not the Russia you left behind. Everything has changed and, for people like us, not for the better.'

'You sound like Afanasyev,' he interrupted bitterly.

'Don't think you rebuke me by saying that, Andryusha. Afanasyev may be a brute, but he is not a stupid brute. He is cunning enough to know which way the wind is blowing. It is no accident that he has joined up with the Bolsheviks. We are supposed to be ruled by the

Provisional Government. But where is it? I am told its representatives are in Samara. But we haven't seen even a tax collector in Golovino! Apart from the Red Cross, who help out at the hospital, the only sign of government has been these so-called commissars from Simbirsk. And you and Goga may have killed them both! We will pay dearly for what you did this morning.'

She sat back, at once astonished and exhilarated by her temerity.

'Stuff and nonsense, woman,' he retorted, with angry contempt. 'These Bolsheviks may have the beating of Kerensky's government – that isn't hard to do. But once Brusilov and Kornilov get organised, the army still has enough reliable regiments to scatter these anarchists to the four winds and order will be restored. What I did in the village this morning was harsh justice, but justice nonetheless. We are nothing if the law is not upheld.'

'Well, Andryusha, you may believe that. But you have been cut off from the world. You forget that our hospital is a marketplace of information. Each week I talk to a new batch of injured officers and ordinary soldiers. They come from all along the front, from far north to far south. And if there's one thing I've learned, it's that the army itself is split down the middle between revolution and the old order. We heard only last week that General Kornilov had failed in an attempt to restore order in St Petersburg and was under arrest. As for this Trotsky you so carefully guarded' – a touch of sarcasm slipped into her voice – 'he is recruiting an army of Red Guards from your mutineers and deserters.'

Andrey realised that somehow the argument was slipping away from him. He was at a loss for words.

'Andryusha, Andryusha!' she continued, pressing her advantage, 'There is no going back to the old ways. We must adapt or die.'

This, he thought, was not the wife he had left behind. In truth, she was not speaking complete nonsense. Her story about Kornilov was news to him. Yet it had the ring of truth, since the man was a fool. And to be honest, he did not know what was going on in St Petersburg. But all that was by the by. A stand had to be taken if Russia was to be saved from the clutches of anarchy. It was a war of civilisations; and, if the Lord so decreed, he was ready to die for what was right.

'All right, Katyenka,' he said, still seething with exasperation. 'What would you have had me do this morning? Nothing?'

'No, of course not. I think you were right to go down to the village, armed to the teeth. But you should also have taken a dozen bottles of vodka with you and, instead of whipping Afanasyev to within an inch of his life, you should have invited him as the village elder to drink with you. He would not have refused because his vanity craves respect. You could have reminisced with the commissars about this Trotsky fellow, shown them the pass and told them how you protected him in Samara, and what happened to what's his name in Lemberg. You could have regaled them with tales from the front. And then, when everyone was drunk, you should have shaken hands on a deal in front of the entire village. That's what I would have done.'

She sat back in her chair, perspiring and exhausted. In six years of marriage she had never addressed her husband in this way. She waited for an explosion of choleric rage.

But, instead, Andrey fell silent. He poured himself some coffee and looked across the gardens to the line of trees beyond. After a few minutes he turned to his wife.

'Katyenka, you may be right. You probably *are* right.' He spoke quietly. 'But I cannot forgive a man who insults and threatens my wife and children, who steals my favourite horse. And after what I have witnessed in the last few weeks, I loathe these Bolsheviks to the depths of my soul. I cannot help myself. This is the man I am. I cannot change.'

He reached across the table and took his wife's hand.

Chapter 10

The waters closed over the incident of Afanasyev and the commissars. Whatever the tensions beneath the surface – and there were many – these took second place to the harvest, which, with the arrival of late summer, had to be brought in.

The Alexandrovs had fields of their own, separate from the peasants' holdings, which they paid the villagers to work. The villagers liked the feel of coin in their hands at the end of every week. This land was the relic of the demesne, which under the old feudal system the lord had retained for his personal use.

Andrey enjoyed rising before dawn to scythe and gather the crops. He enjoyed working the long back-breaking days with the peasants, who soon forgot his presence. He enjoyed listening to their conversations, which told him much about village life. He enjoyed coming home at sunset, soaking in a bath and having dinner with Katyenka. He enjoyed sleeping like a babe afterwards. He enjoyed his bowl of *kasha* by candlelight in the kitchen the next morning, with Stenka pushing and nuzzling his shoulder. He enjoyed the first sniff of the early morning air. Then, in his white collarless shirt, trousers and boots, with bread, cheese and a bottle of *kvass* slung in a napkin over his shoulder, he would stride towards the fields, his straw hat jammed on his head.

He also enjoyed examining his body each night, as his scars faded, his muscles strengthened and his hands became as rough as emery paper. Katyenka appeared to like his abrasive touch and their lovemaking every Sunday was the better for it. He often feared that his hands were too rough for his daughters, whom he picked up and kissed each evening when he returned from the fields. They did not seem to mind his touch either, as they giggled and gurgled in his arms.

This is the way country life should be, he thought, landowner and peasants working together for the same cause, led by his example. Even Katya fell for a while under the harvest's spell. Villagers, who had quit working at the house, drifted back, claiming that they had never wanted to leave but had been terrified of Afanasyev's threats. Andrey did not want disloyal servants back in the house, but Katya prevailed, insisting that repairing relations with the village was more important.

She had been much influenced by her elderly cousins, the Suslovs, a noble family who owned a huge estate at Gradov, a day's carriage ride to the east. They had had similar problems with their villagers, though without the violence seen at Golovino or direct interference from the Bolsheviks. Old General Suslov's grandfather had supported Tsar Alexander II's decision to free the peasants from serfdom. He was a firm believer in the estate and village as a single family, which it was the Christian duty of the landowner to nurture and cherish. It was a way of thinking that was partly fed by the teachings of the Church, partly by a mystical, sentimental view of the Russian countryside, partly by the ancient tradition of the Tsar as 'little father' of the Russian people. It was at once paternalist and pragmatic, a defensive shield against peasant disaffection of the kind that had plagued the countryside in recent years.

Katya went further in her thinking. She loved to read the literature of Western Europe in its native languages. She had graduated from poetry to novels, French and English above all. But the more serious side of her was drawn to philosophy and political ideas. She was attracted to the liberal thinking, particularly German, that had swept through Europe after the Year of Revolutions in 1848. She had a vision of a Golovino where ancient Russian traditions would be leavened by modern liberal ideas from Western Europe. She dreamed of putting an end to strife between landowners and peasants. She yearned for a model of harmonious coexistence that would, as she liked to say, spread from Golovino throughout Russia like the rays of the sun. Without telling Andrey, she even submitted an article on the matter to a learned magazine in St Petersburg. The editor turned it down, saying that, though it was quite interesting, it was too naïve and needed further work. She was stung by this patronising rejection, convinced that he would have published her article had she been a man.

Andrey had little time for any of this. For him, a military man of the old school, the organising principles of society were discipline and rank. He had an especial aversion to liberal thinking. He believed that it had wrecked the finances of his family estate when the serfs were freed and had weakened Russia itself. He looked askance at the monthly arrival from St Petersburg of the German, French and English publications to which Katya subscribed, though the very same post sometimes brought him a bundle of his favourite newspaper, *The Times* of London.

To all outward appearances Andrey's violent reprisal against the Afanasyevs had put a stop to disaffection in Golovino. He and Katya spoke no more about it. A new village elder had been chosen by the villagers. He was literate, quite well educated and seemed respectful enough. He was another prosperous *kulak*, with holdings also in the neighbouring village. But, though his name was Safin, he was a member of the extended Afanasyev clan.

Safin chose to live in the Afanasyev compound in Golovino. Yuri Afanasyev's legs had been amputated above the knee since his shattered kneecaps and whipped legs had become gangrenous. He had gone mad from the pain.

Katya had seen him once. Each day he was placed on a child's small cart, where, balancing on his stumps, he could propel himself by pressing his fists on the ground. The massive head and torso would race demonically around the village, ranting and howling, no longer capable of normal speech. His hair and beard had grown to such a degree that he looked barely human. The villagers, in their intense superstition, feared that the devil himself had taken up residence in his soul.

Afanasyev was a constant reminder to his family of the humiliation they had suffered. Katya had no doubt that in the privacy of their compound Afanasyev's two brothers never stopped talking of revenge. Fortunately, they had neither the courage nor the gumption to do anything. But Safin worried her. He was an enigma behind his mask of deference. He never showed emotion and he never smiled.

Andrey and Goga had meantime become close companions. They hunted and rode together. Andrey taught him how to handle his Mauser, army rifle and pistol. He gave Goga a horse – a good one with speed and strength – and told him always to have the shotgun on his shoulder, with a supply of shells in his saddlebag. He taught him basic husbandry. Goga became the son that he'd never had and was never likely to have, as Katya could not survive another childbirth.

Katya also took to the boy and taught him to read and write. He was a quick learner with a particular facility for mathematics. She liked Goga as much as Andrey did, but for different reasons. He had a quick wit and a sense of humour. He made her laugh. He helped her with the household accounts, which, since the steward's desertion, were the bane of her life. He was infinitely curious. He would sometimes appear at the hospital and make himself useful as an orderly. The nurses said that he had even learned how to dress simple wounds.

One day, as she was tending the fruit orchard with the gardeners, she heard Svyet screaming and laughing. Oksana, the nanny, had instructions not to go with the girls into the field beyond the orchard because of the grazing animals. What did Oksana think she was doing? She hurried to the end of the orchard, her long white skirt streaming behind her, to see Svyet riding Goga as if he were a horse, while little Gulya watched from Oksana's lap. Goga crawled through the grass, roaring like a lion. With each roar Svyet screamed with delight, while Gulya gurgled and spluttered, waving her chubby arms. Then Goga said in the deepest voice he could muster that he was feeling tired and wanted a rest. He gently rolled over onto his side so that Svyet tumbled off him into the grass without hurting herself. He started to snore. Svyet shouted in each of his ears in her high piping voice, 'Get up! Get up!' She pulled his hair and ears, squeezed his nose, until he suddenly jumped up with a mighty roar and she ran away squealing, to hide behind Oksana's skirts. The old woman, her white scarf tied tightly around her head in peasant fashion, had tears of laughter running down the lined cheeks of her wide Slavic face.

Katya's first instinct had been to scold all concerned for playing in the field, but it was such a scene of innocence and pure joy. What a shame to spoil it!

She must have been standing there under the apricot trees for a good ten minutes. Suddenly Svyet noticed her and raced over, crying 'Mama, Mama!' Little Gulya stretched out her arms, as she started to wriggle and squirm on Oksana's lap. She and Goga looked up, surprised and guilty. They knew that it was a golden rule not to take the children into the field. Goga started to explain that it was all his fault. Katya, with tears in her eyes, kissed him on the forehead and did likewise to Oksana. Then she swept Gulya up in her arms and, taking Svyet by the hand, went into the house, leaving Goga and Oksana stupefied.

Goga became almost a member of the family. He was given a bedroom in the attic with a table and chair for his studies. He helped Oksana with the care of the girls. Like Molnya the stallion and Stenka the hound – and his own horse, Mars – they loved him.

From time to time he would go down to the village on his horse, shotgun on his shoulder, Stenka by his side, to deliver messages and collect gossip.

Goga had another reason for these excursions. He had met a girl he liked – Mara – and she liked him. He had found himself alongside her on the first day in the harvesting line. Despite the heat and gruelling work, they had never stopped talking to each other. As the sun went down, she appeared as lively and energetic as at the dawn. She was the daughter of the cobbler, a man of substance in the village. After the harvest, Goga took her for walks and rides – with, of course, her father's permission. Her family liked him: he was a boy with prospects, an excellent catch for their daughter, who was becoming increasingly difficult to handle.

Goga would pull Mara into the saddle behind him. This gave her an excuse to hug him tight, as Goga had intended. She was slim and lithe.

Unlike most of the village girls, she had wild black hair and a copper skin. Her mother always said that there must have been gypsy blood in the family. She was illiterate and unschooled, but she was no fool and, like Goga, was full of curiosity and an urge to learn.

Goga found in Mara an outlet for all the things he wanted to say. There was no one in the big house of his age in whom he could confide. He had begun to feel that he would explode if he could not unburden himself of all the extraordinary things that had happened so quickly to him. One sunny autumn afternoon, when they were sitting under the birch trees beside the lake, where geese, ducks and moorhens were navigating together like three foreign fleets, he told Mara everything.

Goga looked into the distance as he spoke, his knees pulled up to his chest. Mara knelt beside him in her white blouse, blue skirt and flowered apron, twirling dandelions between her fingers.

His reversal of fortune had been a miracle, he said incredulously. From an orphan who slept on straw in the stables, he had become overnight a trusted member of the household with so many responsibilities that it frightened him when he thought about them. He was treated almost like the son of the family. The *barynia* had even kissed him on the head! The other night, when they had returned from shooting grouse, the *baryn* and he had sat together in the stable, drinking vodka, while the master told him stories from the war. Mara's mouth fell open when she heard this. 'I had to pinch myself!' exclaimed Goga.

Mara wanted to know what the Polkonins were like. Was the *baryn* as harsh and cruel as everyone said he was? He always looked so fierce. She had been asleep when he had shot and whipped Yuri Afanasyev. She had sometimes seen the *barynia* with her babies. She seemed nice and people in the village liked her. Her parents always spoke well of her; they had played together as children. Mara's dream was to work in the house as a maid and to learn needlework.

Goga told her that the *baryn* Andrey was a hard man – but what did you expect after so many years at war? For some reason he had found extraordinary favour . . .

'Oh, I know why!' interrupted Mara, her eyes shining with love and admiration as she looked at his quizzical face. 'The whole village has talked about it. There you were, as cool as could be, standing on that cart with your guns, protecting the *baryn*'s back. My father said that nobody wanted to take any chances with you. He said that you had real balls – Mama was so cross with him for using that word in front of me. The *baryn* must have seen what a good, brave man you are.'

Goga blushed and Mara covered his face in kisses. They sat in silence for a while. 'Go on,' said Mara.

The Polkonins, said Goga, had transformed his life. Thanks to them he had three meals a day and a proper bed to sleep in. He could read! He could write! He was doing sums! He hunted with the *baryn*, he helped look after the children with the *nyanya*. ('I would like to have babies,' Mara said.) He could herd cows and milk them. He still looked after the horses, especially the *baryn*'s hunter. They were good people. He would go with them to the ends of the earth. ('Will you take me, too?' asked Mara.) He would defend them to the death. ('And me?' pleaded Mara.)

Goga turned to Mara. All the earnestness in his expression dissolved, to be replaced by a tenderness and love that bathed his eyes and face. Goga took Mara by the hands and told her that he could not live without her.

Mara gave him regular reports on the village. It was not really a contented place, despite the excellent harvest. People like her parents, who had detested the Afanasyevs, were delighted at the punishment meted out by the *baryn*. But they were worried about the dead commissars. Sooner or later people would come from Simbirsk in search of them. Then what would happen? Others in the village, who had profited from stealing the *baryn*'s animals or from grazing on his pastures, were angry that they had to return everything they had taken. Still others, who had been close to Afanasyev, were true believers in revolution and looked forward to the day when they could sack and pillage the big house. Some even talked of killing everyone inside.

Mara found Safin, the new village elder, a sinister figure. She hated his cold eyes. He certainly managed to keep things calm in the village. He was always telling people to be patient. But patient for what? wondered Mara.

The villagers treated Goga with wary respect. A few started to talk to him, even Safin. News of his privileged position in the *baryn*'s house had spread like wildfire. He had faced down and shot a commissar with a coolness and accuracy that Safin secretly admired.

Early one morning in late autumn, when the east wind was starting to chill the air, Safin stopped Goga in the village square as he was riding through. As usual he was calm and respectful, though his eyes were as cold as marble. Stenka disliked him and began immediately to growl.

'I have something important to tell the *baryn*. Please can you give him a message. It will be quicker.'

'Of course,' said Goga.

'Some people with Red Stars – they called themselves Red Guards – came from Simbirsk yesterday, looking for the commissars. We didn't tell them what your father had suggested, because they would have shot my cousin Afanasyev. Though,' he said, with a tiny light of humanity in his eyes, 'it might have been better to put him out of his misery. His shouting is driving us all mad. We just said that the commissars had come and left. Then they got angry and asked us why we hadn't occupied the house and taken the animals, as the commissars had ordered. We said that this would have been difficult, as the *baryn* had just returned from the wars wearing a *budyenovka* and carrying a document signed by some big chief from St Petersburg called Trotsky. We told them that the *baryn* had said that he was a Red Guard himself and that he had been a bodyguard of this Trotsky. And the villagers had added that the *baryn* had changed so much in appearance since he'd first gone off to war that some still thought it was a different man.' He went on. 'This made these people from Simbirsk think a while. They talked a lot among themselves. I heard the name Trotsky frequently mentioned. Then they said they would be back and would want to talk to the *baryn*. Just as they were about to spur their horses, they said to us, "Isn't it splendid that the revolution has taken place?" We said, "Yes, but that was months ago." "No," they said, "the revolution of workers, sailors and soldiers. It's just happened. The Bolsheviks have taken power in St Petersburg. Woe to anyone who takes sides against the revolution – and that includes you and your so-called *baryn*!" And that was that.'

'Did they say when they were coming back?' asked Goga.

'No,' replied Safin. 'But I doubt it will be very long. A week at the most.'

Goga thanked Safin and trotted calmly from the village. As soon as he was in the cover of the wood, he galloped like fury to the house.

Andrey and Katya were having breakfast when they heard the sound of hooves. They both got up from the table and saw Goga jump off Mars and tie him to the post outside the front door. He raced into the house with a panting Stenka and rapped fast and loudly on the breakfast room door. They called to him to come in. Stenka burst in with him.

For all his sense of urgency, and a hard gallop notwithstanding, Goga was calmness itself as he carefully recounted everything Safin had said. As she listened, Katya's heart sank: this, she thought, is the beginning of the storm. Her mind began to turn to what they would take and what they would leave if they had to flee the house at short notice.

Andrey was yet again impressed by Goga's coolness under pressure. God, he would make a fine officer! Then he started to think hard. The Bolsheviks in Simbirsk had been bound to return in search of their companions. That was hardly a surprise. He was prepared for it. But this talk of another revolution was very worrying. If true, it meant that the Bolsheviks had seized power. A visit from their people in Simbirsk would now be a much more dangerous proposition. They would have the wind in their sails and would be eager to assert control over all Russia. It was vital to find out exactly what had happened. He would ride to Syzran immediately where there was a telegraph. If he took Molnya and a spare horse, he could be back by early next morning.

He caught Katya's anxious look.

'Are we going to have to flee the house?' she asked.

'I don't think so. But first we need to find out exactly what has happened to the government in St Petersburg,' he replied. 'I'll be back before tomorrow's dawn.'

'Do you want me to come with you?' asked Goga, eager for another adventure.

'No. You will stay here and look after the house. I don't want anyone in the village getting ideas about attacking us, if they learn that I am away. Use the roof as an observation point – the staircase is next to your room – and take all the guns with you plus a good supply of ammunition. Patrol regularly around the house on horseback, but not at too great a distance. Always have Stenka with you, because he will smell out people before you see them. If the peasants decide to attack us, it may be at night. You have my authority to shoot anyone who looks like a threat. Stenka will kill if you set him on someone.'

This, thought Katya, was what Andryusha must have been like on the Galician Front.

'What if the people from Simbirsk return before you do?' asked Goga.

'Let us pray that they don't. If they do, treat them with respect and give them beds in one of the hospital barns. Don't let them into the house, if you can avoid it. Katyenka, you could say that one of the children has scarlet fever, which is highly contagious. Tell them I will be back before dawn and that I have gone to Syzran to get my orders by telegraph from Trotsky. Play for time. If they do come before I return, leave a light in the pantry.'

'Don't forget,' said Katya quietly, 'that I can shoot, too. Let me have one of the shotguns.' Andrey hesitated, but Goga immediately replied, 'Of course.' Without giving Andrey an opportunity to interrupt, Goga agreed with Katya that while he was on the roof or patrolling, she should take up position in her bedroom above the front door. Andrey smiled and said nothing. Then he put on his brown leather coat with the fur collar, donned his *budyenovka* and strode to the stables, the army rifle on his shoulder and a pistol at his waist. He jumped on

Molnya, seized the reins of the other horse that Goga had prepared for him and disappeared into the night.

In Syzran, after a four-hour ride, he went straight to the headquarters of the local gendarmes. He convinced them easily of his Bolshevik credentials. He found out what had happened in St Petersburg. The Kerensky government had been scattered to the winds. The Bolsheviks had seized power under that villain from Simbirsk, Ulyanov, now calling himself Lenin. Andrey did not recognise any of the other Bolshevik names except Trotsky's. He was to be head of the Red Guards, a new army of volunteers and professionals who would guarantee the security of the state. The gendarmes told him that anyone who had military experience would, under pain of death, be obliged to join the new army. Samara, now under Bolshevik control, had become a regional recruiting centre.

'You'll be joining Trotsky's army, then?' said the captain of gendarmes.

'Of course. Without delay,' replied Andrey.

Chapter 11

Andrey had been ready to race back to Golovino and tell Katyenka to pack up and leave, but with the big rail junction at Samara in Bolshevik hands, it would have been impossible to escape by train in any direction. And they couldn't go to St Petersburg or Moscow in any case. The only way out was east or south. If they could get to Odessa on the Black Sea, they could find a steamer that would take them to France or England. But the two babies ruled out the long and dangerous overland route, which was the only alternative to the railway. They had no choice but to stay at Golovino for the time being.

One thing comforted him as he rode back home in the dark. He had been surprised at how easy it had been at the gendarmerie post in Syzran to pass himself off as a Red Guard. Trotsky's signature on his travel pass with its red star had had a magical impact.

It was around three in the morning when he approached Golovino. A cold wind blew hard from the north, which got inside his coat and chilled him. In his haste he had forgotten to bring a proper fur hat with ear flaps. The felt *budyenovka* offered little protection against the elements. His face felt frozen, his ears numb. He rode round the back of the house. There was no light in the pantry. He continued to the stables where, as he fed and watered the two horses, he was joined by Goga.

'Anything to report, Goga?'

'Not really, Andrey Andreyevich. Around twilight Stenka started to point at the woods between us and the village and growl. I couldn't see anything and didn't want to investigate too far from the house. Somebody may have been watching us.'

'What does that girl of yours tell you?'

'I haven't seen her since running into Safin. She has promised to warn us if the Bolsheviks come.'

'But she doesn't have a horse, Goga.'

'Andrey Andreyevich, she can run like the wind and has the stamina of Molnya. She won't let us down.'

And she didn't. Later that day, after Andrey had snatched a few hours' sleep, Mara came to the house, somewhat breathless, to announce that a dozen men had arrived from Simbirsk. They were Red Guards. They were perhaps fifteen minutes behind her. As Goga took her down to the kitchen to get something to drink, Andrey changed into his common soldier's uniform and *budyenovka*. He had a pistol and a bayonet on his belt. As they had previously agreed, Katya put on a plain blue dress with a long white apron, covered in blood stains, as if she had just come from the hospital.

Holding Stenka on a tight leash, Andrey went out to greet the troop of horsemen as soon as he heard the sound of hooves on the drive. They were dressed in long black leather coats, which were draped over the flanks of their horses. Beneath these they appeared to be wearing the same uniform as Trotsky and his companions – drab grey tunics with black boots. Each wore a cap with a red star just above the peak. They all carried the standard army-issue rifle.

Andrey greeted them heartily, 'in the name of the Revolution'. Katya, who had also stepped out, heard Andryusha's unfamiliar tone and accent. He did not sound like a nobleman anymore. She also noticed that he was affecting a slight limp.

The leading horseman, who looked like a tax collector, with his rimless spectacles and tiny, short-sighted eyes, returned the greeting with cold formality. A typical Bolshevik, thought Andrey. Underneath their coats and uniforms the rest of the riders looked like a regular cavalry troop from the old army. He knew how to handle men like that.

'Comrade, my name is Commander Z. You need not know more than that. I am here in the name of the Council of People's Commissars, the supreme organ of the Russian state,' announced the little tax collector with puffed up self-importance, leaning forward in the saddle.

'Since,' he continued, 'our beloved Motherland is beset by enemies without and traitors within, it is our task, Polkonin, to establish where you stand. We are conducting an investigation into the fate of two commissars sent here from Simbirsk a few months ago. We do not believe that they simply left the village. I should warn you that if you lie to us, you will be taken to Simbirsk for execution and your property will be confiscated.'

All this was delivered in an unpleasant, high-pitched voice. This runt will be dangerous, thought Andrey, unless I am very careful and very clever.

'Commander, that is a damnable lie. Never listen to evil tongues. The villages are full of would-be informers, who hope to earn a few roubles from the revolutionary authorities.'

'Prove it,' said Commander Z.

'May I ask – did you serve at the front against the Germans and Austrians?' enquired Andrey, going off at a tangent, all false respectfulness, looking up at the little man on his horse. He instinctively knew the answer: the runt had not, but most, if not all, of the riders had.

Commander Z was embarrassed by the question, but it was one he had to answer, if he were not to lose face in front of his men. This was the first time that he had been given an active command.

'I don't know what this has to do with the charge levelled against you,' replied the commander, 'but to my eternal regret my eyesight stopped me from serving the Motherland as I would have wished. Please obey my order.'

Good, thought Andrey, I have put you on the defensive. Now, let's drive a wedge between you and your men.

He turned to face the rest of the troop, praying that his gamble would pay off.

'How many of you lads were at the Filatov ridge outside Lemberg in '16 when we whipped the Austrians?'

Seven heads nodded in unison.

'Why do you ask, comrade?' asked one of the troopers.

'I always ask cavalrymen this when I meet them. That charge led by

Burin up the ridge saved the day. And saved me and my men. I was commanding the guns on the other hill. I was lying in the grass, my leg broken, a piece of shrapnel sticking out of my calf, bleeding like a pig. We had shells for just one more salvo. Then the word came that the Austrians were in full retreat before your sabres.'

He limped a little ostentatiously towards the seven horsemen who had nodded and shook each by the hand. For soldiers, to have been comrades-in-arms in a desperate battle transcended everything. He had now established a closer bond with the horsemen than with their officious little commander, who sensed that he was losing the initiative.

'These war stories are all very well, but we need to get to the point without further delay,' said Commander Z, turning and twisting in the saddle as he looked in irritation at his men.

'That,' replied Andrey, 'is exactly what I am going to do, Commander. It was only by putting your life on the line at the front that you could experience at first hand the sheer rottenness of the system that was conducting the war.'

This provoked nods and murmurs of approval from the troopers.

'I see our revolution as a disinfectant purging a gangrenous wound. Do you think I would otherwise have been chosen by Comrade Trotsky to guard him against counter-revolutionary forces in Samara, which, thank the stars, is now in our hands?'

Katya could barely conceal her astonishment at her husband's eloquent expression of ideas that she knew he abhorred. Who would have thought he had it in him?

The little commander was blinking furiously behind his pebble glasses. Mention of Trotsky had made him deeply uneasy. He could not afford to get on the wrong side of the newly appointed commander of the Red Guards. But what if this Polkonin was bluffing?

'Comrade,' continued Andrey with a warm smile and a cold eye, 'it is chilly out here. Why don't we talk further inside? Your men can feed and water their horses in our stables – Goga, will you see to it? – and get bread and cold cuts in the kitchen. Meanwhile, you and I can go to my study, where there is a samovar brewing.'

'Very well,' said Commander Z slowly, after a moment's hesitation. 'I will bring three of my men with me to ensure you are not tempted to do something rash. I would like your wife to be present during our conversation.'

'That will not be possible,' said Katya with calm authority. 'I am responsible for the hospital and we have desperately wounded men there, most of them just young country boys abandoned by their officers. I am needed urgently. By all means come and visit me there later.' Now it was Andrey's turn to listen in admiration. That was a clever touch about being abandoned by their officers.

Once again Commander Z had an uneasy feeling that he was being outmanoeuvred. Without even awaiting his order, the troopers pulled their horses aside to let Katya through. She disappeared down the drive towards the hospital barns painted with large red crosses on their sides.

Goga took care of the horses and led the rest of the troop to the stables while Commander Z dismounted and, with three of his men, followed Andrey into the house. They went straight to his study, a small room off the main hall, which was barely big enough for the five of them and Stenka. Andrey sat behind his desk, Stenka tied to its leg, and invited Commander Z, who looked even more diminutive out of the saddle, to take the chair opposite. Stenka would normally have fallen asleep, but the great hound, who had already caused several of the horses to rear, sat watchfully at Andrey's side.

The room was furnished very much in Andrey's style: spartan and practical. His guns were lined up against the wall behind him. The shrapnel that had been pulled from his leg lay on the desk next to his *budyenovka* and a bayonet. A newspaper, which he had bought in Syzran, announcing the Bolshevik Revolution on its front page, lay on top of a low bookcase filled with military manuals. There was a large, framed engraving on one of the walls, depicting the dispositions of the Russian and French armies before the Battle of Borodino in 1812. On the wall behind him hung small portraits of the great Russian generals, Suvorov and Kutuzov. It was the study of a serious military man.

Commander Z's men recognised this immediately and stood respectfully. The commander sought to reassert his authority.

'What do you know of the fate of our two commissars? There is considerable suspicion at headquarters in Simbirsk that they have been victims of foul play and that you had some role in it.'

'I know only what the villagers have told me. They came, they went. I wasn't here. I was with Trotsky in Samara. Here is the travel pass he signed for me,' said Andrey in a matter-of-fact way.

Commander Z peered shortsightedly at the card, turning it over in his hands. He flicked his fingers and said 'Trotsky's order-of-the-day' to one of the guards, who produced a creased single-page document. The little commander looked at the signature on each. They were identical. He returned the travel pass to Andrey.

'How did you meet Trotsky?' he asked, his voice now slightly less accusatory.

'In a cemetery behind a church. The one behind the first-aid post opposite Voronezh station. I was there to have my wounds dressed. I was approached by a group of men, dressed like you, one of whom was Trotsky. I had heard of him but had never met him. He had been on "Wanted" posters in the name of Bronstein, distributed by the High Command. We had been under orders to arrest or shoot him on sight. Trotsky and I had a long discussion about the conduct of the war. He knew what he was talking about. I was impressed. But the gap in his knowledge was artillery, which is my speciality. He asked me to help organise the artillery regiments of what he called the Red Army. Of course, I agreed. When I told him I was heading for Samara on my way home, he said that so was he and he asked me to take charge of a platoon who were acting as his bodyguard – which I also agreed to do. He had received, he said, many threats to his life.'

'Why aren't you with him now?' said Commander Z.

'Well, in Samara, just after Trotsky had addressed an infantry company in the main square, we were ambushed by Cossacks loyal to Kerensky and one of our men was killed. We saved Trotsky's life, but he was arrested. Before he was taken away, he ordered me to escape if I could and await instructions in Golovino to join this so-called Red Army. I managed to escape and that's what I am doing now. He and his staff know where to find me.'

Once again, he related this to Commander Z without bombast or embellishment. It was the more convincing for being understated.

'All right, Colonel Polkonin,' said Commander Z, even more respectfully than before. He turned to his three guards and saw that they were spellbound by the story. 'But tell me this. What made you desert the Imperial Army in the first place?'

Andrey leapt to his feet, genuinely enraged at being accused of desertion by this half-blind dwarf who had never smelled cordite. It startled everyone, even Stenka.

'Desert? Desert? I didn't desert. *It* deserted *me*!' The guards smiled and relaxed again with their tea. Commander Z stopped fumbling for his pistol, whose holster was anyway too stiff to undo. Stenka resumed sitting.

'I crawled out of my tent one fine morning in Galicia and there was nobody there. My men had gone. They had spiked the guns so the Germans couldn't use them, left me my horse and disappeared. The High Command had already disintegrated and stopped sending orders. So, I had nobody under me and nobody above me. All I knew was that, not far behind, several thousand angry and mutinous Russian infantries were in full retreat. If they caught up with me, they would almost certainly shoot me as an officer. That is why, Commander Z,' he added, a mocking smile playing on his lips, 'if you had looked more carefully at my travel pass, you would have seen that I was travelling as Sergeant Vlasov, not Colonel Polkonin!'

The guards began to guffaw as Andrey invited them to look at his pass. Commander Z blinked furiously in embarrassment and sank deeper into his chair. He looked balefully at Andrey through his pebble lenses, his little black eyes like poisonous raisins. He had been outmanoeuvred again.

'Damn my eyesight!' said the commander.

Time to be nicer to him, thought Andrey. He decided to resort to a risky gambit.

'But here's the real answer to your question,' he said, now looking the commander earnestly in the eye and grasping his arm across the table in manly fashion. 'I will be frank with you. After the collapse of our army, I did not at first know what to do. I found myself in Lemberg looking for a train to take me back to Russia. Then I had the good fortune to meet an extraordinary man, a former Tsarist officer who had seen the light and had taken control of Lemberg on behalf of the St Petersburg Soviet . . . '

'His name?' interrupted Commander Z, sharply curious.

'Lebedev, Commissar Lebedev, an admirable man, hard but fair. I don't know his other names. We met at Lemberg station where he had his headquarters.'

The commander and his men looked at each other, nodding approvingly.

'Comrade Lebedev,' said the commander, 'is one of the heroes of the Revolution.'

'Well, while I had been fighting on the southern front, he had commanded an infantry regiment in the north. We talked long into the night about Russia's destiny. At the end of it, as the sun was rising, I agreed to follow his footsteps and support the St Petersburg Soviet. Just as we were shaking hands, German aircraft bombed the city and hit the railway station. I was cut to shreds by flying glass and he was very badly injured. I pulled him out from under a heavy table. He was unconscious. His arm was terribly crushed and he had a bad wound to one of his eyes. After I had handed him over to the Red Cross, I continued my journey eastwards by rail, but now with a new sense of purpose given me by Commissar Lebedev. Do you know what happened to him?'

'Ah, you were privileged to meet him. I am not surprised you fell under his spell. Any friend of his is a friend of mine.' An obsequious smile spread across Commander Z's lips. 'I have heard that he has lost an arm and an eye, but has not allowed these disabilities to hamper him in any way. In fact, the latest news is that he has been recalled to St Petersburg and has become one of Trotsky's political officers, responsible for discipline and ideology.'

At this point Katya walked into the room. She had been worried, but immediately she entered she could tell that things were going well. Both Andrey and Commander Z were leaning back in their chairs, talking as if they were at the Naval and Military Club in St Petersburg. The three guards had put down their rifles and were leaning on the wall, drinking tea and listening to the conversation.

Commander Z even made to rise as she entered. She wondered what his real name was and what he had done before the Revolution. He was a little man, drunk with power, who probably liked to be cruel – and to be flattered. Andryusha seemed to be making a fine job of him.

'I am sorry to interrupt, but I have finished my rounds and I know you wanted to see me,' she said, looking at Commander Z with a slight smile.

'Why don't you and your men have something a little stronger than tea,' Andrey said, before the conversation could go any further. 'I have some Georgian *chacha* you might like.'

Chacha was something the Georgians brewed from grape skins. Even for vodka drinkers it was a potent brew. It went to the stomach like a stream of fire, tempered only by an aromatic aftertaste akin to cognac. Andrey poured the glasses. Katya refused to touch it. The commander had never experienced it before. He looked fearful and hesitant. The guards, peasant soldiers all recruited from around Yaroslav, eyed the *chacha* with relish. One of them muttered with a grin, 'I had this once in the Caucasus. It will set fire to your hair.' Katya, perched on two stacked military drums from the Crimean War, demurely poured herself a glass of water.

Andrey gave a toast to the Revolution. As custom demanded, he and the guards knocked it back in one, heads thrown back. After various noises and exhalations of pleasure, he immediately refilled the glasses. He gave a toast to Mother Russia. Once again four of the five *chacha* glasses were drained. Commander Z, meanwhile, was still toying with his first glass. He took a tiny sip and coughed. His guards, emboldened by the alcohol now coursing through their veins, shouted, 'Go on, Commander, *do dna, do dna*, down in one, down in one!'

Andrey added pressure. 'Lebedev and I drank this all through the night in Lemberg.'

The mere mention of Lebedev's name jolted Commander Z into action and he drained his glass. He began to cough so violently that Katya feared he would choke. Just as she was about to reach out to him, he suddenly stopped coughing and screamed at the top of a strangulated voice, 'More, give me more! We must drink to Lebedev! To Lebedev!'

Andrey gave him another glass, as he did the guards. They all toasted Lebedev in a single gulp. Then, in the Georgian manner, toasts followed in quick succession to Trotsky, to the St Petersburg Soviet, to the Simbirsk commissars, to parents, to children and to the harvest, each toast with a freshly filled glass downed in a single shot. Andrey appeared wholly unmoved by the *chacha*. The guards were holding up well enough, though two of them were swaying and the third was holding onto the wall.

But something odd was happening to Commander Z. His eyes had lost focus behind his pebble glasses. His head was jerking from side to side. Without warning, he lost consciousness, his head falling onto the back of the chair. He appeared not to be breathing. Katya became anxious. Just when she thought he might be dead, he awoke with a start. He stood uncertainly and, saluting, began to sing a nursery rhyme in a high, almost childlike voice, his pebble glasses hanging from one ear, his cap high up on his forehead. He smiled angelically at Andrey. Then, kneeling before Katya, he took her hand and began to kiss it repeatedly. Katya sat horrified, trying to withdraw her hand. He held on ever more tightly and started to kiss her bare arm, making catlike sounds. The guards were laughing so much that one of them wet himself.

Finita la commedia, thought Andrey. He was about to pull Commander Z off his wife, when he yawned loudly and rolled senseless to the floor. Katya hurried from the room to wash her arm.

Andrey ordered the guards to carry the commander outside and tie him to his horse. Even through an alcoholic haze, they recognised the voice of authority. Andrey knew that the *chacha* would not affect him for at least another hour. A delayed reaction was always the way with him and drink. He had to get the Red Guards off the estate by then. He sent for Goga and the rest of the troop, who had been taking their ease in the stables. There was a sergeant among them who was happy to assume command. Andrey explained that the commander must have had an attack of indigestion. He and the sergeant looked at each other completely straight-faced.

The horsemen formed up in two columns of six, with one of them holding the reins of the commander's horse. He was snoring loudly. Andrey and Katya stood together in the courtyard to bid them farewell. It was a jovial departure, with many expressions of thanks from the riders.

The troop disappeared behind the firs at the bottom of the drive. As they did so, it started to rain. Grey clouds whipped across the sky. Rooks and crows wheeled in the early winter air. Leaves rushed across the gravel. Katya and Andrey stood there, coatless and in silence. Goga and Mara stood a little way off, their hands touching, and Stenka sitting at their side.

'Well?' said Katya after a while.

'Well?' replied Andrey.

'Do we leave or do we stay?'

After another pause, Andrey said, 'We stay. We have bought ourselves enough time to be safe for the winter, maybe longer. We so entangled truth and falsehood that they will be very hard to untie. We won't be seeing Commander Z again. After his performance we can effectively blackmail him at long range. It's a shooting offence to be drunk on duty. I get the sense these Bolsheviks like to appear as puritan as they are ruthless. His troopers don't like him. I'd wager we won't see anyone from Simbirsk or Samara until the spring sowing season.'

As he paused, he looked up and saw that he was part of a circle that now included Katya, Goga and Mara. He greeted the tall girl. He liked her style. She held her head high. She was resourceful and brave. He thanked her for her timely warning. She in turn thanked him with a glorious smile. No wonder Goga was smitten. He turned to the group.

'Do you think I'm right?'

'I think you are, my dear Andryusha,' Katya replied. 'You did well today. I was proud of you.' If only you had been as clever with Afanasyev and the commissars, she thought.

It was a long time since Andrey had received a compliment from his wife. He smiled at her. His chest swelled a little.

Much to her own surprise, Mara then spoke.

'*Baryn*, I was not witness to what happened just now. Nor was Goga. We trust your judgement as our lord and master. And yours, too, *Barynia*. Our great anxiety is Safin. We are both convinced that he means you no good. We think he keeps in touch with the bad people in Simbirsk and that he wants vengeance against you as much as the Afanasyev brothers. You cannot afford to hibernate for the winter and wake up only in the spring. Your enemies could strike at any time.' Mara stopped for a moment and then said, 'There, I have said my piece and forgive me if I have spoken out of turn.'

'Mara, of course you have not spoken out of turn,' said Katya, looking at her with warm affection. 'I am beginning to think that this family will not be able to survive without you and Goga at our side. If Safin is as evil as you say, what then should we do?'

Now it was Goga's turn.

'I don't think you should leave now. But you must get ready a store of clothing and supplies, loaded onto two carts, so that you can leave at a moment's notice. You must have enough for the four of you and *Nyanya*. I will have two strong ponies always ready to pull the carts. Mara and I will warn you if danger approaches. No one knows better than Mara the wood's secret tracks between the village and the house.'

Andrey and Katya both had the same idea.

'If the enemy returns, you two will be in as much danger as we—' said Katya.

'Exactly,' interrupted Andrey.

'You must come with us!' Katya exclaimed, seizing Mara by the arm.

'Yes, please!' said Mara and Goga almost in unison, grinning from ear to ear. Katya hugged them both, tears in her eyes. Andrey gave them gruff handshakes, knowing that even his eyes were a little watery. Must be the *chacha*, he thought. He must now say what he thought before the alcohol rendered him incoherent.

'Goga, Mara, you are quite right to have us prepare for departure at short notice. We must do that first thing tomorrow. We are safe unless and until that merciless devil Lebedev turns up in Simbirsk. If that happens, we shall have to run for our lives.'

Suddenly they all felt cold and turned to go indoors, Stenka bounding ahead. Andrey was beginning to feel very unsteady. He put a hand on Katya's shoulder. His last thought before he passed out was how strong and warm she felt.

Chapter 12

Andrey had guessed right: after Commander Z's visit to Golovino, the estate was left undisturbed by the authorities in Simbirsk until the following year.

Safin and the villagers had fully expected Andrey, maybe Katya, too, to be taken away in chains to Simbirsk by Commander Z, never to return. They were astonished when the horsemen passed through the village on their way home, not only without Andrey, but with their commander tied to a horse. When Safin had asked what was wrong with Commander Z, the sergeant had told him to mind his own business.

After this, the villagers, including Safin, treated Andrey very differently. They now took seriously the notion that the *baryn* was part of the new dispensation and had influence with the Bolshevik authorities in Samara and Simbirsk. The rumour reached them that he was personally acquainted with Trotsky, soon to be the commander of the Red Army.

All this was reported by Mara and Goga. Gradually Katya and Andrey began to relax. Even Stenka, with his extraordinary sensitivity to danger and the anxiety of others, stopped padding watchfully around the house during the night, grumbling and rumbling at the slightest noise.

For the first time ever, the family spent Christmas in Golovino. Before the Revolution it had been the custom for the nobility to attend the Russian Orthodox rituals in one of the great St Petersburg cathedrals, with the Tsar and Tsarina and *le tout* St Petersburg. Katya remembered her excitement at going for the first time to the Christmas service as a young girl. She had put on her best dress and coat and had learned to curtsy for the moment when the Tsar and Tsarina passed.

Now, with Andrey, Svyet, Gulya and the entire household, she was squeezed into the little Golovino church with all the villagers. Everybody stood, Katya and Andrey at the front. Father Nikolai had conquered his fears and returned to his priestly duties. Candles burned brightly everywhere. Old women were on their knees, scarves tied tightly around their heads, crossing and recrossing themselves as they muttered prayers. Father Nikolai had a good voice and, in the Russian style, chanted the prayers and incantations at speed, but loud enough for all to hear and say their amens. He had put together a makeshift choir, which added its contribution lustily and entirely out of tune. Around the church flitted the grey shapes of the village spinsters, whose task it was to help the priest in his ministry.

The scent, the priest's voice and the dancing candlelight had a reassuring effect on Katya, renewing her confidence in the unshakeable solidity of old Russia and its customs. Atheist agitators from the big cities would have their comeuppance in the ancient Russian countryside. The old ways would prevail.

She said as much to Andrey, as they drove back from the service and she put her arm in his.

'You may be right,' he replied. 'We have become so accustomed to the hammer blow of events that we have given in to an unworthy fatalism.'

He had to pause as the cart slipped sideways into a snowdrift and came to an abrupt halt. The snow was deeper than he had expected and it took a good ten minutes to dig out the wheel and get the cart back onto the hard, icy track leading through the wood. As he jumped back on the cart and whipped the ponies, his breath coming in short, rapid bursts of condensation in the icy air, he continued talking as if uninterrupted.

'Katyenka, I have always thought that we would be safe until the spring, when the big roads are passable again. That's when the Bolsheviks will come looking once more for their commissars. But what if,' he asked, looking earnestly at his wife with his dark, luminous eyes, 'things were to go our way again? Why do we assume that God will allow the Bolsheviks to prevail? I have heard things that have made me think.'

'What do you mean, Andryusha?'

'These are no more than straws in the wind. They are so thin that I haven't even bothered to mention them to you. But consider this. Last week, when I was in Syzran, I dressed up as usual in my Trotsky uniform with *budyenovka* and red star. It did not work its charm as it did the time before. Some of the gendarmes gave me a dirty look. I asked one of them I knew slightly what the problem was. He whispered – he was very uneasy about being seen talking to me – that changes were coming, not only in Syzran but in Samara, too. I pressed him further. But he was too junior and too stupid to understand the import of what he was saying. Then, a horse-wrangler I've known for years said to me, again his hand in front of his mouth, that the next time I came to Syzran I would do well to be rid of the Bolshevik paraphernalia. He, too, refused to enlarge on what he meant. Finally, when I was riding back, I encountered that band of tinkers who often camp on our common land. I have a passing acquaintance with their leader, Isaak. He has never caused us trouble and, when we meet, we drink vodka together.'

'I remember the last time,' Katya laughed. 'You fell asleep on your horse.'

'Anyway, for donkey's years he and his troupe have followed the same route – Golovino, Syzran, Samara, Kazan, Simbirsk and Golovino again. He told me that this year he was giving Samara, and possibly Kazan, a miss. There was mischief in the air and he didn't want to get caught up in it.'

'Mischief in the air? You're talking in riddles, Andryusha.'

'I know. But I'm not certain myself what all this means. My guess is that forces are gathering along the Volga to throw out the Bolsheviks.'

He paused. There was some tricky driving to do if they were not to slide off the track again. Once safely on the driveway to the house, he continued.

'There is one last piece in my jigsaw. It may mean something, it may mean nothing. That post rider, who came by the house yesterday, was carrying a message from my old friend Misha Chazov, the naval commander who was with me in Galicia. He said to expect a visit from him.'

'Oh, I have been longing to meet him!' Katya exclaimed.

'He could not say when, but it would be quite soon. He wrote, using a code we had learned at naval academy, that he had an important matter to discuss. Most mysterious. So, my dearest Katyenka, there may be something stirring.'

*

It was not until winter was giving way to a chilly spring that Misha Chazov appeared one evening at the front door. Stenka's stentorian barking had given them early warning. Andrey threw open the door to see Misha's slim figure astride a muscular pony trotting up the drive, with two more in tow behind. He was dressed in some appallingly shabby outfit with a moth-eaten *shapka* perched on his head.

Stenka knew instinctively that this visitor was friend, not foe, and, wagging his tail furiously, he raced around the little group of ponies. The animals reared a little at the sight of a hound almost as big as they were, but they had been well broken in and Stenka appeared to intend no harm. After the ponies had given him a good sniff, and Stenka had put his front paws on Misha's shoulders, they calmed down, glad to be at rest after an arduous day's travel.

'Best way to travel, Andryusha, in these troubled times,' said Misha, laughing, after he and Andrey had embraced. 'Take a train and, if you don't give the right answer to some brute of an inspector, you won't arrive at your destination. You'll be six feet under!'

Andrey looked at Misha's keen, humorous eyes.

'By Jove, am I glad to see you!' he replied with unusual warmth. 'Katya and I have been living here virtually imprisoned in our own home, isolated from anything resembling civilisation, waiting for the local *jacquerie* to rise up and slaughter us in our beds.'

'Where is Katya? I must meet this astonishing woman!'

At that moment, wrapped in a blue cloak, she appeared at the front door. Misha skipped towards her with his ineffably light step and, taking her hand, bowed low to pass his lips over her fingers.

'Ekaterina Alexandrovna!' he exclaimed, 'I have been waiting for this day. In all our perilous scrapes last year, your husband never ceased to talk of you and how he longed to return to the family.'

Katya, astonished, assumed this charming young man was seeking simply to flatter her.

Misha, as if sensing what was passing through her mind, added quickly, 'He may behave like a block of wood, but beneath the surface he's a sensitive fellow, who can sing and paint.'

'Sing and paint?' exclaimed Katya, laughing. 'That's the first I have heard of it!'

She went on, 'My dear Mikhail Dimitrovich, the feeling is mutual. When Andryusha told me about your boldness and courage, I longed to meet you, too. How many times have I said that to you, Andryusha?' Katya, still smiling, turned to Andrey.

'Many times, Katyenka, many times.' He winked at Misha.

It was almost dark and they were still outside. Katya shivered. 'Let's go in,' she said. 'Misha – from now on I am going to call you Misha and you will call me Katya – you must have a long, hot bath and then we will all have dinner. After that you can go into the library with Andryusha and discuss what you have to discuss in front of a fire with cigars.'

'I can think of nothing better,' replied Misha. 'But, if you can bear the cigar smoke, I think you should be with us. What I have to say concerns you both. Besides, Andryusha and I think too much alike. We need another point of view.'

Katya smiled, delighted at Misha's suggestion. Andryusha would not, of course, object, but he would never have thought to include her.

'I would like that, Misha,' Katya replied. 'And I'll have one of my cigarillos.'

A couple of hours later they were seated around the dining table. As usual the room was lit with a profusion of candles, carefully arranged to illuminate the table, while leaving the rest of the grand room in near darkness. To the servants, as they entered the room, the three figures around the table looked disembodied, as if levitating. Katya liked the cosiness of it, the sense of being protected within a magic circle of light.

She insisted on a fine dinner to mark Misha's visit. It was like the old days, a lavish meal of celebration. They put serious matters to one side. They gossiped and told stories about life before the war. Misha and Andrey recounted their naval academy escapades, slapping their knees and roaring with laughter. Katya could barely believe that her serious, even severe, husband could once have been so carefree and mischievous. They exchanged tales about Rasputin and the Imperial family. Misha had had a bit of a crush on the Grand Duchess Maria Nikolaevna, one of the Romanov daughters, which he thought had been reciprocated. Who knows where it might have led, but for the interruption of the Revolution, said Misha rather wistfully. He had romantic visions of freeing her and her family from captivity through some act of derring-do.

For those two hours they were able to forget the dangers that lurked outside their little pool of candlelight. Then Misha picked up a candelabra and placed it atop the small Steinway that Alissa, the family matriarch, had first brought to the house. He started to play the songs of old Russia, his light tenor voice extracting from the music every last drop of its plangent nostalgia. Katya became lost in a memory of her grandmother singing to her when she was a child. She looked up at Andrey and saw tears streaming down his face. This man is a mystery to me, she thought.

Misha stopped playing and closed the piano. They were all silent for a while, each lost in a reverie that transported them far from Golovino. Katya broke the spell. 'Let's take our coffee in the library,' she said in a businesslike manner, 'and hear what Misha has to tell us.'

They left the dining room and crossed the hall to the library. A fire had been lit, and Stenka was already asleep before it. Three armchairs were arranged around the fireplace. Andrey and Katya sat on either side of Misha. The men went through the fussy ritual of lighting fine Cuban cigars. Katya was as good as her word and lit a cigarillo. On a small table Valentin had left a pot of coffee, a bottle of whisky, a bottle of brandy and a soda syphon with glasses.

Misha looked around at the serried rows of books. It was a veritable store of learning and history, an accumulation of human experience. He thought of all the lessons that might be learned from their pages, lessons which would have to be learned again and again from bitter experience and at goodness knows what cost in pain and suffering.

He drained his coffee, poured himself a whisky and soda and began to speak.

'Katya, Andryusha, you cannot imagine the joy I feel at being here with you both – at finding my old *sputnik* Andryusha alive and well, at meeting you, Katya, the light of my old friend's life. I will never forget this day.' He paused to take a sip of his whisky and soda and then resumed.

'I'm sorry for being so mysterious in the message I sent you months ago, sorry, too, for resorting to that old naval code.' His brow furrowed in deep-set lines as he continued. 'But, in these perilous times you do not write things down only for them to be intercepted and read by the prying eyes of the censor's office.'

He took another sip of his whisky and drew deeply on what was left of his cigar. Andrey and Katya watched him intently.

'I am afraid it's quite a long story and you will have to be patient with me before I get to the point,' he said a little shyly, with his disarming smile.

'We have all the time in the world, Misha,' said Andrey, as the ash fell from his cigar onto the sleeping Stenka.

'Andryusha, when you and I parted at the station in Samara some nine months ago, I went, as I had intended, straight to my family's estate in Vologda. I arrived there to discover that my father had just been killed by a German shell on the northern front. The local peasants had taken advantage of his death and my absence to burn down our house and parcel up the land among themselves. All this had been encouraged by our traitor of a steward, whom, in my grief and rage, I despatched with my father's shotgun.

'There was nothing I could do on my own to get my estate back. So I went to St Petersburg to see if I could get help from Kerensky. He was still running his provisional government. I had known him a bit before the war and we had got on well enough. There's no doubting his brains and he is quite a charmer. He agreed to see me. All I needed was a squadron of gendarmes. It was hopeless. He was in despair, beset by problems on every side. He had put Kornilov in charge of the army to restore order in St Petersburg and deal with the Bolsheviks once and for all. But a few days before our meeting, Kornilov had run amok, botched the whole operation and was now himself under arrest. Kerensky felt his position hopelessly undermined. Of course, he never recovered and, not long after, the Bolsheviks delivered their *coup de grâce*. I never got my gendarmes.

'I am not proud of what happened next. It was my turn to fall into despair. I hung around the old haunts in St Petersburg, got drunk most nights, won and lost money by the barrel-load, fought a couple of duels without harm to myself or my opponent, and took a room at the Astoria Hotel with one of the Tsar's courtier's old mistresses, Suzi d'Anjou. This went on for several months. I was drunk, in bed with Suzi (forgive me, Katya), when the Bolsheviks threw out Kerensky.'

Misha paused again for a sip of whisky and a pull on his cigar. Andrey got up to put more logs on the fire. Katya threw her cigarillo butt into the flames and helped herself to soda water from the syphon.

'Try as I did,' continued Misha, 'I could not pull myself out of this downward spiral of self-destruction. Then, one evening late last year, I was invited to dinner by friends of my parents, the Kolchaks. The old boy, who's now very ancient, had been in the marine artillery and had fought the British and French in the Crimean affair. As a child I used to love listening to his war stories and it was because of him that I decided to become a naval gunner.'

'Any relation to the polar explorer who used to lecture us from time to time at the academy?' asked Andrey.

'Absolutely,' replied Misha, 'he is the father of Commander Alexander Vassilyevich Kolchak of the Imperial Russian Navy, famous explorer and hero of naval operations against the Japanese, Turks and Germans. He, too, was at the dinner along with a colonel from your old outfit, the Life Guards Second Artillery Brigade. A tough-looking fellow called Diterikhs, who remembered you well. He said he would go to hell and back with you!'

'He was my commanding officer in the Galician campaign in '14,' interjected Andrey. 'He was one of the few senior officers who knew what he was doing.'

'Well,' continued Misha, 'when the ladies retired and we were sitting round the table with the port, Kolchak and Diterikhs spun me a yarn. After the Revolution they were both out of a job, as it were. Like a lot of former officers of the old army, they were being pressed by the Bolsheviks to help organise this new Red Army, which our old friend Trotsky is going to lead. If they didn't agree, they would likely end up in prison or before a firing squad. Except that, as Kolchak put it – he's a cold fish, by the way – the wheels were coming off the Revolution.

'I won't bother you with all the details, but I found them pretty persuasive. Kolchak, who did nearly all the talking, said the country was a seething mass of disaffection, with groups of all kinds at loggerheads with the Bolsheviks and jostling for power. The Ukrainian, Finnish and Baltic provinces were breaking away from Russia and going to form their own independent states. Even the Cossacks were trying to establish their own territory. Something was stirring in Siberia, while Bolshevik authority was being challenged along the Volga, especially around Samara down the road from here.' Andrey and Katya glanced at each other. 'The Germans were stirring the pot in Ukraine, and there was no sign yet of a peace treaty. This was last December, don't forget. All that was needed, said Kolchak and Diterikhs, was for this rebellious mood to be properly harnessed and the Bolsheviks could be swept from power.

'Then they turned to me,' he continued, 'and asked whether they could count on me when the moment came to roll back the Revolution. I, of course, said "yes", though I had a thousand questions. But our conversation was interrupted by the urgent arrival of one of Kolchak's aides, who whispered a message into his ear. At that Kolchak and Diterikhs departed into the night like scalded cats. I later learned that the secret police were hard on their heels. Kolchak eventually found refuge in Harbin in northern China, where there is a large Russian colony, while Diterikhs went to Vladivostok in the far east.'

'All this was three months ago. Where are things now?' asked Andrey, eyes bright with impatience.

'I am coming to that,' answered Misha. 'By the way, both Kolchak and Diterikhs know I am here.'

Katya asked anxiously, 'Is that wise? Can you trust them?'

'Katya, I asked myself the identical questions. The short answer is yes. I decided to find out for myself whether they were telling the truth. This gave me a new purpose in life and the willpower to abandon my debauched existence. A few days later I moved out of the Astoria and said farewell to Suzi. We were growing tired of each other anyway and, ever sensitive to the way the wind was blowing, she moved in with some big shot on the Petrograd Soviet. I went into the countryside and bought three tough ponies from the Mazur brothers, who, you will remember, Andrey, supplied horses to the army. I also got hold of a job lot of pots and pans, some saddlebags and the shabbiest clothes you have ever seen. With an old military coat and *shapka*, I was the very model of a wandering tinker – and that is what I became.'

The burning logs tumbled with a loud report in a shower of sparks. Stenka jumped up in alarm. Once he realised there was no danger, he stretched, shook himself and yawned, before collapsing again on the rug. Andrey poked about in the fire before piling on fresh logs. The house clocks started to chime midnight. Misha refilled his whisky and took a deep swallow.

'I travelled the land west of the Urals. I began to live the part of a tinker and got pretty good at it. I traded furs, pots, nails, brushes, hammers, you name it. I sat in scores of marketplaces and pubs and listened to the conversation. I broke bread and drank vodka with every kind of ruffian from Zaporozhia to Vilna. I was never once stopped by the police, though I sold horseshoes to the gendarmes in Kazan and Tula. Because it was winter, I first went south to the Cossack territories, where I found complete turmoil. They hate the Bolsheviks and are determined to create their own homeland. In Ukraine, all the talk was about independence. It's the same story, by the way, in the north – Finland, the Baltics – just as Kolchak described. For a while I helped an innkeeper in Samara serve beer. Most of his clients were Bolsheviks and Socialists, whose talk gave me a very good idea of what was going on along the Volga. The days of Bolshevik authority in Simbirsk and Samara look to be numbered. There is talk even of creating a Volga republic.'

Misha leaned forward in his chair, his eyes flashing.

'But here's my greatest discovery. I don't think, Andryusha, you ever came up against the Czech regiments of the old Austrian army.'

'You're right. I didn't. But they had a first-rate reputation as fighting men,' replied Andrey, 'much better than the Austrian or Balkan regiments. I even think we had a few Czech and Slovak regiments on our side, who were keen to be rid of the Austrians.'

'Then listen to this,' said Misha. 'Last month the Bolsheviks signed a peace treaty with the Germans and ever since have been emptying the camps of their prisoners of war. These have included thousands of Czech soldiers, who have kept to their old regiments and joined forces with those of their countrymen who were fighting on our side. There are half a dozen well-armed and well-trained divisions. They have been granted safe passage by Trotsky to go home to Bohemia, but via the long eastern route – the Trans-Siberian railway and the port of Vladivostok. The railway, of course, passes through Samara, your backyard. Soon thousands of Czech soldiers will be assembling there to continue their journey to Vladivostok.'

'And . . . ?' asked Andrey.

'And, if we are canny, the Czechs will come over to our side – the

White side – against the Reds. Four divisions of seasoned troops with impeccable fighting credentials.'

'Why on earth should they do that if Trotsky has granted them safe passage?'

'Because Trotsky wants them to give up their arms before they leave Samara. The Czechs know very well that Bolshevik authority east of the Urals is patchy at best and that Siberia is infested with hostile guerrillas and irregular forces. Safe passage means nothing if they don't have their own weapons to enforce it,' said Misha with a sweep of his arm, as if solving a complex mathematical problem.

Now it was Katya's turn to press Misha.

'Yes, I grasp all that, but what to the Czechs is the attraction of fighting for the Whites – is that how we are going to call ourselves, by the way? – when, if I understand you well, all they want to do is to get home as fast as possible?'

'Booty, money, victory – especially the last, since they will be able then to take the short route home through Europe. They will be travelling forever over sea and land if they go through Vladivostok,' Misha replied, fixing his gaze on Katya.

He went on, speaking more to Katya than to Andrey.

'But you're right. They are not yet persuaded that fighting for our side is in their interest. Kolchak, who has set up shop not far from Omsk just the other side of the Urals, has had some exchanges with senior Czech officers. But they don't like him much – he is an arrogant navy man with no understanding of warfare on land. Diterikhs is much more to their taste – an experienced gunner, used to command.'

Stenka stood up, bored with all this talk. He broke wind loudly and left the room to find his usual sleeping place in the hall. The fire had burned down again, but nobody was minded to put on fresh logs. They all sensed that the conversation was near to its climax and that it would be a watershed in their lives.

'Now,' said Misha, 'I come to the heart of the matter, because, make no mistake, my presence here tonight is not just a joyous reunion. It is also a sacred mission to save Mother Russia from the clutches of evil.' His voice caught as he spoke the last few words. He paused to collect himself and finish the last of the whisky in his glass.

'Andryusha, your country needs you. Diterikhs is holed up in Samara, incognito, protected by a squad of Czech soldiers. He, too, is in regular touch with Czech commanders. He judges that he has brought the Czech horse to water, but he has not yet persuaded it to drink. He believes that, with your help, he can accomplish the final step. What say you? Will you come with me to Samara?'

It was again Katya who spoke.

'Dear Misha, are you telling us that if your admiral's scheming . . . '

Misha interrupted, 'Alexander Vasilyevich Kolchak.'

'. . . if Kolchak's scheming goes to plan, Russia will be plunged into civil war?'

'Yes, Katya. But war has already started. In the north, the Caucasus, Asia, Siberia, soon the Volga. It is the only way to save our country. Kolchak is recruiting among the Cossacks and the old Imperial Army. Thousands are coming over to him and the White cause. It is not just him, of course. Other generals, who served the Tsar, have joined the crusade – Denikin, Wrangel, Yudenich.'

Without even looking at Andrey, Katya could sense his fierce eagerness to join Misha and go to Samara. The atmosphere between the three of them became electric. A moment of truth had arrived.

Andrey asked in as matter-of-fact a voice as he could muster, 'What, Misha, are the qualities that Diterikhs sees in me that could possibly persuade the Czechs to join the White side against the Reds?'

'First of all,' answered Misha, 'you are an artillery man with recent experience of combat. Secondly, like Diterikhs, you would be a welcome antidote to Samara's squabbling politicians – Mensheviks, Socialist Revolutionaries and other curious breeds, whose aim is to unseat the Bolsheviks. Your presence would reinforce the notion that this is a serious military enterprise with a clear political goal, which stands a good chance of success.'

A silence fell in the library. The fire was almost out. It was starting to get cold. Misha looked exhausted.

'How long are you staying with us?' Andrey asked Misha.

'I must ride at dawn and return to Samara as soon as possible,' he replied.

'Then,' said Andrey, without looking at Katya, 'I will ride with you.'

Chapter 13

It was well after midnight when they went to bed that evening. Katya, anxious for the children and the house, immediately reproached Andrey for what she considered the unconscionably rash decision to ride with Misha to Samara. They argued fiercely and angrily until the dawn.

Katya liked Misha. She had found him persuasive and impressive, but she demanded more evidence that the Bolsheviks could be defeated. It would be the height of folly to abandon the family and the estate at the very moment of greatest vulnerability. Surely Andrey could see that! He was proposing to embark on a quixotic exploit out of loyalty to his old friend and a love of adventure. He should wait and see if Kolchak's enterprise prospered before leaving Golovino.

Andrey would have none of it. The success of Kolchak's enterprise, as she put it, could hinge on help from the Czech Legion and that help itself could depend on his joining Diterikhs' staff. This was a golden moment to save Russia itself. If he did not go with Misha, he would never be able to live with himself.

They went round and round the same arguments until the sky began to lighten. They heard Misha saddling up the ponies with Goga's help. They got out of bed and faced each other, their expressions hard and angry, stubborn and unyielding.

Without another word, Andrey fetched some clothing from a wardrobe, put on his boots and walked out of the bedroom. Katya heard him march along the corridor with quick military steps and then clatter down the main stairs to the hall. Ten minutes later there came the sound of hooves, and then there was nothing but the dawn chorus and the sighing of the wind.

Over the next few months Katya felt ashamed of what she had said. Ever since their altercation, the news had consistently proved her wrong. The weekly post began to bring a news-sheet which, as the summer progressed, reported victory after victory. Simbirsk, Samara, Syzran and Kazan all fell to the Whites. A Volga Republic had been declared in Samara, a provisional government of Siberia in Omsk. There were rumours of the British and French, even the Americans, sending troops to support the Whites.

Katya stopped worrying. She turned her energies to converting one of the barns of the old military convalescence home into a dispensary for Golovino and nearby villages. She had plans to offer positions to doctors from neighbouring towns in return for board and lodging at the house. Her relations with the villagers had never been better. Goga and Mara, who planned to marry as soon as the summer harvest had been brought in, had not heard a whisper of discontent or conspiracy for months.

She received regular bulletins from Andrey – a rider with good horses could make the journey from Samara in a few days. Soon after he had arrived in Samara with Misha, the Czech Legion had joined the Whites. They had made all the difference in defeating the Reds and now controlled the great railway which crossed Siberia to Vladivostok. Diterikhs had taken command of the Czechs and had appointed Andrey his chief of staff.

Katya enjoyed three of the happiest months of her life. She watched with satisfaction as Svyet and Gulya grew up. When not working on her plans for the clinic, she read from the large backlog of magazines that she had neglected in the times of stress and anxiety. She was fascinated by the new philosophical thinking springing up all over Europe.

This period of fruitful tranquillity was brought to a cruel end when, in mid-summer, shocking news came to Golovino like a wolf among sheep. She was in a clearing in the wood with the village carpenter, discussing the design of a dormitory where people with infectious diseases could be quarantined. She heard the sound of hooves and looked up to see Goga riding towards them at a brisk canter.

'*Barynia*, I have terrible news. The Tsar and all his family have been shot, murdered. It happened last week in Yekaterinburg, where they were being held prisoner.'

'*Bozhe moi*, my God! And the girls and the Tsarevitch?'

'I am afraid so, *Barynia*. Even the servants were killed. No one was spared.'

Katya crossed herself, as did Goga and the carpenter.

'But why?' asked Katya, her face twisted in anguish.

'Well, according to the postman from Syzran, the Reds didn't want the royal family to be rescued by the Czechs, who are closing in on Yekaterinburg. They feared they would become a rallying point for everybody who's against the Revolution.'

Katya stopped the work that she was doing with the carpenter and sent him back to the village and, in a trance, started to walk home. Out of the trees Stenka suddenly appeared, with his sixth sense for human distress. He leaned slightly against her as she trudged through the woods, a gesture of comfort and protection. Katya patted the giant hound, muttering, 'Dear, dear Stenka.' He nuzzled her, grunting faintly.

She emerged from the wood into the sun's oppressive heat. She began to feel faint and leaned on Stenka for support. He stiffened his body to take her weight and guided her to one of the benches scattered around the park. She sat down heavily at one end, where a small tree offered some shade. She closed her eyes and fell instantly asleep. Stenka sat, alert and on guard.

Katya awoke with a start. For a moment she fancied that she was under some physical threat and looked around her in alarm. Stenka barked at her, as if to say, 'Don't worry. I'm here.' This brought her to her senses. The Tsar, the Tsarina, the four handsome daughters and the little haemophiliac boy – shot to death. She prayed that their last moments had not been too terrible.

As she got to her feet to return to the house, she was suffused with the most terrible sense of foreboding. Holy Russia was holy no more. It had destroyed God's anointed representative on earth. Russia would become a cursed land.

*

Andryusha's messages became less and less frequent and the few he did send were short and hurried. As they were bringing in the harvest, Goga began to hear stories from travellers passing through the village of setbacks for the White army. Without telling Katya, he rode to Syzran to get more reliable news. The White garrison, a mixed force of Russians and Czechs, was moving out.

He rode alongside a marching column and asked where they were going. A young lieutenant replied, 'We've had orders to march to the Volga and join the main force. The Reds have launched a counterattack on Kazan. Where are you from? A fit young lad like you should be marching with us.'

'It may yet come to that,' said Goga grimly. 'I am the steward of the estate at Golovino, to the west of here.'

The lieutenant barked a humourless laugh. 'Well, you had better pray our line holds. Sounds to me like you could be right in the path of the Reds' offensive. If Kazan falls, it will be Simbirsk next and then the big prize, Samara.'

Goga wished the lieutenant Godspeed and rode as fast as he could back to Golovino, deeply troubled. What if the Reds decided to march in the direction of Golovino on their way to the railhead at Syzran? How much warning would they get?

He arrived at the house in time for supper. At first he had thought of concealing from Katya his purpose in going to Syzran. She was still depressed about the murder of the Romanovs and sat in her bedroom all day, lost in dark thoughts. But he changed his mind. If there was a real danger to her and the girls, she must know about it. He consulted Mara, who agreed.

The following morning Goga spoke to Katya. They went to the library together and pulled out a map of the region. It was as he had feared. If the Reds took Kazan and moved south down the Volga towards Samara via Simbirsk, Golovino could well be at risk, especially if the Reds wanted Syzran as well.

By the middle of September the bad news came thick and fast. Stragglers and deserters from the White Army, some of them still armed, dribbled through Golovino, stealing chickens and goats. Goga had to fire at two of them who were trying to rape a village woman. Then they brought the news that Kazan had fallen to the Reds, followed a few days later by Simbirsk. The Red Army, the deserters said, was far better equipped than they were. It was cruel and vengeful. Prisoners were shot without mercy.

The mood of the villagers had changed yet again. Already disgruntled by a poor harvest, now they became positively surly towards Katya and Goga. The *baryn* was absent and anyway fighting for the other side – word had soon got around. They sniffed which way the wind was blowing and began to dream again of looting the house and stealing the land. The newly built dispensary was mysteriously burned down. Goga once again went on his nightly patrols. On one of these his horse, fortunately not Mars, was shot from under him by an unseen assailant, just as the sun was rising. Safin disappeared from the village.

'He's gone to Simbirsk to meet up with the Bolsheviks,' said Mara.

For once Goga's decisive mind was defeated by the situation. To stay or to go? The *barynia*, as before, did not want to leave before the return of the *baryn*. But she had not heard from him for weeks. Days passed in an agony of tension and dread. Most of the servants, terrified out of their wits, fled back to the village. Storm clouds gathered every afternoon, unleashing thunder, lightning and hailstones the size of pebbles, as they often did in September. The peasants saw this as a sign from an angry God. It stoked their superstitious restlessness and belief that great changes were coming.

Then, one morning, Andrey rode back home bringing terrible news. The White forces were in full retreat. The Red Army was on the march towards Golovino.

Mounted reconnaissance units could arrive at any moment. The family would have to leave the house that night.

There was worse news still, Andrey added. Trotsky's new Red Army had political officers – commissars – to maintain discipline and loyalty to the Bolshevik government, now installed in Moscow. The commissar commanding the political units on the Volga front was none other than Maxim Konstantinovich Lebedev, *his* Lebedev. He hoped and prayed that Lebedev had not found out who lived at Golovino.

Katya, Andrey, Goga and the children were standing in the great hall. Svyet was holding one of Andrey's legs, Gulya the other, each trying to catch his attention. Katya said, 'Mara reports that Safin has been to Simbirsk to make contact with the Bolsheviks. He will certainly have betrayed you, perhaps personally to Lebedev.'

'Damn,' said Andrey. He looked at Katya and then at the floor. He looked up again into her eyes.

'You were right and I was wrong – and not for the first time. I am sorry for what I said the night before I left.'

Katya, ignoring Andrey's apology, walked briskly out of the hall, saying in a cold, hard voice that they must get ready to leave. Andrey picked up one daughter in each arm and went to look for the nanny.

Because of their previous preparations, they were ready to go well before nightfall. Goga went to fetch Mara as soon as dusk fell. But she too refused to leave. By now the village had guessed that she was an informer. Her parents, Vanya and Oleg, were tainted by association. Mara felt that she could not abandon them.

This time Goga's brain was working.

'Then your parents must come with us. There is no future for them here. Only death awaits them. Your father could drive one of the carts and your mother help with the children. I could not leave without you, Mara, and I could not desert Andrey Andreyevich and Ekaterina Alexandrovna. I would kill myself first,' he said passionately.

It was all agreed with surprising speed. Mara's parents had needed little persuading. Their closest neighbours now regarded them with hard suspicion. They had found their dog hanging lifeless from their gate. With a couple of saddlebags apiece, Mara's mother climbed onto the back of her daughter's horse, her father on Goga's. They crept out of the village and, once in the wood, galloped away furiously into the night.

Chapter 14

It was ten in the evening and the little convoy of two carts made ready to leave Golovino. A huge moon was beginning to rise, throwing a strange red light. A blood moon, thought Katya ominously.

Oksana hobbled awkwardly towards one of the carts, where Svyet and Gulya, furious at being awoken, were crying inconsolably. She put her hands on their heads, bent low to kiss their foreheads, whispered prayers and made the sign of the cross. Then, deeply distressed, she turned to walk back to the house. Katya wept. Oksana had been her wet nurse and nanny from the day she was born.

Andrey and Valentin, the major domo, shook hands. Katya, increasingly in the grip of her emotions, hugged him tightly. He had been with the family as long as Oksana. Andrey had asked him whether he would prefer to get out before the Reds arrived.

'*Baryn*,' Valentin had replied, 'my only home is this place. I will stay, look after the house and put my fate in the hands of God. I ask only that you leave me Stenka. He strikes terror into the villagers, who think he's the devil's hound.'

Andrey readily agreed though it hurt him to leave Stenka, whom he had reared from a puppy. But he was really too big to come with them. This was the best solution.

Stenka howled in grief as the carts departed. He broke away from Valentin and ran to Andrey, looking up at him with pleading eyes and pawing at Molnya's flank. Andrey dismounted. He dropped to his knees and held Stenka's head in both hands, looking up into his eyes. Those on the carts could see Andrey's lips moving as he spoke to the dog, caressing his ears. Then he rose to his feet and pointed to the house. Stenka turned round and walked slowly back to Valentin. Mara could have sworn that the hound was weeping.

'Andryusha,' asked Katya, 'what did you say to Stenka?'

'I told him to look after the house and obey Valentin. He understood.'

Andrey and Katya had debated taking the family silver with them, but there was too much of it and it was too heavy to fit on the carts. As soon as the sun had set, Andrey, with Valentin's help, had wrapped it in blankets and buried it in a large hole in the soft earth of the vegetable garden. God willing, he would one day be able to retrieve it.

Katya, however, insisted on bringing the family's icons and all her jewellery. Andrey raised no objection. The large pouch of silver roubles would not last forever. Though he did not say as much to Katya, her jewels and icons might well have to be sold to keep the family alive. Who knew what fate awaited them? The same thought had occurred to Katya.

She drove one cart with Vanya sitting alongside her. Svyet and Gulya were behind, and were soon rocked to sleep by the swaying of the cart. It was filled with all the paraphernalia of young children as well as some food and clay jars with water and *kvass*.

Oleg, his daughter at his side, drove the other cart, with two spare ponies hitched behind. This cart was filled with small trunks and suitcases, containing what Andrey and Katya considered to be the bare necessities for restarting life in Samara, or wherever fate decided to deposit them.

Andrey, holding a large burning torch, rode in front on Molnya, who fretted at having to walk so slowly. He was heavily armed, as was Goga, who took up the rear on horseback, also carrying a burning brand. Katya, Oleg and Mara each had a shotgun to hand.

The plan was straightforward – to get to the railway station at Syzran and take a train to Samara, where they would find accommodation – but it was also perilous. Andrey calculated that it would take two days to reach Syzran. It was quite possible that Red cavalry would overtake them. Even if they arrived safely, they might find the town in Red hands. He had brought what he called his Trotsky uniform. He would then have to pretend that they were fleeing from drunken White deserters, who had seized their house. In all the confusion the bluff might work. But then they would be confronted by another problem. If Samara were still in White hands, there would almost certainly be no trains going there from Syzran. To stay in Syzran for any length of time would be dangerous. Their bluff could be called at any moment. Lebedev himself might appear. They would then have no choice but to continue driving eastwards until they reached White-controlled territory – if the Reds allowed them to go on their way.

He explained all this to Katya, Goga and Mara. Nobody had a better plan.

It was Katya who proposed stopping a few hours at Gradov, where her cousins, the Suslovs, lived. It was halfway on the road to Syzran. There they could rest the horses and ponies and take on fresh water. The Suslovs might know more about the military situation and who held Syzran. Andrey immediately accepted the wisdom of Katya's suggestion.

They made slower progress than Andrey had hoped. After the summer rains, the road had turned into a heavily rutted mud track. It was impossible to go faster than walking pace without risk to the axles and wheels. Added to which, the weather was still very hot. They all, horses and ponies included, needed frequent stops to refresh themselves, much to the frustration of Andrey. The animals' muzzles were plagued with flies. It took a sweating Oleg almost an hour to reshoe one of them, as the sun was at its zenith. Svyet and Gulya played quietly in the back of the cart, under the shade of a little canopy, their energy sapped by the heat. Katya kept watch for wasps, but one finally broke through her defences and stung Svyet, who cried for a good hour. To console her, Vanya and Mara quietly sang old songs of the countryside. By mid-afternoon, the little party had fallen silent, exhausted by the journey and the heat.

They passed through flat open country and woodland. They did not meet a single traveller.

The sun was low in the sky as they trundled up the driveway to the

Suslovs' house at Gradov. It was an imposing structure, built in a neo-classical style. As they pulled up, however, the place seemed deserted. Andrey knocked on the door. There was no reply and no sound from within.

'Look, Andryusha,' Katya suddenly called, pointing to an upper window, where she had spotted the face of a woman. 'I'm sure that's Vera.'

Vera was a spinster of uncertain age who looked after the Suslovs, both now in their eighties. It had never been clear whether she was a relative of the family or a governess who had grown old in her service. The Suslovs' only child, a daughter, had long since married and left the family home with her new husband.

The Suslovs were cousins of Katya's and also the family's nearest neighbours, but because of the distance and difference in age, they rarely saw the Suslovs in the summer months. Nor were they that close in St Petersburg. Old General Suslov bored everyone rigid, his conversation confined exclusively to matters military. Andrey had at the beginning found his war tales quite interesting. But at the fourth time of telling, the Battle of Shipka Pass, and the Turkish bullet that had passed through his cap, had begun to pall. His wife, the Countess Suslova, a delicate, bird-like creature, had taken refuge in religious mysticism, like many Russian women of her advanced age. At receptions she would find herself a chair and sit alone, a beatific smile playing on her face.

Andrey banged more loudly at the door. It finally opened a fraction and a shotgun barrel emerged through the crack.

'General, don't shoot! It is Andrey Andreyevich, your neighbour!' Andrey shouted. After a pause, the door swung wide to reveal General Suslov in full military uniform, a blue and gold tunic adorned with medals and a great silver star, finished off with a sash in the blue, white and red of the defunct Russian Empire. A curved sabre in a scabbard hung from his side. With shaking hands, he pointed his shotgun at the party. Partially hidden behind him stood the countess, leaning on two sticks, and Vera, both with expressions of fearful apprehension.

The old general lowered the shotgun and leaned on the door jamb, wheezing heavily. A shock of white hair leading to bushy side whiskers framed a deeply lined, craggy face, out of which rheumy old eyes still blazed with fierce defiance.

'Ah, Polkonin, it's you. Thought it was one of those brigands from the village. You were lucky. I was about to give you both barrels,' said the old general in a rasping voice, pausing to get his breath between sentences. 'Come in, come in. Your men can take the ponies round the back to the stables. The stable boys have gone, but there should be feed and water. Then you can tell us what on earth you are up to.'

Goga and Oleg took the animals, while the rest of the party entered the gloomy hallway. It was unbearably hot and stuffy. A slight smell of urine hung in the air. They followed the Suslovs into the drawing room, the general leaning on Vera while his wife hobbled on her sticks. Vanya and Mara hung back in the hallway, afraid to enter a nobleman's drawing room. Seeing their hesitation, Katya waved them in. After the harshness of the carts, the party sat down on the heavily cushioned chairs and sofas with sighs of relief. The children were placed on the floor, where Svyet constantly scratched the wasp sting on her arm.

'Why are you alone, sir?' Andrey asked. 'What has happened here?'

The countess waved her arms around, eyes bright with alarm, but no sound came from her mouth. The general made a croaking noise and, after what seemed like a Herculean effort, finally managed to tell Vera to explain the situation.

Crossing herself every other sentence, Vera explained that two days previously they had woken up to find the house deserted and all the servants gone. She had heard a noise coming from the stables and had run outside to find out what was happening. She came across two men from the local village in the process of taking the three horses that the Suslovs still kept. When she remonstrated with them, they laughed and threatened her with obscenities, which made her blush to recall. They then said that she and the Suslovs would do well to quit the house as soon as possible. The village had nothing against them personally – the general had always treated them fairly

– but the Red Army was coming and would destroy people of their kind without mercy.

At this point in Vera's tale, the Suslovs recovered their voices. The old countess exclaimed that she could not believe the villagers would be cruel or disloyal to them since, for as long as she could remember, they had lived together as one happy family, united in their love of the good Lord. She too crossed herself.

'Countess, with respect,' Andrey interrupted, 'the villagers may or may not stay loyal to you, but that is not the point. As the village men told Vera, it's the Red Army that you have to fear. They are merciless and cruel. If they come here, you will not survive. I'm sorry to speak so bluntly.'

Vera took out a handkerchief from her sleeve and began to sob. The countess's mouth began to work like a goldfish's. Katya could not tell whether she was praying silently or trying to say something. The old general, who had somewhat recovered, slammed his fist down on a coffee table.

'Look here, Polkonin, I was born in this house and I shall die in this house. In my time I have been in a thousand tight corners fighting the Turk – these desperados hold no fears for me.' General Suslov spoke with an intensity that was surprising for someone so infirm. 'When they see the uniform and medals of an old soldier who has fought all his life for Mother Russia, they will not dare lay a hand on us.'

'Sir,' said Andrey, 'I beg to differ. Your fine reputation as a fighting man will not protect you. If they have gone as far as to massacre the Tsar and his family, they will kill anyone who represents the old order. For goodness' sake, come with us to Syzran – before it is too late!'

The Suslovs were clearly unaware of the slaughter of the Romanovs. There was a silence in the room that seemed to go on forever. The general, who had hung his head at the terrible news, looked up at Andrey with a withering eye.

'If what you say is true, Polkonin, it would be better to die here defending ourselves to the end than to run away in the face of the enemy like weeping women.' As he said this, the general turned with a face like thunder to Vera, who was sobbing uncontrollably. She stopped immediately under the harshness of his gaze.

Andrey was cut to the quick by the general's scathing answer. As he was considering his reply, there came a knock on the double doors and Goga entered the room.

'Who is this?' asked the general irritably.

'This is Goga, our steward,' Andrey answered. 'I think he has something important to tell us.'

'I do, *Baryn*,' Goga replied. 'I have just been to the top of the tower at the back of the house. Though the light is fading fast, I was able to see a large column of smoke on the western horizon. It looked to me as if Golovino was on fire.'

Andrey looked out of the window. There was still some light. He jumped to his feet.

'Show me, Goga.'

They ran outside into the dusk and went round to the back of the house, where an outdoor iron staircase led to the top of a tower. Andrey and Goga clattered up the staircase as fast as they could. At the top they found themselves on an iron platform, which encircled the pointed spike of the round tower. Andrey, breathing heavily, pulled a military spyglass from his tunic pocket and looked to the west. He put the glass to his eye and saw a plume of smoke in the distance, silhouetted against the dying light. He could not be absolutely sure that it was Golovino, but to his artillery man's eye the distance and the direction suggested that his wife's family home was indeed ablaze.

If that was the case, Gradov would be next. It had taken the family the better part of a day to make the journey from Golovino. Fast-moving cavalry could do it in a couple of hours. There was no time to lose. They had to leave, with or without the Suslovs.

Goga broke into his thoughts.

'What shall we do, *Baryn*?'

'We must assume that Gradov is next, as it lies directly across the road to Syzran,' Andrey replied. He paused. 'Though, knowing soldiers, they will have drunk our cellar dry and be sleeping it off as we speak. Have you fed and watered the animals?'

'Yes, *Baryn*. We have also refilled the water containers. The horses and ponies could do with more rest. But as we travel so slowly, they will be good for another few hours. If you wish, we could leave right now.'

As Goga spoke, the sun disappeared below the horizon, leaving behind a dimming afterglow. They both returned to the house. When they entered the drawing room again, they found everyone asleep except for Vera, who, having lit the oil lamps, was nervously pacing the room.

She ran up to Andrey and, clutching his arm, said in a loud, trembling voice, 'We should leave, shouldn't we? You must persuade the general. I could not leave if he and the countess decide to stay.'

Her pleading tones awoke everyone. Svyet began to cry, which set Gulya off. The noise was ear-splitting. Katya tried to calm them.

Andrey was torn. He was anxious to leave and get the family to safety. But his conscience was deeply troubled at the thought of leaving an ancient couple and a spinster to the mercies of a brutal army and greedy peasants. The general's caustic comment had wounded him more than he liked to admit.

'Sir, I have been to the top of the tower and this is what I saw.' Andrey decided to adopt an unadorned military tone, as if he and the general were on campaign together – which, in a manner of speaking, they were. That might prove more persuasive.

The general looked at him coldly.

'Go ahead, Polkonin.'

'Sir, with the aid of a spyglass I was able to discern a large plume of grey smoke on the western horizon. In all probability it is your cousin's – my wife's – home.'

The general grunted, then coughed violently to clear his congested lungs. Andrey went on.

'The fire will be the work of the Red Army or of local peasants or of some combination of the two. We must assume that since the capture of Syzran is one of the Red Army's strategic objectives, they will travel the same road as we do, and loot and burn Gradov. The cavalry vanguard could appear at any moment. Your defensive position is impossible. You are condemning the countess and Vera to death. The right thing to do, if I may say so, General, is to beat a tactical retreat, save your family and live to fight another day. You could achieve all of that by coming with us to Syzran.'

The general grunted again.

'Polkonin, you are not thinking straight. Fear has warped your judgement.' Andrey winced. 'Listen, man. If these brigands are about to descend on us, they will get you, too. How fast can you travel in those carts? They will catch you up in no time. You won't stand a chance!'

The general collapsed onto the sofa in a coughing fit, which Andrey thought would kill him. He struggled in great wheezing gasps to find just enough breath to make his lungs function. Andrey watched, horrified. But, more than that, his mind had been set running by the general's words. Suslov was right. Unless the Reds decided to rest at Golovino, they would be caught on the road to Syzran – out in the open, hopelessly vulnerable.

Vera had given the general smelling salts to clear his airways. Gradually he regained his composure and his shallow breathing returned to some kind of normality.

'Then, sir, what would you have us do?' Andrey asked.

The general paused. His voice now came in a whisper and he beckoned Andrey to come and sit next to him.

'Your family must leave for Syzran tonight, now. Your wife in command. She's a capable woman. Gives them a few hours' start, with luck. You and your men stay here with me. We are four guns. If we position ourselves well, we can hold off a larger force. Make them think we are more. Did it at Shipka Pass. One man in the stables. One in the tower. Two in the house. Get 'em in a crossfire. With luck we'll drive them off. Put your horses at the back. If we are overwhelmed, you make a run for it and ride like hell down the road to Syzran, catch up your family,' the general whispered.

'What happens to you?' Andrey asked.

'If we are lucky and they lose a few men, they may decide we aren't worth the candle and give up the fight. If we look like going under, I'll retreat to the cellar. The countess and Vera must go there now. There's a secret tunnel which runs from the cellar to a hedgerow behind the apple orchard. My father built it for a situation like this.' The general, despite whispering, was again running out of breath.

Andrey looked around the room. Svyet and Gulya were curled up on a sofa, asleep. Everybody else was looking expectantly at him and the general.

He explained the general's plan to the room. It was all desperately risky, and could end in death for everyone, but, said Andrey, overall it gave everybody the best chance of survival. He expected fierce protest from Katya at the mention of separating, but Katya had that steely look in her eye that Andrey had first noticed on his return from the wars and, far from objecting, agreed that it was the best thing to do.

So did everyone else. Mara jumped up from the sofa and hugged and kissed Goga. Vanya did likewise with Oleg. They went outside to prepare the carts. Katya and Andrey embraced perfunctorily. Katya picked up the girls and followed the others.

Outside, few words were spoken.

'Godspeed,' said Andrey, 'see you in Syzran.' But Katya and Mara were already whipping the ponies forward, while Vanya tended to the girls in the back of Katya's cart.

Chapter 15

They came just after dawn. Red Army cavalry. Two parallel columns of ten, an officer at the front, riding at a canter up the drive. They wore grey uniforms and *budenovkyi*, rifles slung over their shoulders. They rode in good order. They looked disciplined and not especially threatening.

General Suslov opened the front door and stepped out in full military regalia. He saluted the officer, who returned his salute.

The previous night, after the carts had left and the countess and Vera had been safely installed in the cellar, the general had held what he called a council of war with Andrey, Goga and Oleg. They decided that, depending on the Red cavalry's approach, they would try at first to deflect them with diplomacy. This would be the general's job.

They abandoned the idea of putting someone in the stables where they could be too easily isolated from the others. Instead, they decided to put Oleg and Goga in the tower, which was connected by a passageway to the main building. It offered an all-round field of vision and would give them early warning of an attack from whatever direction. Each of them was armed with a rifle with a range far longer than that of a shotgun. Oleg, like Goga, was no mean shot, having served five years in the army. They decided that if it came to fighting they would each deliver rapid fire, creating the impression that there were more of them. To reinforce that impression, they would move from window to window and floor to floor.

The general, to steady his shaking hands, brought out of a cupboard a contraption first used by musketeers in the sixteenth century. It was a wooden cleft pole – a 'rest' – almost as tall as a man. The general placed it before the smaller, front-facing windows. He leaned two shotguns against the wall with a large box of shells.

Andrey, it was agreed, should give the order to shoot by firing first. He should otherwise have a roaming role on the first floor, bringing his rifle, shotgun or pistol to bear wherever they were most needed.

As the general exchanged salutes with the officer in command of the cavalry troop, Goga's keen eye atop the tower spotted movement towards the west, where the Suslovs' fields met woods. Beyond the woods lay the village of Gradov. He took out Andrey's spyglass and saw a group of men emerging from the trees. Most were carrying billhooks and scythes. A few had ancient muskets and shotguns.

Goga raced down the interior staircase two steps at a time and ran to find Andrey. He came across him hidden behind a curtain on the first floor, listening through an open window to the conversation between the general and the cavalry commander. He was frowning.

'This is not going well . . . ' he muttered.

Goga whispered what he had seen. Andrey snatched the spyglass from him and, crossing to the other side of the room, peered through the window into the distance.

'They mean mischief, Goga. Take up your position and await my shot. If we drive them off, we'll meet in the drawing room to decide what next. Leave Oleg in the tower as a look-out. If we have to make a run for it, you'll hear two shots fired in quick succession and then another two. Then go to the horses and have them ready.'

'Yes, *Baryn*,' said Goga, sprinting from the room.

Andrey returned to his curtain by the open window. He could hear the officer's voice.

'General, I repeat. You cannot stay here. We are in a state of war. I am under orders from Moscow that, as we advance against the Whites under that dog Kolchak, I must do whatever necessary to help the peasants take what is rightfully theirs – the land and properties of people of your parasite class. This, don't forget, is a revolution of workers and peasants! Now stand aside. In the name of the Supreme Military Council I declare this house requisitioned.'

Andrey now had his rifle in his hands. The officer jumped from his horse and, taking a piece of paper from inside his tunic, stepped forward briskly, pushing the old general to the ground. Andrey fired, killing the officer instantly. Then he shot three cavalrymen out of their saddles. Goga and Oleg joined in. Another six fell from their horses. By the time they stopped firing to reload, more than half the troop were dead. The survivors, who had had no chance to return fire, disappeared at a gallop down the drive.

Andrey ran down the stairs, opened the front door and helped the general to his feet. He was shaken but unhurt. They went back into the house and just as they were locking and bolting the great door, Andrey heard the crackle of rapid rifle fire from the tower. He looked again to the west. The peasants had almost reached the stables. They were dropping like flies. Corpses littered the ground. Some tried to reach the shelter of the stables, but were immediately cut down. Dropping their billhooks and scythes, the survivors ran back as fast as they could to the safety of the woods.

'Misjudged you, Polkonin,' said the general, eyes ablaze with the excitement of battle. 'That was fine musketry. Fell from their saddles like the Turks at Shipka Pass. What do you propose we do now?' His breathing had become easier as adrenalin surged through his body.

They were gathered in the drawing room, with Oleg on watch in the tower.

Andrey spoke. 'The Reds will not tolerate setbacks. We rebuffed them today and we inflicted severe casualties. As night follows day they will be seeking revenge. Because we killed so many of them, they may think that the house is defended by the White Army. I wouldn't be surprised if they brought up a cannon or a machine gun to obliterate us. We have a day, two at the most.'

The general thought for a moment and then said, 'You should leave, catch up your carts and take your family to safety. We have given the Reds a bloody nose and taught the peasants who is master around here. Honour has been satisfied. I thank you all for that. You were right, Polkonin. To their eternal shame, they showed no respect for the uniform of the Tsar's army, in which, I'd wager, most of them had served. Don't delay. Go now. I will retire to the cellar.'

Goga was the first to react to the general's unexpectedly generous words.

'Sir, they will burn the house down. You will die from the flames or the smoke, not from a bullet or a bayonet.'

'No, young man. My father thought of that. We will take the tunnel to the hedgerow and hide there. There is a concealed door between cellar and tunnel. So long as it is closed, very little smoke will get in. Besides, there is ventilation at the other end of the tunnel.'

For a moment Andrey considered disobeying the general's wishes and putting up a last stand when the Reds next attacked, but that would be utterly futile. The element of surprise was lost. More to the point, Andrey had won the general's respect. His sense of honour would not have allowed him to leave if he were still the object of the older man's scorn.

Goga ran to get the horses ready with Oleg. Andrey helped the general take his shotguns and ammunition down to the cellar, where a waist-high buttress pushed out from a wall. It was a superb firing position, which gave the general both cover and a place to rest his shotgun as he fired.

The door to the tunnel was cleverly placed in the angle made by the rear wall and one of the side walls so that it was almost impossible to see where they met. The general pulled on one of the hooks set into the wall for hanging salted beef and sheep carcases in the winter and the door swung open.

'If we are lucky,' he said, 'they won't find the door and they certainly won't find how to open it.'

A hand grenade would blow it open in a second, thought Andrey. But he decided not to say anything.

The general, despite the extreme and imminent danger, seemed to be in the highest spirits as he prepared for battle. He looked ten years younger, his breathing continued to flow more easily and he moved with greater ease.

Neither the countess nor Vera shared his optimism. They were seated on an old sofa. There was a generous supply of bread, dried meat, apples and water on a table. A chamber pot had been put in one of the cellar corners. The countess held an icon of the Virgin and was praying to herself. Vera, clutching a handkerchief, looked at them all in anguish, her eyes red from weeping.

Suddenly there was the sound of running feet. Vera cried out in fear, but it was only Goga, in a high state of alarm.

'*Baryn*, there is movement again to the west on the tree line. And something is happening at the bottom of the drive. We can't see well because of the trees at the bend in the road. I think the Reds are about to launch a two-sided attack. They may have a truck or armoured car at the end of the drive.'

'Polkonin, I command you to leave without further delay!' said the general sternly.

'Yes, sir!' replied Andrey. He bowed to the women and shook hands with the general. They looked each other in the eye. No further words were exchanged. With Goga, Andrey walked rapidly out of the cellar.

They went straight to the horses, where Oleg was waiting, then they mounted and rode carefully to the eastern edge of the house. Andrey peered round the corner and, thanks to his spyglass, could see two open trucks filled with infantry waiting at the bottom of the drive, cavalry behind them. He dismounted and ran back to the western side of the house. There he looked through his glass again and saw an armoured car starting to move across the hard, dry fields to the house.

He ran back to the horses, exclaiming in an urgent whisper, 'Time to go, fast. There is a two-pronged assault about to begin. The main force must have been much closer than I had calculated. We must ride out of here towards the north, since that is their blind spot. Then in due course we can loop round towards the east and Syzran.'

They spurred their horses and galloped hard for half a mile, stopping in the concealment of a small copse. There they turned to look behind them: no one was following. They could see the armoured car behind the stables. The sound of a rattling machine gun came to them on the mild breeze of the Indian summer. There were other reports from what sounded like rifle fire.

'May the Lord be with them,' said Andrey quietly. Goga and Oleg muttered 'Amen' and crossed themselves. Then they turned their horses' heads and continued north.

Chapter 16

Once free of Gradov's bumpy driveway, Katya and Mara were able to go at a steady trot. The surface of the straight road to Syzran began to improve, turning from rutted mud to a flat gravel. The ponies strained forward eagerly, liberated from the slow pace of the previous day.

A bright moon lit their way. The countryside appeared flat and formless, punctuated by the ghostly shapes of occasional woods and hedges. A warm breeze blew in the women's faces and the carts swayed from side to side in an agreeable rocking motion. The harnesses jingled. In the back of Katya's cart Svyet and Gulya were asleep, protected by blankets. Vanya was still awake, singing to herself the lullabies that had soothed the children earlier. The more Katya saw of Vanya and Mara, the more she liked them: tough, kind, courageous, practical, ready to laugh at the drop of a hat.

Katya had never felt such exhilaration. Driving the other cart, Mara was grinning broadly. What was it that had driven the fear and anxiety from them? Katya and Vanya had abandoned a husband, Mara the love of her life. They might never see them again. Her ancestral home was probably a smouldering wreck. They had lost everything. The future was uncertain and probably dangerous. Within twenty-four hours they might all be in prison. Or worse.

But, on the road, under the great orange moon, driving the ponies forward, a shotgun by her knee, she was mistress of her destiny. The sense of freedom and independence was intoxicating. She was certain that Mara shared her exaltation.

Her mind drifted to Andryusha. Why had she felt no sorrow at saying goodbye to him? In truth, after each of his prolonged absences, she had begun more and more to see the family as just herself and her children. His absences had also given her greater confidence in her own abilities. Had she not set up and managed a hospital at Golovino, for which she had received a commendation from the Tsarina? Had she not continued her education, opening her mind to the latest philosophical and scientific thinking? She was itching to set up a salon which would range far more broadly and deeply than the one in St Petersburg. The Lord only knew when she would have the chance to realise her dream.

A thought was knocking at her mind's door, to which she would not yet allow entrance: that Andryusha was a constraining and negative influence on her life.

A shout from behind broke into her reverie. Mara was asking to stop. They brought their carts to a halt and jumped down onto the road. Vanya joined them. The moon was now very close to the horizon and would disappear within the half-hour. Mara spoke first.

'Barynia . . .' She was immediately interrupted by Katya.

'Don't call me that. Please call me Katya. You, too, Vanya.'

The two women smiled at Katya and, on an impulse, they hugged each other under the dying moon and a billion stars.

Mara started again. 'Katya, we've been on the road for some three hours, maybe more. When the moon goes, which will be very soon, the night sky won't be bright enough to light our way safely. I think it would be better to rest and water the ponies – and give ourselves a break – and start again as soon as the sun rises. I know there's a risk that the Reds might catch us, but if they are that close behind, they'll get us anyway.'

Mara spoke with a calmness and authority that belied her years. Katya looked at her admiringly, at her beauty and her physical toughness. Mara was wearing only a sleeveless bodice above her long skirt, exposing the hard muscles of her arms. There was an inner resolution there, too. She turned to Mara's mother, whose expression was a mixture of love and wonder at the prodigy she had produced.

'She's right, Katya. Ponies are tougher than horses, but not that tough.'

'Right,' said Katya, 'it's agreed. We'll rest till dawn. We'd better take turns with hourly watches.'

'No,' answered Vanya, 'I'll take the watch. I have fired a shotgun before, you know.'

Katya and Mara slept the few hours till dawn, when Vanya awoke them. They had a hurried breakfast of fruit, bread and water. The sun rose straight at them. The girls continued sleeping, even when the carts started moving again.

They all had a greater sense of urgency than before. The spirit of adventure and optimism that had run through them was now tempered by an uneasy feeling that danger lay not far behind. Katya and Mara repeatedly turned their heads to see if the enemy was on their heels.

When danger came, however, it was not from behind, but from in front. They mounted a slight incline – it could hardly be called a hill – and when they reached the top, they saw in front of them a caravan of six covered wagons on the downward slope moving slowly towards Syzran.

Vanya stood up to look.

'Tinkers,' she said contemptuously. 'Thieves and murderers. We must be careful. They will want to rape and rob three women on their own, maybe kill us and sell the babes.'

'Hide your shotguns, but be ready to use them. I'll try to drive past,' replied Katya.

But, as they got nearer the caravan, they could see that there was no room to pass the wagons, which sat like fat ducks in the middle of the road. Then the wagons stopped. They had been spotted. Two men jumped from one of them and stood in the middle of the road, barring their way.

Katya brought her cart to a halt about ten yards in front of the men. They were young, swarthy, unshaven. They wore waistcoats over filthy white shirts.

'Good morning,' she called out. 'I would ask you to please let us pass. We have two sick children in the back – it's cholera or typhoid – and we must get to the doctor in Syzran as fast as possible.'

'Good morning, mother. Let us see,' said one of the young men. They walked round the carts slowly, almost languidly, peering inside. Their small, black, predatory eyes did not miss a thing: the supplies of food and drink in Katya's cart and the trunks and boxes in Mara's. They looked at Mara like hungry animals. In the middle of this tour of inspection, Svyet suddenly woke up and, with a smile on her face, asked Vanya for something to eat. She waved cheerily at the men.

'Cholera or typhoid, eh, mother?' asked one of the men. They had returned to face the carts, but were now very close, holding the ponies' bridles. The smell of them was almost unbearable.

'Get down from the carts, please, ladies, and come and enjoy our hospitality before you resume your journey.'

Both men laughed out loud at that, their eyes glittering, like hyenas about to go in for the kill. One of them reached for Katya's skirt to pull her off the cart. As he flicked the fabric aside, he saw the shotgun beneath. His hand closed brutally on her wrist to stop her reaching for the weapon. He looked up at her, grinning. She tried in vain to pull away. Then she was deafened by a blast just behind her head and the man fell backwards as if pulled by a mighty hand. A bloody mess had taken the place of his face and skull.

'Bastard,' came a voice from behind her.

Katya turned to see Vanya, shotgun aimed at the other man, one barrel smoking. She turned further to see Mara also standing, with shotgun held across her breast. Svyet and Gulya were howling in fear. The other young tinker stood rigid with shock.

The women noticed another man walking towards them. He had emerged from the front wagon. He was older and had an air of authority. He carried a shotgun. Katya, Vanya and Mara all levelled their weapons at him.

Katya shouted at him, 'Come no closer or we will shoot you. All we want to do is continue our journey to Syzran. But we will kill anyone who tries to rob or attack us.'

The older man also had the swarthy features of a native of the

Caucasus region – bald, a large, hooked nose and a bushy, black moustache set in an unshaven face. There was something both brutal and humorous about his expression. In dress he was altogether tidier and cleaner than the younger men. Behind him faces were peering out of the wagons.

He stopped and looked at them quizzically.

'Who are you?' he asked Katya.

'We have come from Golovino, where the Reds burned our house. I left my husband at Gradov. He's helping the owners protect their property against the advancing troops.'

'Reds!' said the man and spat on the ground. 'Who is your husband?'

'Colonel Andrey Andreyevich Polkonin,' replied Katya.

'Polkonin, Polkonin,' said the older man almost to himself. Then he relaxed and lowered his shotgun, smiling broadly.

'Colonel Polkonin! I'll be damned! So you are the Countess Polkonina.' He inclined his head in a slight bow. 'My name is Isaac and I am the head of this band. Your husband was always happy to let us use your land for a night or two. We used to drink together when our people came through Golovino. By God, he was a tough nut. By the time we had knocked back a few bottles, I was unconscious, but he could still ride a horse.'

Isaac looked at Katya unthreateningly, while he seized the younger man by the collar. Katya took a gamble. She had heard Andryusha tell of Isaac. She put down her weapon and told Vanya and Mara to do the same. She spoke to Isaac in a tone of respect.

'I have heard much about you. It is a pleasure to meet you. What you didn't know, Isaac, is that when my husband got home, he fell off his horse and had to be carried to bed.'

Isaac slapped his thigh and laughed out loud.

Katya jumped down from the cart and walked straight towards him, her hand outstretched. They shook hands.

'I am sorry about this man, but he and the other one here attacked us,' she said.

'Damned good-for-nothing got what he deserved,' Isaac replied.

Then he turned to the young tinker, cuffed him hard around the head and told him to go back to his mother.

'That's my son. Let that be a lesson to him. Vartan was always a bad influence.'

After that the deal was rapidly struck. Katya gave five silver roubles to Isaac for the family of the dead man. Isaac asked for nothing more out of respect for her husband, but she gave him a sack of grain and a jar of *kvass* nonetheless. Isaac said that he and his band were going to camp somewhere nearby. If the Reds came looking, he would think of something to put them off the scent.

The wagons pulled to the side of the road to let their carts pass, and Isaac walked alongside the two carts until they were safely past the caravan. There was a lot of wailing and sobbing in one of the wagons from the family of the man Vanya had killed. 'Five silver roubles will soon put paid to that,' said Isaac with a sardonic smile.

He and Katya bade each other goodbye with a warmth that surprised both of them. As they disappeared from sight, Isaac shook his head and smiled to himself. It was not every day that you came across two carts occupied by three armed women, one of whom killed a member of your family, another who was a noblewoman and the third beautiful enough to break your heart. These were strange times.

Katya set off at a fast trot, filled once again with the exhilaration that had swept through her at the outset of the journey. With a mixture of violence and diplomacy, the three of them had just faced down some of the biggest cut-throats on God's earth. Mara and Vanya congratulated her elatedly on the way she had handled Isaac. Katya in turn covered Vanya in praise for shooting one of the tinkers. Vanya wondered whether God would forgive her. Katya replied forcefully that of course he would. She had saved two innocent babies.

Of course, luck had played a considerable part. If Andryusha had not made friends with Isaac years ago, Lord knows what would have happened. A pang of conscience piqued her as she recalled her uncharitable thoughts about her husband.

They reached Syzran within the hour. It was a scruffy little place of no distinction, save for its rail terminus and waterfront on the Volga. Katya stopped her cart at the entrance to the town.

'We'd better smarten ourselves up if we're going to find rooms in a hotel,' she said to the others. 'Then I suppose we just wait for our menfolk.'

'We'll also need a safe place for the carts or else we'll have to sleep in them,' Mara reminded her. 'We can't leave them unattended, otherwise everything will be stolen.'

'True,' Katya agreed, pouring water from a pitcher into a bowl. She plunged her face into the water and wiped it with a small towel, then passed the pitcher and bowl to Vanya, remarking, 'If I don't have a bath soon I'll smell worse than those tinkers.'

It was barely a joke. There was a pause. The three women looked at each other, then they burst into wild, almost hysterical, laughter. It was a moment of explosive release from tension. They all embraced tightly.

'I smell worse than you, Katya!' exclaimed Vanya, laughing so hard she could barely stand.

'No, Mama,' screamed Mara, 'I am worse than both of you!' as she exposed and sniffed her bare, tufty armpits. The street resounded to their whooping mirth. Then Vanya saw a horseman approach.

Katya looked up, wiping the tears of laughter from her eyes. There was something familiar about the rider. The three women stood watching, serious again now. Could it be, thought Katya? Surely not . . .

The rider stopped. He was in a plain brown military uniform with a carbine over his shoulder and a sword at his side. He had a pleasing open face with a wisp of a beard.

'Good morning, ladies, may I be of service?' he asked, removing his cap and bowing from the saddle with exaggerated courtesy. Then he leapt from his horse and ran to embrace Katya.

'Katya, Katya, thank God you are safe – and the children!'

She returned the embrace. They held onto each other for a moment. Then she broke away and, turning to Vanya and Mara, said, 'May I introduce Commander Chazov, a very old friend of our family? Misha, this is Vanya and Mara, mother and daughter, two of the bravest women on this planet.'

'I have been expecting you, but with Andryusha. What happened?' asked Misha anxiously, after shaking hands with Vanya and Mara.

Katya gave him a brief account of all that had taken place since their flight from Golovino. Misha looked at once astonished and concerned.

'I salute you, ladies,' he exclaimed, looking admiringly at each of the women in turn. 'I wouldn't have bet on any woman escaping the clutches of a band of tinkers. That you killed one of them and then parted on good terms with their leader is extraordinary.'

The three women beamed at him, not unaffected also by his charm and good looks.

'And talking of tight spots,' Misha continued, 'there are few more resourceful individuals than your Andryusha. But to defy an entire Red Army with three rifles and a shotgun carried by a wheezing ancient is, even for him, setting the bar pretty high.'

Misha looked each of the women in the eye as he asked, 'But, surely, he didn't intend, with Oleg – it is Oleg, isn't it? – and Goga, to fight to the death?'

'I don't think so,' Katya answered evenly, 'they wanted to give the Reds a bloody nose and allow us a chance to get away. I can't speak for General Suslov. He and the countess said that they had no intention of leaving. We must just pray to God that the Reds don't find their hiding place.'

'Knowing old Suslov, he'd keep on blazing away with his shotgun till the last,' said Misha, rubbing his chin. 'Let's think a minute. The Reds in my experience don't like attacking at night. Let's assume they moved on Gradov yesterday at dawn or thereabouts, some eight hours after you left. Let's assume that your menfolk held them at bay for a while, say two hours, and then made their getaway.'

The sun was getting hot as it rose higher in the sky. The Indian summer, with its blue skies and fluffy clouds, was still with them. The three women, fatigue starting to set in, leaned against one of the carts, grateful for their straw hats. Svyet and Gulya lay peacefully in the arms of Katya and Vanya. The ponies stamped and shook their heads as the usual cloud of flies buzzed round them.

'Look,' continued Misha, 'this is no better than informed guesswork. But if I were Andryusha, I would not have gone galloping down the road to Syzran, since there would have been a real risk of the Red cavalry catching them. I would have taken a roundabout route, from the north or approached Syzran from the east – safer, but a much longer way round. But, I'd expect your menfolk, who would be desperately worried about you, to have taken the shorter, but more risky, route. That would, I reckon, put them on the Syzran road not far behind you.'

Misha paused and raised his face to the sky. The three women looked at him expectantly. He thought for a few moments, lowered his head, looked at his boots and then raised his head again, saying firmly, 'Right. I'll get together a patrol and head in the direction of Gradov to find out what I can. But, first, let's get you installed in the hotel, where I can give you some of the officers' accommodation. It's no great shakes, but at least it's clean and there's hot water. We are all leaving tonight on the last train to Samara. After that it will only be a matter of time before Syzran is taken by the Reds. If Andryusha has not appeared by this evening, you will have a difficult decision to take – to stay or leave with us.'

Chapter 17

Misha had guessed correctly. At that very moment, Andrey, Oleg and Goga were about forty minutes away on the highway to Syzran.

They had ridden hard from Gradov all the previous day, across flat and occasionally wooded country. Their great fear was that if the Reds discovered their tracks behind the house, the cavalry would follow in hot pursuit, eager to avenge their fallen comrades.

They followed a wide arc, which, by nightfall, brought them to the top of a ridge, facing due south. They had been able to water the horses at frequent streams and lakes. They had had enough feed in their saddlebags for the animals and plenty of dried meat for themselves. They had avoided villages, in case the inhabitants gave them away to any pursuers. They pitched camp on top of the ridge, each of them taking sentry duty every two hours. Looking south and east, Andrey could see a small cluster of twinkling lights. It had to be Syzran.

They rose a little after dawn. Andrey first scouted northwards with his spyglass and immediately saw just what he had feared – a column of horsemen heading in their direction, enveloped from time to time in a cloud of dust. They would be up the ridge in under an hour. Suddenly the column stopped. Andrey realised that its commander was looking at him as he was looking at them.

They moved off the crest. The road looked deserted. To the east, a series of vague shapes where the lights had been revealed the town of Syzran. They could just see, beyond the shapes, a change in colour that was the Volga river. It would be a good two hours' ride to the sanctuary of the town – if sanctuary it were. It would be a desperately close-run thing to outride the pursuing Red cavalry. They left the ridge without further delay and joined the highway to Syzran.

The Red horsemen drew ever closer. Molnya would have outrun them easily, as would Goga on Mars, but Oleg's horse, though good enough and from the Golovino stables, was not in the same class and began to tire before the others. After an hour or so the pursuing cavalry became identifiable as individual horsemen. Andrey's spyglass showed them to be riding in single column, with one of them near the front flying a red pennant. He reckoned they would be caught on the outskirts of Syzran. Everything depended on the town still being controlled by an effective force of Whites.

Andrey ordered everyone to stop as they came to a little roadside stream. The panting, sweating horses drank greedily from the water. Andrey looked again through his spyglass. There were fewer horsemen than before. Several of them must have fallen behind, unable to keep up the pace.

'We have only a minute,' said Andrey. 'I have the fastest horse and will ride ahead to get help from the town. If there is none to be had, I'll return and make a stand with you. Before the Reds get too close, you should find a ditch or a wood, where you can take up a good defensive position and hold them off until I return. There were around forty of them this morning. They look to be half that now. Those are manageable odds! Goga, take my spare carbine and ammunition!'

Andrey soon pulled away from Goga and Oleg, as the mighty Molnya showed his strength and speed. But even he, after the exertions of the last day and a half, was blowing heavily as Andrey rode into Syzran twenty minutes later. It was nearly noon and the small town appeared for a moment deserted. Then he heard the sound of hooves and around a corner came a troop of lancers, led by a young officer. They were neither Reds nor Cossacks, but wore a brown uniform he had never seen before. They rode aggressively towards him, only pulling up at the last minute. Andrey, blinded by sweat and fearing the worst, reached for his pistol. A familiar voice shouted at him,

'Hold hard, Andryusha, it's me, Misha, and these are my Czech lads!'

Andrey said one word: 'Katyenka . . . '

'Safe and well with the babes and the other ladies, enjoying the spartan delights of the best and only hotel in town,' replied Misha, saluting.

Andrey looked at Misha's boyish, laughing face, now adorned with a smudge of a beard. He could have wept with relief. But this was no time for sentiment – or questions. He had no idea how Commander Chazov, a naval gunner and intelligence agent, had managed to transform himself into a Czech cavalry commander. The last time he had seen him, he had just got back from one of his secret missions for Kolchak.

Andrey rapidly explained the dire situation of his companions.

'Then we must go at once to their rescue! Just like old times, eh, Andryusha?'

Misha's habitual enthusiasm appeared to communicate itself immediately to his troopers, a tough-looking bunch of eighteen hardened veterans. They grinned broadly at the prospect of action. Andrey quickly handed the exhausted Molnya to one of the troopers – who was not happy to stay behind on stable duty – and jumped on the man's horse. He took his place alongside Misha. Together they and the troop rode hell for leather down the road from where he had just come.

After twenty minutes' hard riding, they heard the sound of rifle fire, sometimes intense, sometimes sporadic with single shots. They could see a small hut in the distance at one side of the road. Goga and Oleg were inside under siege from the Reds, who had dismounted and looked to be firing from a small ditch that gave them cover on the opposite side of the road.

Misha stopped the troop for a minute to consider tactics. He was for sending a couple of men forward to reconnoitre. A grizzled sergeant growled, 'And by the time we all get there, sir, the colonel's men will be dead and we'll have to bury them. Better to go straight in and hit the Reds hard and fast.'

Andrey was intensely relieved at the sergeant's words. He looked at Misha, who raised a quizzical eyebrow.

'Misha, I don't want to risk your men, but there's no time to lose.'

Misha turned to the troop.

'Advance at the gallop towards the firing. At my command, wheel to the right and then turn sharply to the left so we catch the Reds in the rear. For the final charge, lances will be deployed in three columns of six.'

Now it was Andrey's turn for exhilaration. Anxiety, his constant companion for weeks, was swept away by the wild gallop, the hot air rushing into his face and through his hair. He had sometimes found a similar exaltation when hunting boar. But this was something else. It was pure soldiering in the face of imminent danger. He forgot Golovino, he forgot Gradov and the poor old general, he forgot his family, he forgot even that the purpose of the charge was to rescue Goga and Oleg.

The Reds were caught at their most vulnerable. They were climbing out of the ditch for a final assault on the hut where Goga and Oleg were holed up. They were too busy firing to their front to hear what was happening behind them. By the time Misha's troop was among them, their own horses had been scattered and the two soldiers deputed to look after them run through with lances.

The fight did not last long. The Reds were tough and experienced, but they never recovered from the surprise. By the time they were able to return fire, half their number was already dead or wounded from the initial assault. Another six were killed, including their commanding officer, who fell to Andrey's pistol. A couple of them were hit by Goga and Oleg. Then they surrendered. Two Czech troopers lay wounded on the ground.

The Czechs disarmed the surviving half a dozen Reds and forced them to sit in the road with their hands on their head. Andrey and Misha hurried to the hut and went inside. Oleg was dead, a bullet hole in his forehead. Goga had been wounded in the shoulder and arm, but was still standing in firing position by the hut's little window.

'Thank God you are here, *Baryn*,' said Goga, his white shirt covered in blood and his pale face shiny with sweat. 'We were about to be overrun. I'm hit but it doesn't feel too bad. We didn't realise how flimsy this hut was. Poor Oleg was killed when one of their bullets came straight through the wall. I was hit the same way. If we hadn't known how to handle a rifle, it would have been over long before you arrived.'

'What shall we do with the prisoners, Captain?' asked the sergeant. 'We can't take them with us. Better to shoot them.'

'No,' replied Misha, 'better still to humiliate them. Make them take their clothes off, please, Sergeant. Then leave them in the road. Only shoot if any of them refuse.'

'Yes, sir,' said the sergeant with a grin.

Andrey saw that Goga was quite badly hurt. He put iodine on both wounds, which made Goga grunt in pain. He put a tourniquet on his arm and told him to hold a bandage to the shoulder to staunch the bleeding. With Misha's help, Goga clambered onto Andrey's horse and, sitting behind him, held onto his waist. Misha then draped Oleg's body in front of him across his horse's saddle. They returned at a canter to Syzran.

Misha and Andrey rode side by side. Goga had to be tied to Andrey as he slipped in and out of consciousness. Misha briefed Andrey.

'Katya, the children and the other two ladies are at the Chaika hotel next to the railway station. They were only a couple of hours ahead of you. They are all in good health. They have quite a tale to tell you. Your wife is an extraordinary woman, of the greatest resourcefulness and most exemplary courage,' Misha said, his voice full of admiration.

'We leave for Samara at midnight,' he continued, speaking fast. 'An armoured train is being prepared, which will carry what remains of the garrison and its equipment. Headquarters have decided to consolidate our forces at Samara. We just can't hold Syzran, the Reds will outflank us. The military situation is not good, Andryusha, I have to tell you.'

'I know,' said Andrey gloomily, 'the front is crumbling wherever you look. What do we do with Goga? He doesn't look good.'

'The train has a carriage for the wounded, where we will put Goga immediately,' replied Misha. 'He seems to have lost a lot of blood, but he should be all right, so long as the wounds don't get infected. We have two compartments for your family, Vanya and Mara – they, by the way, are almost as remarkable as your wife! We should be able to fit all your personal things in one of the wagons. What shall we do about poor Oleg? In this heat we must put him in the town morgue immediately. But after that?'

'I don't know,' said Andrey, already tormented at the thought that he was responsible for Oleg's death. If he had stayed with Oleg and Goga, they might with an extra rifle have been able to drive off the Reds and make it to Syzran. Dear God, if Goga dies too . . .

Goga, who had just emerged briefly from unconsciousness and had heard Misha's question, suddenly spoke up.

'You must fix me up enough to let me break the news to Vanya and Mara. They will want to bury Oleg in Syzran. He was born there, you know. He's the son of a ferryman.'

'Then,' said Misha, 'if that is their wish, we will do so with military honours before we leave tonight.'

In the shabby surroundings of their bedroom in the little Chaika hotel, Andrey and Katya were reunited. Neither showed much emotion; they were too drained. Something had once again shifted between them, of which each was only dimly aware. Katya had come through the most testing ordeal without any help from her husband. She had displayed a strength which most would have considered the unique preserve of men.

Goga, sitting up on a stretcher, in desperate pain, was carried into the next-door bedroom, where he broke the news of Oleg's death to Vanya and Mara. Both reacted with the stoicism of the Russian peasant. They hugged each other, but neither shed a tear. They were in any case prepared for the worst. An ironic thought pierced Vanya's silent grief. Her man, who had survived five years' murderous campaigning under the Tsar's flag, had fallen to the Bolsheviks – they who had come to Golovino preaching an earthly paradise for peasants such as Oleg.

Mara was more concerned with Goga's condition. He had fainted at the effort of speaking to them. He lay motionless on the stretcher, his face as white as alabaster. The two orderlies hurried him away to the station and the train's hospital carriage.

Vanya agreed that Oleg should be buried with his parents and forebears in Syzran's cemetery. It sat high on a bluff with a magnificent view of the Volga. Misha organised a priest, a coffin and a grave. That same night, an hour or so before the armoured train was due to leave for Samara, the priest, heavily bearded and in a plain dark habit, waited for them in the cemetery's gloom, lantern in hand. Misha had arranged for the small honour guard of Czech cavalrymen to carry flaming torches. The graveyard looked fantastical in the dancing light. As Oleg's coffin was lowered into the ground to the priest's muttered incantations, Vanya, Mara, Katya and Andrey, following the rite of the Russian church, each threw a handful of earth onto the coffin's lid. At Misha's order, the Czech troopers fired three fusillades in salute to Oleg. Only then did Vanya and Mara weep for their dead husband and father.

After the funeral the little party returned to town on horseback, as they had come. They dismounted at the brightly lit station. Katya and Andrey, with Vanya, took their places in the two compartments reserved for them by Misha. Olga and Svyet were already there under the watchful eye of a military nurse. Wide awake, they greeted their parents with glee. Mara went straight to the hospital carriage to look after Goga. All their personal belongings had been loaded into the freight car, while Molnya and Mars joined the other horses in one of the cavalry's wagons. The ponies and carts had already been given to a man who had come to the Chaika hotel claiming to be Oleg's cousin.

Just after midnight the heavily armoured train trundled painfully out of the station. It was shrouded in grey smoke, which billowed from the stack with thunderous explosions. Two sweating, half-naked engineers furiously stoked the furnace to get the great steel beast to move. Once the soldiers' cordon had been removed, several of the more agile townspeople ran along the platform and managed to get aboard before the train picked up speed. In the rear was a platoon of soldiers in an open wagon with a machine gun. Misha took up position on the roof of a carriage in the middle of the train with another machine-gunner. They were showered with cinders and coal dust from the smoke.

As soon as the train began to move, its rocking motion sent Katya and Andrey into a dreamless sleep of utter exhaustion. In the hospital carriage, Mara wiped Goga's brow. He was starting to run a fever: it would be touch and go for him. Svyet and Olga were once again asleep. Vanya looked out of the window at the Volga. She thought of how she had first met Oleg at the water's edge, as he helped his father and uncles paint the ferryboat.

One life was over, for all of them. Heaven only knew what the next would bring.

Part II

HARBIN

Chapter 18

There is no Chinese city quite like Harbin. For Russian exiles in the 1920s, this Manchurian city bordering Russia's far east was a haven that provided a sense of the Motherland. They could imagine that, with the Russian cathedral, the Russian opera house, Russian clubs, Russian newspapers, Russian hotels and Russian shops, they were living in a large, sophisticated Russian city.

In 1898 the Tsarist government had struck an agreement with the Chinese to finance the building of the China Eastern Railway, linking the Russian city of Chita to the port of Vladivostok. Harbin became the railway company's headquarters. It was a magnet for Russians – engineers, navvies, managers, adventurers, businessmen – and Jews fleeing the pogroms. Then, with the latest influx of refugees from the civil war, Harbin grew into a sophisticated metropolis, often referred to as the Paris of the East.

The Polkonins, Mara, Goga and Vanya had arrived safely in Samara, where Mara dedicated herself to nursing the desperately wounded Goga. The others found a large, comfortable flat, but the White forces cracked after only a month; the Reds took over Samara in October of 1918, and the Polkonins were once again in exile. All through 1919 they followed the fighting across Siberia, from Omsk in the west, through Irkutsk, to Chita in the east. It was a time of panic, and of long, horrible journeys in trains full of drunken soldiers. In Omsk they found a decent apartment, but Irkutsk was cold and bleak, and Chita even worse: a rat-infested, foul-smelling flat. Katya contracted typhoid and would have died were it not for Vanya's nursing. Then, early in 1920, the Whites lost Irkutsk, where Andrey narrowly escaped death and Admiral Kolchak was betrayed to the

Reds and shot. They managed to retreat to Chita and continued to fight for a while, but it was hopeless. So, towards the end of 1920, Andrey found space for his family, Vanya and himself in a Red Cross ambulance taking wounded men to the Chinese border, where he paid a large bribe to a customs officer to allow them all to cross into Harbin.

*

The rich, mainly Russians and Jews and a few Chinese, lived on the heights of Harbin, in an area called Novy Gorod, or New Town. The Polkonins did not have any money left to afford one of its mansions. For the first few years they rented a small, single-storey house at the foot of Novy Gorod's hill, the closest they could get to the great mansions, and even that was beyond their means. It was one of four identical buildings in the Russian village style, constructed around a central courtyard, in the middle of which stood a pretty medlar tree. Each house had one large room with a stove and two smaller rooms. There was a communal kitchen, bathroom and lavatory for the four houses, all of which were inhabited by Russians. A low wooden fence ran around the compound.

Two of their neighbours were engineers, employed by the China Eastern Railway, and their families. The third house was occupied by Madame Frolina, the widow of a colonel killed fighting for Denikin. She was an austere, unbending woman, invariably dressed in permanent mourning. The girls decided she must be a witch.

These were the early, brief, happy times in Harbin, with everyone piled into one little house. Katya and Andrey took one room and Svyet and Gulya were put in the other. Vanya, who had become both cook and nanny, had a couch in the big room, which she put by the stove in the winter and by the window in the summer. As soon as the weather became hot, they were plagued by wasps and mosquitos from the river, joining the enormous population of roaches that seemed to infest every dwelling in Harbin, rich or poor.

In winter, after supper, they would all gather round the great stove.

Sometimes Andrey and Katya together would tell the girls of their great escape from Golovino to Samara.

Katya would often wonder what happened to the little hospital, which had housed so many young, wounded soldiers. She had warned those who could walk and the remnant of the staff that they should flee before the Red Army arrived, but she never found out how many of them did. She would wonder too whether any of the badly wounded soldiers were spared from the guns of the Bolsheviks. But she never found out.

The only thing she did discover, many years later, was that Golovino had been burnt down to the ground and so had the village on their estate. Only a wooden road sign had been left standing.

Still, for those first few years the Polkonins kept up their hopes. They created quite a life for themselves. Andrey wrote a column in the émigré newspaper *Russky Golos* and gave lessons at the tennis club. Katya took on language pupils. She set up her literary salon, which met once a week, modelled on her salon in St Petersburg before the Revolution. People were encouraged to read their own poems. She banned politics, however, much to the frustration of her husband.

The salon was something of a hub in Harbin for Russians with literary pretensions. Katya was at first overwhelmed by numbers, as people turned up hoping for a free meal or drink. So she introduced a rule that you must bring either a bottle of wine or a bowl of food. This kept the numbers under control. She made an exception only for young people, whose writing she liked to encourage. She thought of them as her protégés.

In their different ways they created quite a position for themselves in Harbin's Russian society. They were frequently invited to receptions and dinners in the mansions high on the hill of Novy Gorod. It helped that they were from grand Russian families. Most of the nobility had fled to Europe or the United States, but some ended up in Harbin, which became an enclave to some 200,000 Russian émigrés. The influx of artists, musicians and intellectuals endowed it with a rich cultural life.

Still, Andrey – unlike Katya – could never shake off the past, or the sense of how different things might have been. The betrayal, capture and summary execution of Kolchak would bring tears to his eyes whenever he spoke of it. Kolchak's courageous demeanour before the Bolshevik firing squad moved him deeply, but it was the collapse of the entire White enterprise that brought him emotionally to his knees. The worst of it was the feeling that if God had existed, he would never have allowed such an abomination. In a single stroke, Andrey lost his faith and his belief in his own abilities, and the black moods that never left him eroded his affection for his family.

Every time a traveller from the new Union of Soviet Socialist Republics fetched up in Harbin, he – or sometimes she – would be passed around the Russian community, to be interrogated about the state of things in the Motherland. Andrey still hoped against hope that the Bolshevik regime in Moscow would crumble. He predicted its downfall in one article after another. This provoked his first big row with Nekrassov, the editor, who one day threw out his copy and told him that it was time to stop baying at the moon. In response, Andrey hurled an ashtray across Nekrassov's office.

Katya had a soothing mantra, which she quoted regularly at supper when Andrey was in a bad mood. 'It's no good thinking of the past. We will never go back to those times. We must make the best of what we have and where we are. At least we have a decent roof over our heads and, thank the Lord, we are living in a Russian city with Russian people.'

*

Then everything started to go wrong.

The Polkonins decided they should start a little school for children between the age of kindergarten and ten. They did not think much of Gulya's primary school and believed they could do better. It mattered little to them that they had never run anything, or that they knew next to nothing about formal teaching and even less about running a business.

They planned on having eight pupils, including Gulya. They

advertised the school in *Russky Golos* six months before the start of term in September and, having set the fees extremely low, were swamped with applications.

Katya intended to teach reading, writing and history, Andrey arithmetic and geography, with half an hour of exercises in the little courtyard with the medlar tree (this immediately irritated Madame Frolina, who complained all the time, shaking her walking stick at the children). School would start at eight o'clock in the morning and finish at half past two after lunch, which they would also provide.

So many things had to be purchased: chairs, little desks, paper, pencils, chalk, books, a blackboard. Then the food for the lunches, which Vanya prepared. Then the bowls, knives, forks, spoons, jugs and glasses.

Their very modest savings vanished in a trice. Worse still, Katya had to abandon more than half her language lessons, while Andrey's output of articles was heavily curtailed. They bet everything on the school turning a profit, and the bet turned sour.

They fell deeper and deeper into debt to Chinese and Jewish moneylenders. None of the Russian community, including the Russian Savings Bank, was willing to lend them a penny. Andrey and Katya found the situation so uncomfortable that they stopped going out in public. Katya shut her salon. Invitations to the mansions of Novy Gorod dried up. The Polkonins' financial disaster was regarded as a contagious disease, something that could easily be caught by those who were themselves living not far from the edge of poverty.

By the summer of 1925 the situation was impossible. Neither Katya nor Andrey had ever had to read a balance sheet. Andrey would disappear rather than admit he was out of his depth.

One broiling afternoon Katya sat at the dining-room table, making calculations on an abacus, surrounded by bills and invoices, a large, black tin box in front of her containing notes and coins. Suddenly she shouted out, 'Dear God, I can't make this work! Nothing adds up!'

With a violent movement of one arm, she swept everything off the table and the tin box fell to the floor with a loud, rattling crash. Svyet and Gulya, who had been reading on the old, sagging sofa, shot to their feet in alarm. Katya sat with her face in her hands, a slight sniffing coming from behind her fingers. At times like this, Svyet liked to affect a tone of exasperation, as if her mother had tested her patience to its outer limits.

'For goodness' sake, Mother, pull yourself together. If you can't do the accounts, find someone who can. I bet you Vera would help. She works in the Gymnasium office.' The Gymnasium was the Russian secondary school, which Svyet attended.

Vera Lassova had already become a feature in their lives. She had attended the salon religiously and developed a kind of jokey, conspiratorial relationship with Andrey, one step short of flirtation. Andrey was clearly flattered by the attention.

Katya could not stand Vera. Nor could Gulya, who hated Vera's habit of pinching her cheeks and mussing her hair. Svyet, however, looked up to her.

'I want to be like Vera when I grow up,' she had solemnly declared one day at supper, apropos of nothing.

Katya came back like a shot. 'You can do far better than that, Svyet. She is a silly, bumptious woman. Her mother was a maid.'

'That's a bit harsh, Katyenka,' Andrey chipped in. 'She is a very capable woman, who, I am told, has singlehandedly reorganised the Gymnasium.'

'I am not having Vera Lassova poking around in our affairs,' Katya retorted.

Vera was in her late thirties, dark and plump, with a kind of vulgar voluptuousness. She had cunning little eyes, which sat atop a broad snub nose that in turn rested on thick lips and a mouth of unusual generosity. She was no fool and clearly very efficient at her job at the Gymnasium. She was also very attractive to men – including, unfortunately, Andrey.

But, even as Katya adamantly refused, another part of her brain told her that Svyet's idea made all the sense in the world. Who better than Vera to sort out what was surely a simple accounting problem?

'Well, maybe you're right, Svyet,' Katya said after a pause.

'I am, Mama, you know it,' said Svyet with a triumphant little smile.

Katya dropped a line to Vera, asking her if she could help, and posted it that night. The following evening Vera, wreathed in smiles, appeared at the front door. Katya was caught by surprise, having expected Vera to send a letter of reply first. It was awkward. She was about to go to the Japanese consulate to give the consul's wife an English lesson.

'That doesn't matter,' said Vera, 'just give me the papers and I will be able to work it out from there. If I get stuck, I can always ask Andrey Andreyevich, if he won't mind my disturbing him.' She looked across the room to where Andrey was working at his desk and bathed him in the sweetest of smiles.

'But he'll be useless,' said Katya. 'He's washed his hands of the accounts and left everything to me.'

'Typical man,' Vera interrupted, giving her broad smile again.

'That's not fair,' said Andrey, pretending to be hurt by Katya's blunt comments. 'I have always stood ready to help with the accounts. I used to do them for my regimental mess. But, as usual, Katya wants to do everything.' Andrey used this little speech to give him cover to move from his desk to the table, next to Vera.

'Anyway, the paperwork's all here on the table next to the tin box,' Katya continued. 'I've tried to organise it in chronological order. I hope you can make sense of it, Vera. Now, I must rush. I'll be back in two hours, maybe less.'

'No need to hurry, Katya. I enjoy this kind of work,' said Vera, her smile somewhere between beatific and predatory.

Chapter 19

It took Vera another session – this time with Katya in the afternoon – to complete the accounts. She was impressively competent and quick. She went home to write them up in due form and returned to the house a third time to hand them over.

'What do they tell us about our little school?' Katya asked, fearing the worst. They were sitting at the dining-room table, while Andrey was across the room at his desk.

'Andryusha, don't be rude. Come and join us at the table. Vera has done all this work. We both need to understand the situation.'

Andrey got up from his desk, somewhat reluctantly, and sat next to Katya on the opposite side of the table from Vera.

'Well, Andrey, Katya, I won't mince my words. The school is doing brilliantly from a scholastic point of view. But your costs are out of control. You will be carrying a significant loss into the next academic year. At the same time, you have several creditors who will expect to be paid before next term.'

Vera paused to let her grim message sink in. 'If you can't pay them, they can force you to close the school. Worse, because you are using your home as school premises, you risk being forced to transfer the lease to your creditors. You are in a precarious situation.'

Katya was pale as a ghost. 'What would you do, if you were in our position?'

'What I would *not* do is take out further loans to pay off the ones you have already. It is always a temptation. But it's the road to perdition. You would be completely owned by the moneylenders and the rate of interest would be impossibly exorbitant, because, to them, you would be a very bad risk.'

Vera paused again. Andrey ran his hands over his hair, cut *en brosse*.

'You have two choices. One, cut your losses and close the school now. Then you can go back full-time to your lessons and articles and gradually pay back the moneylenders. It will be humiliating, perhaps, but it's the safe option. Or, two, raise the fees by thirty to fifty per cent and stop the lunches and the physical exercise class.'

Andrey began to move his head from side to side. Katya put hers in her hands.

Vera continued. 'Unless you change course, radically, you face ruin.'

The room fell silent. Outside, in the little courtyard, came the voice of a Chinese woman singing quietly. She worked for one of the Russian engineers and liked to do her sewing under the cool shelter of the medlar tree. Birdsong was coming from within its branches and a breeze whispered in the leaves. The sun was starting to set now, throwing an oblique light into the room so that half was brightly lit, half in shadow.

What a beautiful day, Katya thought incongruously. Her mind wandered in search of an old Russian saying about bad news coming when nature has put on its finest coat.

Her mind refused to grapple with their predicament, so brutally described by Vera. Perhaps that was because she so detested the messenger. She could see that there was a mutual attraction between Andryusha and Vera. Vera was not much younger than she was, Katya thought ruefully. But she had not dried up like an old prune in the struggle to make a living. Katya counted the months. She and Andryusha had not made love for nearly a year.

Her disconsolate thoughts were interrupted by Andryusha's harsh bark.

'I don't know what Katya thinks, but that's impossible. To close the school now would bring humiliation down on our name. To raise the fees to the level you suggest, Vera, would be as good as closing the school. None of the parents would be able to afford them. The Krasnevs, the Polyakovs, the Semyonovs can barely pay the fees now! Semyonov and I were both wounded the same day outside Lemberg. It is unthinkable!'

Vera remained impassive. Then she asked, in a voice of wheedling insinuation, 'Isn't it worse for you, a nobleman, to be in hock to the Yids and the Chinks? What if they seize your home? I can think of no greater shame.'

Vera had used the most vulgar Russian expressions she could find. Andrey flinched, as if struck in the face. Katya suddenly realised what a formidable adversary she had in Vera Lassova.

'What do you think, Katya?' Vera asked.

The gears in Katya's brain finally engaged. Andryusha was right. They could do none of the drastic things Vera wanted without closing the school. But they could shorten the school day to cut expenses and allow more time for her language lessons. She could even take the translation job that the Japanese were offering her. The lunches should cease. So should Andryusha's physical exercises.

She said as much to Andrey and Vera, in a tone that brooked no contradiction. Vera knew not to pick an unwinnable fight. In the end, things would go her way. She just had to be patient.

As Katya spoke, another part of her mind was wrestling with a dilemma. It suddenly resolved itself and she turned to Vera.

'It would be a very great reassurance to us if, Vera, you were able to keep an eye on the administration of the school. The blunt truth is that, in our previous lives, we always had stewards and comptrollers to do all this for us. That's why Andryusha and I are so hopeless at things like accounts. We would, of course, be happy to pay you a stipend – it couldn't be very much.'

'My dear Katya, I would be happy to do this and, of course, I couldn't accept payment.' Vera said this with an expression of such unctuous piety that Katya immediately regretted making the offer. She noticed Andryusha's satisfied smile and twinkling eyes.

'That is most generous of you, Vera,' he said. 'How do you want to organise this?'

Katya had a sense of imminent danger, as if everything was about to change. Her heart began to pound.

'Well, my duties at the Gymnasium will obviously have to come first . . . '

'Of course, of course,' interrupted Andrey, a little too eagerly.

'. . . but this should still give me time to do your accounts, pay bills and address anything else that may be needed.' Vera said this with a flirtatious giggle that Andrey found delightful and Katya disturbing.

'Then perhaps we should agree to meet once a fortnight here on a Friday or Saturday,' Katya said to Vera, in a tone that was meant to be businesslike but sounded as if she was talking to one of the maids.

'If you won't consider me rude, I think our meetings should be weekly,' Vera replied evenly, 'because your costs are so out of control and demand urgent attention. Of course, the meetings don't always have to be here. We could do them at my little place in Novy Gorod.'

And that was their agreement. The new term began. The parents grumbled, but nobody withdrew their child from the school. Each week Vera sat down with Andrey and Katya to explain what was happening. For a while it all seemed to be going swimmingly. The Polkonins got into the habit of meeting Vera on Friday nights: a business session over a glass of wine, followed by a simple supper. They went once or twice to Vera's place. She was renting rooms in the first-floor corner of a sugar trader's mansion. She seemed to have money of her own. She had a Russian maid to prepare and serve supper. Katya had a glimpse of her bedroom, where an enormous bed was decorated in the same colours. There was not a book to be seen in the entire flat.

Katya was now earning good money at the Japanese consulate, translating into English articles in newspapers from across Europe. The Japanese were especially interested in the French, German and Russian press. She realised that both the school and her family now depended largely on Japanese money and that sometimes worried her. It was Japan's defeat of Russia in the war of 1905 which had led to the first revolution, which in turn, according to the Russian community in Harbin, had paved the way for the Bolsheviks in 1917.

The Japanese consul, Mr Amae, and his staff appeared to appreciate the speed and accuracy with which she completed her translations, as well as her courteous, reserved approach to giving language lessons.

Katya realised that she was being paid a very great compliment when Mr Amae asked her to give English lessons to his children.

*

It was early in 1926, the second year of the school's existence, when the Japanese asked Katya to do extra translations into English. They would be sent by special courier each weekend to their embassy in Pekin to be read by the ambassador and his senior staff on Monday morning. It would mean coming into the consulate on Friday evenings. The Japanese were prepared to pay generously.

The money had become essential. Vera had shown at their first meeting of the Easter term how the gap between income and expenditure was starting to widen again. There were no more economies to be made, she said. Vera was also worried about one of the Chinese creditors, Je Jin, who had, without warning, doubled the rate of interest on their loan.

'But he isn't allowed to do this,' Katya protested. 'The courts won't permit it.'

'I am afraid that he is very rich and powerful. I am told he has links to criminal society,' said Vera. This was the kind of worldly thing that Vera knew. 'No judge will go against him. What worries me is that he hates Russians. If you don't pay him, he will seize your home.'

Katya told them about her new job at the consulate and suggested moving their meetings, as she would now be occupied on Friday evenings.

Without missing a beat and with an expression of earnest sincerity, Vera said, 'I am afraid that won't work for me. I have constructed my timetable at the Gymnasium around our Friday evenings.'

Katya knew what was coming. She was trapped.

'Katya, I know it would be better with you present. But why don't you brief Andrey on things that bother you and then leave it to him and me to sort out? I will write down anything of importance in case he forgets to mention it to you,' Vera said with an arch little smile. 'I can even give him supper at my flat, which will save Vanya having to prepare something late in the evening when you return from the Japanese. How is that for a suggestion?'

How indeed, thought Katya.

'I can't have that, Vera. You know what Russians are like. It only takes one of them to see Andryusha going into your apartment and all Harbin will know. Your reputation would be destroyed and our school might have to close down.'

Andrey, who was standing, stared silently at his boots.

'Katya, Katya, you misunderstand me,' said Vera, holding Katya by the upper arms. 'My aunt, Lidia Sorokova, would be there as well. She is a widow, who works as an administrator at the railway. I always call on her to chaperone me when I have business meetings in my flat. I am happy to introduce her to you. She is rather stern, of the old school, the height of respectability.'

Vera allowed an expression of pained mortification to linger on her face.

'For goodness' sake, Katyenka,' said Andrey, 'this is the 1920s! What's more, our school, our home and our honour are all at stake.'

'Well, if you say so, Andryusha. But even with a chaperone, it had better not be too often. We don't want to set off what the French call *les mauvaises langues*.'

Our honour, Katya repeated to herself. She felt sick to her stomach.

Chapter 20

The Japanese consulate threw so much work at Katya – language classes and translations into English – that it became almost full time. The money was good. She saved as much of it as she could. She had a premonition that disaster lay just around the corner.

Andrey tried to get his hands on some of it to pay for a new tennis racquet and a set of whites. Katya refused him. She would not even tell him how much she earned. In her imagination a red line now ran through the family. She and her daughters were on one side, Andrey on the other. Their relationship had become a wasteland, in which there was minimal communication and no affection. Nobody told stories around the stove any more. The evening silence was broken only by rustling pages, the clicking of Vanya's knitting needles and Andrey sucking on his pipe.

*

Vanya knew what was going on between Andrey and Vera, but she couldn't work out whether Katya realised. How could she miss it? It was so hard to tell. Katya was much less lively than she used to be. She hardly said a word to Andrey and sometimes even the children found it hard to get a response out of her. But that could be money worries and tiredness from all the work the Japanese piled on her.

Then something happened that, for Vanya, put the matter beyond all doubt. She ran into Vera's chaperone and aunt, Lidia Sorokova, at the Saturday street market. She was not an unpleasant woman and, unlike many of the snobbish Russian bourgeoisie, was perfectly happy to be seen talking to Vanya in her peasant headdress and apron.

They were surrounded by a sea of Chinese shoppers, crowding

round the market stalls. The noise was deafening – stallholders and hawkers proclaiming their wares, shoppers bargaining at the tops of their voices, cart-pushers and rickshaw-pullers demanding passage through the narrow lanes between the lines of stalls. Here and there a European was visible above the bobbing Chinese heads like a volcanic peak in the ocean. Occasionally there was the impatient horn of a motor vehicle – a chauffeur stupid enough to drive into the market and now unable to get out, trapped by the press of pedestrians and carts.

Vanya, who was forceful and boisterous in manner, deliberately playing up her peasant roots, greeted Lidia Sorokova with a laugh in her voice. 'I bet you never expected to play chaperone again at your age, Madame Sorokova!'

'It didn't last long,' she replied with a smile. 'I felt a complete fool sitting there with two adults working on accounts. After a couple of sessions, I told my niece that there were plenty of other things I could be getting on with. Vera agreed and we stopped the arrangement over a month ago. Hadn't you heard? The idea that my niece is in moral danger from Colonel Polkonin is absurd. As for their reputations, they are perfectly capable of looking after themselves.'

This was delivered in brisk, businesslike tones. Mrs Sorokova turned to the market stalls. 'Vanya, excuse me, but I need to buy some of those aubergines before they are all snatched up. Please give my regards to the Polkonins.'

Over a month ago, thought Vanya. That was when Andrey started going to Vera's every Friday, while Katya was kept late by the Japanese. He would return, go straight into the bedroom where there was always a large bowl of water, and wash. Sometimes he went to the communal bath house. He always changed before Katya's return. Vanya knew why. He smelled of sex, sometimes strongly. It was the juice of that overripe melon, Vera.

It kept Vanya awake at night. Should she mind her own business? It was not for her to speak to her mistress on such matters. But after their miraculous escape from Golovino, Katya felt more like a sister. She was sure Katya felt the same way about her; they exchanged so many intimacies. Then again, if she did raise the affair, what advice would she give? As she tossed on her pillow, the answer became suddenly obvious. Katya was the breadwinner. She should tell Andrey: give up Vera or get out! Things could not go on as they were.

Vanya chose her moment a few days later, when the children were playing with friends and Andrey was at the newspaper. She got straight to the point.

'Katya, what's going on between Andrey and that Lassova woman? My nose tells me something's not right. He follows her around like a lovesick dog. What do they get up to on Friday nights?' There, I've said it, she thought.

'Don't be silly, Vanya. Yes, she's a bit too forward and plays on Andryusha's masculine vanity,' Katya replied, putting down her French novel. 'But the accounts have to be done and Vera's aunt is there when Andryusha goes to her apartment on Friday evenings.'

'It's not as you think, Katya,' said Vanya. 'I ran into Lidia Sorokova at the market last Saturday and she told me she had stopped chaperoning Vera a month ago.'

For a moment Katya did not reply.

'Are you sure? Neither Andryusha nor Vera has said anything to me.'

'Well, they wouldn't, would they? Madame Sorokova has no reason to lie.'

Katya was silent again, a frown carving deep furrows in her forehead. She knew this was one of those moments in life you don't forget, like when they left St Petersburg for Golovino back in 1917. She watched as two sparrows sitting on the windowsill were chased off by a magpie. 'One for sorrow,' she murmured.

She passed a hand over her eyes and sighed, turning to Vanya.

'So, you think they are lovers.'

'No doubt about it,' replied Vanya unsparingly. 'I can smell it – literally. It's a good thing you're not around when he comes home from her place, stinking of perfume and the Lord knows what else.'

If the truth be told, Katya had herself smelled the heavy, gamey scent when she went into Andryusha's wardrobe, but had not wanted to believe it.

'Isn't this what men do?' said Katya, almost pleadingly. 'We've been married for almost twenty years. My mother told me that sooner or later Andryusha would stray. She said it was perfectly normal and I shouldn't make a fuss. My father was the same. The world, she said, was unfair. A man could have a mistress and his reputation remain untouched. If a woman took a lover, she could be expelled from society forever. I shall just have to put up with it and wait till they tire of each other.'

'I beg your pardon? Is this the woman who faced down the tinkers on the road to Syzran?' Vanya stood up, arms akimbo, her eyes flashing thunderbolts. 'This is Harbin, not St Petersburg. You are the breadwinner. Andrey lives off what you earn. His articles hardly buy a beer. And while you are exhausting yourself working late for the Japanese, he's lying in the arms of his mistress. It's disgusting.'

'So, what would you have me do?' asked Katya.

'Tell him if he doesn't stop seeing this Lassova woman, you'll throw him out. It's you who pays the rent.'

'But all that would do is drive him into Vera's arms – and leave the children without a father!'

'Maybe, maybe not. Knowing your husband's temper, he probably would storm off to Lassova's flat. But how do we know she'd welcome a lover who lives off her and hangs round her flat all day? It's just as likely that after a month or so she would send him packing and he'd crawl back here, tail between his legs.'

'But what if she doesn't do that and he doesn't come back?'

'Then good riddance!' said Vanya. 'I know it's a horrible thing to say. But, to be honest, what's left of your marriage? What's left of family life? Andrey doesn't talk to you or Svyet, and Gulya just irritates him. The way he is now, you'd be better off without him.'

'Vanya, even if you are right, you've forgotten one thing. What about the school?'

'What about it? You have to give it up. It was always a foolhardy thing to do. As long as you have it, Vera is in your lives. Get out while you can!'

'I'll think about it,' said Katya, utterly crushed. 'All this drama has given me a headache. I'm going to sit in the garden.' She turned her back on Vanya and walked out of the house.

Chapter 21

Vanya had put into words the fears that had been racing through Katya's mind for weeks. Once again, the school had started to lose money. For over a month, there had been unexplained outgoings every week. Another few weeks and there would be nothing to pay the creditors at the end of term – including Je Jin, Harbin's most notorious moneylender of last resort, with a reputation for unforgiving ruthlessness. This was the man who, according to Vera, wanted to seize their home.

Je Jin lived nearby, in a large house situated on the frontier between the Chinese and Russian quarters of the city. Katya had to pass it on the way to the market. It was guarded by a large, menacing Chinese man, bald except for a long pigtail that fell to the waist, and dressed in the red tunic of the Boxer rebels of the great 1899 uprising against foreign occupiers.

She found that she was forever running into Je Jin in the street and began to suspect that this was deliberate on his part. She and Andryusha owed him a lot, as he liked to remind her. But he was always courteous. Sometimes he had one of his guards with him. Most of the time he walked alone or with one of his children. Such was his reputation that he feared attack from no one.

The day after her devastating conversation with Vanya, Katya again ran into Je Jin on her way back from giving an English lesson. He had his little daughter with him. As usual he greeted her in his excellent English. He cut an impressive figure in his *changshan*, the traditional full-length robe often worn by more prosperous Chinese men. He was tall, early middle age perhaps, with high cheekbones, even features and an unusually aquiline nose. His black hair was brushed tightly back from his forehead in the style of Rudolph Valentino, who was all the rage, even in Manchuria. He was a handsome man. On an impulse, Katya invited him to tea. It would do no harm to show him some respect, after all.

Je Jin accepted without hesitation and they walked together. His daughter hopped and skipped in front of them, from time to time racing back to hug her father and once, shyly, to put her hand in Katya's. As they entered the compound, Madame Frolina was coming out. Her habitually severe expression turned to shock, then horror, to see Katya taking a Chinese man into her home. She clasped her scrawny bosom as if about to faint.

'Good afternoon, Madame Frolina,' Katya called out cheerily, 'warm for the time of year.' Madame Frolina scurried away without a word.

'Who is that?' asked Je Jin.

'Madame Frolina, our neighbour, who has never forgiven us for being of higher birth than her. If you take possession of our house,' said Katya, looking Je Jin in the eye, 'you will have the joy of living next to her. She hates the Chinese.' She allowed a hint of humour into her expression, suddenly realising that, for some mysterious reason, she was enjoying herself.

'Please come in. I will make some tea. Your daughter can play with Gulya's toys.'

Katya brewed tea, placing glasses in their silver holders on a black lacquered Russian tray decorated with roses. Je Jin wandered round the room, picking up and putting down family photographs, each time asking Katya who was in the picture. By the time they sat down with their glasses of tea, he had received a potted history of the family.

'It must be hard for you – to have fallen from such a great height and now be forced to live cheek by jowl with people like me,' he said.

'It was hard to leave everything behind and to see our country estate burned to the ground,' she admitted. 'My mother still lives in St Petersburg with many of our relatives. It's difficult to get news of them, the post is so unreliable. Some may be in prison, like my uncle Alexander. His health was always frail and I don't think he will survive.'

'Why put him in prison? Was he a rebel against the regime?'

'On the contrary. He is a gentle, bookish man. They imprisoned him for being what he is, a scholar of noble birth, whose studies of insects and small birds is of no use to the Bolsheviks.'

Je Jin grunted and nodded.

'That can happen anywhere if your face doesn't fit.'

'For a long time we thought this nightmare would pass and we would be able to rewind history and return to Russia. My husband believed that very strongly. He thought the Bolsheviks could not last. Now, years later, we have given up hope. It has hit Andrey and many of his friends very hard. Some have taken their own lives.'

'Your husband hates us Chinese, doesn't he? He's like that woman we met as we came into your compound.'

Katya took a deep breath, painfully aware of the sensitive ground on which they were treading.

'He's like many Russian men with a military background. For him it is a humiliation to have to seek refuge in China and to depend on the Chinese for the basics of everyday life . . . '

'. . . including money,' murmured Je Jin.

'Including money,' Katya nodded. 'That is a particular humiliation for him.'

'For you?'

'I just don't like owing money. And I worry about our school. But I don't feel humiliated. Destiny has cast us on China's shores. I'm grateful to find a roof and a home here. China – its history and civilisation – are of endless fascination to me.' Again, she looked Je Jin in the eye.

'You say that, but after years here you don't speak a word of our language.' His reproach was sharp and Katya replied in kind.

'To survive in Harbin, I teach Russian, English, French and German to the international community. I don't have a minute to myself all day. I have one or two Chinese pupils. But for the most part the Chinese show not the least interest in foreign languages or culture.'

'*Touché*,' said Je Jin with a slight smile. 'I tried to send my eldest son to the Russian Gymnasium. He's a brilliant child with good English. But they turned him down just because he is Chinese. I wasn't surprised, mind you. I have experienced nothing but sorrow and insults from Russians. You are the first to show any sign that we Chinese belong to the human race.'

'But Mr Jin,' Katya hesitated and then took the plunge, 'it is said that not only are you a moneylender, but that you are cruel and that you have criminal connections. It's hardly surprising that the Gymnasium wanted nothing to do with you.'

'Then, Madame Polkonina, you are unusually courageous to allow into your home a cruel criminal who is Chinese to boot!'

They held each other's gaze without rancour. Then each burst into laughter.

'You have been very candid with me, Madame Polkonina. I appreciate that. It is a sign of trust. Now allow me to repay you the compliment.

'My family also lost everything. We were very rich farmers and grain traders. The business had been built up over centuries. My father had land and estates all over Manchuria. He was powerful and wealthy, but not very educated. He wanted me, his only son, to be everything he was not. He sent me south to Hong Kong to be educated at an English school, St George's Academy for Boys. The English are terrible snobs, but in their funny way they get on quite well with the Chinese. My school had only a few Chinese boys, because it was so expensive. The English boys called us Chinks. It was hard for me in the beginning. But I was taller than most Chinese and I could box. I was good at football, too. That earned their respect. In the end they made me Captain of School. Can you imagine that happening at the Russian Gymnasium?'

Je Jin fell silent. His eyes had a distant look as he recalled the happiest days of his life.

'Go on,' said Katya.

'Anyway, it was in Hong Kong that I acquired a love of European music. My father liked the idea of a son who was both good at sport and wanted to be a musician. He loved my stories of bossing English boys around as Captain of School. I told him I was really keen on a musical career. He was so pleased with me, he granted my wish and despatched me to Vienna to be trained as a violinist. But by the time I returned to Harbin, two years later, to play a concert at the opera house, he was a ruined man. It was the most bitter of moments, just when it should have been the most triumphal and gratifying. He had borrowed heavily to finance the building of a brewery modelled on the one in Tsingtao, which the Germans had started. His many farms were his collateral, all of which were mortgaged to the Russian Savings Bank here in Harbin. Unfortunately, when the debt came due, it was after three disastrous harvests. He begged the bank for more time – one good harvest would have been enough – but they refused. They seized all his land, leaving him with only the house where I live today. On the night before I was to play my opening concert, my mother and I found him in his bath, his wrists slit wide open.'

Katya had been listening, enthralled, in one of the two armchairs, her chin resting in her hand. When Je Jin came to the end of his story, she sat up sharply. Her eyes began to prick with tears. She could not control them.

'You wanted revenge,' she whispered to Je Jin.

'Yes, with a ferocity, Madame Polkonina, you cannot imagine.' His eyes too were luminous with tears. 'Until this moment I have never told this story to anyone outside the Chinese community.'

For a while a silence fell between them.

'I decided to turn myself into a mixture of Manchurian bandit and Boxer nationalist. I decided to be the very opposite of everything my father had educated me to be. I decided to be a moneylender, specialising in Russians like you and Jews. I decided to lend money at exorbitant rates. I decided to use criminals and violence to get my money back. And when that didn't work, because there was no money there, I would seize their property and throw them onto the streets. But I never gave up the violin.'

Katya noticed the beads of perspiration on Je Jin's brow. He was a little breathless. His eyes were as black as a shark's.

Suddenly his daughter ran into the room, breaking the spell. His expression immediately softened. She jumped onto his lap. She was a sweet child.

'Why don't you send her to our school?' Katya asked on another impulse. 'It would do our Russian and German children a world of good to meet a Chinese girl. We would make sure she wasn't teased. The children would soon get used to her. And we do most of the lessons in English.'

'What about their parents? They would hate the idea. Wouldn't they withdraw their children?'

'I doubt it. The main thing is, do you like the idea? It would only be for the remaining school year, another three months or so. I don't think I can stand the strain of running the school after that,' Katya said, realising that she had just taken a very big decision even as she spoke. 'Of course, there would be no charge.'

Je Jin and his daughter spoke to each other in Chinese.

'She would like to come. She says you are kind and that she would like to play with your daughter.'

'Then that is settled,' said Katya briskly.

'I will also reduce your debt by ten per cent. Tell me, by the way, about the school's finances.'

'We should break even this term, which will enable us to pay most of our creditors,' said Katya, coughing awkwardly.

Je Jin looked at her impassively, nodding slightly, noticing everything.

Then, on yet another impulse, she continued:

'No, I am not telling you the truth.' Katya was stunned by her own indiscretion. Even Je Jin looked a little surprised.

'We were doing quite well until about a month ago. Since then, I have discovered expenditure which I cannot account for.'

'Who does the accounts? You?' asked Je Jin.

'No, a woman who is an administrator at the Gymnasium, Vera Lassova.'

'Vera Lassova,' repeated Je Jin, a sardonic grimace passing across his face. 'It was she who stopped my son joining the Gymnasium, despite his qualifications. An arrogant, vulgar creature.' As he spoke, Katya could see the anger boiling up in him.

Silence fell between them again as Je Jin let his anger subside. Then he said, 'Perhaps I should see the books? Maybe I can help,' he finished, with a slight smile.

In for a penny, in for a pound, thought Katya. 'Please do. They are here on the table.'

She poured him another glass of tea as he settled down with the file.

After ten minutes or so, Je Jin looked up from the file, taking off his rimless spectacles. 'These accounts are not complicated,' he said. 'You are losing money quite badly, at least you have been for the last month or so, as you yourself have spotted. It's not the fault of the school where, again as you say Madame Polkonina, you were almost breaking even. Your recent losses are for quite different reasons. Someone is stealing from you. Here, sit next to me and I will show you.'

As she sat next to Je Jin, she detected the faint scent of sandalwood. She wondered what Andryusha would think if he walked in now. She rather wished he would.

Her mind was jolted out of its musings by Je Jin's ominous words. He showed how, under the guise of work on the accounts or obtaining supplies for the school, cash was being paid to two unnamed parties.

'Madame Polkonina, do you have an explanation for these unusual items? Have you needed recent supplies for the school?' asked Je Jin.

'No, we order all our supplies before the term begins,' replied Katya. A horrible suspicion was growing inside her.

'I conclude, then,' said Je Jin, sounding a little like a prosecuting counsel in an English court, 'that as the accounts have been prepared by Miss Lassova, she must be taking some of the money. If indeed she is one of the guilty parties, who then is the other, unless she has decided to take two identities to cover her tracks?'

Katya replied so quietly that Je Jin could barely hear, 'No, I fear it is Vera and my husband, Andrey. They must be conspiring together.'

Je Jin turned to Katya and put his hand on hers. It was warm and dry. She did not pull away.

Then, with his hand lightly resting on hers – if his father were watching from a heavenly cloud he would have savoured the irony, thought Katya – he made her an offer.

Without repayment of the debt, he would take over the lease of the house. Instead, he would install Katya, Svyet, Gulya and Vanya in an apartment in a large, three-storey house shared with two Chinese families, where they would have their own bathroom and kitchen. He owned it. It was in one of the best Chinese neighbourhoods in Harbin. The rent would be modest. If his daughter were happy at Katya's school, he would keep it afloat until the end of the academic year, another three months. If she were not – he thought this most unlikely – he would insist on its immediate closure. If she could establish that Vera and Andrey had stolen money, he would ensure it was returned. If it had been spent already, he would expel them both from Harbin.

'And what must I do in return to deserve this generosity?' asked Katya, gently withdrawing her hand from under Je Jin's.

Je Jin thought for a moment.

'Nothing. I like and admire you, my first Russian acquaintance. That must be our secret, since I don't want my reputation for cruelty and ferocity compromised.' At that he laughed uproariously. 'You could, I suppose, teach me some Russian, if you have the time. I might as well get to know my enemies better.' He let out another explosion of laughter, louder than the first. His little daughter came running into the room to find out what was so funny. I doubt she often hears her father laugh like that, thought Katya.

'But,' he continued, the humour fading rapidly from his expression, 'I am not sure you have fully considered the implications of accepting my offer. The breach with your husband will soon be known throughout the Russian community. His running off with another woman, if that is what he chooses to do, will cause an almighty scandal. Your moving to a Chinese house will be seen as a great fall from grace for a Russian noblewoman. But nothing will damage your reputation among Russians more than the knowledge that you are beholden to me for your salvation. Have you thought of this?'

Katya considered for a moment. She heard Vanya's words ringing in her ears.

'I have and I don't care. We are beholden to you anyway. I must be able to provide a roof and a hearth for my daughters. Why should anyone find out that you and I have reached an agreement on the repayment of our debt? And even if they do, why should anyone object, since there are dozens of indebted Russians trying to find an accommodation with Chinese moneylenders?'

'All that is true. But sooner or later people will begin whispering about our . . . ' He hesitated, gesturing with his hands, '. . . our personal relationship. It doesn't matter, let us say, whether you come to my house or I to yours for Russian lessons. Tongues will start to wag. I know many Russian men who have relations with Chinese women. No one cares about that. But, for a Russian woman to have a personal relationship *of any kind* with a Chinese man . . . ' he said this with great emphasis, '. . . breaks a taboo. Particularly when the Chinese man is a moneylender with, so it is said, criminal connections. Your reputation would be in shreds.'

The implication of what he was saying sent a little thrill through her, like a charge of electricity. He was trying to protect her. He was right: she would probably start to lose some of her regular language pupils. But, in truth, that would be no bad thing. The work given her by the Japanese consulate, who, she was sure, did not care anything about her private life, had already caused her to discard one or two of her pupils. As for her reputation – this was Harbin, not St Petersburg, as Vanya never ceased to remind her!

'I still don't care. I would love to teach you Russian so that one day I may introduce you to our literature and poetry. I know you would appreciate them,' Katya said enthusiastically. 'I used to have a salon in St Petersburg, where we held poetry readings every week. I even managed to recreate it for a while in Harbin. That's how my Andryusha met Vera Lassova.'

Je Jin looked at Katya. She saw that there were again tears glistening in his eyes. Somehow she had moved him. Then he collected himself.

'Very well. That is our agreement. What is the next step?' he asked.

'Today is Tuesday. On Friday Andryusha will, as usual, expect to go to Vera's to do the accounts, so-called. But, I will say that, given the deterioration in our finances, I want to be present and that the meeting should take place here in our home. I will tell the Japanese that I am unwell.'

'Then,' continued Katya, 'I will confront them. I know what to say as far as the accounts are concerned, as you have just told me. I will say that unless the money is returned within a week, they must answer to you, since, strictly speaking, the money is yours. That will frighten them. I will then take advantage of their disarray and tell them that I know about their affair. I will ask Andryusha to leave the house immediately, since . . . ' Katya thought for a moment, '. . . I can no longer bear to share my bed with a man who smells of another woman.'

Katya stopped, slightly out of breath.

'You should come and work for me,' said Je Jin admiringly. 'Do you wish me to be present?'

'No. I must do this myself, otherwise they'll think you're twisting my arm. You could perhaps visit the following morning and I'll tell you what happened.'

Je Jin nodded his assent, astonished at this admirable, courageous Russian woman, who somehow had succeeded in reviving his better instincts, for years suffocated by a bitter longing for vengeance.

Vanya, with Svyet and Gulya, returned just as Je Jin and his daughter were leaving. Hands on her hips, Vanya asked Katya what they were doing in the house.

'I invited Mr Jin to take tea. We have had a very constructive and amicable conversation. His daughter will join our school until we break up for the summer holidays.' Je Jin, who understood Russian better than he let on, gave Vanya the warmest of smiles, as Katya blushed scarlet.

Chapter 22

Three days later, on Friday evening, Katya despatched the girls to the circus with Vanya, and summoned Andrey and Vera to a crisis meeting to discuss the school's finances. She served no wine, placing only a jug of water and a lamp on the table with the accounts.

Katya was polite, cold and self-assured. There was no smile of welcome, no kissing, despite Vera's attempt to place her full lips on Katya's pale cheek. She barely gave the time of day to Andrey.

Katya's demeanour disconcerted Andrey and Vera. It was utterly unexpected. They had braced themselves for an anxious, fearful woman, who would need to be calmed, blinded by science, or at least accounting terminology.

It put both of them instantly on the defensive – which was what Katya had hoped – but for different reasons. Andrey feared that his infidelity had been uncovered; Vera her dishonesty. He'd been vaguely aware that Vera might be taking money from the school, but he hadn't asked and she hadn't said.

They sat down at the table. Andrey began to fiddle irritatingly with his pipe, which refused to light.

In as relaxed and friendly a voice as she could muster, Vera asked, 'Katya, darling, do you think I might have a tiny glass of wine? It's been such a long day?'

'This is not the moment for alcohol, Vera. We need clear heads,' Katya replied curtly.

Vera sat as still as a statue, her face cast in a smile that was as false as it was patronising. Andrey, having finally succeeding in lighting his pipe, was concentrating intently on a moth that kept flying into the lamp Katya had placed on the table.

Behind her rictus smile, Vera was in turmoil. This was not how things were supposed to unfold. Her carefully worked plan would have had them slip away from Harbin in three weeks' time, finding refuge in the coastal town of Tsingtao. The money she was surreptitiously taking from the school – it was at least as much Andrey's as it was Katya's – plus what she had saved from the Gymnasium would give them a sufficient financial pillow to begin with. She had no intention of staying in Tsingtao forever. Her ambitions extended to Pekin or Shanghai, and, beyond there, perhaps to Paris. All in good time, she always said to herself. But for her ambitions to be realised, she needed right now, before she got too old, a husband of noble birth, who would give her the respectability and entry into Russian and European society that she craved. Andrey fitted the bill perfectly. She did not love him. He would not be forever, but for the time being she had him on a tight leash. He was besotted with her and with the sex she gave him every Friday night, unlike anything he had ever experienced.

Vera's mind was racing. Surely Katya did not have the skill to spot the anomalies in the accounts? She might, on the other hand, suspect Vera's affair with Andrey, particularly if she had found out that Aunt Lidia had stopped playing chaperone. She had agreed with Andrey that they would deny emphatically and indignantly any charge of immoral behaviour.

Andrey and Vera had without thinking sat down together, on the opposite side of the table to Katya. Well, that's a giveaway, Katya thought.

'Vera, Andrey' – Andrey's head shot up and the pipe fell from his mouth at being addressed by his wife in such a formal way – 'I thought we should have this meeting, since it is plain that our school, and therefore we, are in deep trouble. If we project forward the weekly losses to the end of term, we will end with a deficit so large that it will be impossible to pay any of our creditors – and that includes the "sinister" Je Jin.' It was he who had suggested that she describe him so.

'But, Katya, darling, let me explain . . . '

'Kindly do not interrupt me, Vera. And do not call me "darling". I know you wanted us to cut our losses and close the school. Maybe we should have done. But we didn't – and somewhat to our surprise, with a few economies, we were able to break even. But then, almost two months ago, our weekly expenditure began to skyrocket and we plunged into deficit. Andrey, did you know?'

Katya looked up from the file and switched her gaze from Vera to Andrey and back again. Vera was now red-faced and sweating, great arcs of dampness forming under the arms of her tight red bodice. The smile was gone, replaced by lips twisted in a silent snarl.

Andrey, as always when his self-esteem was at stake, resorted to anger.

'For God's sake, Katyenka, this is not the Spanish Inquisition. Vera offered her help from the goodness of her heart and you now accuse her of incompetence or worse – what ingratitude! You don't know what you are talking about! It's a disgrace!'

Vera made to calm Andrey. But it was too late.

Katya replied in cold fury, 'I'll tell you what is a disgrace. It is a disgrace that Vera has stolen money from the school account. And it is a disgrace that you, Andrey Andreyevich, come home every Friday night, stinking of Vera's cheap perfume and the smell of her sex.'

Andrey was speechless. Vera tried to rally, concentrating on the more serious of the charges against her.

'Are you accusing me of theft? How dare you! Where is your evidence?'

'It is here,' said Katya, cold and implacable. 'Let us take the expenditure entries for 4 February and 3 March. Where are the school supplies to which these apparently refer? We purchased all our supplies last September. There are, by the way, eight other entries I could show you.'

Vera grabbed the pages, but Katya could see that she was not really looking at them. It was a manoeuvre to gain time and come up with a convincing reply.

Suddenly Vera dropped the pages on the table, turned to Andrey and said, sobbing, 'I told you this would happen. I told you she would find out. But you wouldn't listen.' Sweat poured down her face.

Andrey spoke. 'Vera, I have no idea what you are talking about. You said no such thing to me.'

'There is no honour among thieves,' said Katya contemptuously. 'I don't know, and I don't care, which of you was responsible for this shabby scheme. But you had better return the money you have taken, and fast.'

'And how do you propose to make us do that?' asked Vera scornfully, her sobbing having passed like a summer storm.

'I don't intend to make you do anything. Je Jin, though, is another matter. After all, the money you have taken really belongs to him.'

At the mention of the moneylender's name, Vera's hand went to her mouth and Andrey became as white as a sheet.

'What on earth do you mean, Katyenka?' he asked.

Katya gave them a bowdlerised version of her meeting with Je Jin.

'Earlier this week, when you were at the newspaper, Je Jin came to our house and demanded repayment of our debt. I was candid with him about our inability to do so. I showed him the accounts. He immediately spotted the dubious expenditure items. The last person who had tried to rob him was Usmanov, the butcher. He was found floating face down and throat slit in the Sangari river. Can't you understand that it is Je Jin you are robbing? You are in peril of your lives!'

Katya had been reluctant to use these lurid details, but Je Jin had insisted.

'You want this to be a decisive battle,' he had said.

Vera was on the edge of hysteria and began to babble. Andrey raised his hand, as if to slap her face.

'Pull yourself together, woman,' he said harshly. It was the first time he had ever asserted himself with Vera. He looked at Katya.

'Do you mean to say that you told Je Jin, a murderer and common criminal, that we were stealing money?' asked Andrey, blazing with self-righteous indignation, shaking the broken stem of his pipe at Katya. 'You are no wife of mine!'

'Too true, Andrey – and with your fornicating and thieving you are no husband of mine,' Katya retorted, raising her voice just a little.

Vera decided to retreat to the sofa.

'You are planning to go away together, are you not? When would you have told me?' Katya asked Andrey, as if enquiring about the weather.

'Yes, we are,' said Andrey, all anger suddenly spent before Katya's remorseless pressing. 'In about three weeks' time. I am sorry it has ended like this. What do we have to do to escape Je Jin's attentions?'

'First, you return directly to him the money you have taken. He will expect it by this time next week. Secondly, you and Vera must quit Harbin by this time next week. Whether you do so in tandem or separately is of no concern to me or to him. If you try to stay, you do so at your peril. Thirdly, you leave this house tonight and never return.'

Andrey's face twitched with Katya's every sentence, as if each were a physical blow. God, he thought, what an idiot I've been. His remorse was not for his faithlessness, nor for stealing money, but for his stupidity in making an enemy of Je Jin. He hoped Vera had not spent the money.

'May I see the children before I go?'

'No. Perhaps one day. But since you've shown precious little interest in them or their welfare in recent months, it will be no hardship for you – or them.'

'Then, Katya, there is no more to be said. I will send Vera's woman tomorrow to collect my clothes.'

'Goodbye, Andrey.' Katya remained seated, stern and unbending.

Andrey went to collect Vera from the sofa. Her face was wet with perspiration and tears. Her mascara was smudged over her cheeks. Mucous dribbled from her nostrils. To Katya, she was a revolting sight. To Andrey, she was, in this state, an even greater object of his lust.

They left. Katya felt exhausted but relieved. There was something else, too. She had enjoyed the cut and thrust. She had routed the enemy. Je Jin would have been proud of her.

She poured herself a glass of Italian wine, lit a Cuban cigarillo and sat down in her armchair. After a while she slept. She dreamed of Je Jin's warm, dry hand on hers.

Chapter 23

Andrey was not missed at home. His baleful presence had worn everyone down. It took Gulya some time fully to grasp what had happened, but home became a more cheerful place, and because those closest to her were happier, so was she. Gulya also had a new friend, Je Jin's daughter Yu Yan. The two girls loved playing together. Yu Yan was desperate to learn Russian, instantly copying Gulya's words and expressions. Then she would repeat them until she got the pronunciation just right. With each attempt she would look up at Gulya, her little eyebrows raised in interrogation, her eyes shining like stars. Then, when she was told it was excellent – *otlychno* – her face would explode into smiles and laughter, as she danced around the room chanting in Russian, 'May I have a glass of milk?' or 'Good morning, Papa.'

Yu Yan was the most cheerful person in the world, not exactly pretty, but cute, as the Americans would say, and a quick learner. Very soon Katya and Gulya were able to hold simple conversations with her in Russian. Je Jin was astonished at his daughter's progress.

Most of the time it was Je Jin's chauffeur and a bodyguard who collected Yu Yan from the Polkonins' school. They came in an enormous dark green Rolls-Royce, the chauffeur resplendent in a uniform of matching green with silver buttons, a peaked cap and shiny black leather boots up to his knees. The bodyguard was an English-speaking Boxer called Fang, who carried a long, curved sword in a leather scabbard covered in metal studs, and would smile when Yu Yan pulled his pigtail, showing a gleaming row of metal lower teeth.

From time to time Je Jin himself would come to fetch Yu Yan after school. This was always a grand treat for Gulya, who had warmed to him from the start. He would walk up to her, bow, and with great formality say in English, 'Gulya, it would make me very happy if you would come home with Yu Yan and me and teach us both some Russian.'

Gulya, as instructed by Katya, would always reply in Russian, 'With pleasure, *Gospodin* Je Jin.'

Then the two girls would race each other to the car and hurl themselves onto the back seat. The other parents and children would look on with a mixture of envy and disapproval as Gulya and Yu Yan sat up straight and waved to them like the King of England, as the car drew away.

Je Jin's house was huge, designed in the Chinese style with four sides and an inner rectangular courtyard, including a vegetable garden. The house was all on one floor, divided into innumerable small rooms with polished teak floors. Each of the rooms had a plain mahogany table, a chair, an adult's cot and a wash-stand. Most were undecorated and spartan, occupied by servants and guards. The bigger and better rooms, set aside for visitors, had a veranda leading into the courtyard. Their white walls were decorated with pictures of flowers and vegetables, or stylised horses racing over hills, or country landscapes where tiny peasant men and women worked in fields or woods. Gulya would peer at them intently, imagining that the figures moved, and always finding something she hadn't seen before.

The full length of one side of the house was reserved for Je Jin and Yu Yan. Each had a large bedroom, which gave onto the inner courtyard, and a proper bathroom with running water. Je Jin's bedroom gave onto his study and his late wife's dressing room.

In one of the larger rooms stood a grand piano, on which sheet music lay open on a stand. Above hung a portrait, executed in the European style, of a beautiful Chinese woman, seated on an Empire chair, dressed in the height of 1920s elegance with a long cigarette holder in her right hand. Gulya asked Yu Yan who it was.

'That's Mama,' said Yu Yan, matter-of-factly. 'She died.'

Gulya wanted to know more, but Yu Yan knew nothing and she did not dare ask Je Jin.

Beyond the northern side of the house was a garden as big as a small park, with a profusion of trees and bushes, their trunks and branches so twisted and intertwined that in some places they seemed to be growing into each other.

There was one room, however – one of the largest – which Yu Yan and Gulya were never allowed to enter. It was what Yu Yan called the Fighting Room. There Je Jin would keep in practice with the sword and dagger in mock combat with his men, as well as boxing and wrestling.

Then there were days when the garden was out of bounds, as targets were put up and Je Jin and his men practised with rifles and pistols. In the central courtyard, Yu Yang had an almost life-size wooden doll's house, into which she and Gulya could crawl. It was her pride and joy, a replica of the traditional Chinese house to be found in a *hutong*, or lane. They played there endlessly.

Je Jin liked to watch them play. When he allowed himself time to relax, he would lie on a hammock, strung between two cherry trees, reading the newspaper and sipping tea. Sometimes Katya would lie on another hammock alongside Je Jin. They rarely spoke. When they did, it was usually because one wanted to show the other what they were reading. Sometimes Katya would place her hand on Je Jin's arm. Sometimes he would take her hand.

Those few months of fleeting contentment and tranquillity – the spring and summer of 1926 – soon passed. With the end of the summer term, the school year was over and so was Katya's little school. Thanks to Je Jin – and Vera's return of most of the money she had stolen – Katya found herself debt-free.

Over breakfast one morning, Katya announced the closure of the school and the family's imminent move down the hill to the Chinese quarter. She described their new home in glowing terms, well aware that Svyet would be horrified. Svyet, in the throes of adolescence, had become increasingly contemptuous of family life.

'It is much bigger than this little house. We will each have our own room, including you, Vanya. There is a big living room, where we can all spread,' Katya continued. 'We will also have two lavatories and a bathroom with a tub and basin. Think of that! What luxury!'

'So where is this beautiful house, Mother?' Svyet asked, her voice drenched in sarcasm. 'It sounds like a palace.' Svyet had long since stopped calling Katya 'Mama'.

'It's not actually a house. It's an apartment on the third floor of a three-storey house. It's light and airy, with windows on three sides. We are surrounded by trees, which protect us from the noise of the city and freshen the air. It's near here, ten minutes down the hill. You will be closer to your school and you, Vanya, to the market.'

'But, Mother, you can't mean that. It's the Chinese quarter.'

'I do mean that,' said Katya, coming to the heart of the matter. 'It's in a street where prosperous Chinese people live. Both our neighbours beneath us are Chinese. One is a teller at the Russian Savings Bank, the other a clerk with one of the shipping companies. They are good people. I've met them.'

When Je Jin had taken Katya to see the apartment for the first time, he had made sure beforehand that the neighbours would be in. He wanted them to understand clearly that the family was under his protection.

'I could never live there,' exclaimed Svyet in dismay. 'What will I tell my friends? You cannot do this to me, Mother!'

Katya began to get cross. 'No one is doing anything to you, Svyetlana. Try not to be so selfish.'

Katya paused for a moment. Then she went on, her expression hardening. 'The cruel truth is that the only money we have is what I earn. I already work fourteen hours a day to keep you in food and dresses. If you want to go to university, we must move somewhere cheaper, so I can build up some savings. The new apartment will be half the price of this place and twice as big. We are not the first Russians to have to do this. Look at the Shuvalovs, a family of higher nobility than our own. They have to share five rooms with a Chinese family.'

Mention of university silenced Svyet. More than anything she wanted to study in Pekin or Shanghai.

Katya had not finished. 'I am very happy, Svyetlana, that your Russian heritage is so dear to you. But never forget that Chinese civilisation has a far more illustrious pedigree than our own and deserves your respect.'

'And my best friend is a Chinese girl, Yu Yan,' Gulya piped up. 'I don't mind living with Chinese people.'

'Yu Yan, Je Jin!' spat Svyet, as if a dam had broken. 'What is this obsession with this Chinese family? Everyone is talking about your relationship with a moneylending Chinese bandit. It brings shame on our family.'

Katya became coldly furious. Because this was so rare, it was far more intimidating than Andrey's repeated explosions of bad temper, and even Svyet was taken aback.

'From the day we fled the Bolsheviks almost ten years ago, we have lived on the edge of the abyss. I have even killed men to stop us tumbling over it.'

Svyet and Gulya looked at their mother open-mouthed. Vanya continued knitting as if Katya had done nothing more than admitted to killing mice.

'All this time,' continued Katya, 'we have been a whisker away from abject poverty and the destruction of our family. Now that your father is gone, if anything should happen to me it's the orphanage for the two of you, where you will find yourselves sleeping three to a bed with Chinese, Mongol and Uzbek waifs and strays. I know Je Jin's reputation. Don't take me for a fool, Svyetlana. You know nothing of the world. By treating him with a modicum of respect, I have saved us from the abyss. He has forgiven our debt. If in the end you go to university, you will have me, Gulya and Je Jin to thank.'

'Why Gulya?' asked Svyet, still in a state of stupefaction at Katya's admission to killing men, while Gulya looked thrilled at the idea.

'Because she has shown Je Jin's daughter only love and kindness. You will do well in life to be a little more like your younger sister.'

To be compared unfavourably to Gulya was an intolerable humiliation for Svyet. She left the table and ran out of the house. That was the beginning of Svyet's estrangement: unable to reconcile herself to the Chinese House, as they came to call it, her absences became longer and more frequent. She never asked for Katya's permission – she simply announced she'd be staying with this or that friend, or sometimes a teacher. Then she stopped doing even that.

Chapter 24

On a beautiful autumn day in late September of 1926, Katya, Vanya and Gulya moved into the Chinese House. Je Jin had made all the arrangements, even sending the Rolls-Royce with his chauffeur and Fang the bodyguard.

None of their neighbours came to say goodbye. Everyone knew why they were leaving and where they were going. Madame Frolina, in particular, took the greatest pleasure in, as she saw it, the Polkonins' downfall. She was friendly with Vera's aunt and had soon extracted from her a lurid and fraudulent account of why Andrey had abandoned the household. According to this, Katya had not only mishandled the school accounts, but had driven her poor husband to distraction through her scandalous relations with a Chinese criminal. The shame of it all had forced him from the family home into the arms of a good Russian woman. Now Katya was leaving to become a Chinese moneylender's concubine! The poor children!

Katya did nothing to fight back against this bile. She simply withdrew from the Russian community. If she suffered from being so cruelly ostracised, she did not show it, and for good reason: soon after the move, she and Je Jin became lovers. Katya had never been happier. She did not give a fig for the Madame Frolinas of the Russian community – bitter, frustrated old women (and men), who were sinking ever deeper into poverty. Indeed, as time passed, several of her most abusive critics came crawling back, begging her to intercede with Je Jin so that they could get a loan on favourable terms or have their debt forgiven.

But from the start Katya had taken the decision not to interfere in Je Jin's business. He appreciated this, though would himself from time to time enquire about Russians who owed him money. The only time she ever asked him to show compassion was when the Shuvalovs, a branch of the family to which she was cousin, fell on hard times. He forgave their debt. Because he was so enraged at the way Katya had been treated by the Russians of Harbin, Je Jin made sure the Shuvalovs knew it was only thanks to her intervention that they had not been thrown onto the street. This had the opposite effect to that intended: far from showing gratitude to Katya, it only increased the Shuvalovs' display of disdain. No good turn goes unpunished, she thought.

Gulya liked their new apartment. It was in the largest house in the street and surrounded by tall trees. The street was not like those narrow, muddy *hutongs* which criss-crossed the Chinese quarters of Harbin. It was wide and properly paved. It had been built for the Chinese *haute bourgeoisie*. On either side was a mixture of houses in Chinese and European styles, most of them divided into apartments. There were cars parked outside – mainly Model T Fords and a few Buicks – at that time a sign of unusual affluence for a Chinese street. It was uncrowded. The occasional pedestrians were all Chinese. Some of them had little dogs on leads, and a few had taken to the French custom of walking their cats.

There was a little collection of shops at one end of the street where they could buy groceries, have shoes mended and clothes washed and cleaned. Every Friday a fishmonger and a butcher would set up their stalls for the morning. After her first visit with Vanya, Gulya never went near them again. The fishmonger sold enormously ugly catfish, with great whiskers. They were not always dead and would suddenly twitch and thrash on their wooden slabs. Worse was the butcher, who, along with cuts of pork and whole ducks and chickens, had dogs awaiting slaughter, crammed together in cages.

From the nearby tram stop they could travel either up the hill to the New Town or, in the other direction, all the way through the town centre and commercial district to the river. It was perfect for getting to school and, in Katya's case, for going to the Japanese consulate. Je Jin had done his research well.

The neighbours were always smiling and courteous, but very shy. Katya was under no illusions. These people did not want to get on Je Jin's wrong side. She had learned basic conversational Chinese – enough to pass the time of day or comment on the weather, and occasionally even to run errands.

*

Despite all the family turbulence, life at the Chinese House was happy. But then Vanya left. Her daughter, Mara, had stayed behind in Russia nursing her desperately wounded Goga back to health. Then, in the chaos that attended the end of the civil war, Mara and Goga had managed to escape to the USA through the port of Vladivostok. They left Russia on one of the last ships which repatriated the Czech Legion to Europe. From Bremen they found a ship bound for New York City. And from there, after a multitude of perilous adventures, including an encounter with the Odessa mob, Mara and Goga had finally settled on a farm in Idaho. Vanya had missed her daughter and she was longing to see her again. When letters arrived from Mara, Katya or Svyet would read them aloud to Vanya. Then, one day, the tone of the letter was different. Vanya could tell, behind the words, that her daughter needed her.

'Vanya, you must go,' said Katya. 'I will, of course, pay for your passage. It will be wonderful to be reunited with Mara and Goga. A whole new life awaits you.'

Vanya nodded, too choked with emotion to speak. The two women embraced. It was decided. Je Jin immediately offered to pay for Vanya's tickets. Katya refused. Her bond with Vanya was too personal, her debt to Vanya, in every kind of way, too great.

But neither Katya nor Vanya declined Je Jin's offer of practical help.

'If I may suggest,' said Je Jin, with Katya translating into Russian, 'there is a ship which goes every month from Hong Kong to San Francisco through the Panama Canal. It is simpler and quicker than changing vessels somewhere in Europe. Since she doesn't speak English, all kinds of crooks will try to take advantage of her on the way. I will send Sam, one of my butlers, with her. He's Chinese, but fluent in English and has even a smattering of Russian. He will escort her.'

Once again, it was quickly decided. Two weeks later, Vanya left with Sam to take the train south to Hong Kong. Sam was a jolly man with a ready smile. He could have been anywhere between fifty and seventy years old, lean, wiry and tall. It was obvious that Vanya liked him.

Gulya was heartbroken to see Vanya go. Everyone wept as they embraced and said goodbye. Je Jin and Sam stood respectfully in the background. Then Vanya and Sam got into the Rolls-Royce and were gone.

Three months later, a letter arrived from Mara containing a photograph of Mara, Goga, Vanya and Sam. They were standing in front of the Idaho farmhouse, grinning and waving, happiness bursting out of them like the rising sun.

Mara's letter said that Vanya had arrived safely after an uneventful journey, except for one extraordinary thing. She and Sam had got married in San Francisco. Love had blossomed during the long voyage from Hong Kong. Now they were building a home for themselves next door to the farmhouse. Thank goodness Mama is here, Mara exclaimed, because I am expecting a child.

'I have had a letter from Sam, apologising for not coming back,' said Je Jin, after hearing Katya read out Mara's letter. 'I half expected it. He's a good man and I wish him well. In a generation's time, God willing, they will all be rich. Please write to them and tell them never to fall into the grasp of the banks.'

Chapter 25

In 1931, Svyet passed her exams for the literature faculty at Pekin University, where courses were taught in Chinese and English. Though Harbin had a well-regarded university of its own, it had grown out of cooperation between Russia and China on the construction of the railways, and its focus was engineering. The ambitious student, Chinese or Russian, aimed for Shanghai or Pekin.

Katya was, of course, delighted for her. But the elder daughter who came home to announce this was like a stranger. She was perfectly pleasant, but in a condescending way. She politely declined Katya's offer of a small party to bid her farewell. Instead, she invited Katya and Gulya to an event high on the hill of Novy Gorod, where a renowned family of musicians, the Feutzes, were giving a grand reception and dinner in her honour. Svyet reached into her handbag and, looking extremely pleased with herself, handed over two enormous envelopes, each containing an embossed invitation.

Katya was hurt, but she was also curious. The Feutz family was half-Swiss and half-Russian. Alfred, the Swiss father, was a conductor of some repute, who each season was hired by this or that orchestra in one of the world's great capitals. His Russian wife, Galina, a soprano of similar renown, sang most of the time at l'Opéra in Paris. Occasionally, their schedules would coincide in Harbin, as they had now. Whenever that happened, it was their custom to give a week's performances of *Carmen* at Harbin's handsome opera house. *Carmen* was Galina's *pièce de résistance*, though she was getting a little long in the tooth for the role. They were throwing their party for Svyet on a Tuesday, which was by tradition a dark night at the opera.

Gulya, too, was curious, but not because she particularly liked opera. The Feutzes had three children, twin daughters and a son, Marcello, in his twenties. He was a budding star of German silent films, reputed to have had an affair with Marlene Dietrich, who liked her lovers young. Gulya had seen every film of his that came to Harbin, and even had his picture pinned on the wall of her room.

Marcello Feutz despised Harbin – he had his eye on Hollywood – but he had landed a prominent role in a Chinese film about the Opium Wars, in which he played a British officer. Most of the time he was holed up at the Hotel Majestic, the best in town. There he indulged in champagne-fuelled orgies with Korean prostitutes, though with the arrival of both his parents in town he affected filial piety and returned to the bosom of the family.

Svyet had been lodging with the Feutzes for the last three months, thanks to her close friendship with the Feutz daughters, who were in her class at school. There, as far removed as possible from the Chinese quarter of the city – and her mother's affair with Je Jin – she had found a comfortable berth to study for her exams. The two sisters were as plain as Marcello was beautiful, which suited Svyet fine. She was herself growing into a lumpy, ugly duckling with her father's somewhat prominent nose. Svyet had elected to use her wit and intelligence to compensate. Part of this persona was to deploy a withering contempt for any woman better-looking than herself – and that included Gulya, who had the good fortune to have inherited the small, upturned nose, petite figure and shapely legs of the Alexandrov women.

Gulya, at fourteen, was beside herself with excitement to be invited to the soirée. She had just finished cutting and sewing a blue dress in the latest fashion, based on a design she'd found in *La Vie Parisienne*, while Katya got Madame Zobel to make her a dress based on a Coco Chanel creation.

On the eve of the party, Katya and Gulya put on a fashion show for Je Jin and Yu Yan.

'Wow!' exclaimed Yu Yan.

'Katya, you have never looked more beautiful,' Je Jin said. 'You, too, Gulya. You could be film stars.' Katya blushed. She *did* look good. Her love affair with Je Jin had taken years off her. The grey, lined, worried face had been banished. As for Gulya, her heart swelled with pride.

'You must take the Rolls-Royce and arrive in style,' he added.

'Yes, we will . . . ' Katya paused and looked at Je Jin, '. . . and I will take you! We cannot arrive unescorted.'

'No, no, Katya, you have suffered enough from your association with me. Anyway, I haven't been invited.'

'I don't give a damn,' said Katya fiercely. Je Jin, Yu Yan and Gulya looked at each other in astonishment at such language. 'You and I have been together for almost five years. People have said everything they could say about our relationship. They can't hurt us anymore. Never forget – you are among the most powerful men in Harbin and I am a Russian aristocrat. Let us behave like it. *Courage, mon amour! A l'attaque!'*

Gulya suddenly heard herself shouting, 'Yes, yes, that will show them – and Svyet, too.'

'I appear to have been outvoted,' said Je Jin mildly.

'Wish I could go,' said Yu Yan disconsolately.

*

'The Honourable Je Jin, the Countess Ekaterina Alexandrovna Polkonina and the Honourable Olga Andreyevna Polkonina,' announced the master of ceremonies in his resplendent red tunic, as they swept into the Feutz house the following evening.

They had arrived fashionably late, and the two large, connected reception rooms were already packed. The guests at first glance looked to be all European, the women in a mix of short and long dresses, the men in black tie.

As for Je Jin, he looked like the Emperor of China. He wore the most wonderful long coat in blue silk, tricked out in gold and silver embroidery. A curved sword in a scabbard of pure gold hung from his waist. His height, slim figure and good looks were stunning. Gulya was sure she could hear exclamations from some of the women.

They started down a receiving line, comprising Alfred and Galina Feutz, Svyet and the three Feutz children.

They had wondered beforehand how Alfred and Galina would receive them, but they need not have worried. The Feutzes were sophisticated citizens of the world, and the evening had a very specific purpose. Alfred was a fading figure in the world of music and Galina's voice was shot. The harsh truth was that their international careers were over. Svyet's success was simply a peg on which to hang a party.

With a keen sense of public relations, they were delighted to have their party adorned by a Chinese guest of such notoriety and power, accompanied by two Russian women of noble birth. They fussed over the three for so long that a small queue of late arrivals built up behind them. Svyet had a place of honour between the Feutz parents and sisters. She gave Katya and Gulya a frigid kiss each and said something about being pleased to see them at 'her' party.

Marcello was at the far end of the line, a smile playing on his divine features. He greeted Je Jin with practised charm and respect, bowing slightly towards him. To Katya he bowed from the waist, allowing his lips lightly to brush her gloved right hand. Then it was Gulya's turn to look into his cobalt-blue eyes. He bowed and kissed her hand with the fullness of his lips. She felt herself swaying.

'My dear Olga Andreyevna . . . ' said Marcello.

'Call me Gulya. Everyone does.'

'May I? Then please call me Marcello. I hope and pray that you will do me the honour of a dance after dinner.'

'Come along, Gulya,' she heard Katya say, 'you're holding everyone up.'

'Really, Gulya,' Katya chided, leading her away, 'You cannot flirt like that in public. Everybody was watching. Don't you think, Je Jin?'

'I'm keeping out of this,' said Je Jin, laughing.

'I was not flirting!' Gulya retorted.

'Just be a little careful with Marcello, Gulya,' said Je Jin, a hand on her arm. 'He's a man-about-town, a ladies' man. He has left a trail of broken hearts from here to the Sangari river.'

The three turned to face the guests.

'Well, I suppose we'd better circulate and meet people,' said Katya, suddenly losing confidence.

'Don't worry, they'll come to us. You'll see,' replied Je Jin, guiding them forward into the throng.

He was right, of course. The power of celebrity swept all before it. They were exotic creatures, rarely seen in public. They had barely stepped five yards when they were surrounded by people keen to introduce themselves. Some of the men gave Je Jin their business cards, while Katya was inundated with invitations to tea and lunch from the Russian ladies of Harbin. Gulya, naturally, found herself at the centre of a group of young men, some of whom she knew from school.

Dinner was al fresco, on a grand terrace overlooking the extensive grounds of the Feutzes' house. The gardens were lit by a semi-circle of burning brands. A wind had come up from the Sangari river, making the flames leap wildly and the shadows dance like dervishes. There was one long table, deep inside the terrace. Three great silver candelabras, placed equidistant along the table, added to a light that was brilliantly refracted through the elaborate formations of crystal and silverware at each guest's seat. Behind each chair stood a footman, dressed in the eighteenth-century style with knee breeches and powdered wig.

'This must have cost a fortune,' Katya whispered to Je Jin. 'I never realised the Feutzes were so well off.'

'They are not,' answered Je Jin. 'This is all borrowed money, half from the bank and half from me.' He gave a harsh little bark of a laugh. 'He is – literally – betting the house on becoming resident conductor of the Harbin Symphony Orchestra and repaying the debt from a handsome salary. That's why the entire board of the opera house is here.'

'And if he doesn't get the job?' asked Katya.

'He probably will, because he would raise standards in the orchestra, which is desperately needed. Though he's past his best, Feutz is still enough of a name to put Harbin on the map. The mayor, of course, doesn't like Feutz and may block him. To be frank, I don't mind either way. If he defaults, I'll pay off the bank and take the house, which Feutz has put up as collateral. I wouldn't mind living up here.'

Katya took her place in the middle of the table on Alfred Feutz's left; the wife of the opera house chairman, Madame Borisova, was on his right – the place of honour.

Alfred Feutz was deeply boring. To Katya's disappointment he was incapable of talking about music in any inspiring way. His conversation was all about ticket sales, the unsubtle message being that the Harbin Opera needed a new broom like him, who had filled concert halls all over the world.

With a small sigh, Katya counted the knives and forks on either side of her plate. It looked as if there would be six courses. She was wondering how she would be able to endure this interminable dinner, when she felt a tug on her left sleeve and turned to see the ruddy cheeks and rheumy blue eyes of the old archbishop, Metropolitan Seraphim. He arrived at a dinner table tipsy and ended the meal too drunk to speak. He was a typical Russian peasant priest. He had escaped the Bolsheviks and, through a mixture of cunning, obsequiousness and luck, had risen rapidly through the ranks of the Russian Orthodox church in Harbin. He was a relief after Alfred Feutz, regaling her with outrageous gossip about prominent Harbin families. He made her laugh out loud, so that everyone looked up to see the source of such merriment. At one point, his old eyes twinkling, he leaned towards her and, breathing Armagnac fumes across her face, whispered that he had forbidden Andrey and Vera to worship in the cathedral.

Then, after draining his glass, he let his chin drop to his chest and he fell fast asleep.

On the other side of the table, Je Jin had been seated on Galina Feutz's left. On his other side was the mayor's wife – his second, a pretty blonde some twenty years her husband's junior. She wanted to be flirtatious with Je Jin, but the hint of menace in his demeanour, which he could turn on and off like a light bulb, extinguished her wilder side.

Svyet, at one end of the table, had to her right Rector Sukhodryev of Harbin University and to her left Saprykhin, director of the Gymnasium. She was more than satisfied with this respectably prominent place.

Gulya, meanwhile, was seated some way down the table on Katya's side, on her right an earnest young man with acne and glasses and on her left, Marcello. Just five minutes' conversation with Marcello left her breathing heavily, as he leaned over her, one arm running along the back of the chair. By the time the cheese course arrived, she was like the proverbial rabbit in the headlights. As his father rose to make the toast, she felt Marcello's hand on her knee, pressing and squeezing as if her flesh were some kind of dough. She pushed his hand away. It immediately returned. She pushed it away again. It again returned. This time she let it stay.

Alfred Feutz embarked on his speech, orotund in style and tedious in length. He felt it necessary to recognise all the dignitaries at the dinner table. People gazed into the distance, eyes focused on nothing. A number of them had joined the Metropolitan in sleep. Some were whispering to each other.

Then Feutz suddenly reached his climax. His guests came to attention at the table. After thanking Je Jin and Katya for coming, he paid tribute to Svyet's astounding intellectual achievement, the diligence of her studies and the honour she had bestowed on Harbin by gaining, against the fiercest competition, entrance to the English faculty of Pekin University.

Feutz's peroration elicited thunderous applause, prompted mainly by a profound and universal relief that the speech was finally over.

Svyet rose to reply. She was dignified but cold. She did not refer to her notes. She thanked a few people, notably the Feutzes. She made no mention of her family.

Svyet's response received polite, but unenthusiastic, applause. Everyone knew that she was just an excuse for a party. More to the point, she was not someone who was likely, now or later, to have influence in Harbin, or to advance – or impede – careers.

No sooner had the applause for Svyet died down than the master of ceremonies announced coffee and dessert in the drawing room and a band struck up in the garden. The Feutzes had laid a wooden dance floor on the lawn, which had not at first been visible. Suddenly, a row of electric Chinese lanterns was lit, which cast a golden glow over the floor and revealed, seated to the side, seven musicians, dressed in black tie, with a piano and a set of drums. They broke into jazz, all the rage in Harbin among both Chinese and Europeans.

The band started playing 'Tiger Rag', an exciting, raucous, fast number. Alfred and Galina rose from the table and, encouraging the guests to follow them, moved to the dance floor, where Alfred made a fool of himself, trying to lead his wife in a fast foxtrot.

Marcello, whose hand was still caressing Gulya's knee, turned to her and asked, 'Can you do jazz dancing?'

'Of course I can,' she replied indignantly, 'I love it.'

'Then, let's show them how it's done!'

He got up from the table, pulling her to her feet. All eyes were upon them. Katya's were filled with alarm. Je Jin was impassive.

Marcello was a wonderful dancer. Gulya responded by unleashing all the steps and moves that she'd practised with her girlfriends. They bounced, twirled and lindy-hopped around the floor at top speed, perfectly synchronised.

Then, with a bravura ensemble finale, the music came to a halt. There were cries of 'Bravo!' and 'Encore!' Even Katya was smiling as she applauded, and Je Jin made Gulya a slight bow of appreciation. Svyet's chair was empty.

The band then began to play a slower number at which the guests poured onto the dance floor. Marcello held Gulya close as they started to move to the rhythm. He took out a silk handkerchief and wiped a sheen of sweat from his face. He lit a cigarette as they danced, blowing smoke in her face. Suddenly he seemed coarser. A large quiff had escaped the carefully lacquered arrangement of his hair, falling over half his brow and upper face, covering one of his eyes. The other returned Gulya's infatuated smile with a strange stare.

'Let's go for a little walk in the garden and get away from this crush,' he said, in a tone that brooked no resistance.

She meekly followed Marcello through the crowd. He held her upper arm tightly as they walked to the trees at the end of the garden. Without warning, he pulled her into the darkness behind the burning torches and kissed her roughly, thrusting his tongue into her mouth. She struggled, but he kissed her again, rubbing insistently against her groin. She bit his lip, hard.

'Why did you do that, you silly little girl?' Marcello raged, blood pouring from his lip. 'You know you want me.' He took out his sweat-soaked handkerchief and pressed it to his lip as Gulya stood, paralysed with fear.

Suddenly, violently, he pushed her onto her back, then fell on her, one hand pinioning her wrists, the other trying to undo his trousers. She screamed, but her voice was swallowed up by the loud music. She twisted and turned with all her strength but Marcello's sweating, bleeding face was pressed into her neck.

Suddenly, she remembered her girlfriends' advice, and jerked a knee upwards into his genitals, which were half out of his trousers.

Marcello rolled off, roaring with pain. For a few seconds he was incapable of speech. As Gulya sat up, and he rose from his knees, he found his voice and rasped, 'By God, I am going to teach you a lesson, you little slut.'

He raised his fist to hit her. She put up her hands to protect her face. Then something strange happened, which at first she did not understand. A shadow appeared behind him. His raised arm seemed to go further and further behind his back until it was in an unnatural position. He looked back and began to whimper. Slowly he was forced again to his knees, and then onto his back. Gulya looked hard at the shadow. It was Je Jin. He towered astride Marcello, who had begun to jabber in German, '*Nein, nein, bitte, nein.*' Je Jin did not say a word. He was holding Marcello by the hand of his outstretched right arm, looking for a moment like a manicurist examining a client's fingers. The music rose to a crescendo. Je Jin began to make sharp jerking movements with Marcello's fingers.

By now Gulya was on her knees and could look down at Marcello's face. It was still contorted, but this time by fear and pain. His eyes bulged as if they were about to explode. His nostrils were flared like those of a panicking horse. His mouth was wide open, screaming. But he could not compete with the final bars of 'Muskrat Ramble'. It was just like one of his silent films.

*

There is an old black and white silent film called *Flames Over the Orient*. It is a Chinese-German co-production about the Opium Wars, in which the villains – the British – are all played by German actors, except for one, a very handsome chap, who is actually Swiss-Russian. He has a significant supporting role as a British army officer. Throughout the film, he has one arm in a sling. This, according to the film, is because he is the hero of a desperate action against the Chinese army. In fact, he wears the sling because he is Marcello Feutz and all the fingers in his right hand have been broken by Je Jin.

Chapter 26

After the party, Svyet's speech was the talk of the town. Russians tend to honour their families. Svyet had ignored hers. The Feutzes did not like the idea of being on the wrong side of a family divide, particularly when the family included Je Jin. So Svyet was politely invited to leave their house. She returned to the Chinese House in the vilest of tempers.

For six weeks, she either immured herself in her room, emerging only to take meals, or left the house early in the morning without telling anyone where she was going or when she was coming back. When she was at home, she refused to speak to Gulya and was barely civil to Katya. The atmosphere was poisonous.

It all came to a head at the beginning of September, as the three sat in the drawing room on the eve of Svyet's departure.

'I am astonished, Mother,' said Svyet with patronising pomposity, 'that a Polkonina, born an Alexandrova, could tolerate living in such demeaning circumstances. The sooner I get to Pekin the better.'

She had not noticed that Je Jin had just arrived and was within earshot behind the door. He came into the drawing room, obviously angry.

'Well, Svyetlana,' said Je Jin, who never called her Svyet, 'you will find yourself surrounded in Pekin by a veritable multitude of Chinese people. Your faculty is but a tiny English-speaking island in an ocean of slitty-eyed orientals. How *will* you manage to cope?'

'I did not mean you,' stammered Svyet, flushed with embarrassment.

'Why didn't you mean me? I am one hundred per cent Chinese. I am responsible for installing you in this Chinese apartment that you despise so much. Don't you think, given your distaste for us Chinese, it would be better to pursue your studies here in Harbin, where the ratio of Europeans to Chinese is far higher than in Pekin? If the Feutzes won't have you anymore, I am sure you will find a Russian family who will let you a room. After all, most of the Russians in this town are short of money. I should know – I'm a moneylender.'

This was delivered in acid, unforgiving tones, as Je Jin stood intimidatingly over her. Svyet had committed the cardinal sin, in his eyes, of showing disrespect to her mother.

'On second thoughts, just go,' he continued. 'Why do you think the Feutzes threw you out?'

'They did not throw me out!' screamed Svyet. 'They needed my room.'

Je Jin pressed on. 'You may have a half-good brain, Svyetlana, but emotionally you are behind. Your jealousy of Gulya defies reason. Just because Marcello Feutz preferred to dance with her . . . '

'That's enough, Je Jin, please,' Katya interrupted, her maternal instinct no longer able to endure the flaying of her older daughter.

Je Jin fell silent for a while. Then he turned to Katya and took her hand.

'I am sorry, Katya. I let my anger get the better of me. That was inexcusable.' With that, he walked out of the drawing room.

Gulya awoke sometime in the middle of the night to the sound of low voices: Katya and Svyet were deep in conversation. Neither of them went to bed that night. Before Svyet left to catch her train just after dawn, she hugged Katya tight and wept again. She was even nice to Gulya.

After she had gone, Katya and Gulya sat at the kitchen table and for a while drank their coffee in silence. Finally, Gulya said, 'Svyet was much nicer when she left. She even said "sorry" to me.'

'I think Je Jin's harsh comments last night were . . . ' Katya hunted for the words, '. . . lanced a boil.'

'Why do you say that, Mama? She got what was coming to her.'

'Gulya, you must try to be a little more charitable. I know she has been horrid to you. But she is your sister. When Je Jin said what he said, it unlocked a mass of emotions inside Svyet. All kinds of feelings and anxieties, which have been pent up for far too long. I talked it through with her all night. By the time it came for her to leave, Svyet was much calmer and full of regret for her behaviour.'

'I'm sure that won't last long.'

'Well,' said Katya, wearily, 'it's true, I suppose, that showing remorse is not in her nature.'

They fell silent again.

Then, as Katya rose to wash the cups and saucers, she said, 'It's just you and me now, Gulya.'

*

For a while, life changed for the better. Gulya became a local hero. The story of her dance with Marcello had swept the Gymnasium – even the teachers were impressed when the report appeared in *Russky Golos*. They treated her with more respect, and she responded by giving them better classwork, to Katya's relief. Meanwhile, Katya reinserted herself cautiously into Russian society, as she took up some of the invitations given her at the Feutzes' house. She was very choosy, determined not to forgive those who had been particularly beastly to her or Je Jin.

But even if she had wanted a more active social life, her work for the Japanese consulate would have got in the way. Katya had given up private language lessons altogether and was now working full-time for the Japanese. More often than not she worked late. She did not mind. The staff were polite and respectful. She counted Mr Amae, the consul, and his family as friends, even though a certain formality imposed limits on their relationship.

She concentrated so hard on getting the translations right, while doing them quickly, that she never dwelt on their content. Yet, with the benefit of hindsight, it was clear that the storm had been gathering for years.

It turned out that the thousands and thousands of Russians and Jews, who had found refuge in Harbin and other Manchurian towns after the great conflicts in Europe and Russia, had not chosen well. Manchuria had become the cockpit of fierce competition between China, Japan and the Soviet Union.

After the overthrow of the last Chinese emperor, the country had become an unstable republic in which warlords fought each other for supremacy. Patriots like Je Jin were tearing their hair out at China's inability, through corruption and incompetence, to extinguish the malign influence of foreign powers. Korea, no great distance from Harbin, had already become a Japanese protectorate. Manchuria was the next target of Japanese ambitions.

As autumn changed to winter in 1930, Gulya noticed that they were seeing less and less of Je Jin.

'Something has been worrying him,' Katya said, when Gulya questioned her, 'and he won't tell me what it is. He also won't let me go to his house anymore.'

Gulya's voice began to quaver. 'It's not over between you, is it?'

'No, no. I think it's something to do with my work for the Japanese. He has always grumbled at how much time I spend with them.'

'At school they are saying there's going to be war between China and Japan.'

'I've heard the same thing,' said Katya. 'Recently there's been a funny feeling in the air at the consulate, as if everyone was holding their breath.'

A few days later, when Gulya was still at school, Je Jin came to the apartment. He looked exhausted and anxious. He sat next to Katya on the sofa, kissed her and took her hand.

'Katya,' he said, 'I know you are worried. I have been absent a lot. And when I'm around, I'm not the best of company. But we have to speak very, very seriously. Some of the things I am about to say are very distressing. The time has come to face a harsh reality. My only aim is to protect you and Gulya from harm.'

'What can you mean, Je Jin?' Katya asked, deeply alarmed.

Je Jin sighed and took a deep breath. 'You must have wondered why I don't invite you to my house anymore.'

'I have,' said Katya quietly.

Je Jin grasped her hand more tightly. 'You can't go there because it's dangerous for you and it's dangerous for me. Even Gulya must stop going.'

Katya remained silent, searching Je Jin's troubled dark eyes.

'There will soon be a war between China and Japan. Relations are going from bad to worse. You must have read this in all those translations you do for the Japanese. They are desperate to know what international opinion thinks of the situation – Russian, French, German and so on. That's why your work has doubled in the last few months.'

Katya sat bolt upright, slowly removing her hand from his and holding it to her mouth.

'It won't be we who strike the first blow, though you never know with our fools of squabbling leaders. It will be the Japanese and the first blow will be here in Harbin. That we know from our spies. We think they want to take all Manchuria and install a Chinese emperor, who would be their creature. They would then have a base for further conquests to the south. This would be done in the name of this puppet emperor, aided and abetted by Chinese traitors.'

'How does this affect you? Us?' asked Katya, still fixing Je Jin with an unblinking stare.

'I am working closely with loyal patriots in the Chinese army to prepare as best we can for a Japanese attack. If it comes to war, my men and I will join the army. We will be defeated, because we are outgunned and have no air force. But we can make the Japanese bleed. Then, if we have not all been killed, we will in time-honoured fashion take to the hills and continue the fight as guerrillas. My home has become the centre of our planning. The Japanese know this and have planted spies outside the gates to see who goes in and out. We seized one of them the other day – a Chinese traitor. He told us quite a lot before we strung him up.'

Katya's heart was thudding.

'This is why,' continued Je Jin, 'it is too dangerous for you or Gulya to be seen going to my house. The Chinese will think you are spying for Japan, because of your long association with Amae and his staff. They are already suspicious of you. People have accepted my assurances up to now. But, as the military planning gets more detailed and sensitive, I cannot protect you forever.'

'Should you even be coming here?' asked Katya. 'Aren't you in danger of compromising yourself?'

'Yes, I am. And you, too. You are not only under suspicion from my fellow countrymen but almost certainly from the Japanese as well. There are several representatives of the *Kempeitai*, the Japanese secret police, working under diplomatic cover in the consulate. You can assume they know about our relationship. They will be asking themselves whether you are spying for us – or whether they can make use of you to spy on me. I think it is called pillow-talk in English.' A watery smile briefly crossed Je Jin's face.

'Then,' said Katya, 'not only should I no longer go to your place, but I must immediately stop working at the Japanese consulate.'

'No,' he said, 'That too would be extremely dangerous, possibly fatal.'

'But I could not possibly work for our enemies!' protested Katya. 'What a silly, blind fool I have been!'

'On the contrary,' said Je Jin calmly and firmly, 'the very best thing for you to do now is to continue at the consulate as before. You would not be safe from the *Kempeitai* by resigning your position. They could come for you at any time, usually at night, to take you away for interrogation. There is no protection to be had from the Harbin police. The *Kempeitai* would probably take Gulya, too. One of their techniques is to torture children in front of their parents to make them talk.'

Katya caught her breath in horror.

This was one of those moments when you see and hear everything around you with the greatest clarity, while your mind finds refuge in the incongruous, unable to take in what you are being told. As Je Jin informed Katya that her and Gulya's lives were in mortal danger, she suddenly remembered she had a coat waiting to be collected from the Jewish tailor.

'The Japanese will approach you shortly and ask you to work for them in another capacity. It will for them be a test of where your loyalties lie. It is a test you must pass if you and Gulya are to survive. They will want you to extract information from me.'

'But, Je Jin, I could not possibly do that,' exclaimed Katya in distress. 'We are trapped!'

'No, you are not, my love. There is a way. It is not one I would wish to force on you, because it will have its own grave dangers. But the only alternative is to leave Harbin without delay and get out of Manchuria altogether.'

'No, never. I am not going anywhere. But what is this "way" you just mentioned?' Katya asked.

'It is this,' said Je Jin, taking her hand in both of his. 'When they ask, you should agree. I will then feed you morsels to pass to them. Most of them will be misleading, even downright false. But there will be enough that is true to protect your credibility – and keep you and Gulya safe.'

'In return,' continued Je Jin, 'we hope you may be able to pick up information of use to us. I don't want you to do anything out of the ordinary that may arouse suspicion. Just observe and keep your ears peeled.'

Once Katya had got over the shock, Je Jin's words began to arouse in her a strange feeling that she could not at first identify. Then it came to her: it was that heady exhilaration in the face of danger that she had first felt all those years ago as she drove the family cart from Golovino to Syzran. A fragment of Shakespeare's *Henry V* entered her head: *stiffen the sinews, summon up the blood . . .*

'What do you need to know?' she asked.

'We do not know when the Japanese will strike. You could be the first to pick up the signal. You have already noticed a change in atmosphere at the consulate. There is bound to be some further change the nearer they get to the attack. They may, for instance, start burning documents. Amae may send his family back to Japan or to Korea. That sort of thing.'

Je Jin paused. He looked into Katya's eyes. He saw no fear. His heart yearned for her. Soon, he thought, we will be separated forever. Cherish every single moment that remains.

He went on. 'Have the Japanese ever asked you about me?'

'Never,' replied Katya.

'Do the Japanese ever try to engage you in discussion of the topics that you translate?'

'I don't think I have ever discussed with anyone what I am translating. As far as Mr Amae and the consulate staff are concerned, I have no interest in international affairs.'

'What do you discuss with Amae?'

'All kinds of things, but not current affairs. He's interested in languages, etymology, literature, history. He's more like a professor than a diplomat. His younger brother was an officer on a battleship at Tsushima in 1905, when the Japanese sank our fleet. We talk about that and the Russian Revolution. I think that I have established a relationship of confidence with Mr Amae and his family – and his staff, for that matter.'

'Then betraying this confidence will be difficult for you, won't it? Are you sure you can do it?'

'Yes. For you. Yes.' Katya said this without hesitation. 'I am actually excited by the prospect.'

At that moment Je Jin realised the full depth of Katya's devotion to him. By God, she would make a good guerrilla, he thought. He tried to cough away a ball of emotion that had suddenly welled up in his throat and caught him by surprise.

'Then it is decided,' said Je Jin, still trying to clear his throat. 'Provided you are not found out, you will be well placed to weather the Japanese occupation, when it comes. The Japanese don't like the Russians. They will be pretty rough on your community here. Your work with the consulate will protect you. You will have a special status in their eyes. But to most Russians and Chinese you will be considered a traitor. That won't be pleasant.'

Katya made a dismissive gesture and asked, 'And you, what will you do? You can't be a guerrilla forever. Where will we meet again? Will you come south, too?'

'No, my love.' Finally, the tears welled up in Je Jin's eyes. 'Never, in my cruel and twisted life, did I think that God would bring me the love that I have shared with you. There is nothing, nothing that I desire more than to live the rest of my life with you, until I am a doddery old fool, fit only to feed the carp in my pond. But it is not to be.

'When I go to war, I will not come back. I may be killed on the first day of battle or years hence on a hillside with my guerrilla band, finally cornered by the Japanese army. I will never stop harrying them and they will never stop hunting me. It can end only in my death. That is my destiny. I can only hope that you and I will one day be reunited in heaven.'

Chapter 27

Je Jin was right. A week later, as she was preparing to go home, Mr Amae asked Katya to step into his office. He looked embarrassed and awkward. She went in to see another Japanese official sitting in a corner of the room. He was bald and hard-faced, wearing a pin-striped suit. Showing his contempt for anyone Russian, he did not acknowledge her arrival in any way. She sat opposite Mr Amae on the other side of his desk.

Mr Amae came straight to the point without introducing his colleague. Katya noticed that his hands were shaking.

'Countess Polkonina, we have become concerned at your relationship with the notorious criminal Je Jin. What can you tell us?' Mr Amae looked forlornly through his round, rimless spectacles, as he nervously tugged his skimpy little goatee beard. This hurts me more than it hurts you, screamed his silent message.

She and Je Jin had carefully prepared and rehearsed her answers to an interrogation. They had expected this question.

'Mr Amae, I can assure you that nobody has been more concerned about this relationship than I. Though it pains me deeply to tell you, and in front of a total stranger to whom I have not yet been introduced . . . '

At this, Mr Amae introduced her to Mr Kamimura, who looked unblinkingly at her. Katya carried on unperturbed.

'I was several years ago abandoned by my husband, who absconded with what was left of the family money. In my desperate situation, I had to borrow money from Je Jin, the lender of last resort for us Russians. He charged me a rate of interest so high I could not afford to pay it. He then used a ploy that he had used on other defenceless

Russian women. He offered to halve the rate of interest and the capital if I would submit to a relationship. The choice for me was between becoming a Chinese concubine . . . ' Katya almost spat out the word 'concubine', '. . . or abandoning my daughters' education. Of course, I could not let down my children. You cannot imagine the humiliation that I, a Russian woman of noble birth, have had to endure!'

Katya paused, taking a handkerchief from her sleeve, to dab her eyes. Both Mr Amae and the other man were staring at her intently.

'Mr Amae, it is only thanks to your confidence in me and, indeed, the generosity of your government, that I have been able to save enough money to pay off Je Jin and meet my children's school bills. As you know, my older daughter is now in her first year at Pekin University. I must say in all frankness that you and your family are among my dearest friends in all Harbin.'

Mr Amae bowed slightly and said, 'Your work has been exemplary.'

He was about to say something else when the other Japanese, to whom Mr Amae clearly deferred, broke his silence in fluent, if heavily accented, English.

'This is a touching story, Countess Polkonina, but I doubt it's the whole truth. If your relationship with Je Jin was so distasteful, what were you doing with him at the Feutzes' big party last summer? You did not need to take him there.'

'Mr Kamimura, I do not think you could ask such a question if you really knew Je Jin. He is a man of violence, who is used to getting his own way. Those who obstruct him are either killed or severely beaten. I have learned not to stand in his way. If he has a weakness, it is his craving, criminal though he may be, for recognition and respect at the highest levels of society. When he heard of the Feutzes' party, he insisted on accompanying me. I could hardly say no to him for fear of repercussions.' Katya allowed her voice to rise in indignation.

Kamimura nodded equably. 'But now that you have repaid him, he has no further hold on you. Surely.'

Suddenly Katya found out why, at a deeper level of consciousness, something had been gnawing at her memory. Mr Kamimura sounded and looked like the police detective Charlie Chan, in one of those new American talking films. She had just been to see it at the Imperial on Kitayskaya Street.

'If only it were that straightforward,' replied Katya. 'He owns the house in which I live. I pay no rent. If I were to try to leave him, I doubt he would let me go.'

'So,' said Kamimura, as if summing up a business meeting, 'you will continue to have an intimate relationship with Je Jin for the foreseeable future, even though you would like to end it.'

'That is exactly the case,' said Katya.

Kamimura began to talk to Amae in Japanese. Amae occasionally responded, nodding in the affirmative, 'Hai, Kamimura-san.' He is getting his orders, thought Katya.

Then Kamimura turned to her and again spoke in English. The likeness to Charlie Chan really was astonishing.

'I am grateful to you, Countess, for your frank answers. I draw two conclusions. Firstly, we would like you to continue your work. Your translations are read every Sunday night by our ambassador in Pekin, who then forwards them to our ministry of foreign affairs in Tokyo. Is that agreeable to you?'

'Perfectly,' answered Katya, with a surge of well-concealed relief.

'Secondly, we do not want you to be in any hurry to end your relationship with Je Jin.' This time sheer joy coursed through her.

'Oh, no,' she said with fake despair, 'is this absolutely necessary? I was planning to escape somehow.'

'I am sorry to ask you to make this sacrifice,' continued Kamimura, 'but it is important to us. We want nothing but peaceful coexistence with China. But Je Jin is fomenting war between our two countries by stirring up Chinese hatred against us. He has a network of agents and spies to do his dirty work. We need to find out about his activities. Who he sees. What he is planning. And so on. We have noticed of late that he prefers to come to your apartment.'

'That's because some of his friends think that I'm too close to Mr Amae, that I am some sort of Japanese spy.'

'Well,' said Kamimura, 'the way to dispel suspicions is to spy on us for him.'

'What on earth do you mean, Mr Kamimura?' said Katya, turning up her nose as if there were a bad smell beneath it.

'It is perfectly simple. From time to time, we will give you information, which you can pass to him. Most of the time it will be misleading, but not always. To start off, in two days' time, you can say that Amae has told you that he is afraid the Chinese are about to attack our forces in Korea. That's completely false, but it's plausible.'

Kamimura paused. Katya's early exhilaration began to turn into a sensation just short of panic. She felt that she was entering a labyrinth with two exits, one leading to Je Jin, the other to Kamimura – and she had no way of knowing if at the end she would find the lover or the torturer.

Kamimura went on, 'You will be well rewarded for this work, Countess. If Je Jin finds you out, we can protect you. When all these matters are, how can I put it, resolved, we will help you leave Harbin and escape Je Jin's clutches once and for all.'

With a satisfied look on his face, Kamimura leaned back in his chair and laced his fingers together over his stomach. Amae was staring at the inkwell on his desk.

Katya's brain had seized up, momentarily unable to distinguish between truth and deceit, fearful of saying anything that might betray Je Jin or herself.

'How does this all sound?' asked Kamimura, breaking the silence.

'I think I could do it,' she said hesitantly. 'I have never done anything like this before.'

'All you have to do is to act normally and keep your ears and eyes open.' The very mirror of Je Jin's instructions, she thought. 'Amae will tell you what to look out for. Most of the time you can communicate with us when you come to the consulate. But in emergencies, we will show you a tree where you can leave messages. It's not very difficult,' said Kamimura with a hint of impatience.

'Very well,' said Katya, 'I will do what you wish.' Kamimura nodded with satisfaction.

When Katya got home that evening, she asked Gulya if she would mind cycling to Je Jin's.

'Invite yourself to supper with Yu Yan and then ask Je Jin to escort you home. Tell him I have some information. Try to say this to him without anyone else hearing.'

She was not quite sure why she was instructing Gulya to take such precautions. There were hardly likely to be Japanese agents inside Je Jin's house, but she had become so entangled in subterfuge that ultra-caution had to be the order of the day.

An hour later, Gulya, Je Jin and Katya were drinking tea in the apartment. Katya gave Je Jin a detailed account of her meeting with Amae and Kamimura.

When he heard the latter's name, Je Jin grunted, 'The head of the *Kempeitai* in the consulate. Not somebody to be trifled with. You did well to persuade him that you wanted to be rid of me. If he had doubted you, Katya, we might never have seen you again.'

In a deliberately matter-of-fact manner, Katya added 'The good thing in all of this is that our old way of life remains unchanged – I continue doing my work at the consulate and we continue seeing each other.'

'Quite so,' said Je Jin.

'What I need by the day after tomorrow is your reaction to my news that the Japanese fear an attack by Chinese forces on their army in Korea.'

'This, dear Katya, is bluff and double bluff. The Japanese want us to focus our attention on the Korean peninsula. But we know from our spies that their attack will be along the axis of the South Manchuria Railway, from Port Arthur on the coast north to Harbin. We in turn must give the impression that we have fallen for this ploy.'

'I will have to be able to tell Kamimura this in my own simple way,' said Katya.

Je Jin thought a while.

'You might say something like this. "When I told Je Jin, he answered that you were lying; that it's camouflage for Japan's own plans to attack China from Korea." That is what Kamimura and his masters will want to hear.'

Ten days later, Katya ran into Kamimura in a corridor of the consulate. 'You did well,' he said. 'Two regiments of Chinese infantry and some artillery have just moved to the frontier with Korea. Perhaps you have a gift for this type of work, Countess.'

Katya, somewhat to her shame, took pleasure in his words. She noted the trace of a smile playing on his lips.

Je Jin was equally content.

Katya had passed her period of probation as a spy with flying colours. She was now a fully fledged double agent.

Chapter 28

As Je Jin had predicted, the Japanese army – the Kwantung – came up the South Manchuria Railway, capturing town after town with ease until they were at the gates of Harbin in early 1932. As the Japanese got ever closer to the city, crowds of Chinese would gather daily outside the Japanese consulate to shout slogans and throw stones. Every day the crowds got larger.

The defence of the consulate was left to the *Kempeitai* officers and their thugs. The inevitable happened. One winter's afternoon, with the sun touching the horizon and the temperature well below zero, a handful of demonstrators, who had managed to get over the railings at the back, were shot dead.

Though Katya was in the building at the time, she did not hear the shots. They were drowned by the sound of screaming voices and banging drums. She was unnerved by the demonstrations. It was impossible to concentrate. She could no longer walk to work. It was too dangerous to run the gauntlet of the crowd. The Japanese sent a car to pick her up every morning and bring her in through the back gate of the consulate. But even there, large crowds had begun to gather. They hammered their fists on the car's roof or spat on its windscreen.

This cannot go on, thought Katya. One day soon they will drag me out of the car and kill me. It was beyond even Je Jin's power to protect her against a mob so inflamed by war fever.

Je Jin had been away on some mission while all this had been going on. On his return he was appalled to discover that Katya was still working at the consulate. He asked her immediately to stop. There would be more violence.

'But I am finding out things every day. The staff, in their panic, have become very loose-lipped,' she protested.

'That is not worth your life,' said Je Jin fiercely.

'All right. I will go in tomorrow and hand in my notice.'

The next morning, the day after the shootings, before Katya could say anything to anyone, Mr Amae, who had already sent his family to safety in Korea, walked into her office and told her that she must leave immediately and not return. A car was waiting as usual at the back. The crowds had dispersed – it was just too cold to be on the streets – but they would be back later in the day, still enraged by the shootings.

'Today,' said Mr Amae, who was in a fever of anxiety, 'we will burn all our sensitive documents and destroy the cypher machines. Then, under the command of Major Kamimura, we will arm ourselves. With any luck we should be able to hold out until the Japanese army arrives.'

Katya had never seen anyone less martial in bearing than Mr Amae, tall, stooped and blinking owlishly from behind his round spectacles. The idea of his actually firing a weapon, or even killing someone, defeated her imagination.

'And when will that be, Amae-san?' she asked.

'In about a week, at the beginning of February. At least that is what we have been told. You would do well to stay indoors when the troops arrive. They are poor country boys with animal appetites, which their officers do little to restrain. The 20th Division have a reputation for violating women. Stock up with food now, before people start to panic.'

'What should I do if the soldiers come to our apartment?'

Mr Amae was carrying a folder, which he handed to her.

'Inside is an official certificate in Japanese, with the Imperial stamp, that attests to your loyal service to the Emperor. During our occupation – I have no idea how long it will last – have it with you all times. If soldiers come to your apartment, immediately show them the Imperial stamp. Unless there is an officer with them, most likely they will be illiterate, but every soldier knows what the Imperial stamp looks like. That should protect you and your daughter.'

Mr Amae stopped. For a few minutes he had been transformed, speaking firmly without his usual hesitancy. Then his old persona returned. He looked at her gravely. 'My wife and my children send their very best wishes. They are sorry not to have had an opportunity to say farewell to you. When everything is calm once more, I hope, we all hope, it may be possible that you will work for us again . . . '

Mr Amae's voice, now soft and barely audible, trailed away altogether. Katya sensed that he had no faith in what he was saying. Nor had she.

They were abruptly interrupted by an aide, who rushed into the room and said something to Mr Amae.

'You must hurry. The mob is on its way,' said Mr Amae.

He shook hands with Katya. They looked at each other for a moment and then he was gone. His distraught face stayed printed forever on her memory.

Her *Kempeitai* driver, with a pistol in his lap, started to drive through the streets towards Je Jin's house. She saw in the distance what looked at first like a burning building. Then, she realised that it was a vast crowd carrying blazing torches. They must be heading for the consulate. She wondered if Mr Amae would survive the night. She shivered and hunched herself in the corner of the car's back seat.

She found Je Jin's house full of men in uniform looking at maps. They all turned to look at her as she walked into the big reception room.

Je Jin, one of the few keeping his cool, said, 'Thank God, you're back. The streets are not safe today. Did you hear anything about when the Japanese army will attack?'

'Amae told me he expects his army to be in Harbin in about a week's time.'

Je Jin translated and there was a babble of Chinese voices. He called for silence.

'What else, Katya?'

'The *Kempeitai* men shot and killed some demonstrators. The consulate is burning documents and destroying their cypher machines. They are arming themselves. Major Kamimura is in command of the defence. They hope to hold out until the Japanese army arrives. But on the way home I saw what looked like a very large crowd, with blazing torches, heading towards the consulate.'

Katya paused and then added, almost as an afterthought, 'My work at the consulate has been terminated. I can do no more for you.'

'Thank you, Katya. We are all very grateful to you. It cannot have been easy,' said Je Jin. He once again translated. The Chinese officers turned to her and bowed.

She went into the kitchen, where she found Gulya and Yu Yan having an early supper. She sat down with them and drank the bowl of soup that Je Jin's cook gave her.

'You look exhausted, Mama,' said Gulya, reaching across the table and holding her arm.

'Pass me that bottle of wine, will you, Gulya.'

She poured some red wine into an ordinary tumbler and drank it straight down. Then she poured another and sipped from it.

Gulya had never seen her do such a thing before. 'Have you had a bad day at the consulate?' she asked. 'Je Jin wouldn't let us go out of the house because the streets are full of people shouting and running everywhere.'

'I have had a horrible day at the consulate. It's surrounded by demonstrators, who are getting more and more aggressive. The Japanese guards shot a group of them who had managed to get over the fence at the back and into the garden. The rest of the crowd ran away. But Mr Amae expects them to return and attack the consulate in revenge. As I was leaving, I saw a huge mob coming down the road. I think they will attack tonight.'

Katya, who had been staring into her glass as she said this, talking in a low, barely audible voice, looked at Gulya and Yu Yan as she finished.

They were speechless.

'Poor Mr Amae,' Gulya finally said. 'What will happen to him and his family?'

'Well, at least he has got his wife and children out. We said our goodbyes tonight, because I obviously can't go back to work. I had this strong feeling I would never see him again. I think he felt the same. He became quite emotional. He gave me, by the way . . . ' Katya hunted around in her bag, '. . . this official Japanese document with the Imperial stamp. He said it would protect us when the Japanese soldiers arrive. We must always have it with us.'

Je Jin came into the kitchen. He was dressed like a Boxer, in a pink tunic with a knotted scarf around his head. He had a sword and pistol at his waist and a carbine slung over his shoulder.

'There's a massacre going on at the Japanese consulate. Chinese demonstrators have attacked the consulate. The Japanese have a machine gun firing from an upstairs window. They are mowing down demonstrators who have got over the rear fence into the garden.'

'And you are going there to fight them.' This was less a question than a statement of fact.

'Yes, Katya. I cannot stand by and do nothing. If I wait for the army I'll wait forever. Something has to be done right now. There may only be twenty of us but we know how to fight.'

'And how will you avoid being killed by the machine gun?'

'We will get into the consulate from the other side, from the front. Now, Katya, my love, I have to go. My people are dying as we speak!'

Je Jin embraced Katya, Yu Yan and Gulya; then, spinning on his heel, he swept from the room. The three sat there in a state of shock.

*

When Je Jin and his men arrived at the consulate, they found a scene of carnage, bodies scattered all over the garden and piled up at the rear gate. The survivors in the crowd had retreated out of the machine gun's range and extinguished most of their brands for fear of becoming targets.

Je Jin's arrival gave them renewed heart. For some in the crowd he was a supernatural figure. He proposed leaving a handful of his best shots at the rear to try to suppress the machine gun's fire. The crowd, or what was left of it, could then attack again. He would lead the rest of his men to the front of the building, get inside and capture it.

Je Jin himself fired the first shot to see if the machine gun would respond. It did, spitting out bullets from a first-floor window in the centre of the building. His sharpshooters returned fire – sparingly, like all good shots – and a body fell from the window. There followed wild firing from the machine gun in the general direction of the rear gate.

The grey light was already fading from the short winter's day. As a decoy, the surviving demonstrators lit burning brands to the right of the garden, while they prepared to attack from the left once darkness had fallen.

Je Jin gave orders to his sharpshooters to lay down heavy fire in exactly five minutes and for the Chinese demonstrators to attack simultaneously. This would give him and the rest of his men cover to enter the consulate and begin their own offensive.

It all went largely to plan. After five minutes Je Jin heard his men firing from the rear. The machine gun started up again and then suddenly stopped. The gunner must have been hit, thought Je Jin, as he and his men scaled the front gate with ease. Then a pistol was discharged from a window on the ground floor and one of his men fell from the gate. Kamimura must have placed a lookout at the front. Je Jin could see a shadow at the window. The lookout had allowed himself to be exposed by a dim light behind him. Je Jin fired his pistol three times at the silhouette, who cried out and disappeared.

Je Jin and his men climbed in through the window from which the shot had been fired. On the floor lay a man, groaning. Je Jin unsheathed his sword and slashed his throat. Then the bulk of his men made their way room by room through the building, slaughtering all whom they found, except for some women and children hiding in the coal cellar.

Je Jin, with a couple of his men, had gone straight to the first floor to find the machine gun. As they reached the top of the stairs, they were confronted by a tall, stooping figure with round spectacles and blinking eyes. His right arm was stretched out before him, pointing a pistol. God, it's Amae, thought Je Jin, hesitating a moment. A gun went off behind him and Mr Amae fell backwards, his arm still extended rigidly in front of him, his pistol firing uselessly into the ceiling. The bullet had passed in perfect symmetry between his eyes.

The machine gun started firing again. It had been moved from the centre of the building to the far end of the corridor, to make it harder for Je Jin's sharpshooters in the garden to take it out. He ran down the corridor to where a door was ajar. The ear-splitting sound of firing came from within. He pushed open the door and saw that it was Kamimura himself manning the weapon, with another *Kempeitai* man feeding in the ammunition belt.

Because of the noise, neither heard Je Jin and his men come in. The ammunition man was immediately shot dead. Je Jin pulled out his sword and, rather than killing him instantly, kicked Kamimura away from the gun. He wanted to see Kamimura's face before he beheaded him. As his sword cut into Kamimura's jugular, the Japanese, with the last physical movement of his life, pulled the trigger of his pistol and shot Je Jin through the heart.

By the morning of 19 January 1932, the Japanese consulate had been burned to the ground and all the staff killed.

Chapter 29

A few days later, on 4 February 1932 – a bitterly cold day, when the temperature fell to twenty-five degrees below freezing – the Kwantung Army marched into Harbin. They had crushed Chinese resistance with ease, helped by turncoat Chinese generals.

Katya, in a state of extreme shock after learning of the demise of both Je Jin and Mr Amae, had wanted to stay on in Je Jin's house. Unlike Katya and Gulya, Yu Yan had not shed a tear when told of her father's death.

'I was expecting it,' she explained. 'Papa said to me that dangerous times were coming and that one morning he might leave the house and never return. I am sure that one day I will cry – but not now.'

Such calmness from one so young was almost shocking.

'Besides,' continued Yu Yan, 'I have you and Gulya. Papa always said that if anything happened to him, I could rely on you to look after me.'

But it was not to be.

Most of Je Jin's men returned to his house unharmed. Two of them carried his corpse and placed it on the dining-room table. The men invited Katya, Yu Yan and Gulya to pay their respects. With heads bowed, they stood as a kind of honour guard around the walls of the room.

Je Jin's eyes had been closed. There was very little blood on his body. He looked to be sleeping peacefully. Katya kissed his lips, said a prayer and crossed herself. Yu Yan hugged him close and said in Chinese, 'Farewell, Papa.' When it came to Gulya, she froze.

'Mama, what do I say?' she asked in panic.

'Say what you feel, Gulya. Listen to your heart,' replied Katya calmly.

'Dear Je Jin, I just don't know how we are going to manage without you. I will miss you so much,' she said in a wobbly whisper, and then burst into tears.

The cook and her husband, who had known Je Jin the longest, assumed the responsibility for preparing the body for burial. They were imbued with multiple customs and superstitions. They cleaned the body and dusted it with talcum powder. They dressed him in a magnificent coat, with his weapons by his side. They avoided the colour red, which, they believed, would turn him into a ghost. Then they burned the rest of his clothing. They went around the house, removing the mirrors. They covered the statues of Chinese gods that were scattered around the house. They placed a gong to the left side of the entrance to the house.

Though all this was done with due ceremony and respect, there was also a sense of urgency. The sounds of artillery and attacking aircraft grew ever more ominous. They had to bury Je Jin and get out of town before they were trapped by the advancing Japanese troops. They laid him to rest deep in the woods at the bottom of the garden. There was no stone or marker, in order to avoid desecration by the Japanese.

When they returned to the house, sombre and, in Gulya's case, tearful, one of Je Jin's men turned to Katya and Gulya and told them in English to get back to their apartment. The piece of paper provided by Mr Amae would offer no protection if they were found in the house of the very brigand who had slaughtered their kin at the consulate.

'What about Yu Yan?' cried Gulya. 'Can we take her with us?'

'No. The *Kempeitai* will know who she is. It would be the death sentence for all three of you if she is found sheltering in your apartment. She will go to relatives in the countryside. She must leave now with the cook and her husband. They will be safer hidden in a stream of refugees. Now, I beg you, please go!'

The urgency of the moment roused Katya from her grief-stricken trance. She hugged Yu Yan, whose self-control began to crumble. Her lower lip quivered and a silent tear rolled down her cheek. She held Katya and Gulya's hands and, looking up searchingly into their faces, said with great solemnity that they would soon meet again – of that she was sure, because she had dreamed it three nights in a row. As Katya dragged Gulya by the hand out of the house, she looked back to see Yu Yan's slight figure standing between the rotund cook and her skinny husband, one hand raised in a farewell salute, anguish written on her face.

*

They hibernated in the apartment, eating from the supplies of tinned food that Katya had wisely stocked before the Japanese attack.

'We must stay indoors until the storm has passed. In due course things will return to normal even if we are ruled by the Japanese,' Katya said.

Gulya had no wish to go anywhere in the freezing weather. She had just embarked on *Anna Karenina* by their distant relation Lev Tolstoy, though her concentration was repeatedly broken by thoughts of Yu Yan. Katya had promised to look after her, yet now Yu Yan had been abandoned into the care of distant relatives. Would she think they had betrayed her?

A few days after Je Jin's death, Katya was awoken just after dawn by a heavy, insistent banging on the apartment door. She opened it to be confronted by a squad of Japanese soldiers. They were small, wiry men in drab olive winter coats, wearing funny little fur hats with a badge in the shape of a star. Each carried a rifle with a long bayonet fixed. They reached roughly to pull her from the apartment. She was prepared for this and held in front of them the document that Mr Amae had given her. She had learned to say in Japanese that the paper was from the Emperor.

This gave the soldiers pause. They peered at the document. They talked among themselves. Then one of their number ran down the stairs with the document, presumably to consult a senior officer. The rest of them stood silently, staring, with their bayonets pointing towards Katya and Gulya. Two of them were smiling in predatory expectation.

Finally, after what seemed an eternity, footsteps could be heard coming up the stairs, slowly and deliberately. There hove into view a bulky figure in a military greatcoat, followed by the soldier who had rushed downstairs with Katya's document. This man was much older than the soldiers, with a lined, weather-beaten face and a straggling, wispy beard. He was clearly in command. He returned the document to Katya and bowed. Katya bowed in return. Immediately the soldiers lowered their rifles and the tension evaporated.

As the soldiers left, Katya closed the door. She leaned against it in relief, taking several deep breaths in quick succession. Then she went to a cupboard in the kitchen, poured herself a glass of vodka and downed it in a gulp.

'Can I have a drop, Mama?' asked Gulya, who had never tasted vodka.

Without saying a word, Katya half-filled another glass and handed it over.

'*Do dna!* Down in one!' she commanded.

Gulya threw the vodka down her throat and immediately began to cough uncontrollably.

'That was terrifying, Mama. How could you have stayed so calm?'

'Gulya, I was very frightened. If things had gone badly, we would have been raped and murdered. But I have learned that if you wish to survive, you must put on a show of utter fearlessness. That was how we managed to escape from Russia all those years ago.'

Katya was thinking back to her encounter with the tinkers on the road to Syzran when she suddenly heard a great commotion in the street, with shouting and screaming in Chinese and Japanese. Katya crossed herself and exclaimed, 'Oh God, our poor neighbours!'

They rushed to the front windows to see the Chinese neighbours from the two apartments below lined up in front of the Japanese soldiers. They were of all ages, from babies to elderly grandparents. The stout sergeant was shouting into the face of one of the Chinese men, Mr Chu, who worked at the Russian Savings Bank. The sergeant suddenly took two paces back, drew his revolver and shot him. Mr

Chu instantly crumpled. The rest of their neighbours began to wail, some of them falling to their knees. The sergeant said something to his men. They advanced and bayoneted all of them, repeatedly. The babies, three of them, were held aloft by the soldiers on the end of their bayonets, as if in triumph. One poor infant continued to wriggle, like a fish on a hook. The soldier brought his bayonet down violently and smashed the child's skull in the road.

Katya and Gulya stood frozen in horror.

'That,' said Katya, 'is what Mr Amae saved us from.'

Having pulled their bayonets from the bodies, the soldiers, at the sergeant's barked command, formed themselves into a single column and marched off. The corpses were left in the street. Katya thought she saw one of them move.

'Shouldn't we go down and see if anyone is alive?' asked Gulya, tugging at Katya's sleeve. The vodka had given Gulya what they used to call 'Dutch courage'.

'We should wait a moment to make sure the Japanese aren't coming back.'

After ten minutes or so they put on winter coats, went downstairs and stepped gingerly into the street. The Japanese troops had vanished, but screams and shouts were coming from the direction of the shops further down the street.

Katya and Gulya got to their knees and examined the bodies of their neighbours. They were all dead. Their wounds were hideous; inflicted, so it seemed, with a deliberate, obscene brutality. Katya said, 'We must pray for their souls. They weren't of our church, but God, in his mercy, will listen.'

They began to murmur Russian Orthodox prayers for the dead, their breath emerging from their mouths in great clouds of steam. 'Heaven knows when they'll be buried,' said Katya. 'We ought to cover them.'

They found sheets and blankets in the neighbours' ransacked apartments. They covered the bodies. The babies looked like little parcels. Then they retired to their own apartment, where they sat and shivered in shock.

As the day wore on, plumes of black smoke from burning buildings rose vertically in the freezing air, undisturbed even by the mildest breeze. When night fell, out of several score inhabitants of the street, only Katya, Gulya and a Franco-Japanese family had survived the depredations of the Japanese soldiery.

Chapter 30

It was astonishing how quickly the appearance of normal life returned to Harbin.

The following morning, they woke to find that the corpses beneath their window had been removed during the night. Unarmed Japanese soldiers were clearing out the ransacked apartments. By the time breakfast was over everything had been taken away in two lorries.

There was a tapping on the front door. Katya and Gulya looked at each other. Without a word Katya got up to open the door, seizing Mr Amae's document from the hall table as she went.

Two Japanese men in uniform were standing on the landing. One was a common soldier, small and bandy-legged, impassive, the other a tall, smiling officer in an expensive-looking winter coat of leather and fur. He allowed it to hang open, revealing beneath a smart olive uniform and polished black boots to his knees. On his head was a peaked cap encircled by a red band.

He clicked his heels and bowed to Katya.

'Major Yamamoto of the military police, the *Kempeitai*. We are sorry, Countess Polkonina, that you were so rudely disturbed yesterday, but there was a misunderstanding. To avoid further . . . ' he hunted for a word '. . . mishaps, we will pin to your door a notice in Japanese and Chinese stating that your apartment is the official property of the Japanese Empire and that you are to be treated with appropriate respect. This will protect you from unwanted callers.'

This was delivered in good English.

Katya's mind was racing. Yamamoto's visit meant that for all practical purposes she was considered to be one of them. She found this abhorrent. The Japanese – and a *Kempeitai* officer to boot – had killed the love of her life. Yet, to be suspected of sympathy for Je Jin and his cause would mean a death of unimaginable cruelty. There was no choice.

'I am honoured, Major Yamamoto.' They bowed to each other.

'Might I enquire,' asked Katya politely, 'whether it is advisable to go into town? And my daughter will need a similar document to mine, if she is to resume her attendance at school.'

'Our plan,' replied Yamamoto easily, 'is for everything to be back to normal by next Monday, five days from now. I would not venture out till then. We are still arresting Chinese criminals and bandits and there is sporadic violence and shooting. If you need supplies before Monday, please call this number.' He gave Katya his card. 'I will ensure that a pass for your daughter – Olga Andreyevna Polkonina? – is delivered here shortly. And, of course, we would like you, Countess, to resume your work for us. You have given us invaluable service in the past.'

'Once again, Major, it would be an honour to serve the Emperor.'

There was more reciprocal bowing. The words had almost stuck in Katya's throat, but she consoled herself with the thought that it was what Je Jin would have advised her to say.

'I am delighted,' said Major Yamamoto. 'Please come to my office – the address is on my card – at ten o'clock next Monday.'

The major, followed by the little soldier, departed in an extravagant swirl of clicking heels, flapping coat and rigid military salute. She barely had time to get her breath back before the telephone rang, making her jump. She had only recently acquired the machine and was completely unused to its jangling bell.

It was the principal of Gulya's school, Mr Saprykhin, announcing his intention to reopen the Gymnasium and resume classes the following Monday. He wanted to know whether Katya would send Gulya back to school next week.

Then, in his falsely intimate and oily voice, he added that he had it from impeccable sources that a new political order was about to be instated. Manchuria would become an independent state under the protection of Japan. This would put a stop to the quarrelling between

Chinese warlords – which had been going on quite long enough, thank you. A bit of Japanese discipline would do everyone some good.

Katya, who loathed Saprykhin, could imagine him in all his puffed-up self-importance on the other end of the phone. He had always sought to convey the impression that he was the confidant of the highest political and social circles, when in reality he was no more than a purveyor of low-grade gossip. It was clear to Katya that he was under orders from the Japanese authorities.

Katya confirmed that Olga would be at morning assembly at nine o'clock the following Monday. She put the phone down in disgust.

*

So began a strange period, both unremarkable in its routine and shot through with tension.

Gulya duly went back to school. An envelope had appeared in the letter box over the weekend, containing a *laissez-passer*, written in Japanese and Chinese and stamped with the Imperial seal. It worked like magic. There were checkpoints all over the city, manned by highly officious Chinese police. They examined minutely people's identity documents and, if there were the slightest irregularity in their papers, hauled them off to the police station for interrogation. As soon as they saw Gulya's *laissez-passer*, she was waved through without further ado.

It was a sort of normality. Gulya took the tram each day to school. The shops reopened at the same time as the schools. Since the Japanese soldiers had killed the shopkeepers as well as pillaging the shops, new occupants had to be found to take over the businesses.

Before long the street markets were in full swing.

But Harbin had changed. Bombed-out buildings lined the riverfront. There was damage in town as well. The synagogue on Central Street had taken a direct hit from the air and was now a burned-out ruin. Part of the Hotel Majestic had also been burned and its walls were pockmarked with bullet holes.

One afternoon, Gulya finally plucked up the courage to go to Je Jin's house. There was no sign of it. It had been razed to the ground, leaving only blackened foundations. Some of the wood at the end of the garden had been burned too, but the clump of trees under which they had buried Je Jin remained intact. She went home to tell Katya, who had been unable to bring herself to go there.

The atmosphere changed as well. Harbin became a more regimented city. There were suddenly lots of Chinese police in spanking new uniforms. The Japanese were deliberately inconspicuous, yet every now and again, as if to remind you where authority really lay, you might see a *Kempeitai* officer out for a stroll with his wife and children.

Katya was now working full time for Major Yamamoto. Among other things, she learned that the Japanese authorities had placed informants everywhere. They were afraid of Chinese resistance to their puppet emperor. They were especially fearful of young people.

'Never, ever, Gulya,' she warned with her most serious face, 'say anything rude about the Japanese or this new Chinese emperor they have put on the throne. You can be quite sure that there is at least one informant in your class. Don't forget also that most of the teachers have to report to the Japanese, and that includes Mr Saprykhin.'

Katya had gone to see Major Yamamoto on that first Monday, after making sure Gulya had got to school safely. The *Kempeitai* had taken over a hotel on Central Street, which had once been called the Paradise. Since there were torture chambers in what had been basement storerooms where people were executed, to be 'sent to Paradise' was acquiring a sinister irony among the Chinese resistance groups.

She took the lift to the first floor, where Major Yamamoto had his office. It was one of those rattling metal cages, operated by an ancient Japanese in a plain blue uniform with three rows of medal ribbons. The lift reminded her of the one in the Astoria, the finest hotel in St Petersburg. The memory gave her a sharp jolt of nostalgia for her homeland.

Major Yamamoto was all charm, courtesy and elegance. He came straight to the point.

'Countess, this is the situation. We have grown tired of the endless fighting and quarrelling between Chinese warlords. Since the Republic of China was created in 1912, the country has been in a state of anarchy, nowhere more so than in the region that used to be called Manchuria.'

'Used to be . . . ?' murmured Katya.

'Yes, used to be,' replied the major. 'It is now Manchukuo. We have suffered intolerable provocations from Chinese bandit generals. We had no choice but to intervene, not only to protect our interests, but to respond to the entreaties of those Chinese – the great majority – who want to lead decent and disciplined lives, free from the threat of chaos. That is why the Kwantung Army temporarily occupied this city. We have, I am pleased to say, routed the forces of disorder. This has been warmly welcomed by the Chinese of Manchukuo, to such an extent that Prince Puyi of the Qing dynasty – the last to rule Imperial China – has agreed to become head of state with the title of Emperor.'

'Now,' continued the major, 'this is where you come in. Our job at the *Kempeitai* is to hunt down and destroy the last vestiges of resistance to the new order. But our initiative in helping to create Manchukuo has aroused the jealousy of the Soviet Union, which has long-held designs on the natural resources of the region. I expect in my lifetime to see another war between Japan and the Russians. Then there is the attitude of the international community in the shape of the League of Nations, this absurd organisation in Geneva. Rather than support our noble efforts to bring peace to northern China, it looks as if the League will condemn us. If that happens, I doubt we will stay a member.'

Major Yamamoto paused, drew deeply on a cigarette, which he had just lit after offering one to Katya, and then came to the crux of his presentation. Somewhat against her will, Katya found herself fascinated.

'We want you to monitor the Soviet press and to translate into English anything written about Manchukuo and Moscow's intentions towards Japan. Secondly, we want you to do something similar with the English, French and German press with regard to action that may be taken by the League of Nations. It will be a heavy job. Do you think you can do it?'

'Of course I can, Major Yamamoto. I am ready to start now.'

The Major leaned back in his chair with a satisfied smile on his face. He again offered Katya a cigarette. This time she took it. She smelled his cologne as he bent forward to light it for her. It was a little too sweet and obvious for her taste.

'My dear Countess, that is wonderful. We will, of course, pay you handsomely.'

Which they did. It was thanks to the Japanese that Katya and Gulya now began to lead a comfortable life in exile.

Chapter 31

One week was much like another. In term-time mother and daughter left home together in the morning. They both liked to rise early, to discuss the previous day's events across the kitchen table. Even in the school holidays, Gulya was at the table at the same time as Katya.

For the first few months their breakfast conversations enabled Katya to grieve over Je Jin. She talked a lot about him, sometimes in an intimate way, and on occasion wept uncontrollably at some memory of their life together. Then, as the time approached for them to catch the bus, she would dry her eyes, get to her feet and say the same thing she always said: '*Bozhe moi*, my God, I must pull myself together. Je Jin would not approve.'

Within about six months she was talking less about Je Jin and, when she did, she remained dry-eyed. There was love, tenderness, amusement, but no longer grief. One of the reasons was that she had found a way of helping Je Jin's followers.

The major had given her an office on the same corridor as his own, at the rear of the building and looking out onto a pleasant formal garden. She was to report directly to him.

Katya threw herself into her work. She summarised and translated vast amounts of material at great speed. After a while certain things became clear to her. There was significant Chinese resistance to Japanese-dominated Manchukuo – fighting was still going on between guerrillas and the Kwantung Army. The League of Nations, though its reaction was slow and indecisive, would in the end condemn Japan and demand its withdrawal from northern China. Tension between the Soviet Union and Japan was also growing. The Russians were spoiling for a fight to avenge their humiliating defeat in 1905. The Japanese were seeking to expand their empire right up to the Soviet border. It made war almost inevitable.

She said as much to the major at her meetings with him. He listened to her with growing attention.

He said to her one day, 'Countess, you are more than just a translator of the press. You are also an astute analyst of international politics. I think my weekly meeting of planning and research would benefit from your presence. I have learned things from you that I have not heard from my staff, who are supposed to follow these matters. You are the first to tell me that our great victory over the Russian Empire in the war of 1905 negatively affects Soviet attitudes to Japan today, even though it hastened the taking of power by the Bolsheviks. I look forward to seeing you every Thursday at eleven o'clock in the meeting room along the corridor.'

'But I don't speak Japanese, Major.'

'That is not a problem. All *Kempeitai* officers on my staff are expected to understand and speak English. If there is a problem, I will have an interpreter present or translate myself.'

The weekly planning and research meetings gave Katya a new reading of the Japanese. She thought that she had acquired a fair idea of their character and way of working from her time at the consulate under Mr Amae. It had been hierarchical, deferential and formal. But that was as nothing compared to the *Kempeitai*.

A dozen uniformed officers entered the room at eleven o'clock on the dot. Each was expected to stand up and give a report. Upon completion, the officer turned to the major, saluted and sat down. If the major asked a question, the officer would again stand to reply. There was no general discussion across the table. Nobody interrupted to make a point. There was no challenging the reports except by the major himself.

Katya noticed something else, something more insidious. It seemed unacceptable for any officer to suggest that Japan could make a mistake or fail to achieve something. As a result, Major Yamamoto and his staff came away from these meetings buoyed by a wholly unrealistic optimism.

Katya's presence in the room was clearly a shock to the major's staff. The major introduced her, explaining her role, and everyone, including Katya, stood up and bowed. He sat her next to him, to his right, a place of honour and seniority. As the meeting progressed, she wondered how she should insert herself, given the major's grip on the proceedings. She need not have worried. After two of the reports, he invited her to comment. She made a few anodyne remarks with mild criticism of one of the points made in the second report.

That was how it all began. As time passed, he called on her to speak more often. When she asked if she might make an intervention, the major readily agreed. Furthermore, when she spontaneously challenged something said by one of the reporting officers, the major indicated his agreement with what she had said. She became more hard-hitting in her comments.

Then the penny dropped. He was using her to change the nature of the meetings. The more he allowed her freedom of speech – a woman and a foreigner – the more his officers dared to loosen up. One day there was even quite a heated debate about Soviet intentions. Katya brought discussions to a conclusion with what the major called a 'magisterial' analysis.

'The meeting is not what it was when I first joined,' she said to the major afterwards. 'It's far less wooden.'

'Thank God,' replied the major. 'We Japanese, locked away on our islands, have to understand that there are things to be learned from abroad. That, after all, has been how we have modernised our armed forces. I inherited these meetings from a colonel of the old school, who discouraged debate. I could not change them on my own. I needed an outsider to show the way.'

In a matter of months the 'Russian Countess' made herself indispensable to Major Yamamoto. This began to open a door to a subject so far never discussed in front of her – the continuing resistance of Chinese guerrilla groups in Manchukuo.

One day Katya came across a lengthy article on precisely this subject in the French socialist newspaper *l'Humanité*. The journalist wrote under the pen name of Charles Martel, the great eighth-century Frankish leader. Martel wrote with a familiarity that suggested he had accompanied a band of Chinese communist guerrillas. He promised a second article, in which he would follow Chinese nationalist forces, who were also inflicting heavy casualties on the Japanese. He suggested that if the two factions could only unite, they would stand a good chance of bringing down the puppet regime of Emperor Puyi. He claimed that clandestine talks were taking place between the Communists and Nationalists in Harbin.

Katya translated and summarised the article and sent it immediately to Major Yamamoto. She knew that it would cause consternation. The Japanese strained every sinew to convey an image of peaceful normality throughout Manchukuo.

With the despatch of the *l'Humanité* piece, Katya found that she had cleared her desk and it was only mid-afternoon. She decided for once to leave work early and buy food in the market near the apartment.

Katya was browsing the fruit and vegetable stalls when she saw a familiar figure behind one of them. It was Fang, the English-speaking Boxer who had been in Je Jin's entourage. He had already spotted her.

'Lovely fruit, lady, lovely fruit!' he called out in English.

She went up to him, showing no sign of recognition. She felt her heart beating a little faster. He hacked open a melon for her to taste. She ate a slice. It was deliciously ripe.

'Very tasty. I'll take one,' she said.

'Have another for half price. Feel it for ripe,' he said insistently, putting it into her hands.

She felt it. It was incredibly light. Then she realised that it must be hollow. She looked at the man and he looked at her. A barely perceptible signal of complicity passed between them. She put the two melons in her string bag. She bought some vegetables as well to make the transaction look convincing to anyone who might be watching.

At home, she told Gulya of the encounter.

The hollow melon was tied with the thinnest strand of white cotton. Excitedly, Gulya undid it and pulled the melon apart. Out dropped a single sheet of paper. It was a message from Yu Yan in English. They read it together.

Dear Gulya, I am very well and the people I am staying with are kind. But I miss you and Katya very much. Please write back. Much love, YY.

'You reply,' said Katya. 'After all, it's addressed to you. Just give her my love.'

Gulya wrote rapidly on a piece of paper and gave it to Katya to sign, too.

'I can't just hand it to Fang,' she said after putting down her pen. 'What if an informer sees me?'

'You could pretend it's your list of fruit and vegetables for next time.'

'Too risky. Most market people can't read or write. What if someone asks to see it? The authorities are very nervous at the moment.'

They thought hard for a while.

Then Katya said suddenly, 'I know. Fang sells fresh juices of all kinds out of those big pots at the back of his stall. You have to bring your own jug or bottle if you want some.'

She went into the kitchen and brought back a ceramic jug with a cork in the top.

'Your message to Yu Yan will fit inside. I'll hand the jug to Fang and ask him to fill it with juice. He will go to the back of his stall and in the shadows should be able to extract the message without anyone seeing.'

'How will he know there is a message inside before he pours the juice?'

'He will know.'

'Let's take it to him now! The market is still open.'

'Absolutely not, Gulya. Going back to the market on the same day would arouse suspicion. We need to wait at least a couple of days. We cannot be too careful.'

Katya had started to worry about her growing absorption into the Japanese machine. Now, in creating a safe means of communication between Gulya and Yu Yan, she might have found a way of helping a cause which Je Jin would have supported body and soul.

That night she slept like a log.

Chapter 32

The article in *l'Humanité* had indeed caused consternation. When Katya went to work the next day, Major Yamamoto had called an emergency meeting of his planning and research committee.

Yamamoto was exceptionally agitated.

'I have been asked a hundred questions by High Command about this article.' He turned to Katya. 'Countess, what is your best judgement of its authenticity? Is Charles Martel a reputable journalist?'

'*L'Humanité* is a serious socialist newspaper,' said Katya without hesitation. 'It will slant the news to convey its anti-capitalist message. It is ideologically hostile to Japan. But I would be astonished if it actually lied about the situation in Manchuria, sorry, in Manchukuo. Charles Martel is almost certainly not the journalist's real name. He's given himself what the French call a *nom de plume*, a pen name to conceal his real identity.'

'Hm,' grunted Yamamoto, looking at Katya, 'how the devil do we find him?'

Katya decided to strengthen her credibility.

'He obviously entered Manchukuo under another name – maybe his own. If I were you, I would check the names of everyone on the staff of *l'Humanité* in Paris and see if any has been given a visa to come here.'

'I fear Mr Martel is right,' said Yamamoto after a pause. 'Headquarters is awash with rumours of disaster. We can no longer dismiss them as Chinese or League of Nations propaganda.'

He looked around the table. Fear and consternation ruled the faces of his subordinates. He spoke, almost shouted, banging the table for emphasis.

'The military have not been straight with us. All of you should have good contacts with the army. So I want to know from you, now, what is happening in the hinterland. What have you heard about insurgent activity?'

There was complete silence in the room. Katya wondered who, if anyone, would dare open his mouth. Each was being asked to go against the habits of his caste and career. Finally, one of Yamamoto's analysts, who had been staring at the table in front of him, began to speak.

'I was having a drink a few nights ago with my younger brother, who is a lieutenant in the infantry. I had not seen him for a long time. He was very unhappy. His regiment is stationed in Inner Mongolia not far from the border with the Soviet Union. It's hilly country, perfect for guerrillas to hide in. His colonel has no idea how to fight this kind of war. His troops are repeatedly ambushed and take heavy casualties. One patrol was massacred to the last man. When we do go after them, the guerrillas just melt into the countryside. My brother suspects that the Russians let them take refuge on Soviet territory. The situation in his area is deteriorating. Morale is low.'

'I thought as much,' said the major, almost to himself. 'What, then, is the right way of fighting guerrillas? Does your brother have a view?'

'I don't want to get my brother into trouble,' said the analyst, hesitantly.

'He won't get any trouble from me. I won't mention your or his name,' replied Yamamoto. 'It is your duty to speak.'

'The junior officers,' the analyst continued, 'have formed up to the colonel and proposed a radically different strategy. They want company-sized sweeps, which will drive the guerrillas into a trap formed by the two other companies of the regiment. Then the full force of artillery and aircraft can be brought to bear on the cornered guerrillas. But he was having none of it. He has no idea how to use aircraft either for reconnaissance or for attack. He said that my brother and the other officers were cowards, who were afraid to die.'

'The old school is the curse of our army. If we lose the countryside, we lose the towns,' said Yamamoto in exasperation. 'I will raise this at our next meeting with High Command. If the situation is as bad as your brother describes, we must fear even more the possibility of the Nationalists and Communists uniting their forces. I have always believed that they detest each other. But what if they are uniting to face a common enemy? I want you all to squeeze our informers to find out where and when this rumoured meeting between the Nationalists and Communists will take place. It is our topmost priority.'

This prompted another of the analysts to speak.

'I think, sir, if we are talking of squeezing, there is more to be extracted from Emperor Puyi's entourage. He has around him generals whose loyalties are constantly shifting. I suspect we are being betrayed by elements in the royal household itself.'

'Then it is time for the Emperor to receive a visit from General Tojo,' said Yamamoto, referring to the commander of the *Kempeitai* in Manchukuo.

That evening, when Katya returned home, she sat down at her desk and, fortified by a small glass of vodka, wrote a summary note in English of the meeting. She did so in capitals, both for clarity and so that her handwriting could not be identified. She put it in the jug with Gulya's note to Yu Yan.

'Well, I have burned my bridges,' she thought to herself with complete calmness. 'If this all goes wrong, Gulya, Yu Yan and I will be dead before the month is out.'

The following day, she went to the market early before work. There were plenty of things she legitimately needed. Like the other stallholders, Fang was shouting enticing descriptions of his wares, especially the different types of melon that sat in piles on his stall. He was doing a brisk trade. Despite the early hour, his stall had a long queue of customers waiting to be served. For a moment Katya hesitated, worrying that someone in the queue might spot her clandestine transaction. But that was the last thing a Chinese housewife or an elderly grandparent would be looking for. She placed herself at the back of the queue and waited patiently as it moved forward.

Finally, it was her turn to be served. She and Fang looked into each other's eyes for an instant, as they exchanged greetings. She went through her shopping list, piling the produce into her basket on wheels. Then she pulled out the Russian jug and asked Fang to fill it with grape juice. He took it to the back of the stall, turned his back on Katya and the queue, then returned the jug with the stopper firmly in place.

'Next time, lady, you should try apricot juice. Very good,' said Fang with his metal-toothed smile, as she paid.

The following week Katya stopped at Fang's stall to buy melons. He gave her two, one of which was hollow. She asked him to fill her jug with apricot juice. This time she had no message to send. When she returned home and broke open the hollow melon, a small piece of paper fell out. On it, written in capitals, were the English words 'Very useful. More please. Take great care. YY happy.' She tore the paper into pieces and burned them in the kitchen sink.

At the next two meetings of Major Yamamoto's planning and research committee, there was no discussion of the military situation in Manchukuo. Most of the articles that Katya translated were about the chances of League of Nations action against Japan. She found, not surprisingly, the Swiss paper *Tribune de Genève* to be exceptionally well informed about deliberations at the League's headquarters. Translations of its articles provided the bulk of her reports to the committee. Since there was no appetite for military action against Japan among the nations of the League, the meeting noted her reports with interest but little concern.

Then she spotted something in *l'Humanité*. Under the front-page headline 'Outrage And Indignation', the paper reported that its special correspondent, Pierre Mestrallet, had been expelled from the puppet state of Manchukuo on the orders of the Japanese authorities. He had, the paper said, been arrested by the secret police, the sinister *Kempeitai*. They had interrogated him and roughed him up. Readers would remember his authoritative account from three weeks before, writing under the name of Charles Martel, of Chinese armed resistance to the Japanese forces. It was this article, and a companion piece planned for the next week, that seemed to have upset the Japanese authorities, who had shown themselves to be as intolerant of free speech as both Hitler and Mussolini.

Katya mentioned the article to Major Yamamoto when she ran into him in the corridor. He put his finger to his lips and invited her into his office.

'You should not speak of this article at our next meeting. I should not even be discussing it with you, Countess. But it is thanks to your suggestion that we were able to identify Charles Martel by his real name. He revealed to us under interrogation that there would be a meeting next week in Harbin of senior figures from the Nationalist and Communist factions of the armed resistance. He even gave us the address. I am in command of the extremely sensitive operation to arrest the lot of them.'

He should not have told me that, thought Katya. For a moment she wondered whether he had let slip the information as a way of trapping her. Maybe her transactions in the market with Fang had revived *Kempeitai* suspicions of her being a Chinese spy. Then she looked at the pride written all over his face. It was Major Yamamoto's weak spot. The elegant, almost dandyish, cut of his uniforms was matched by a vanity of character which he found impossible to hide. My goodness, she thought, he actually wants my approbation.

That night, she emptied the Russian jug of its dregs of apricot juice and washed and dried it. Then she wrote a summary of her conversation with the major, with the word 'WARNING!' at the top of the page. Then she folded and placed it in the jug.

The following morning she went very early to Fang's stall.

'Apricot juice? Very fresh, very sweet, lady.'

'No, grape this time, please, Mr Fang.' Once again, he went to the rear of the stall and, turning his back, ladled the juice into her jug. Then he selected a large bunch of carrots – 'Gift for very good customer. Eat them and you see at night,' and, coming round from behind the stall, dropped them all into Katya's basket. As he did so, some of the carrots fell on the ground. Katya and Fang both bent down to pick them up. As their heads touched, Katya whispered, 'Urgent. Read my message. There is great danger.'

'Thank you, lady,' shouted Fang to Katya as she went on her way. 'Next week, lovely cherries. Yes!'

On the following Wednesday, Major Yamamoto's planning and research committee meeting was cancelled. Katya had seen him the previous day in the corridor. He was so preoccupied that he had barely acknowledged her. That was the last time she saw him alive. Wednesday passed like any other day of the week. She did her translations and summarised a piece in the *Manchester Guardian*, based closely on the Charles Martel article in *l'Humanité*.

When she came to work the next day, Thursday, she immediately realised something was wrong. A guard tried to stop her going to the first floor. She had to show him the Imperial document as well as her daily pass in order to gain access to her office. As she emerged from the lift, she saw at the end of the corridor, where she and the major had their offices, a large group of *Kempeitai* officers. She walked towards them.

They were talking among themselves in urgent whispers. Every now and then they would look into Major Yamamoto's office. Their faces ran the gamut from serious to grief-stricken. As she approached the group, they all turned to look at her. She felt her heart start to race and butterflies took control of her stomach. The officers were looking at her in confusion and embarrassment. This, they evidently thought, was no place for a Russian woman.

As soon as she saw that there was no hostility in their gaze, her nerves calmed and she asked, 'What has happened? What is going on?'

One of Major Yamamoto's analysts, Lieutenant Goto, who had good English, and a *Kempeitai* officer whom she had never seen before, stepped out of the group and invited her to go with them into her office.

'Countess, there has been a tragedy,' said Goto, as Katya took off her coat and placed her briefcase on the floor. She invited them both to sit as she took her place behind the desk. 'Major Yamamoto is dead. He committed *seppuku* sometime very early this morning.'

'Why, why?' she asked, looking at each in turn. There was no need for her to call on any histrionic skills to convey extreme shock and horror. It was exactly what she felt and it was written on her face for all to see.

Katya knew what *seppuku*, sometimes called *hara-kiri*, meant. It was a form of ritual suicide carried out by the horizontal slitting of the belly below the navel. The motive was usually shame at failure or defeat. Despite attempts to stamp it out, *seppuku* was deeply ingrained in the culture of the *Kempeitai* officer class.

'He was in charge of an operation last night,' continued Goto in a matter-of-fact tone, 'against Chinese rebels here in Harbin. He had information from what he thought was a reliable source. But when he got to the address, there was nobody there. After he and his men had entered the premises, the rebels dynamited it. Major Yamamoto was one of the few to survive the explosion. But he was terribly wounded and, refusing all medical help, returned to his office to commit *seppuku*.'

This is my doing, thought Katya. I had better weigh my words very carefully.

'We have a traitor in our midst,' said the unnamed *Kempeitai* officer, his eyes filled with tears. 'No punishment for him will be too harsh.'

'Am I allowed to ask the source of the false information about the meeting? The major never mentioned anything to me, but I would not have expected him to do so.'

The two *Kempeitai* officers looked at each other. A few words in Japanese were exchanged. Goto replied.

'It was the French journalist, calling himself Charles Martel, who gave Major Yamamoto details of a meeting between Chinese Nationalists and Communists in Harbin. The major acted on his information. It was a trap.'

'In my humble opinion,' she said after a moment, 'you need look no further than Martel. I doubt he knew that he was passing false information. There is quite a history of journalists being used as useful idiots, who can be manipulated for propaganda or other purposes.'

'Useful idiots?' asked Goto.

'"Useful idiots" is a phrase invented by the Bolsheviks for foreigners, usually journalists, who can be easily manipulated. I suspect that

Martel was deliberately betrayed to the *Kempeitai* by the Chinese, with the express purpose of his revealing under interrogation the time and place of the bogus meeting.'

'You yourself, to your credit, told us how to identify Martel,' said Goto.

'True. But I didn't tell you where he was hiding.'

Chapter 33

For most of her three years at Pekin University, Svyet barely kept in touch with her family.

She wrote occasionally, brief, sketchy letters that conveyed little of her life. She always said that she was well. She always trumpeted her academic successes, which seemed to have been considerable.

When Katya suggested going to Pekin to visit her, Svyet put her off with one excuse or another. But she did come to Harbin once, when Katya's mother, Alissa, was visiting from Leningrad (which, like all the Russians in Harbin, she persisted in calling St Petersburg). Svyet had not seen Alissa for well-nigh twenty years. Unlike Gulya, she had distant memories of staying with Granny. This gave them some common ground on which to rebuild a relationship. Alissa got Svyet to talk about her life in Pekin in a way that Katya had not been able to manage. In a few days, she learned more about her daughter's studies and friends than she had in two years. Then, one lunchtime, Svyet came to interrogate Granny Alissa about life in Imperial Russia and how the Revolution had changed things. She took copious notes. This material, she explained, would make an important contribution to research into the pre- and post-revolutionary periods. She intended to use it for a doctoral thesis. Then, after three days of relentless interrogation, Granny began to feel exhausted. She had run out of things to say. At that, Svyet returned to Pekin as abruptly as she had appeared in Harbin a week earlier.

Katya was surprised that Alissa had been allowed to travel to Harbin. As the thirties progressed, the Soviet authorities had become more and more repressive. The families of the *ancien régime* were particular targets. A request for an exit visa to visit relatives abroad more often than not led to a ten-year sentence in a labour camp. As it was, most of the male members of the Polkonin family who had not fled the Bolsheviks were sent to the camps, never to be seen again. But somehow or other, perhaps because of her age, Alissa had slipped through the net.

She had arrived in Harbin little the worse for wear, despite a gruelling train journey which had taken almost a week. A tall woman, she must have been in her late seventies, possibly older, but her erect posture and elegant, though understated, dress made her look ten years younger. She came with precious little luggage and carried a stick which she seemed barely to need.

Katya's plan was to persuade her mother to come and live with her and Gulya. Alissa certainly seemed happy enough in Harbin, but then, after about three months, she announced out of the blue at the breakfast table that she wanted to go back to St Petersburg. Despite the privations of life there – the family apartment had been turned into a communal flat, which she shared with three other families – she could never, she said, abandon Russia. Like for so many Russian refugees of that generation, the pull of the Motherland, the *rodina*, was greater even than the delight she took in being reunited after so many years with her daughter and granddaughter. Simply, she longed to return home.

They tried in vain to make her change her mind. For Gulya, her presence had helped fill the hole in the family left by Andrey, and over time they had become a close and affectionate three-generation trio. But Alissa was implacable.

*

Alissa left for Leningrad a few days later, laden with supplies for the week's journey. The farewells at Harbin station were cheerless, Katya and Gulya both sensing that they would never see her again.

After Alissa's departure, Katya was depressed for days. She felt that her life was losing value and direction. Her marriage had long since collapsed. Je Jin was gone. Svyet was gone. She knew that Gulya was itching to leave home.

Katya might not have felt all this so acutely had she not sensed that her Japanese days were coming to an end. The *Kempeitai* never discovered who had betrayed Major Yamamoto. If Katya had ever come under suspicion, she was not aware of it. The Japanese continued to treat her with the greatest courtesy and respect. Fang went on working at the market, unmolested.

But the day soon came when she was summoned for a final interview. It was conducted by the colonel, whose name she never discovered. He told her that General Tojo himself had decided that security inside the Harbin *Kempeitai* was too lax and must be tightened. One of General Tojo's edicts was that all foreigners working for the *Kempeitai* office in Harbin should be dismissed forthwith. That, most unfortunately, would include Katya.

The colonel had tried, to no avail, to make the case for her continued employment on the grounds that she had given exemplary service over many years. But there had been an interesting postscript to this stern message: Countess Polkonina's employment in some other capacity was not to be excluded.

'What does that mean? What do they have in mind?' asked Katya.

'Should you decide to move to another town – to Pekin or Shanghai, for instance – there could be openings. It is no secret that we may well have to extend southwards our cooperation with friendly Chinese elements. If, like so many of your compatriots, you decide to move south, please let us know before you go.'

They stood up and bowed to each other. Like Mr Amae before him, the colonel gave Katya a printed scroll with the Imperial stamp, testifying to her loyal work for the Japanese Empire.

As she stepped out of the building for the last time, she reflected on the colonel's final words. It raised her spirits a little. She was still appreciated and had the scroll – now tightly rolled inside her bag – to prove it. But to move south? Why would she wish to do that? For better or for worse, Harbin was now her home.

Yet the colonel had planted a seed. As she walked briskly along Central Street to catch the tram home, it had already started to swell and germinate inside her.

*

Gulya left school at the age of eighteen. She graduated from the Gymnasium with respectable but unremarkable grades. University was ruled out: as Mr Saprykhin, the principal of the school, put it with oily spite, she could become a shop assistant or, if she really put her mind to it, train at a secretarial college.

Katya's solution to the 'Gulya problem' was to marry her off. Katya took it upon herself to organise a programme of Sunday tea parties with rich and carefully chosen Russian couples who she knew would be happy to forego the customary ample dowry if it meant bringing noble blood into their family. The invitations were delivered by telephone, enabling Katya to add as a seemingly throwaway line, 'Bring Sergey/Mikhail/Genya/Boris, as Gulya will be there.'

Katya dragged out what remained of the family silver – the rest had been buried at Golovino by Andrey before the escape.

For Gulya, these were grisly occasions. The boys ranged from acned youths who had barely the courage to look at her, to young sophisticates who would eye her up and down and ask her out on the spot. Whenever Gulya went on one of these dates, Katya would stay up and interrogate her as soon as she returned. Gulya only saw drudgery and the narrow horizons of petit bourgeois existence. Her mother's response, 'romance doesn't put food on the table', drove Gulya mad.

'Mama, is it too much to ask that I should try to find someone I love?'

Katya sighed deeply and stared into the distance. Then she said, very quietly, 'No, Gulya, no. It's not asking too much. In St Petersburg I turned down the man I loved and in the end had to marry your father as a second best. Look how that turned out. I can't risk inflicting the same fate on you.'

Katya felt humiliated by the failure of her ill-fated tea parties. Yet it was all for the best. Relations with her daughter had become strained. Now they embraced, both a little tearful.

Through the harsh winter of 1935–6, Katya's energy centred on rebuilding her language teaching business. It was not long before she had once again a substantial network of students, such was the hunger to learn English. Meanwhile, with heavy heart, Gulya went to work at

Madame Zender's haberdashery. Madame Zender was a ghastly old Swiss crone who had agreed to employ Gulya for a pittance. Mother and daughter had come to an unspoken understanding. If Gulya would endure Madame Zender's store until she found something better, Katya would not complain about her going to dance halls and fashionable cafés to let her hair down. Katya's instincts told her that while Gulya loved flirting with boys – she had a terrible reputation as an '*allumeuse*', a prick teaser – she was not going to give herself easily to any man.

One Friday evening, when Gulya was about to go off to her favourite haunt on the river, the Seagull Café, she looked back at her mother after kissing her goodbye. Katya looked tired. She had long since lost the glow that Je Jin had given her. She was, Gulya knew, desperately lonely. She needed a man in her life. On an impulse, Gulya paused at the front door and said, 'Mama, why don't you come with me? It would do you good to get out.'

'No, Gulya. It's kind of you, but I am past all that now . . . I would just spoil your fun.'

'Nonsense, Mama. Everyone who is anyone goes to the Seagull, even some of the Japanese. You'll love it!'

'Do you really think so?'

'Of course! It's not just a place for the mindless young! Come on! Get your coat!' Reluctantly, Katya agreed.

They found a taxi without difficulty. As they got into the cab, there was much tutting and clucking, puffing and blowing from Katya, as if it were all too much effort. The taxi turned into Central Street, which would take them straight to the river and the Seagull. As Katya looked out of the window at the brightly lit Christmas streets and the crowds thronging the pavement, a transformation began to come over her. Her eyes shone.

The taxi dropped them at the Seagull's brightly lit entrance. There was quite a queue of those leaving, who were waiting for a cab. As they arrived and stepped out of the taxi, a cheer went up from the jostling line and they were greeted with good-natured ribaldry. Gulya was used to it, but suspected it was the first time in her life that Katya had been publicly congratulated on her figure and her legs. They were a long way from old St Petersburg.

'Mama, I do believe you're blushing!' she said, laughing.

'Really, Gulya,' Katya replied with faux indignation, a smile flickering across her face. Gulya seized her mother by the arm as they pushed through the crush of customers going in and out and plunged into the spinning maelstrom. 'Here we go!'

In a trice they were spat out into a scene of light and noise and conviviality. The Seagull, with its red velvet seats and brass fittings, designed to look like a Parisian brasserie of *la belle époque*, was heaving. The gypsy band was playing at full tilt, just about audible above the crashing waves of conversation. All the tables were occupied, including the two or three in a kind of alcove reserved for Japanese officers. Waiters raced between the tables. The huge, bearded Zoltan – the Hungarian owner of the Seagull – moved with slow but amiable menace among the throng to ensure that all were being properly served – especially the Japanese and Manchukuo officials – and that no one was getting too unruly.

Gulya looked around for her friends. She could hear Katya behind her, muttering, 'Well, I never.' From across the room, she spotted one of her school-friends with a dozen companions. As Gulya and Katya began to fight their way to the table, Zoltan suddenly appeared before them. He bowed elaborately to Katya, his lips brushing her gloved hand.

'Countess, you honour me by your presence. Follow me, if you please.'

Like an Arctic icebreaker, his vast bulk carved a way for them. Gulya remembered that he and Je Jin used to go hunting together. That was how he knew of Katya. From then on, they were always guaranteed the best table at the Seagull.

There was a hardcore of Gulya's closest girlfriends at the table. They had become known as the Friday Night Club. Zoltan gave Katya the seat of honour in the middle of the table, facing the interior of the café, so that she could see everything that was going on. Around them would gather a varying cast of a dozen men and women – young, middle-aged and elderly. The only criterion for admission to the Friday Night Club was to be *sympathique* and interesting.

Katya fell in love with the Friday Night Club. Their table, with its ever-changing cast of characters, became Katya's salon reborn. Unlike its incarnation in her first Harbin home, it was not the St Petersburg model exhumed – staid and dignified, with formal readings. This was something modern, less disciplined, less respectful, with opinions on every conceivable subject hurled back and forth across the table, stoked by Hungarian wine, beer and goulash. Only mention of the Japanese and the Manchukuo regime was taboo.

In the early summer of 1936, when the Seagull threw open its windows to the Sanguri river and you could hear the strains of its gypsy band from the far bank, a newcomer joined the table at Katya's invitation. She was called Anna Pugacheva, a Russian from Vladivostok, married to Mikhail, a distant cousin of Katya's.

Anna came to Harbin each spring to recruit staff for the summer season at the resort she and her husband owned on the north-east coast of Korea, near a village called Romina. Rumour had it that she was by origin a peasant, whom Mikhail had plucked from a tumbledown village while out hunting. Katya was fond of her, though Anna was absolutely not her type.

In Romina the Pugachevs had set out to create an exclusive resort for the rich and famous, run by Anna. In her youth she had been a voluptuously beautiful blonde, and had found fleeting fame as a film actress. She sought to exploit this in order to bring to the remote Korean coast members of the international *beau monde*.

But Korea was too remote, and Anna's glamour too faded, to achieve in full their dream. In 1936 Romina was, as usual, fully booked through the summer season, but by a pretty raffish bunch of Europeans, Americans and Russians. One or two were film actors of some repute; rather more were stars firmly on the wane.

Many of the guests were drawn by Romina's decadent reputation. For this the resort had to thank Emperor Puyi of Manchukuo, installed in his lofty position by the Japanese, and Wangrong, his wife. They stayed at Romina as Anna's guests, since she regarded a real live emperor as one of the hotel's more exotic attractions. The couple had a reputation for sexual deviation and opium addiction. They both loved dancing, and Wangrong was a good tennis player.

Mikhail Pugachev's family had made a fortune in the timber trade under the Tsars. After the Revolution, nothing changed much. They bought protection from Communist Party officials in Vladivostok, who were no less corrupt than their Tsarist predecessors – sometimes they were the very same individuals. Nonetheless, Mikhail had taken the precaution of creating a business base in northern Korea, close to both the Soviet and Chinese frontiers, but under the control of the Japanese. There he had a dozen local officials on his payroll. His system began to break down only when Stalin's purges swept through the Vladivostok *nomenklatura*.

While Anna was with Katya and Gulya at the Seagull, Mikhail was in Romina, sitting out a prolonged period of turmoil in Vladivostok during the latest Stalin purges. He was not sure that he would ever return to the Soviet Union, as it was getting too dangerous. So he had moved all his business operations into the resort hotel.

As Gulya returned to the table from the ladies' room, she noticed Anna looking her up and down. She asked Gulya what she was doing for the summer.

'Dear Gulya, I have a better idea,' said Anna. 'Why don't you come and spend the summer season with us by the sea at Romina?' Anna leaned across the table towards Katya, who was deep in conversation with Jean-Jacques Martinet, who had just arrived from Hanoi. Jean-Jacques, the nephew of a French composer, was a debonair French widower who lived in Hanoi most of the time, but came frequently to Harbin for business. He was something in dyes and textiles. He was amusing, with a waspish wit, and he and Katya had struck up a friendship.

'Katya, Katya, forgive me for interrupting. I need your daughter. She tells me that she is condemned to spending the summer in a haberdashery shop guarded by an old Swiss witch. I can offer her instead sun, sea and sand!'

Katya, a little inebriated and heavily occupied with Jean-Jacques, replied distractedly, 'I don't know, Anna. Come for tea tomorrow and we'll talk about it.' Then she returned to her conversation with the Frenchman.

The following afternoon, after Katya had poured tea from the samovar, she said to Anna, 'Now, Anna, what was all that about Gulya going to the seaside, instead of earning her living through the summer?'

'Katya,' replied Anna, 'I fully intend for her to help out. We have an unusually large number of guests this year. It would be a real boon to have a beautiful young Russian aristocrat to help us look after the guests. We wouldn't pay Gulya, but she would have full board and lodging – and she could take part in all our entertainments as if she were a guest. It would be far healthier than being stuck indoors in a shop.'

'Oh, yes, please, Mama!' cried Gulya.

Turning to Anna, Katya declared, 'That's very kind of you, Anna. But Gulya is far too young and all your guests will be so sophisticated. Perhaps next year or the year after.'

'Nonsense, Katya,' retorted Anna. 'Of course, it's a pretty sophisticated crowd. But there are all sorts, of many different nationalities. Gulya will learn so much – like tact and firmness, when to say "yes" and when to say "no" to their endless demands. She will be able to perfect her English and French. Her Russian will be invaluable. She will acquire knowledge of hotel and restaurant management. She will improve her tennis and dancing, since I would expect her to partner the guests.'

'But, Anna . . . ' said Katya. Anna cut her off immediately.

'Katya, it's the university of life. She will come out of the experience with new skills and accomplishments that are unobtainable in Harbin. You can't deny your daughter this opportunity. Besides, Mikhail and I need her! The season starts in two weeks' time!'

'*Please*, Mama,' begged Gulya.

Anna promised to play the role of chaperone, and further reassured Katya that Gulya would be sharing a room with a well-bred English girl of her age called Susan Carleton-Sinclair, whose family were traders in Shanghai and Hong Kong.

Katya acquiesced, albeit with misgivings, and less than a fortnight later, Gulya left for Romina.

Chapter 34

That summer dragged by for Katya. It was the longest time she'd ever been separated from Gulya. When she finally returned at the end of September, their reunion at Harbin station was joyous. As soon as they were in the cab, Katya began to ply her daughter with questions and observations, words tumbling from her mouth in her excitement.

'My, you do look well. You're so tanned. Your hair is almost bleached white. You've let yourself get a little skinny, mind . . . '

'That's the hard work and the tennis. It was non-stop almost every day.'

For the rest of the journey Gulya described the daily routine, the resort, the guests – including Marlene Dietrich and Ernest Hemingway – the Emperor and Empress, and Mike and Annie, in a rather bowdlerised version of events.

They were stuck in traffic for a while. Katya looked at her daughter intently.

'You have changed, Gulya. Did you make any special friends?'

Gulya described Sue Carleton-Sinclair, and how well they got on together.

'And men? Boys? You have always been very attractive to them.'

Gulya decided to get it over with. 'I had an affair with an older man. It didn't last long.'

She was expecting a cry of anguish. Instead, Katya looked at her evenly. 'I thought that might happen. I never believed Anna would chaperone you properly. You are not pregnant, I hope?'

'No, I was careful and I've had my period since.'

'Thank goodness for that.'

'Why did you let me go, if you thought Anna would not look after me?'

'In the end I could not say no. Je Jin wouldn't let me. I dream of him most nights and he usually talks to me. He was all in favour of you going. Anyway, I trusted your common sense. It is no big thing to lose your virginity, so long as there's not a child as well. I lost mine far too late.'

Gulya was stunned by Katya's calmness.

Once back at the apartment, they sat in the kitchen drinking tea for what remained of the afternoon. Katya admitted how lonely she had become in Harbin without Gulya. She had wearied of Jean-Jacques.

'I just got tired of him. He was quite amusing. We had some good times together. But he was no substitute for Je Jin,' she said a little sadly.

'What about the Seagull? Do you still go? I missed it.'

'I didn't want to go on my own, without you. But do you know what happened? A couple of weeks after you left, there was a knock at the door. It was the doorman at the Seagull, in full uniform. He bowed low and told me that the pleasure of my company was requested at the Seagull and that a carriage awaited me. Well, you know me, I made a thousand excuses for not going but was thrilled to be invited. The doorman said to me, with that magnificent Mongolian accent, that he would lose his job if he did not return to the Seagull with me. Zoltan would not take no for an answer. So, I went.'

Gulya clapped her hands in delight.

'I arrived, the band played "Here Comes the Bride", would you believe, and, when I got to our usual table, everyone applauded, banged their fists on the table and cheered. I was quite overwhelmed. I wept. I laughed out loud. Zoltan hugged me so tight I could hardly breathe. Even the Japanese officers smiled from their alcove.'

'We must go next Friday,' said Gulya, moved by Katya's story.

'Well, everyone's expecting you.'

At last they fell silent. It was already past six o'clock. They cleared away the teacups and Katya opened a bottle of Meursault, courtesy of Jean-Jacques. She paused and took a deep breath.

'I am thinking of moving away from Harbin. There.' Katya crossed her arms, terrified that Gulya would raise a violent objection.

'Where would you go?'

'Shanghai.'

To Katya's bemusement, Gulya jumped up from the table, skipped round to Katya's side and gave her an enormous hug of relief and joy.

Gulya explained that Sue, her roommate in Romina and now a close friend, had proposed that they share an apartment in Shanghai, where her father, who owned the Victoria Trading Company, had offices. Sue was sure that her father would offer Gulya a job, and planned to ask him as soon as she returned from Romina.

'I'd been so worried about leaving you in Harbin. Now we can go to Shanghai together!'

'God moves in mysterious ways,' said Katya, crossing herself.

'I don't want to hear about God, I want to hear why you have decided to move!' exclaimed Gulya, bursting with impatience.

'Shh, dear! Don't blaspheme. The idea came from Svyetlana.'

'What?'

Katya made a calming motion with her hand.

'While you were in Romina, I got a letter from Svyet. It was quite different in tone from anything she had written before. Kinder, nicer, with lots of news. For the first time she sounded happy. Then, another letter arrived a week later. I had never received two in such quick succession. Again, it was full of happy chatter. But it contained a nugget of news – that she was thinking of transferring to the philology faculty of Shanghai University, where there was a better Russian department than in Pekin. Then came a third letter in which she announced that she had fallen in love with a Russian professor of philology, who had come to Pekin on a one-month sabbatical. He was, she said, a wonderful and unusual man, older than her, of aristocratic background. He seemed to have fallen equally in love with her. His name is Maxim Konstantinovich Lebedev.'

'Have you heard of him?' asked Gulya.

'The name means something to me, but I can't put my finger on it.

There were Lebedevs we knew in St Petersburg, a nice family. He might be one of them. Anyway, he proposed, she accepted, and she was moving to Shanghai, where they would marry in two weeks' time.

'As if this weren't exciting enough,' Katya continued, 'Svyet went on to invite me to Shanghai – to move there for good.'

'Did she mention me?'

'Oh, yes. At the very end of her letter – I only got it the day before yesterday – she confessed to not having been the nicest daughter or sister, and hoped that in Shanghai we could all start afresh.'

They looked at each other.

'So, Gulya, what do you think?' Katya asked.

Without hesitating, Gulya said, 'We should go. I think we've exhausted Harbin.'

Katya nodded.

'Je Jin wants us to go. But he's asked me to find Yu Yan and take her with us.' Katya spoke of Je Jin as if he were still living among them. In a way, he was.

The next morning Katya wrote Svyet a warm letter of congratulations and good wishes, confirming that she would accept her proposal to come to Shanghai. Gulya added a paragraph to say how thrilled she was at her news and that she could not wait to get to Shanghai. With the envelope sealed and stamped they set off together to the main post office. Then, with a skip in their step, set off for the market to buy food for the next few days.

They went straight to Fang's fruit and vegetable stall. When they reached the front of the queue, Katya gave him a bottle in which she had inserted a handwritten note and asked him to fill it with peach juice. He went to the rear of the stall and returned with the bottle full of juice. He had found a cork and stuck it in the bottle. Katya bought some vegetables, paid for everything and said a perfunctory goodbye to Fang. He was already engaged with the next customer.

As they left the market, Katya said, 'Fang will get the message to Yu Yan and her guardians in the countryside.'

'But there is more to him than that, isn't there?' Gulya asked.

Katya stopped walking. She looked up and down the street. Then she took Gulya by both shoulders.

'Never mention Fang again. Above all, say nothing to your friends at the Seagull. That place is full of Japanese informers.' Her voice, already deadly serious, now took on an anguished tone. 'It is a matter of life and death, for Fang, for Yu Yan and for us.'

She let go of her daughter abruptly and they resumed walking.

After that, things moved quickly. They returned home from the market to find Sue's promised letter offering Gulya a job as an assistant to Mr Montgomery Carleton-Sinclair, her father. She would share Sue's large flat on the Bund. There would only be a nominal rent, to be paid to Mr Carleton-Sinclair's company. Almost every sentence ended with an exclamation mark. 'What fun we are going to have!!!' she wrote.

Gulya replied by return, explaining that her mother and sister would also be moving to Shanghai. She did not mention Yu Yan.

With a job and accommodation in Shanghai arranged, there was not much more for Gulya to do other than to say goodbye to her friends and to pack.

It proved a little more complicated for Katya.

Chapter 35

The Friday after Gulya's return from Romina saw a raucous dinner at the Seagull. The usual gang was there, plus a few newcomers. They gave Katya and Gulya a heartfelt welcome, cheering and clapping as they took their places at the table. Zoltan presented Gulya with an enormous bunch of flowers and, on the house, placed a magnum of champagne at either end of the table, each in an enormous ice bucket.

Gulya was teased mercilessly about what she had got up to in Romina, especially when she revealed that she had danced with Errol Flynn and Ernest Hemingway and had had to dodge the attentions of Marlene Dietrich. One of the newcomers asked about the Emperor and Empress. Gulya noticed one of the waiters prick up his ears at the question, as he bent down to serve the baked sturgeon, Zoltan's speciality. She spoke respectfully of them and changed the subject. A little later she saw the waiter in conversation with a Japanese officer.

On the way to the Seagull Gulya and her mother had debated whether to reveal that they would soon to be moving to Shanghai. Katya advised discretion. It would not be tactful, she said, to make such an announcement at the very moment Gulya's return was being celebrated. Gulya did not agree – but for the sake of an enjoyable evening she held her tongue.

Katya, meanwhile, was thinking of her final conversation with the colonel at *Kempeitai* headquarters. The colonel had hinted that Harbin might not be the limit of Japan's territorial ambitions. And now, it seemed, trouble was brewing again between the Japanese and Chinese, with rumours that Japan threatened to occupy Pekin and Nanking, perhaps even to go as far as Shanghai.

If they would have her, she would go to work again for the Japanese, the dangers notwithstanding. It had always been interesting, even congenial. But behind these superficial considerations, there burned the pure, blinding flame of revenge. The Japanese had killed the love of her life.

About a week after Gulya's return, Katya concluded her internal wrestling, in which reason, conscience and emotions had jostled for domination. She had consulted Je Jin, who, as usual, had appeared at the foot of her bed. He was so real that she could not believe that it was a dream. He had liked the notion of revenge. But he feared for her and for Yu Yan, who would, he had said, come and live with her in due course. If I did not seek to avenge you, she had replied, my conscience would never rest easy. Then it is settled, he had said.

When she awoke, her mind was at peace. She knew what she was going to do.

She dressed with the severe elegance that she knew the Japanese liked. She took a taxi to the *Kempeitai* office in Central Street. She asked to see the colonel and was invited to take a seat in the entrance hall. There was a lot of phoning and muttering. Then the double doors behind the entrance barrier were thrown open and out strode a smart young officer with shaven head and moustache.

'Countess,' he said in lightly accented English, 'Captain Abe at your service. Please follow me to the colonel's office. What a pleasure to see you again in our building.'

The colonel was alone in his office. Captain Abe took a seat next to him. He interpreted for Katya, who, as usual, sat opposite the colonel. She came straight to the point. They liked that.

'The last time I was here you explained to me, Colonel, why it would no longer be possible to work for you after the tragic death of Major Yamamoto. You also said that I should let you know if I were to move elsewhere from Harbin. I am here today to inform you that I plan to move soon to Shanghai.'

The colonel and Captain Abe listened intently.

The colonel extracted a gun-metal case from an inside pocket, opened it and offered Katya a cigarette. She declined. He then took one for himself. He ignored the captain.

'May I ask you a few questions about your move, Countess? When will you go? Why are you going? What will you do in Shanghai?'

'In about two weeks' time, Colonel.'

Katya had decided to conceal nothing. They would find out anyway from their own investigations. She explained how her older daughter, who had just married a Russian professor of philology, had invited Olga and her to move to Shanghai to be near her.

Katya paused. Captain Abe had been furiously scribbling. The colonel, too, had made the occasional note.

'What, Countess, is the name of your older daughter's husband?' asked the colonel, looking unblinkingly at Katya through the cloud of cigarette smoke.

'Maxim Konstantinovich Lebedev.'

'Do you know anything about him?'

'Only what my daughter has told me. He is older than her. He is of aristocratic origin. He may be from a St Petersburg family known to us before the Revolution. He, like us, has taken refuge in China. He is, according to my daughter, rather distinguished in his field.'

The colonel and Captain Abe had taken careful note of Maxim's name.

'Well, Countess, that is all very interesting. It is, I think, as far as we can take matters today. Just to be clear. You would be prepared to do the same kind of work in Shanghai as you did for us here?'

'Absolutely, Colonel.'

Katya took her leave of the colonel with Captain Abe once again at her elbow. She heard coming from somewhere in the bowels of the building a distant shouting and screaming. That had occurred quite often when she had worked there before. It reminded her that this was a place not just of amiable colonels and elegant captains, but of torturers and butchers, too.

Only a couple of days after visiting the colonel, she returned to the market. There was Fang. She felt her pulse start to beat a little faster. Her life was picking up pace, her senses on higher alert.

Now that she had informed the colonel, there was no reason not to tell people that she was moving to Shanghai. It was the natural thing to do. So she told Fang and anyone in earshot.

'When you leave, lady?' Fang asked.

'At the end of the month, Mr Fang,' Katya replied.

'Lovely. I will tell my cousin and his wife. They sell very lovely fruit and vegetable at the great market behind the Bund. Do you want coconut? Lovely, just arrived.'

'Yes, please.'

Their eyes locked for a moment.

When she got home, she found the coconut cut in half and put together again with a nail. She opened it on the kitchen table. Out fell a piece of paper, on which had been written a short message in English. The handwriting was a little laborious. Katya had a flash of memory: Yu Yan sitting at the table, exercise book before her, her tongue poking out of the corner of her mouth in concentration, as she copied a poem.

Thank you for message. I am well. Tell me Shanghai address and I will come. I miss you and Gulya. My father wants us united. Love YY.

Katya wondered if Je Jin spoke in dreams to his daughter as he did to her.

Gulya had everything in place for the move to Shanghai. She had received another letter from Sue suggesting that she start work on the first Monday in October, only two weeks away. Meanwhile, Svyet had sent Katya the postal address of her apartment. She had immediately passed it through Fang to Yu Yan with the date of their arrival.

After that, Katya waited for the colonel to contact her. She could not leave without seeing him again.

Only a few days before they were due to leave, the colonel's office telephoned to invite Katya to stop by as soon as possible at *Kempeitai* headquarters. Captain Abe was there again to greet her and escort her to the office.

'Major Seko will also be present. He is the head of our Russian section. He does not speak English and I will have to interpret for him as well.'

'Why will he be there?' Katya asked.

'Colonel Yamashita will say,' replied Abe.

Ah, it's Yamashita. She had got so used to thinking of him as 'the colonel' that it had never occurred to her to ask his name.

Colonel Yamashita and Major Seko rose smartly to their feet as Captain Abe ushered her into the room. They might have been twin brothers: plump, with dyed black air swept back from the brow, *pince-nez* perched on the nose and a pencil-thin moustache. It was, she realised, the *Kempeitai* look for senior officers.

The colonel greeted her with a warm handshake. The major just clicked his heels and bowed. She took the chair on the other side of the desk. There was a slight whiff in the air of an unpleasantly sweet cologne. She wondered whether there was a *Kempeitai* cologne, then immediately scolded herself for such frivolity.

'Thank you for coming so quickly, Countess. When exactly are you leaving?'

'In three days' time, on Friday. That will give Olga the weekend to settle in before she starts work.'

'Where will she work?'

'With a British trading company, the Victoria, based in Shanghai and Hong Kong. It's owned by a Mr Montgomery Carleton-Sinclair. Olga is sharing a flat with his daughter.'

As the colonel put his questions and Katya gave her answers, Captain Abe gave a rapid translation. In the background, from the adjoining office, she could hear the sound of the swiftly tapping keys of a typewriter.

The colonel pressed on. Katya gave him her Shanghai address and that of Svyet and her new husband. She did not know Gulya's. Then the colonel paused and exchanged words with Major Seko.

'My colleague, Major Seko, would now like to ask you a few questions about your new son-in-law. Have you discovered anything more about him since we last spoke?'

'Nothing at all, I am afraid, Colonel. I have told you the little I know.'

'We have made some enquiries about him and have had some

interesting results. Major Seko, will you please explain to the countess?'

The major spoke rapidly in short, staccato sentences, pausing frequently to allow Captain Abe to interpret into English.

'At first,' said Major Seko, 'Maxim Konstantinovich Lebedev appeared to be exactly what he claimed. His papers are in perfect order and give us a detailed account of his life – born near Novgorod, lived with his parents in St Petersburg, went to school and university there, did a year's postgraduate work in Heidelberg in Germany, served in the Tsar's army in the Pripet Marshes during the war and then, after the Russian Revolution and the civil war, fled to China, finding his way to Shanghai, where he had contacts at the university.'

Major Seko stopped for a moment as he leafed through papers in the file before him. Silence fell on the room. Katya was fascinated.

The major continued. 'His family had an estate near Novgorod. Just before the war, Lebedev's father killed himself after shooting his mother. It was, we think, a suicide pact because they had fallen into bankruptcy. The estate is now a collective farm. Lebedev is forty-one years old. He was badly wounded during the war, losing an eye and an arm.'

'Thank you,' said Katya. 'I may have known him. My family certainly knew some Lebedevs who had an estate near Novgorod. I vaguely recall some kind of terrible family tragedy. That apart, he does not sound like someone who has led a life of unusual interest.'

Major Seko allowed himself a wintry smile and raised his hand in a gesture to command patience.

'Ah! But that is not all,' said the major with something like a triumphant flourish. 'I now come, Countess, to the crux of your question.

'We have found in our files traces of an alternative biography for Lebedev. If this alternative biography is to be believed, your son-in-law changed sides in 1917, deserting the Tsar's army and becoming an officer in the OGPU, the Bolshevik secret police. He is today a senior serving member of its successor organisation, the NKVD, a spy working under deep cover in the guise of a respectable academic at Shanghai University.'

'*Bozhe moi!*' Katya exclaimed. 'What does this mean?'

Major Seko turned to Colonel Yamashita. They spoke for a few moments in Japanese. Then the colonel nodded to the major, who nodded back.

'Countess,' said Seko, 'because you are a woman of confidence, who has rendered invaluable service to our Emperor over many years, there are certain things I can tell you about your son-in-law and what he is up to. But they are of the utmost secrecy. I have to say to you, that if you are found to have revealed to any unauthorised person, even inadvertently, what I am about to say, the punishment is summary execution by beheading – for you and for me. Do you understand, Countess? There is nothing personal in this.'

All three Japanese fixed their gaze on Katya. She held it steadily, without blinking. This was a moment, she sensed, that would govern the direction of her life for the foreseeable future.

'I would expect treachery to deserve no less,' she replied.

It was exactly what the Japanese hoped to hear. All three relaxed and the chill in the room began to evaporate.

'The Kwantung Army in Manchukuo will soon undertake operations well to the south of Harbin,' said Major Seko. 'We are tired of endless provocations from the Chinese – warlords, Communists, and the so-called Nationalists. They must be crushed once and for all. We shall soon move to occupy Pekin and Nanking. We will in due course move to bring order to Shanghai as well. We did it once before and we need to do it again.'

The major's revelation came as little surprise to Katya as rumours to this effect had been ripe in Harbin for some time. It was in any case dwarfed by the shock of being told that her older daughter had married an NKVD officer. It had made her head swim. Maxim Konstantinovich Lebedev. The name chafed her memory like a piece of grit in her shoe.

'But,' continued the major, 'there is a far greater matter than General Chiang Kai-shek and his Chinese rabble.'

He paused, so it seemed, for dramatic effect.

'It is our old enemy to the north and west, now going by the name of the Union of Soviet Socialist Republics. Your countrymen, Countess, have hostile designs on the lawful Japanese presence in Manchukuo. They are poisoned by a baleful desire to avenge their humiliating defeat by our glorious forces in the war of 1905. They hope that we will become so preoccupied with the Chinese renegades that they will be able to attack and catch us unawares. Mark my words, Countess, it will come to war once again between Japan and Russia before the decade is out.'

At first Katya did not respond. She was trying to take in all that she had just been told. Then she spoke.

'What is it you want me to do when I get to Shanghai?'

Part III

SHANGHAI

Chapter 36

Since Katya and Gulya were taking the early morning train on the last Friday in September, their bacchanalian dinner of farewell at the Seagull took place on the Wednesday of that week. Zoltan honoured them by closing the café to the public, filling it with their friends and giving them all dinner on the house. Any attempts to pay, or at least contribute to some of the cost, had vehemently been rejected.

It was an evening of endless food and drink, raucous laughter, many speeches, music, dancing – even Katya took a turn on the crowded dance floor – and, in the end, hugs and tears. Everyone, including Zoltan and his waiters, seemed to be weeping, as, at the evening's end, long after midnight, they all tumbled out onto the pavement. The Chinese lady who drew up the bills, sitting on a high stool behind a wooden desk adorned with a lamp and a pewter seagull, was inconsolable. They exchanged pledges of eternal devotion with each of their friends, promising to keep in touch. Then they climbed into the Seagull's carriage to be taken home by the Mongolian driver and his old nag.

Just before they went to bed that night, their emotions now in calmer waters, Katya said, 'You know, Gulya, most of those people we will never see again or even hear from.'

'But, Mama, why not?' Gulya replied, a little shocked, even irritated, at this douche of cold water all over her sleepy contentment.

'Because, dear, that's the way of the world.'

A handful of Katya's closest friends came to the station to see them off, along with three of Gulya's classmates. But as the train clattered through the Chinese countryside, Harbin itself was already acquiring the quality of another planet.

Katya was very quiet during the first hours of the journey. She opened a book of German poetry as the train pulled out of the station, but let it fall into her lap and instead stared out of the window. Gulya took out a book of her own, assuming Katya wished to be left alone to her memories of Harbin.

That was not the explanation at all. She certainly wanted to be left to her thoughts, but they had nothing to do with nostalgic contemplation of *temps perdu*. In the middle of the farewell dinner at the Seagull, Katya suddenly remembered who Maxim Konstantinovich Lebedev might be. Wasn't Lebedev the name of the dreaded commissar who, back in 1919, Andryusha had feared would descend on Golovino? Hadn't Andryusha first run into him on the Galician Front and just managed to escape his clutches? Wasn't Lebedev blown up somewhere, but managed to survive?

These fragments of memory fluttered through her mind like leaves in the wind. She urged her brain to do better and to put some ballast into her flimsy recollections. But everything she knew about Lebedev had come from her husband's telling. That was the problem.

Katya had a troubling presentiment. If the meticulous *Kempeitai* had identified Svyet's husband as an intelligence officer, that was what he was. An army of questions marched into her mind. If he were Andryusha's mortal enemy, what was he doing marrying Svyet? Was it love and an extraordinary coincidence? Or could it be something darker and more calculated? If she knew where Andryusha lived, she could have written to him. There were one or two people in Harbin who, she knew, had kept in contact with him. Perhaps she would write to one of them for his address.

Meanwhile, she concluded, it would be safer to assume that Maxim Konstantinovich Lebedev was indeed the 'devil incarnate', as Andryusha had once described him.

Major Seko had asked her to get very close to Lebedev and find out what he was up to. He explained that Lebedev's spying activities were almost certainly linked to possible conflict between Japan and the Soviet Union. This was what they wanted Katya to focus on. Their intelligence sources told them that, like common rumour, Moscow expected a drive south soon by the Kwantung Army against the Chinese. But the Soviets had got it into their heads that this would be a feint to disguise an attack westwards against the Soviet Union. Their paranoia was extraordinary. The same intelligence sources were saying that, on the principle that attack was the best means of defence, the Soviets were therefore contemplating a pre-emptive strike east against the Kwantung Army.

'And Russian fears are without foundation?' Katya had asked.

'Yes – and that is what we shall want you to convey to Lebedev. We shall talk more about how you do it in Shanghai. As you may imagine, Countess, it would be highly inconvenient, to put it mildly, if the Soviets were to attack us while we were dealing with the Chinese. The time for war between us is not yet.'

Then Colonel Yamashita, who had been smoking silently, took over. Looking solemnly at Katya, he said, 'Countess, we are asking much of you on a mission that could prove personally dangerous. But you have proved your courage time and again in the service of our Emperor.

'The stakes, Countess, could not be higher. We shall want you to put all that courage to work again as never before and help us find out whether the Soviets intend to attack us within the next twelve months. We must be ready to repel them when they come.'

She should report, the colonel had said, to Major Seko, who, with Captain Abe, was to be transferred to the consulate in Shanghai. They would give her more detailed instructions. She need not hurry. That only led to mistakes. They would give her a month or so to get Lebedev's measure. The colonel liked the idea of her return to giving language lessons. It offered her a valid reason for travelling around Shanghai and cover for her visits to the consulate.

The Japanese had assumed that Katya would be appalled at her daughter's marrying an NKVD man. This, they had calculated, would provide more than sufficient motivation for her to work against the interests of her mother country. But she did not tell them that she and Lebedev might also have a shared past founded in mutual, murderous intent. That was something to keep in reserve against the day when it might be necessary to buttress still more their belief in her.

She reopened her book of German poetry.

The journey was tedious and they were relieved to reach Shanghai in the early hours of Saturday morning. As they climbed down from the carriage, Svyet was waiting on the platform in a sea of scurrying Chinese travellers. They had little luggage, having used a French removal company to send their belongings ahead in a locked railway wagon.

Svyet seemed genuinely pleased to see them. Her eyes filled with tears as she hugged them tightly in turn.

'Mama, Gulya, I cannot tell you what joy it gives me to see you, how happy I feel that we shall soon be the closest of neighbours! Shanghai will be a new start for all of us. How pleased I am that we can put that horrid Harbin behind us!'

As Svyet made her little speech, Gulya was able to make a swift appraisal. She was slimmer and more elegant. Her hair and make-up were done rather well. She was wearing a nice coat with a decent piece of jewellery at her neck. She looked really happy. So that was what marriage and a man could do for you, she thought.

The rising sun threw a brilliant horizontal light across the station, creating deep shadows behind pillars, kiosks and carts piled with luggage. Gulya suddenly became aware that a figure, half hidden in shadow, was standing a little behind Svyet.

'You must meet Maxim!' exclaimed Svyet, as if he had been forgotten. 'Max, stop hiding and come out and meet my mother and sister.' The figure stepped into the bright morning sun. It was a shock. Maxim, who must by now have been used to this, swiftly filled with practised ease what could have been an awkward moment.

He reached out to shake hands with Katya and then with Gulya. His manner was elaborately deferential.

'Dear Ekaterina Alexandrovna – may I call you Katya? – dear Olga Andreyevna – may I call you Gulya? – it is a great honour and a great pleasure to meet you. I have heard so much about you both from Svyetlana that I have been barely able to contain my impatience.'

Another pretty little speech issued from a hideously disfigured face, which had been terribly lacerated and burned. Its right side was a lumpy mess of pink and white scars straggling across small craters like the surface of the moon. Its right ear was just a small shapeless protuberance. The right eye was covered by a dark blue eye patch, onto which had been sewn the Russian Imperial eagle.

Yet, strangely, for all his disfigurement, Maxim was an attractive man. He exuded an almost intimidating self-confidence. It was easy to understand why Svyet had fallen for him. The other side of his face displayed regular features and a piercing blue eye. Enough of his mouth had survived to permit a charming smile, embellished by the whitest of teeth. His greyish hair was cut *en brosse*. He presented a trim, youthful figure – not the tallest of men – and though he had lost his right arm just below the shoulder, this paradoxically added to the impression of agility and energy. He was unmistakably, in speech and in manners, from an aristocratic family.

Without missing a beat, Katya answered with a warm smile, 'Maxim Konstantinovich, of course you may call me Katya. You are now a member of our family and we of yours.'

'My old friends at cadet school and in the army used to call me Max. Then the name fell out of use. Professors are so much more pompous than soldiers. I would be delighted if you were to revive dear old Max.'

All this was said with self-deprecating charm, his one eye lit from within by friendly humour. For the rest of the day Max, as he was thereafter called, slipped into the background and Svyet took over. There was a lot to do.

First, they went to Max and Svyet's apartment to bathe and breakfast. They lived in what was known as the French Concession, an area of Shanghai that the Chinese had leased to the French under duress in the nineteenth century. It ran west from the Wangpoo river and, with its elegant apartment buildings and shops, looked a little like a French town. Tree-lined avenues and streets heightened the impression. Foreigners of all kinds lived there. It was a favourite of Russian exiles, who had sought refuge in Shanghai in their thousands. Their number had been recently swelled by those who wanted to get away from the Japanese occupation of northern China. There was even, as in Harbin, an Orthodox cathedral.

Max and Svyet's fourth-floor apartment was in a modern block called the Gascogne, on the Avenue Joffre, a very smart part of town. It was large and comfortable, decorated in the Art Deco style. They rented it, they said, from a wealthy Russian fur and diamond trader. They had found not far away a slightly smaller flat for Katya in a block called the Normandie. Again, it was on the fourth floor and owned by this Russian businessman. Like the Gascogne, the Normandie had the luxury of an electric lift.

Katya liked it immediately and wanted to move in without delay. If all had gone well, her personal belongings and furniture could not be far behind. Max asked Gulya several questions about where she would be working, most of which she was unable to answer. He said that he knew Sue's father, who was a bit of a swell in Shanghai's foreign community.

The telephone in Katya's apartment was already connected, so Gulya was able to call Sue and arrange to go round to her flat the following morning, Sunday. She would have preferred to go on her own, but there was a chorus of protests from Katya, Svyet and Max. So, next morning, they all piled into Max's large American Buick and drove to Sue's flat.

It was in another part of Shanghai wrested from the Chinese in the nineteenth century. This adjoined the French Concession and was called the International Settlement. In character it was largely English and American, though once again it was home to many nationalities, in particular Russians, Jews and well-to-do Chinese.

Sue's flat was on the top floor, the eighth, of a building on the Bund, with a great terrace overlooking the Wangpoo river and the famous promenade. The view was magnificent. The flat was enormous, as befitted the boss's daughter. It allowed Sue and Gulya to be completely independent in their own wings at either end of a large drawing room.

The flat was shabbily comfortable in the style of an English country house, with a random collection of sofas, armchairs, small tables and a very large brown-haired dog of indeterminate breed called Toby. He had the run of the flat and was allowed onto the chairs and sofas. According to Sue, Toby was usually well-behaved and friendly.

Sue greeted them all like long-lost friends. Gulya had managed to warn her beforehand about Max's face. She did not bat an eyelid when she saw him. But Toby was another matter. Having done what dogs do, trying to sniff under everyone's skirt, he suddenly spotted Max. Toby took a few steps back and his legs went rigid. He bared his teeth and began to growl, while the hairs along his spine rose vertically. Then he started to bark furiously in a deep baritone and moved in a crouch towards Max, as if to attack him.

Katya feared the worst but Max didn't move. He simply stared hard into the dog's face. This seemed to give Toby pause. As he hesitated, growling and frothing at the mouth, Sue got a lead on him and pulled him back. She tied the lead to a curtain hook and made Toby sit by a window, where he carried on rumbling like a volcano about to erupt.

'That's odd,' said Sue, somewhat flushed and embarrassed. 'The only time I've seen Toby do that before was when we ran into a wolf on a hunting trip. I am awfully sorry, Mr Lebedev.'

'Don't worry, Sue; I am afraid my face scares dogs. They have never seen anything like it before. Come to that, nor have most people,' said Max nonchalantly, trying to put everyone at ease. 'By the way, it's Max.'

Sue served sherry in enormous brown crystal goblets.

They stood in a semi-circle and drank several toasts to mark Svyet's and Max's marriage and Katya and Gulya's arrival in Shanghai. As is the way with Russians, they drank to the future children and grandchildren of Svyet and Max, then to Gulya's, then to Sue's, and then, when they were all fairly drunk, to Katya's next lover – this proposed by Gulya, to screams of laughter at her audacity. Katya went bright red with embarrassment and mirth. Toby joined in, barking furiously, until given a bone to gnaw on.

All the time, even when she had become quite tipsy, Katya kept an eye on Max. He appeared to join in the merriment without inhibition, laughing with the best of them and proposing some of the toasts. But he drank barely a glass and surreptitiously poured much of what Sue gave him out of the window or into the plants.

After a while, they walked round the corner to a Russian restaurant. A great lunch followed that must have lasted a good three hours.

Chapter 37

Shanghai dwarfed Harbin. It was far larger, far busier, far more prosperous, far more cosmopolitan, far more sophisticated, enhanced by the broad river, heavy with barges and junks, running through its centre. The city was more impressive than beautiful – it was too crowded for beauty and its architecture was a complete jumble of styles. It had three distinct atmospheres, belonging to the Chinese, French and British districts. As you went from one district to the other, it was like crossing a frontier, with the feel of the place changing immediately.

The French had gone out of their way to make their quarter look like a cross between the 16th *arrondissement* of Paris and a solid French provincial town. The British preferred an orderly street plan and functional but handsome buildings, like the Customs House and the Hong Kong and Shanghai Bank, where business could be properly carried on. They enjoyed the inestimable advantage of having most of the Bund, along which they had erected their imposing buildings.

The Chinese areas were like any of their large cities, disorderly and crowded, crammed with rickshaws, palanquins, carts drawn by donkeys and the odd car or lorry. Every street seemed to be a market and the noise was indescribable. Among the alleyways and *hutongs*, where people lived in modest single-storey dwellings, some no better than hovels, you might suddenly come across a temple or a pagoda of great beauty. Here and there in the teeming Chinese streets you could find a more substantial house, surrounded by a high wall, its entrance guarded by large stone dragons with fire-breathing muzzles. But, by and large, as soon as Chinese merchants made any money, they wanted to move into one of the foreign quarters.

To Gulya, Shanghai was the most exciting place on earth. She loved going to work at the grand Victoria Trading Company building, where she began as receptionist, gatekeeper and diary secretary for Montgomery Carleton-Sinclair. It wasn't long before Monty, as he was known, recognised her talent for handling people and her ability to navigate the complex layers of Shanghai society, and promoted her to his personal assistant. At the tender age of twenty, she became – along with the British consul-general's social secretary, who was twice her age – a social figure of some heft in the International Settlement.

*

Katya, too, was rising to prominence in the French Concession. Within a month of arriving in Shanghai she had accepted an invitation, which included Gulya, from General Socquet de la Tour, commander of the French garrison, to dine at the Officers' Club. An invitation to one of Socquet's dinners at the Club was much coveted in the foreign community. It marked your 'arrival' in Shanghai. Such an invitation was rivalled only by one from the French Chief of Police or the British consul-general.

The Shanghai foreign community was rigidly layered, dividing along lines of class, rank, profession, wealth and race. The great divide, of course, was between the expatriates and the native population: the latter were virtually invisible to the former. Only a few Chinese, either of great wealth or great power or of some other distinction (a few professors at the university, for example, or an artist) were received into foreign society.

Katya had Max to thank for the general's invitation. He had cultivated a web of contacts all over the city, including with the press. Just after they arrived, he dropped a story into the French-language *Le Journal de Shanghai* that the Countess Polkonina, a noblewoman from one of Russia's most ancient families, had arrived in the city from Harbin, accompanied by her beautiful younger daughter. There followed a few lines about Max and Svyet.

Two things then happened. Katya's language teaching exploded into life, so that, within a matter of a few weeks, she was offered more work than she could handle and her income shot up accordingly. Life in Shanghai was comfortable from the very beginning.

Secondly, they were bombarded with invitations from the foreign community – especially the Russians and the French. She was asked to join this or that Russian club or benevolent society. Representatives from the Orthodox, Catholic and Protestant churches of Shanghai descended, hoping to claim the countess as their own. Even the Rabbi asked to pay a courtesy call. A group of wealthy Chinese businessmen invited her to become an honorary member of their chamber of commerce. She received similar invitations from their French and British counterparts.

As this whirligig gathered pace, Gulya began to get invitations from the French and Russian communities in her own right – from mothers who wanted to introduce her to their sons and from young men directly. The mothers sent letters. The boys just called her up.

All this was, for both Katya and Gulya, at once exhilarating and overwhelming. Until they found their feet, they relied enormously on Max and Svyet – especially Max – to guide them through the social jungle of the French Concession. Once a week they would meet over a drink at Katya's to decide which invitations to accept, which to discard, who to cultivate, who to ignore. Max was in his element. There seemed to be nobody he did not know.

Max was truly a phenomenon. Someone less sure of himself, with a lesser personality, would have been crushed by his disfigurement. But Max made a virtue of it. There can never have been a professor of philology as gregarious and social as Max. Because he was witty and a great conversationalist, at ease in several languages, he was hugely in demand. Hostesses saw him as an exotic adornment to their parties, not an object of horror. His presence, they thought, bore witness to their courage and generosity of spirit in inviting someone so less fortunate than themselves. Women adored him and men admired him – he had seen action, had been terribly wounded and had triumphed over adversity.

There was no social circle in which Max did not shine. You could see him deep in conversation with politicians; military men, European, Japanese and Chinese; the great property developer and businessman Victor Sassoon; and the Rector of the University. Max could even be seen occasionally at the salon of the avant-garde painter Macron O'Reilly, one of the few places in Shanghai where Chinese, Europeans and Americans mixed socially.

Gulya went out with lots of young men, but kept them at arm's length, the better to judge them dispassionately. She was starting to look for a husband and did not want to make a mistake like her poor mother. She gained a reputation for being charming, amusing and a great dancer. But there was no boy in Shanghai who could truthfully claim to have kissed her – which, of course, only enhanced her appeal.

Katya, meanwhile, was observing Max with a keen eye. If he were a spy, he had perfectly positioned himself for the role. She found the dinner at the Officers' Club intriguing. Max had effectively got her the invitation. Why?

By the time she was in a taxi on the way home, she had a shrewd idea of the answer.

She had been given the place of honour to the right of General Socquet. To his left was a good-looking Chinese woman. She was the wife of the Chinese general sitting in an ornate dress uniform, covered in medals, to Katya's right. Katya peeped discreetly at his place card. It read Chiang Kai-shek.

'We call him the "Generalissimo", not entirely without irony,' Socquet muttered discreetly in French to her, as they sat down to dinner. 'He is China's military dictator and, for everyone who wants some peace and order in this benighted land, Chiang is the great white hope.' He said this with a mocking lift of the eyebrows. 'He is competent enough but capable of very great cruelty. He has done terrible things here in Shanghai. Anyway, his task is impossible. He is trying to modernise the country, defeat the Communists, suppress the warlords, resist the Japanese and heaven knows what he is up to with the Soviets.'

'Perhaps I should ask him,' replied Katya. 'I am after all Russian.'

'Perhaps you should,' said Socquet. 'Tell me what he says. He speaks quite good English and Russian.'

With that, they turned away from each other as social etiquette demanded. Katya heard Socquet start a conversation in execrable English with Madame Chiang.

She turned to Chiang. He was thin and small, a large moustache compensating for the near-baldness of his head. With his high cheekbones and wide face, he was not unattractive. He could have been a Siberian.

To Chiang's right was the enormously fat wife of the German consul, her blonde hair piled on top of her head in a ziggurat of curls, waves and ringlets as if she were a sixteen-year-old. She was probably the wrong side of fifty. She was giggling flirtatiously, her rolls of flesh wobbling to each peal of merriment. The source of her entertainment was the handsome, darkly moustachioed man to her right, who looked like a tango dancer in a Hollywood film. He was in fact an American petroleum trader.

'Well, General Chiang, to what do we owe the honour of your presence in Shanghai?' Katya asked in English. She immediately regretted the unintended condescension in her question. Chiang turned slowly towards her, his eyes cold and hard in implicit rebuke.

'Countess, do you find it odd that China's senior general should be inspecting the defences of its most important city, given that the Japanese army is but a few days' march away?'

'I am sorry, General, I did not mean to sound . . . flippant. I have just moved from Harbin. I could no longer bear living cheek-by-jowl with the Kwantung Army,' replied Katya, seeking to make amends.

'What was so intolerable about the Japanese occupation?' the Generalissimo asked, a flicker of interest beginning to soften the icy edges of his stare.

'I am a Russian. The Japanese are our enemy. They are imperious and cruel. They treat us foreigners with a modicum of respect, but are abominably harsh to the Chinese population. The secret police, the *Kempeitai*, strike fear into everyone.'

Chiang grunted and returned to his soup. At first, she thought that he was deliberately ignoring her. Then she realised that he was thinking about what she had just said.

He finished his soup and put down his spoon. The fat German woman tried to engage him in conversation. He shocked her by brusquely turning his back in response and looking at Katya again. She heard the German exclaim 'Pah! These Chinese . . . ' She was about to say more when the American whispered in her ear and she fell silent, her mouth set in a sulky pout.

'I know what you mean. I was partly educated in Japan. But tell me more about life in Harbin,' the Generalissimo said. 'How did you come to live there?'

Katya gave him a condensed history. She stopped at one stage, thinking that she was talking too much.

'Go on, go on,' he responded impatiently. 'I find this of the greatest interest.'

She decided to admit to having done translation work for the Japanese and to her friendship with Je Jin. She had a feeling that he could find out anyway. Perhaps he knew already.

'Je Jin, Je Jin – ah yes, a bandit but a patriot. He died for his country. I met him once.'

Katya was suddenly caught unawares by a surge of emotion. Her eyes filled with tears and her voice broke as she said, 'He was a very great and wonderful man.' She had to say that. Je Jin could not be dismissed as a bandit.

Chiang rested his hand for a moment on her arm and nodded. He understood. The entire character of their conversation changed.

'That's how I started,' he replied, a little wistfully.

Then it was Chiang's turn to talk. It was as if Katya had turned on a tap. He waxed lyrical and at length on his ambitions for China – to restore its dignity and greatness, to wipe out the shame of treaties forced on the old Qing Empire by the western powers. One day, he said, even this very agreeable French enclave – a favourite of his wife – would have to be fully restored to China. No nation worthy of the name could tolerate great chunks of its land being torn away by foreigners.

He went on to talk of a great revolution that he was trying to push through in industry and education. But there were, he said, so many obstacles, so many forces, standing in the way of progress.

Katya found all this of huge interest. She had not said a word for almost ten minutes. He was starting to sound as if he were addressing a public meeting, and she thought she had better remind him of her existence. She took her chin from her hand and asked, 'How will you overcome these obstacles and forces? In my country we had a violent revolution.'

The question snapped Chiang out of his reverie. He answered Katya with a question of his own. 'You left Russia because the Bolsheviks were your enemy?'

'Aren't they yours, too?' she countered, after nodding in the affirmative.

'Who knows? My enemy's enemy is my friend, as someone once said. But that's not a sound basis for an alliance. The Soviets helped against the warlords and the Japanese. I even sent my son to Moscow for his education. That proved to be a mistake. He is now more a prisoner than a pupil. They don't like my campaign against the Communists. They want me to join forces with them against the Japanese. I don't want to do that. China can handle the Japanese on its own. I have trained an entire army for the purpose.'

'But what about your son?' Katya exclaimed. 'He's Moscow's hostage.'

'He knows his duty. Even my wife, who longs to see her child again, doesn't want me to hold hands with Communists. I have slaughtered so many of their Chinese brethren, traitors all of them, including in this city, that there can be no real trust between us.'

'Honour and trust mean nothing to the Bolsheviks. Expediency and violence are all they know. I sometimes feel shame at being a Russian.'

When she said that, Katya did not really mean it. She was never ashamed of being Russian. But she had this feeling that if she said it, shook the tree a little, she might learn something of interest from

Chiang. The Japanese would soon find out about this dinner – the guest list was invariably published in *Le Journal de Shanghai* – and would expect a report. Max, too, would want to know what had passed between her and the Generalissimo. It would be interesting to see how he approached her. She had to come up with something of consequence to both the *Kempeitai* and the NKVD which did not damage the Chinese.

Chiang thought for a moment and then said, 'Countess, it is not easy, I know, but you should not confuse Russians with Bolsheviks. You still have family there?'

'If the Bolsheviks haven't sent them to the Gulag,' Katya interrupted bitterly.

Chiang looked her in the eyes. He is weighing me up, she thought.

'Shanghai is a great city and a more comfortable refuge for a foreigner, I imagine, than Harbin. But it may not stay peaceful for much longer,' he said. Katya made to interrupt again, but he held up his hand.

'The Soviets fear a Japanese attack,' Chiang continued. 'They recall all too well Russia's crushing defeat in 1905. They would like me to commit to a pincer movement, with my forces attacking the Japanese from the south and the Soviets striking through Mongolia from the west. It may well come to that. I expect the Japanese army to make a thrust south to Shanghai and Nanking sometime quite soon. I will throw my new model army at them if they do. Then the Soviets can attack the Japanese – and release my son.'

A silence settled between them. Katya was committing to memory what Chiang had just told her. Then she sensed Socquet trying discreetly to get her attention. She turned towards him. As she did, Chiang spoke across her.

'Forgive me, General, I have monopolised the countess. But it is not often that you come across a woman of such interest and intelligence, if I may say so.' Chiang inclined his head to Katya and then at last turned to the wife of the German consul.

'Countess,' said General Socquet in French, 'you may consider this a gross impertinence, but I would like to say to you now what I had intended for a later date, when we had got to know each other better.'

Socquet stopped to clear his throat. His pudgy hands shook slightly. He tapped his beautifully manicured fingers on the table. He is nervous, thought Katya.

'You have obviously made a great impression on the Generalissimo. This will have been noticed by all at this table. He is perhaps the most important personality in China. Normally he gets bored after ten minutes and leaves. I have never heard him pay a compliment to a woman – to anyone – as he did just now to you.'

Katya smiled at the general, not quite knowing what to say.

'You flatter me, General. Most of the time I was simply listening to him.'

'Knowing how to listen is itself a great skill, Countess. Which brings me to my point. It is a matter of some delicacy.'

His face was very near to hers, his breath slightly sour.

She examined Socquet more closely. He was not a bad-looking man, in his late fifties or early sixties, bulky, running to fat, but still suggesting physical strength inside his bulging uniform. His hair was a lacquered snowy white, brushed back from his forehead with a parting as straight as a Roman road through the centre of his skull. He had a thin, white toothbrush moustache over fleshy lips that suggested self-indulgence. He was otherwise clean-shaven with a complexion a little too florid for Katya's taste.

'Countess,' continued Socquet, 'I am delighted that you have been able to grace this dinner. In the two years that I have been in command here, these occasions have acquired an importance, both social and political, that I never expected when I started them.'

'How often do you give them?' Katya interrupted.

'Once a month. Always at the Officers' Club, always twenty-four guests around this table. In the beginning the guest list was fairly random. Then Monsieur Sotieu, the French consul-general, a very experienced diplomat, explained to me one day how I should make better use of these occasions. It was he who suggested I move them from my dreary barracks to the Officers' Club, an address of high standing, to which everyone would want an invitation. Like many good ideas, it was obvious – I should have thought of it myself!

'Sotieu wanted me to do as the best diplomats do – plan my guest lists methodically, focusing on those of influence in Shanghai, who had information of value to France. People, he said, tended to indiscretion after a couple of glasses of good wine. We agreed a plan. I would always invite him or his deputy, we would split the guest list and we would afterwards pool the intelligence that each of us had gathered.'

The general was interrupted by an aide whispering in his ear. Socquet brushed him aside.

'They want me to propose the toasts. But that can wait five minutes. I must get to my point, otherwise, dear Countess, your patience will snap.'

Katya smiled, but this time said nothing.

'Sotieu was absolutely right. The dinners have provided a harvest of intelligence. But there is one thing that they lack – or, rather, that I lack. Now, I come to my point!'

Socquet paused for dramatic effect. Was it her imagination or were the other guests falling quiet in the hope of hearing what the general would say?

'Protocol demands that men and women should alternate around the dining table,' continued Socquet. 'That means the guest of honour should always be flanked by two women, the senior hostess and another. But my wife is in France, her health too fragile for her to join me in Shanghai. I need a hostess who can sit next to the senior guest, entertain him, win his confidence, extract information from him. Dear Countess, I believe that you are that person. I have just witnessed your mastery of the Generalissimo.'

Socquet paused and took a deep breath. Then he said with something of a flourish, 'In consequence, I extend to you an invitation to a permanent seat at my table as my hostess. There is, of course, no need to give me your answer now. I would just ask you to reflect, benevolently I hope, on my offer and let me know your response before too long.'

Katya decided silently to accept Socquet's offer. It would put her at the very centre of things. It would delight the Japanese and Max in equal measure. It would make her intelligence work immeasurably easier. It would cement her standing in Shanghai, thus reducing her reliance on Max, which made her uncomfortable. But before giving the good news to Socquet, a few things had first to be made clear.

'General Socquet, you flatter me with this offer. In truth, the Generalissimo had very little to tell me . . . '

'But you didn't know what to ask,' Socquet interrupted impatiently.

'Be that as it may, but wouldn't people assume that you and I had a relationship of some intimacy? You are a man and can survive these things. But I, as a woman, alone in Shanghai, for whom reputation is everything, cannot afford to be tainted by rumour.'

Katya had, of course, already compromised herself in Harbin with Je Jing. But people in the end had got used to it, thanks to Je Jing's influence and wealth. By contrast, rumours of a liaison with a lonely, albeit married, French general at the pinnacle of French society in Shanghai would barely disturb the surface of the waters. They were, she thought, something she could easily survive. But she still wanted to hear Socquet's reply.

'I would rebut them in the strongest possible terms,' said Socquet vigorously, almost explosively, his face turning puce and his fist banging the table. The noise attracted the attention of some of the guests. 'I would seek satisfaction from any man who suggested such a thing. I would demote to the ranks any officer who dared give voice to such a slander. And, Countess, you can rest assured that any woman who spread gossip of this kind, would be cast into the outer circle of social hell.'

'I see,' said Katya, wondering if he was protesting just a little too much.

Then she posed her second big question. 'Are you not asking me to spy for France, when I am Russian-born?'

'Dear Countess, there would be nothing clandestine about this arrangement. I would actually make an announcement that, given your illustrious background, I had invited you to become official hostess at my dinners, and that you had accepted. All I would suggest is that after dinner, or even the next day, you give me your impressions and tell me whether our guest of honour had anything of interest to say. As for your being Russian and I French,' Socquet's voice dropped, 'are we not as one in our hatred of the Bolsheviks and the Japanese? Besides, you speak French like a Frenchwoman.'

Socquet's responses were good enough for Katya. But she would not tell him straightaway. Wasn't it the great French diplomat Talleyrand who once said, '*Surtout pas trop de zèle*' – 'Above all don't be too keen'?

'General Socquet, I am, I repeat, flattered by your offer and will give it the most careful consideration.'

General Socquet de la Tour rose to his feet, requested silence and proposed a toast to the President of the French Republic and then to the Generalissimo. Chiang returned the compliment with a toast to the French President. He sat down again but did not stay for dessert and coffee. He made a sign to his wife and they rose together from the table. He said a warm goodbye to Katya, expressing the hope that they might meet again. Then, accompanied by General Socquet de la Tour, he and Madame Chiang left the room, acknowledging and bowing to the polite applause that accompanied their departure. A small bodyguard of smartly turned-out Chinese soldiers, led by an officer, awaited him just outside the dining-room door.

After the Chiangs' departure, the life went out of the evening and the dinner rapidly broke up. Katya and Gulya – who had spent a much less interesting evening than her mother – said goodnight to General Socquet, thanking him profusely for his hospitality.

'Dear Countess,' he said to Katya, 'you will not make me wait too long, I trust.'

'Dear General, not a minute more than I have to,' replied Katya.

'What was that all about, Mama?' Gulya asked as they stepped into the taxi. 'You are surely not considering him as your next beau.'

'Don't be silly, Gulya. Of course not. Wait until we get home and I'll explain.'

Bozhe moi, thought Katya as they drove through the Shanghai night, I shall be working for the *Kempeitai*, the NKVD *and* the French army.

She should have found the prospect terrifying. Instead, she was exhilarated. She could hear Je Jin chuckling.

Chapter 38

When they got home from the Officers' Club there was a letter on Katya's hall table with a Chinese stamp and, on the back of the envelope, an almost indecipherable Harbin address.

It was the reply to a letter she had sent to Andrey via a Harbin friend who kept in touch with him. Her letter to him had contained a photograph of Max, snipped from a picture taken at the Russian restaurant, where they had all lunched together on that first Sunday in Shanghai.

Andrey wrote in Russian:

My dear Katya,

I am happy to hear from you. You and the girls seem in good health. You are well out of Harbin, I can tell you. It's become drab and sad under the heel of the Japanese. I would hate to think that the girls were still growing up in this cursed place. I cannot wait to get away myself, but the Japanese have just issued an edict which stops people leaving without a ticket to a final destination. I want to get to Switzerland, where there are some Russians my family used to know, but I don't yet have the resources.

Now, Lebedev. I looked closely at that picture. It was hard to tell after all these years and those terrible injuries. But, yes, it is he. You don't forget easily someone you were about to shoot and who was about to shoot you.

It fills me with dread that he has married our daughter. He is

*cruel and vengeful even by the standards of the NKVD. I would not
be surprised if he thought his injuries were in some way my fault.
Then we outwitted him at Golovino and made our escape to Samara.
I have always had the feeling that he has been after me ever since.
Now I fear he may have decided to track me down through you or
even to take his revenge on you and the girls. I know it's twenty
years after the event, but that's the kind of man he is.*

*My advice? Get out of Shanghai and find refuge with the
British in Hong Kong or the French in Hanoi.*

Give my love to Svyet and Gulya.

Yours ever,
Andryusha

*Post-scriptum. By the way, Vera and I have long since separated. I
was a fool to leave you and the family, but it's no use crying over spilt
milk. I have taken a little flat near the river. It's all I can afford.
Perhaps I will come and visit you one day.*

Katya sat down to compose an urgent reply. She thanked him for
confirming Max's identity. She led him to think that she would flee
Shanghai, taking Svyet and Gulya with her. The last thing she wanted
was his turning up on her doorstep in some quixotic attempt to protect
her from Max. Despite the late hour, she hurried to the main post office
to ensure her letter caught the milk train north.

With that done, her mind could turn, uncluttered, to the nub of the
matter: was Max a threat to be deflected or an opportunity to be
embraced? The answer, she decided, lay in her own hands. She had
been given her marching orders by the Japanese. It was her task to turn
him into an opportunity. Despite his disfigurement she had smelled a
massive vanity in Max. That was her opportunity, a weakness waiting
to be exploited. She decided that it would not be she who first

mentioned the Socquet dinner. Max would ask her about it soon enough, of that she was sure. That would be the start of the great game between them. Heaven knew who, in the end, would come out on top.

The thought occurred to her that she would do better to put Andrey's letter in her safety deposit box at the bank.

*

The following Monday she paid her first visit to the Japanese consulate. It was a huge building at the northern extreme of the International Settlement. On arriving she asked for Major Seko and Captain Abe. She was almost immediately escorted to a third-floor office, which looked onto an inside courtyard. Seko and Abe were not so much pleased as relieved to see her. Despite the smiles and bows, there was a tension in the air. With one thing and another – settling in, registering with the authorities, starting her classes, making sure Svyet and Gulya were all right, getting to know Shanghai and creating a relationship with Max – several weeks had passed since she had seen her Japanese contacts. They had obviously been worried that she might have changed her mind.

By the end of the meeting all tension had been expelled from the room. Seko and Abe thought Kaya had excelled herself by getting an invitation to General Socquet de la Tour's dinner. The news had caught them off guard. *Le Journal de Shanghai,* with Socquet's guest list, would not emerge till the following day.

Their usual inscrutability was further punctured when she gave them an account of her conversation with Generalissimo Chiang Kai-shek, edited to omit anything that she thought might prejudice the Chinese position. She decided, for example, to hold back the information that he would not enter into formal alliance with the Soviets against Japan. But she confirmed that the Chinese were preparing to defend themselves against a strike southwards by the Kwantung Army. She exercised some poetic licence by underlining how well prepared Chiang considered his forces to be, some of them having been trained and armed by Germany.

This information – a bonus, considering her brief was to probe Max for Soviet intentions – was more than adequate compensation for her having nothing yet to report from her son-in-law. She emphasised how sensitive and delicate it all was. She had, she told the Japanese officers, to start on the right foot and not disclose in any way that she suspected Max's real role. She wanted him to approach her first. That might give her an opportunity to start finding out things.

Seko and Abe nodded their approval and rose to conclude the meeting. Katya did not move.

'I have something else to tell you,' she said.

They sat down again.

'General Socquet de la Tour has given me a standing invitation to attend all his dinners as his official hostess. He wants to make an announcement shortly.'

Seko jerked his head up from the note he was making. The breath escaped audibly from Abe's mouth. For the third time in twenty minutes, in a growing crescendo of surprise, the Japanese faces opposite her had lost their composure. It gave Katya almost unreasonable pleasure. But she knew that she had to be careful. She had got to know the *Kempeitai* mind. On the whole it did not like surprises. Suspicion could all too easily follow.

'Countess, you are full of surprises today,' said Seko. 'May I ask how you achieved this extraordinarily privileged position in so short a time?'

Yes, the seed of suspicion was there in his voice.

'It wasn't so difficult, Major,' Katya answered easily. 'I don't know how it is with the Japanese, but the foreign community – that is the Europeans and the Americans – are terrible snobs. Once the word got round that I am from the old Russian aristocracy, and that my younger daughter, Gulya, has been made personal assistant to the head of the Victoria Trading Company at the tender age of twenty, we have been submerged in invitations. One from the commander of the French garrison was inevitable.'

'But a standing invitation, Countess?' interrupted Seko.

'Even I was a little surprised,' said Katya, smiling. 'At first, I suspected him of harbouring unworthy desires – which may actually be the case. We'll see. But these dinners are chiefly intelligence operations, jointly organised by Socquet de la Tour and the French consul-general. The missing piece in their jigsaw has been an official hostess for the general, whose wife remains in France. He saw me in conversation with General Chiang Kai-shek and decided on the spot that I fitted the role. I have not yet told him that I have accepted his invitation. There are, as you may imagine, possible difficulties for my reputation.'

Seko rubbed his chin, the light of ironic amusement in his eyes.

'I understand,' said Seko. 'We do not want you to do anything indelicate that will make you feel . . . awkward, because that is when mistakes are made. But these dinners have truly become a marketplace for intelligence and gossip. We have tried to get someone into them on a regular basis, but in vain. General Aiko is invited only three times a year and is always stuck between women of incredible stupidity. So we would very much appreciate it if, despite the possible embarrassment, you were to find your way to accepting the general's invitation.'

'Don't worry, Major, I have already decided to accept. I will tell General Socquet de la Tour before the end of the week.'

At the end of the meeting, all three were smiling when they rose and shook hands. How strange the world was. They were her mortal enemies. But, up to a point, they had become friends. The familiarity helped, of course. It was well over ten years since she had given Mr Amae his first Russian lesson. But, with the *Kempeitai*, she knew the bonhomie could be stripped away in a trice.

Abe drew a piece of paper from his pocket.

'I almost forgot, Countess. Here are details of three members of the consulate staff who are keen to have English or French lessons for themselves and their families.'

Abe bowed. Katya thanked him and Seko profusely. As she stepped out of the building, she felt a surge of relief. She had cleared the first hurdle. Now for Max.

Chapter 39

It had instantly become a ritual for Svyet and Max to invite Katya and Gulya for supper on Thursdays. These were quite jolly occasions. Svyet's transformation into a normal human being continued. Her bossiness and sharpness had been blunted by her devotion to Max, and she broke the habit of a lifetime and stopped picking quarrels with her younger sister.

On the Thursday following the garrison commander's dinner, they arrived as usual at seven o'clock sharp at Svyet and Max's flat in the Gascogne apartments. Svyet threw open the door and greeted them with a shower of kisses. Max was standing behind her, smiling, as elegant as usual. He affected a British-style blue double-breasted blazer, a Shanghai Club cravat and smart grey flannel trousers. He wore cream and brown correspondent shoes, which were all the rage. Katya always said that you could judge a man by his shoes. She was never convinced by these two-tone abominations, which she found somewhat vulgar.

Max and Svyet looked the picture of devotion. But something was not quite right: both Katya and Gulya sensed it.

Not for the first time, Gulya found herself struck by the apartment's comfort and touches of luxury. How could they afford it on a professor's salary? The truth was that their landlord – who also owned Katya's flat – was a Russian businessman who traded commodities on behalf of the Soviets in an elaborate international barter system. The Victoria Trading Company got involved in some of the deals. The Soviet Union had depended for decades on barter – wheat for ships and the like.

The businessman was an old Chekist, close to the NKVD, one of the Cheka's successor organisations. He had let the apartment to the

NKVD at a heavily discounted rate. They had then installed Max, so that he could use it as a fashionable base from which to spin his web of high-powered contacts.

Max and Svyet paid not a penny in rent. Katya paid only a token sum, thanks to Max's relationship with the businessman. It troubled her sometimes, but if it gave Max comfort to think that he had Katya in his debt, it well suited her purpose.

It was Svyet, not Max, who broached the Socquet de la Tour dinner.

'Gulya, how did you wangle an invitation to the general's dinner? Your name and Mama's are all over *Le Journal* today. Was it fun? Did you meet anyone interesting?'

They were sitting in the drawing room drinking a glass of sherry before dinner. This was another English affectation of Max's.

Max had one leg languidly crossed over the other. His one eye was fixed on Svyet and Gulya. It was astonishing how, without its twin, it could still convey mood. The eye was signalling keen interest.

'I was dragged along in Mama's wake.'

'Don't be so modest, Gulya!' Max interrupted, a little sharply. 'Now that you have become Monty Carleton-Sinclair's personal assistant, your celebrity has spread into the French quarter. You're a personality in your own right. How did you find this dinner for VIPs?' His one eye now shone like a searchlight.

'Well, that may be, Max,' replied Gulya, slightly taken aback. 'But I was bored stiff and stuck between two old men. Mama, though, seemed to be having a whale of a time. She spoke for ages to a Chinese general with stars and medals all over his chest.'

'That must have been our Generalissimo, Chiang Kai-shek,' said Max, as his one eye swivelled in Katya's direction. 'How did you find him, Katya?' His voice shed a few layers of nonchalance as he put the question.

Katya had prepared herself for the moment. She had decided to be deliberately vague about the very thing in which she knew Max was most interested.

'Amiable enough, but hard work,' she answered. 'There was lots of stuff about armies and war, which is really not my strong suit. I found him more interesting when he got on to his plans for China. Reform and all that. By the way, like many Chinese we meet, he really resents the foreign enclaves up and down China's coast, including in Shanghai. He's determined to be rid of us all one of these days. He talked a lot about the unjust treaties of the last century.'

'That's all the thanks we get for bringing them modern civilisation,' said Max contemptuously. 'What did he say about war? Is he going to fight the Japanese again? There was terrible bloodshed and destruction after the last conflict a few years back. Part of the city was flattened. We don't want to see that again.'

'To be honest, Max, I don't remember much,' she sighed. 'He's afraid the Japanese will advance south. He's determined to stop them. But haven't we been reading about this for weeks, ever since we first arrived in Shanghai?'

'Surely he had a bit more to say than that?' said Max, with more than a hint of exasperation in his voice. Katya in turn was starting to sound just a little irritated.

'For goodness' sake, Max, we're here for supper, not an interrogation. The Chinaman wasn't going to reveal his war plans to a Russian he has never met before. He did tell me, however, that he had sent his son to Moscow for his education. Why Moscow, do you think?' asked Katya, seeking to change the subject a little.

'Why not? I don't know.' Max's exasperation was palpable. 'I suppose he went to army officer school,' he continued, making an effort to sound more equable. 'The Soviets have one just for foreigners from countries where they sell military equipment. Like China.'

Svyet said with an attempted tinkle in her voice that came out like a cracked bell, 'You are incredible, Max, darling. You know so much for a philology professor. How on earth do you know about military schools for foreigners in the Soviet Union?'

Because you have a husband who is an NKVD officer, thought Katya. There was definitely something off-key between Svyet and Max. Did Svyet have any idea who Max was? Surely not. Then again . . .

Max had, for a moment, revealed a crack in the shiny carapace of his affability. It was no more than the slightest breath of wind on the mirrored surface of a pond, the whisper of a dragonfly's slipstream. But it had been there.

Max was saved from answering his wife's question by the arrival of a Chinese maid, carrying a large porcelain tureen of soup.

'Ah! Thank you, Chang-Wei. Let's take our places at the table,' said Svyet a little too loudly. 'Mama, I hope you like the soup. It's grandmother's old recipe.'

The soup was indeed excellent and lunch passed pleasantly enough, but Katya and Gulya sensed an underlying tension between Max and Svyet.

As they enjoyed their coffee at the end of the meal, Katya said out of the blue, 'Oh, going back to our conversation about General Socquet de la Tour, I forgot to tell you – Svyet, Max – about his offer. He wants me to play the role of hostess at all his Saturday night dinners. His wife is an invalid in France. He thinks I handled the Generalissimo so well that I would be invaluable looking after each guest of honour.'

'Won't everyone think you're having an affair with him?' asked Svyet with a frown.

'Of course they will,' Gulya chipped in with her usual lack of tact. 'The gossips will be out in force, especially those who don't get invited to the dinners!'

Max, whose eye had switched on again like a piercing light bulb, sat bolt upright and said, 'Oh, I don't know, if it's handled right. It just needs to be announced officially from the garrison HQ.

'The family reputation was my first concern,' said Katya. 'But after thinking about it, I have come to the same conclusion as Max. As it happens, the general readily agreed to make an official announcement and told me he would cashier any officer spreading scandal.'

'So, you have accepted?' asked Max.

'Yes, of course. It will be fascinating. If I have decided to make my home in Shanghai, I need to learn about it. What better listening post could I have? It will also help my language lesson business and you can all bathe in my reflected glory!' Katya said with a beaming, teasing smile.

'Do you actually like the general, Mama?' Gulya asked.

'Yes, well enough – but not to become his mistress! He has bad breath and spits when he's eating!' All three Polkonin women shrieked with laughter.

Max maintained a serious expression through all the merriment.

'This is quite something, it really is,' he said quietly, rubbing his chin.

'Well, Max, it's you I have to thank,' said Katya with the look of laughter still in her eyes.

'Now I come to think of it, my article in *Le Journal de Shanghai* probably helped. But, dear Katya, you could return me the favour. You see – and I haven't yet told Svyet – I am about to embark on a second career.'

She stared at Max and suddenly found him hideous.

'What, Max?' Svyet cried out shrilly. 'Do tell!'

'I am going to write a weekly column for the *Shanghai Times*.'

Svyet clapped her hands in delight and looked lovingly at her husband. Katya and Gulya offered congratulations. Svyet filled small glasses with Georgian cognac and they drank a toast to Max.

Except that it was not true at the moment Max announced it. The idea had just come to him, prompted by Katya's own disclosure. He had been agonising for months as to how best to take advantage of fate delivering the Polkonin family into his hands.

In the beginning, a prisoner of a twenty-year obsession, he had picked Svyet as a stepping stone to a final settling of accounts with Andrey Polkonin. But, to his disappointment, she had no interest in her father and no idea where he was living. He found this out too late. He deeply regretted marrying her. He did not love her. He had certainly not revealed to her that he was a serving NKVD officer.

For the first time in twenty years he was starting to question his obsession with revenge. It clearly triggered his 'turns'. The doctors in Moscow had warned him of the lasting cranial damage inflicted by the German bomb. He had to try to dig this Polkonin business out of his soul.

Max's exile to Shanghai had already provoked a profound disillusionment with the Soviet regime. The realisation that marrying Svyet would do nothing to help find her father had sapped still further his energy and motivation. His reports to Moscow became increasingly thin and insubstantial. He ran agents who delivered very little. His taskmasters in Moscow were growing impatient. They were always suspicious of the loyalties of those, like him, who came from the old aristocracy. This was not a good time to arouse Moscow's suspicions. He did not have long before he was recalled. Execution or hard labour in some hellish Siberian Gulag would inevitably follow.

Just as he was starting to despair, and even to consider flight, Katya had entered his life, offering a possible lifeline. It would oblige him to keep up appearances with Svyet, but that was a small price to pay for buying time with Moscow and possibly resurrecting his career.

Even Gulya might drop a few crumbs from her job at the British company. It was easy to dismiss her as a pretty, brainless blonde. But Monty, a no-nonsense businessman, must see something in her. Like her mother, Gulya had a quality which warned him not to underestimate her and their ability to survive despite the odds.

The *Shanghai Times* was the city's best English-language newspaper. He knew its editor, Alan Broadwick, all too well. They visited the same brothel together. At the end of the entrance hall were two doors, one green, the other red. Max took the green door, which led to the pubescent girls, Alan the red door to boys of the same age. Should Broadwick resist hiring him, Max had photographs of him *in flagrante delicto* at the brothel, courtesy of the NKVD.

'I wonder, Katya,' Max continued, as he downed his cognac, 'if I could come and see you after these dinners on the off-chance you have picked up something which I could use in my weekly column. It's going to be difficult for me until I get into the habit of writing. I am not asking you to breach any confidences, just to throw the old dog a bone from time to time!'

'Of course, Max. I used to help Andryusha with his columns for the *Russian Voice* in Harbin.'

Chapter 40

As she lay in bed, her mind drifting before the onset of sleep, Katya for some reason started to think about Vladimir Lenin. Wasn't he supposed to have asked 'Who, whom?' about the struggle between communism and its enemies? The phrase in Russian – '*Kto, kovo?*' – buzzed around her head like a trapped bluebottle. Perhaps she was already dreaming.

It had always struck her as a great coincidence, of some unclear metaphysical importance, that Lenin had been born in Simbirsk, just to the east of her family home in Golovino. Later she had found out that Alexander Kerensky had also been born in Simbirsk. Since he had in 1917 opened the door to Lenin, the Russian Revolution and, ultimately, Max himself, wasn't she in some significant way riding history's wave with the three of them?

Then, as sleep overtook her, the god of dreams, erasing grandiose visions of history and waves, mined instead that great seam of fears which lay buried in the dark cave of her consciousness.

She dreamed that she was a juggler. On a boiling hot day, she was standing on the Bund in the shade of a plane tree, performing to a large group of passers-by. She was sweating uncomfortably. She had only three red balls. One spoke to her in Chinese, the second in Russian, the third in Japanese. She kept dropping each in turn. The ball would shriek with anger and pain. The spectators jeered and booed. They closed in on her until she was unable to move. She began to suffocate. As she fell to the ground, she spotted Je Jin, waving, as if oblivious to her plight.

She awoke with a start, clutching her pillow. She was dripping with perspiration. She emerged from under the bedclothes, plumped up her pillow and lay back, glad to breathe the fresh night air coming through the open window and cooling her body.

She went back to thinking of the strange evening she had just spent chez Svyet and Max.

There was something clearly wrong with Max, and not just his face. Another letter from Andryusha had followed hard on the heels of the first. It was filled with warnings and forebodings. By its telling, Max had been born ruthless, vengeful, merciless. Certainly, Max's suaveness and easy self-deprecation were a veneer, and a thin one at that. But Andryusha's judgement had been formed in the heat of war some twenty years before. Now there was something else, the vulnerability of a damaged man, sustained by a monstrous vanity.

Who knew at what cost he had bent his true character to fit the persona of devoted husband and popular professor-about-town? It would have broken a man of lesser powers of dissimulation. But this, Katya thought wryly, was the essential quality of the spy. Now, the cracks were beginning to show. Tension ran through him like an electric charge. Sue's dog had detected this immediately, as dogs do. A horrible thought came to her. When would Toby start barking and snarling at her?

She saw also, from little signs that only a mother can spot, how Svyet's adoration for Max was mixed with anxiety.

This had not been apparent when Katya and Gulya had first arrived in Shanghai. Now, she was concerned for her older daughter. Svyet was the fourth ball in her juggler's collection. Please God that she did not drop her like the others.

For a moment Katya thought of giving up her spying. Je Jin would understand. It was too dangerous. She should slip away from Shanghai before it was too late, and find refuge with the English in Hong Kong. Gulya would grumble, she thought, but with Monty's help she should be able to get a job with the Hong Kong branch of the Old Vic, as he called it. Svyet was a different matter. She would refuse point blank to leave her husband.

I cannot abandon Svyet to Max, she said to herself. I have to stay in

Shanghai. And I cannot stop working for the Japanese without arousing their intense suspicion. I am trapped. Who, whom, indeed!

Katya knew what she had to do to calm Max. He was desperate for information, that was obvious. When she had revealed her new role as General Socquet de la Tour's official hostess, he had pounced on the news. What an odd coincidence that he too had just got a new job, and as a journalist.

'Who, whom.' She would find out soon enough. But if her reading of Max was right, he would try to make her a regular source. She would have to play to this and turn it to her advantage.

'*Bozhe moi!*' Katya muttered, 'when at the age of eighteen I curtsied to the Tsarina at the debutantes' ball in St Petersburg, could I have ever imagined this would be my fate?'

She plumped the pillow again and lay her head down. That was enough thinking for one night. She closed her eyes and fell immediately into a dreamless sleep.

The alarm woke her at eight o'clock. Katya was on the phone before breakfast. She juggled some of her lessons to create a two-hour space to see Major Seko and Captain Abe. She needed a plan and the Japanese had to help her create one.

She wrapped up warm and took a taxi to the consulate general. It was mid-afternoon but already dark. The city blazed with electric light. It was now mid-February 1937. The weather was damp and cold, but still mild compared with the rigours of a Harbin winter.

She was again swiftly ushered into the bare, utilitarian office on the third floor. Major Seko, as usual sleek and plump, and Captain Abe, as usual tall and elegantly thin, were waiting for her. She could not help thinking of those two American comic actors, Laurel and somebody, who appeared in films at the Picture Palace.

They had the briefest exchange of courtesies. For the first time Seko essayed a couple of phrases in halting English. Then he handed back to Abe the role of interpreter.

Katya came straight to the point.

She gave a full account of Max's behaviour the previous evening, including his announcement that he was to become a columnist at the *Shanghai Times*. This aroused the keen interest of the two Japanese. They nodded energetically when Katya pointed out that Max now had a perfect excuse to question her about Socquet de la Tour's dinners. He had become frustrated beyond reason at her inability to tell him much about her conversation with General Chiang Kai-shek.

'You don't think he suspected an ulterior motive behind your reticence?' asked Seko. 'After all, he will be well aware of your Chinese preferences in Harbin.'

'I don't think so,' replied Katya. 'He will also know that in Harbin I had a long relationship with the Japanese consul-general and his family.'

'That relationship,' countered Seko, 'was not of the same nature as that you had with the Chinese warlord.'

'Quite true,' Katya answered, as if they were discussing the weather. 'But the impression I have sought to convey is of having little interest or expertise in military matters. I believe I have been convincing. Nor, so far, has Max shown the least interest in my lessons to Japanese students.'

Seko grunted and gave a short nod of his head.

'I have spoken of Max's frustration. But in truth he is showing signs of severe stress. If I don't give him some information from the next dinners, I fear for his stability and my daughter's wellbeing. It is at the same time an opportunity for you to insert something into what I pass him,' Katya concluded.

'Very interesting, Countess,' said Seko. 'When do you think Max will want to interview you?'

Katya noticed that this was the first time he had called him Max rather than Lebedev.

'Sunday evening. I don't yet know when his column will come out,' she replied.

Seko got up from his chair, took a key from the table drawer and walked to a small safe, from where he withdrew a single sheet of paper. Katya noticed that the sheet had a red border on all four sides. He returned to the table, sat down again and, holding the sheet of paper in both hands, he began to read it to himself.

Silence fell on the room as Seko studied the paper. Abe adopted his usual posture, folding his arms, stretching his legs in front of him and looking at the ceiling. The radiator was making hissing and knocking sounds as it heated the room to an almost uncomfortable temperature.

Five minutes must have passed before Seko abruptly looked up. Abe came to attention in his chair, as it were, ready to interpret his senior officer's words. Seko still held the piece of paper in both hands. He began to read aloud, looking up at Katya from time to time.

'Basically, my instructions to you remain unchanged from our last meeting. But we have refined them to take account of latest developments. Again, I am instructed to stress the extreme sensitivity of what I am about to tell you and the draconian penalty for letting any of the information fall into unauthorised hands.'

Seko paused. He fumbled in one of his pockets and found his gun-metal cigarette case, from which he took out an American Lucky Strike. As he lit it, there was the slightest tremor in his hands. He drew heavily on the cigarette. Katya suddenly realised that he, usually the most imperturbable of men, was under great strain. I know why, she thought. He is about to tell me something so secret that he is almost overwhelmed by its sensitivity.

'This is quite complicated,' said Seko, looking Katya in the eye. Then his own eyes dropped to the document in his hands. He began to read.

'Reinforcements are arriving weekly from Japan so that our forces will be strong enough to overcome Chinese resistance in Shanghai, Pekin and Nanking. We will drive out Chiang Kai-shek's army from the three cities and place them under Japan's authority. We plan a campaign of approximately six months.'

Seko drew again on his cigarette.

'We do not want the Soviets to think that the movement of large formations of Japanese troops is directed at them, even though we will have two divisions placed along our western flank to deter any Soviet attack. We want you to convince Max that these divisions have no aggressive intent. As I have said before, we do not want to become embroiled in a war with the Soviet Union just as we are dealing with the Chinese army.'

'Major Seko,' Katya brusquely interrupted, in genuine puzzlement, 'would you care to tell me how I of all people, a teacher of foreign languages, will be able to persuade a professional spy, who was himself once a soldier?'

'Because the military attaché, General Aiko, will be at Socquet de la Tour's next dinner. Max will not be persuaded by you, Countess, but by the words of our general. You and he will be introduced by his military secretary and you will converse in German.'

'How,' asked Katya, 'do I broach the subject with him?'

'You don't,' Seko briskly replied. 'General Aiko knows nothing of your mission. He's a cavalryman, who likes birds, insects, sailing and the works of Richard Wagner. He's an old-fashioned nationalist. He regards women as inferior beings!'

Seko said this with an almost impudent smile, his yellow teeth showing behind the cigarette smoke.

Before Katya could say a word, Seko went on, 'Don't worry. He will be easy to talk to. We will see to that in the briefing we provide him about you.'

'What have you said about me?' asked Katya, overcome with curiosity.

It was Abe who replied. 'We have said that you are as brave as a *samurai*. That will catch his attention and it has the merit of being true.'

Katya could not remember a time when she had been more thrown off balance by a compliment, because compliment it was – perhaps the highest a Japanese officer could pay. She blushed scarlet. When had she last done that? She had been caught completely by surprise.

For a few moments they were a frozen tableau: the Russian noblewoman and her two mortal enemies. The sorrow and the pity of it was that, so as to thwart them, perhaps destroy them, she had also to befriend them.

Seko coughed and said, 'We must press on.'

Katya pulled herself together. Her complexion returned to normal. She felt that she ought to say something, but words escaped her. Seko saved her the trouble.

'You should tell Max four things: that you met General Aiko, that you had a conversation with him, that he emphasised Japan's wish to avoid hostilities with the Soviet Union and that he told you that Tokyo would soon propose to Moscow a mutual non-aggression pact. It is this last piece of information that will interest Max and his NKVD masters because it will be new.'

'So, you will become friends with the Soviet Union?' asked Katya.

'Oh no, dear Countess. That is a smokescreen. After we have crushed Chiang Kai-shek, we will turn right and smash the Soviets. This is the deepest secret of them all.'

Chapter 41

When Katya returned to her apartment from the Japanese consulate, she found a grubby-looking Yu Yan sitting with her small brown suitcase on the steps leading up to her front door. Her hair was matted. It looked like she had soot marks on her face. She was singing to herself.

Sitting with her were a pair of tough-looking Chinese men in traditional dress. Each had knives at their waist. They reminded Katya of Je Jin's foot soldiers, because that was what they were. They jumped up, bowed deeply and greeted her with elaborate courtesy. They bowed also to Yu Yan. Then they said goodbye. Yu Yan tried to thank them, but, like phantoms, they were gone.

Yu Yan's face lit up on seeing Katya. She raced into her arms and the two hugged each other tight. Katya was overcome. Tears streamed down her face. Yu Yan made funny little noises. She smelled of coal. They clung to each other for several minutes.

Yu Yan had grown enormously. She had come to resemble Je Jin more and more. With her father's slimness and fine features, she was becoming a beautiful woman.

They broke apart and looked at each other. Katya held Yu Yan by the shoulders.

'I am so happy to see you,' she said to Katya in English in that solemn way of hers. 'It has been such a long, long time.'

Katya was incapable of speech. She knew that she would cry again if she tried to answer. She nodded and smiled. Her eyes filled with tears, nonetheless. Another part of her brain noted Yu Yan's flawless English accent, that and the roughness of her palms.

*

Out in the countryside, living with a family of modest farmers who were distant relations, Yu Yan had kept up her English. She had worked her way through the entire works of Charles Dickens, which a retainer had rescued from the smoking ruins of her father's house.

She loved all Dickens' books. *A Tale of Two Cities* was her favourite, because it was a story of romance and redemption. Each night she would open the book at its end and read aloud Sydney Carton's noble last words, as he sacrificed himself on the guillotine for the woman he loved. Ah! To be loved by a man like that.

Then she would kneel over her thin mattress and its threadbare cover and ask God to look after those she loved. She said the prayer in English. It had not worked in Chinese for her mother and father.

The farmers, two brothers and two wives, who were sisters, were kind to her and fed her well, but expected her to help on the farm. Yu Yan had no objection and, with her usual energy and enthusiasm, threw herself into gathering, bundling, raking, picking, hoeing and sweeping. The family was delighted with the little girl, who they had feared would prove a burden. They were prosperous enough, but knew how quickly the fates could turn against them. They were always at the mercy of the weather and tax collectors.

Fang, the fearsome Boxer, kept an eye on Yu Yan from a distance. He regarded it as his sacred duty to ensure that no harm came to Je Jin's daughter. He would suddenly appear in the farm courtyard on the back of a mule or donkey, to avoid attracting attention.

It was through him that Yu Yan, Gulya and Katya kept in touch. When the time came for Yu Yan to leave for Shanghai, Fang explained his plan. 'I have brought two friends. They fought with me and your father. They have known you since you were a baby. I will drive the three of you to the station to catch the express to Shanghai. And they will travel with you until you get to the Countess's apartment. They will protect you against inquisitive gendarmerie patrols or attacks by the Communists.'

The sun rose the next morning on what would be a hot day. Yu Yan had already said an emotional farewell to the farmers before going to bed the previous evening. She had thanked them from the bottom of her heart for the sanctuary they had so generously given her and which could yet cause them much trouble.

As the car drove off, she waved furiously out of the passenger seat window of Fang's Citroën. Then, suddenly, the farm, the farmers and the pigs disappeared from view in the cloud of dust kicked up by the vehicle.

It took Yu Yan and her escorts over two hours to reach the mainline station and climb into the packed express train. The heat and smell of their carriage were suffocating. Yu Yan felt sick. Though she knew it was dangerous, she put her head out of the window, but that was worse. Her head was enveloped by smoke and cinders from the engine's stack. She arrived in Shanghai with soot on her face and ash in her hair.

*

Gulya was also overjoyed at seeing her beloved Yu Yan again. Her friend had matured fast in their two years of separation, and the gap in their ages seemed to have shrunk. Their relationship picked up instantly from where it had left off.

A few days after her arrival in Shanghai, a big family discussion was held about Yu Yan's schooling. Katya was inclined to send her to the French *lycée*, because of its high academic standards. It would also be near to her apartment. Yu Yan was not at all keen. Her two years in the countryside had destroyed her modest knowledge of French and she was way behind in the Chinese syllabus.

Max came to her rescue.

'My dear Katya, we tend to forget that Yu Yan is Chinese and that it's going to be the devil's own job for her to make up for lost ground in the Chinese educational system. Yet she will have to do that if she wants to go to university.' Katya marvelled at Max's use of English idiom.

'No Chinese is taught or spoken at the *lycée*, where they rigidly follow the French national syllabus. But if she went to the Anglo-

Chinese College in the International Settlement, she would have the best of two worlds – no, three. The pupils are a mix of English, American and Chinese. They are very well prepared by the time they get to university.'

'Yes, please,' said Yu Yan, her slim hands with their long fingers clutched together as if in prayer.

Katya's own background and breeding told her that no well-brought-up woman was complete without a knowledge of French culture and the French language. But she was not going to be dogmatic.

'Max, how do we get Yu Yan into the college?' she asked briskly.

Yu Yan jumped up from her chair and flung her arms around her neck. 'Thank you, Katya, thank you!' she cried. Then she walked over to Max and, without hesitation, kissed him on his ruined cheek. 'Thank you, too, Max,' she said with a little smile.

Max's one eye shone with a tear. He spoke again. He was in control of the proceedings, and everyone deferred to him. It just seemed natural. Katya began to understand why Svyet was so in thrall to him.

'The Anglo-Chinese is not easy to get into. But I think I am right in saying that your boss, Gulya, is a college trustee. You should ask Monty to put in a good word for Yu Yan.'

'I will speak to Monty,' replied Gulya, smiling at Yu Yan. 'I am told I have unusual influence with him.'

'Perhaps he is in love with you,' said Svyet, turning to her husband, with just a touch of the old familiar acid in her voice. 'Max says he's been terribly lonely since his wife died.' Max nodded in agreement.

Gulya sprang indignantly to Monty's defence. 'He may have a soft spot for me, but he is the most respectable man on God's earth!'

Next, they had to decide where Yu Yan should live. She agreed that it would be best for her to stay with Gulya during the working week and spend the weekends with Katya. Gulya would have to ask Sue, of course, but she didn't expect any difficulties there, especially if Yu Yan took Toby for a walk every now and then. With both Sue and Gulya out at work, the dog was well-nigh uncontrollable for lack of exercise.

Having taken all these decisions, Katya decided they should

celebrate at the cinema. The latest Fred Astaire and Ginger Rogers was showing at the Rialto. She started to clear the table. Max sprang to his feet and said in Russian, 'Let me help you, Katya.'

He went into the kitchen with her, pulling the door to without quite closing it.

'I must say,' he said, continuing in Russian, 'Yu Yan is very impressive. I think those are good decisions we have taken about her future.'

'Thanks in large part to you, Max. Give me those plates, I'll deal with them,' she replied, also in Russian. She sensed that Max was about to change gear.

Max made a self-deprecating gesture before handing Katya the dirty crockery.

'By the way, talking of the future, I have definitely got that job at the *Shanghai Times*. My first column will appear next Tuesday. I want to catch the readers' interest with a bit of a bang. I'm thinking of writing about tensions in our Chinese neighbourhood and the danger of war. Do you think you may have something of interest from your dinner tomorrow?'

Here we go, thought Katya. She started washing the plates. As often happened when she needed to focus single-mindedly on something, an extraneous thought wandered in from outside. I must look again at getting a maid, she mused. I will ruin my hands in this water.

'Max,' she said, 'everyone is writing about a coming war between China and Japan. Can't you find something more original?'

There, she thought, that will sting him.

'Oh, but I plan a new angle, if I can gather the evidence. That is where Socquet de la Tour's dinner comes in. I am told there will be a Japanese general present.'

'As usual, Max, you are so well informed,' she said with a little smile. 'There will indeed be a Japanese general present. He's called Aiko. He's the military attaché at the consulate general, says Socquet de la Tour. Do you know him?'

'I certainly know the name,' Max replied, 'but I can't put a face to it. Something tells me he's rather important. Go on, Katya.'

'There's not much more to tell. He's apparently a contender for guest of honour. His rival is the Archimandrite of Shanghai, or whatever he's called. It's all turned into a nasty spat over protocol. Poor Socquet de la Tour is in an agony of indecision. I told him that in the old days in St Petersburg the priest would have outranked the soldier. Anyway, I'll probably be stuck between the two of them. What's this about a new angle?'

Katya was now washing teaspoons and forks. Max was drying the plates.

'Well, what if we are too fixated on a Sino-Japanese war to the exclusion of something much bigger?'

'What do you mean, Max? I don't understand,' she replied, looking up as she placed the silverware on the draining board.

'What if, Katya, despite all the talk to the contrary, the next war is going to be between Japan and the Soviet Union? All this massing of Japanese troops, as if in preparation for an assault on China, may be nothing more than a feint. That would be typical of Japan. What if our poor, ravished Motherland is the real target of Hirohito and his army?'

Max's scarred face was once again going various shades of pink as he warmed to his subject.

'Do you have any evidence?' Katya asked. 'Don't forget it was Chiang Kai-shek himself who told me that he expected a Japanese attack this year.'

'I know. And, right now, I have only rumours, straws in the wind. But enough to make me think it's a story worth pursuing.'

Max put the last of the dried plates into a cupboard beside his head. Then he turned rather dramatically towards Katya.

'It's what I'd like to put into my inaugural article.'

'Well, Max, I'll see what I can do.'

'I would be most grateful.'

Chapter 42

As it happened, General Socquet de la Tour seated Katya between M. Delvaux, a senior executive from the Renault car company (the general hoped to get a job with them after he retired from the army); and M. Renard, the Roman Catholic Apostolic Vicar of Shanghai ('Almost a bishop,' explained Socquet de la Tour). They were both garrulous Frenchmen. All Katya had to do was to look interested, smile and from time to time say *'Vraiment?'* or *'Vous avez raison'* or *'Formidable!'*

The encounter with General Aiko ('Frightful bore,' said Socquet de la Tour, just before introducing him to Katya) took place in German before dinner. He was actually quite interesting with a profound knowledge of German literature and music. Katya and he had a lively conversation. Then things took a darker turn.

'My dream,' said Aiko, 'is to watch Wagner's Ring Cycle at Bayreuth with Herr Hitler.'

'Why with Herr Hitler?' asked Katya.

'Because Wagner is made for Hitler and Hitler is the greatest European statesman of his age. We could do with someone like him in Japan. Civilisation demands order.'

Katya was taken aback. Shanghai was remote from Europe. But even at such a distance she could feel Hitler's belligerent menace.

'But, General, Hitler threatens another Great War.'

'Dear Countess, war cleanses the impurities of a nation. I look forward to the coming conflict with China.'

Katya did not know how to respond. She was saved by the gong and General Socquet de la Tour's coming to escort her into dinner.

Two hours later, after the guests had left, she sat down with him and his aide-de-camp at one end of the dining table and let them debrief her.

She was exhausted and did not have much to tell. The Renault man had talked, not uninterestingly, about the strikes in the company's factories, caused largely, he said, by the Communists. They should all be gaoled. At the same time, the situation in Europe was darkening. Perhaps Renault could find a market in China. He was going to see an Englishman, M. Montgomery Carleton-Sinclair, to discuss the possibilities.

The Apostolic Vicar had had his own lament. His French flock had left behind in *la Belle France* every vestige of morality and decent living. All they wanted to do in Shanghai was frequent clubs of ill repute. Of course, it did not help living cheek-by-jowl with the Chinese, who smoked hashish and sold their womenfolk to satisfy the lusts of decadent Europeans. It was time for the Church to set up a new organisation and take the fight to sin. He would call it the Catholic Daughters of Virtue. Would the countess care to be its first president? Katya had no wish to do any such thing. She had an easy excuse. She reminded him that she was Russian Orthodox. The Apostolic Vicar turned his back on her without another word and started a conversation with his other dinner partner.

As for General Aiko, said Katya, he admired most things German, in particular Adolf Hitler, and welcomed war as a purifying force. He had been in no doubt that a conflict with China was coming later in the year.

Socquet de la Tour seemed inordinately satisfied.

'I knew, dear Countess, that it was an inspired idea to have you as my official hostess – and so it has proved. There is much of interest in what you have just related. Now, I can see that you are tired and we must detain you no longer. Lieutenant Combloux, please be kind enough to escort the Countess to her abode.'

'*Oui, mon Général. C'est un honneur, Comtesse.*'

The young officer (he could only be in his twenties, thought Katya) closed his notebook and bowed to her. Then he walked round the table and gave her his arm. Katya took it gratefully. He was tall and good-looking. I would like to have a man in my life again, she thought. Even Je Jin had been pressing her to find one.

Lieutenant Combloux held open the door of the army staff car for her. He then moved to sit in the front next to the driver. A glass partition separated the front and back seats of the vehicle.

'Lieutenant Combloux, please sit with me. I would like to ask you a question,' Katya said in French.

The lieutenant climbed in beside her, his expression a mixture of curiosity and mild embarrassment. They were soon speeding through the night streets of Shanghai.

'Lieutenant, is it true what everyone is saying? That before the year is out there will be war between China and Japan?'

'That is our belief, Countess. We are braced for a Japanese attack on Shanghai sometime in the summer months. My leave has been cancelled for the rest of the year.'

'But surely the Japanese will not attack the foreign enclaves?'

'We don't think so. They do not want to do anything now to alienate the big foreign powers. But war is not as precise and scientific as we soldiers sometimes claim. Shells and bombs go astray all too easily. I don't believe that the French Concession and the International Settlement will be under deliberate and direct attack from the Japanese. But Shanghai will become a dangerous place.'

'Some Russians I know have got it into their heads that the Japanese manoeuvres are a distraction and that they will attack the Soviet Union through Mongolia. What is your view, Lieutenant?'

'I don't think that it is a distraction. The Japanese want to consolidate their position in China. If they don't, they in turn will be vulnerable to attack from the Soviet Union.'

Combloux paused, his brow furrowing. They were not far from Katya's street.

'Not all my superior officers agree with me. But I think that as soon as Stalin has replaced the senior officers he purged last year, it is he who will be ready to strike the Japanese from the west. In my personal view there will be two wars. The first will be between Japan and China, very soon. It will be ferocious and Japan will prevail. The second will be between Japan and the Soviet Union, perhaps next year. It is hard to predict who will emerge the victor.'

Lieutenant Combloux finished his little speech just as the car was pulling up to the kerb by Katya's block of flats. He leapt from the car to open her door. He helped her from the vehicle and gave a little bow, as they stood facing each other on the pavement. He brushed his lips over her outstretched hand.

'Thank you, Lieutenant, that was most interesting.'

'It was an honour, Countess.'

'What is your name?'

'Stéphane, Countess.'

'Stéphane, please give my regards to the General.'

Stéphane looked at Katya. He coughed and hesitated.

'Yes, Stéphane, what is it?' she asked.

'I think I may have been more candid this evening than my senior officers would have wished . . . ' Stéphane's voice tailed off.

Katya smiled. The boy really was charming. Ideal for Gulya.

'I will not breathe your name to anyone. Thank you for seeing me home. Good night.'

Katya sat up in bed, a cup of herbal tea in her hand. She had more than enough material to give Max tomorrow night and the Japanese the day after. Stéphane had been a bonus.

It was only a small step for her mind to turn once again to the vexed question of Max. He was a traitor to his class. He represented a regime that had smashed everything she believed in, that had stolen her family's property and that had exterminated those of her relatives who had chosen to stay behind in Russia after the Revolution. He had been Andryusha's mortal foe and would have killed him if he could. It was possible that his presence in Shanghai and courtship of Svyet had something to do with his vendetta against her estranged husband. He was a senior member of the Soviet state's most pitiless and implacable agency. Svyet had grown fearful of him. He had not hesitated to turn her – his own mother-in-law – into one of his sources of information, possibly endangering her life.

That was pretty damning.

On the other hand, much of the evidence was circumstantial. Max was after all her older daughter's husband, even if Svyet was coming to realise that she might have bitten off more than she could chew. Much could be explained by coincidence. And though she loathed the Soviets, both parties had a common enemy in the Japanese. At the very least she and Max were temporary allies of convenience.

There was something else. Her instincts were screaming at her that Max was deeply troubled. His astonishing self-assurance marched in harness with a matching vulnerability. The tension between the two must be all but unbearable. It might be something to be entered in mitigation. She needed to find out yet more about him.

The jury was still out.

Just before she fell asleep, another thought washed over her. It had been lurking nearby for some time. If war was coming to Shanghai, what did that mean for her daughters, for Yu Yan and for her? She had read about the conflict of 1932 and the terrible damage it had inflicted. Would 1937 be like that? Should they stay or should they go? They had only just arrived.

Chapter 43

Max arrived at Katya's flat as if he had come straight from playing in an entertainment by Ivor Novello. Under his blue and white striped blazer and blue and red Shanghai Club cravat, he was a vision in white – shirt, trousers, socks and shoes.

'Max, you look the perfect Englishman,' she said, believing nothing of the sort. He embodied the foreigner's idea of an upper-class Englishman. He looked like a certain type of hanger-on at the Tsar's court when she was a debutante. It was at one of the Romanovs' summer receptions at the Peterhof that the French Ambassador, who had taken a bit of a fancy to her, had muttered in her ear that it all looked like a fancy-dress party with an English theme.

*

He had just come from the Sunday *thé dansant* at the Shanghai Club, an occasion for which he had dressed carefully. He thought it most important that he should fit in with the many Englishmen who were invariably present. It was all about instilling confidence in those from whom you wished to extract information. One Englishman always trusted another Englishman from the same background. If you could not be an Englishman – and were badly scarred to boot – the next best thing was to dress and speak like an Englishman.

The NKVD, which was set up under cover of the Soviet Trade Office in the International Settlement, followed Max from time to time on the good Stalinist principle, borrowed from Juvenal, of '*Quis custodiet ipsos custodes?*' – 'Who watches the watchers?'

The NKVD noted that Max spent a lot of time at the cinema. One day they called him in and asked why, suspecting that he was guilty of sexual deviancy pursued in the darkness of a picture house. Max had laughed out loud, much to their irritation. They should have noticed, he said, that the film was invariably one starring the famous English actor Leslie Howard. It was on Howard that he modelled his English accent, better to penetrate the inner workings of English society in Shanghai.

He had also, he told them, carefully studied, for sartorial guidance, illustrated editions of novels by the equally famous English author P. G. Wodehouse. His NKVD colleagues should congratulate him on his assiduous preparation and attention to detail. They did no such thing, of course. Max knew that he would not be forgiven for making them look like fools.

The *thé dansant* was always a hive of intrigue and gossip, most of it frivolous or adulterous. It was one of those rare places where a man could invite a woman who was not his wife to dance without immediate damage to the reputation of either.

Equipped with his Leslie Howard accent and Bertie Wooster clothes (he would never grasp, unlike Katya, the essential absurdity of Wodehouse's characters), Max moved among the guests with practised ease.

The room was packed with a dozen different nationalities. There was a small dance floor surrounded by crowded tables and people standing in groups. Waiters in white tunics, in the main Chinese, moved from table to table. A quartet of Russian musicians, all in dinner jackets with slicked-back hair and pencil-thin moustaches, played dance hits from New York and London shows. Most of them were refugees from the Astoria Hotel in St Petersburg. Unknown to Max, the bass player was a captain in the NKVD.

Max moved clockwise around the outer edges of the room. He stopped at this and that group, picking off individuals who might have something of value to say. He never danced, because, though he loved women, he had decided that they were usually poor sources of useful information.

By the time he had to leave for Katya's, Max was worried. He had gathered quite a few nuggets of information, but they did not add up. On the contrary, they pointed in opposing directions, above all on the matter to which, so he had been told, Comrade Stalin, with mounting impatience, wanted an answer.

Stalin had survived and prospered by judging others by his own standards of deceit and violence and by moving against them before they could move against him. It was now the army's turn to feel the lash of Stalin's obsessive persecution complex, which presented itself as a dread of traitors and counter-revolutionaries. Marshals, generals and the officer class as a whole were being hacked down indiscriminately. Even Marshal Tukhachevsky, the victor of the civil war, had not escaped the executioner's bullet. You can never feel safe, thought Max, particularly if you come from a noble background like the marshal and myself.

The Red Army was now in no condition to fight a major campaign. One of Stalin's rules of life was always to exploit weakness. He could not believe that Japan, which had always coveted Russian territory, would not choose 1937 to take a bite of the Soviet Union. He had demanded that the NKVD confirm his suspicion or present clear evidence to the contrary.

Max could do neither. He feared that if he had not come up with something credible by the end of the week, the NKVD's – and Stalin's – patience would snap.

As he drove to Katya's flat, he laughed sardonically to himself. Could he seriously look to his mother-in-law to save him from Stalin? It was absurd to think so. He would have to make something up for his next report to Moscow. Then just disappear: make a run for Hong Kong and there take a ship to Manila. He could go anywhere from there. If he refused an order to return to Moscow they would murder him, and maybe Svyet. She was getting on his nerves more than he had expected. He could just slip away. She knew very little about him.

*

Max settled down with a gin and tonic in Katya's drawing room. She had a glass of white wine.

'So,' asked Katya, 'your first article comes out when?'

'Wednesday,' replied Max. 'I hope it will become a regular feature.'

Broadwick had not needed much persuading to take him on. Max had no need to wave pornographic pictures at him. He gave Max a contract for four weekly pieces. If the readers liked them, he would extend the contract to a year. He agreed to Max's proposal that he should write anonymously under the byline of The Thunderer.

'You remember, Katya, don't you, my hunch that the Japanese troops massing to the north would suddenly turn right and attack the Soviet Union, not China? Did you get the chance to mention this to the Japanese general?'

'Max, let's first be clear about something. I am happy to help you. But that help depends on your never mentioning my name in any of your articles. General Socquet de la Tour relies on my utmost discretion. You must never write anything that would compromise me.'

'But of course, Katya,' said Max, attempting sincerity. 'You have my word as a Russian nobleman. What I write will be without attribution. The last thing I want to do is compromise a valuable source. I would be shooting myself in the foot.'

His foot, thought Katya, was a thousand times more reliable than his word. But as long as she was useful, he would protect her.

'Good. I'm glad we understand each other, because it is the *only* way this arrangement can work.'

Max nodded vigorously. He took out of a white canvas bag a pad and a pencil. He leaned back in the armchair, crossed his legs and perched the pad on his thigh.

'I'm ready when you are, Katya.'

Katya was clear what she was going to say. It would be enriched with a little poetic licence mixed with an anonymous contribution from Lieutenant Combloux.

'I spoke to General Aiko – in German – for quite a while. Most of our conversation was about German art and music. He worships Wagner and the Ring Cycle. Quite interesting, actually.'

Katya noticed that Max's foot was starting to twitch with impatience.

'He loves all things German. He is an admirer of Hitler,' Katya continued, as Max's foot twitched ever faster.

'Then I told him that there were many in the Russian community who thought that Japan would attack the Soviet Union this year and that its mobilisation in the north was a feint. Who should I believe?'

'Precisely the question, Katya. Brilliant.' Max's foot stopped twitching abruptly.

'Aiko, Max, could not have been clearer. They have no plan to attack the Soviets. The last thing they want is a war on two fronts. To emphasise their peaceful intentions, they will soon offer Stalin a mutual non-aggression pact. The Japanese foreign minister will himself go to Moscow and put it on the table, with full powers to negotiate on the spot.'

Max's eye blazed more brilliantly than Katya had ever seen before.

'A mutual non-aggression pact! The devil! *Chyort!* That's the first I have heard of such a thing. If the Japs are bluffing, it's the bluff of the century. My God, what a story, Katya. This is explosive.'

'Really, Max?' she said, feigning innocence. 'I thought everyone did these pacts nowadays.'

'That's as may be, Katya. But to the best of my knowledge, this will be news to the Kremlin.'

And what knowledge is that, thought Katya. Max's excitement had dislodged a few bricks from his wall of discretion.

He could not wait to write his column. He rose to leave. She tugged at his sleeve.

'Don't be in such a rush, Max. I have something else to tell you,' she said. He reluctantly sat down again. This time his whole leg began to shake.

'After dinner I found myself sitting with Socquet de la Tour and some of his officers. They were half discussing, half complaining about the cancellation of leave for the rest of the year. The general told them in no uncertain terms to stop whining. The order had been inevitable. There would be a Japanese attack on Shanghai, though not one, according to intelligence sources, directed at the French Concession or the International Settlement. But, Socquet de la Tour said, you never knew. The garrison would have to be on high alert.'

'A fat lot of good that will do them,' said Max fiercely. 'They have maybe fifteen hundred men, a few guns and tanks and a squadron of mixed aircraft. There are tens of thousands in the Kwantung Army. It would be over in a day, a morning. May I now go and write my piece, Katya?'

'No,' said Katya, her hand now resting on Max's wrist. 'There is a postscript.'

'Can't it wait till tomorrow?' Max was seething with impatience.

'I think, Max, you will want to hear this before committing pen to paper.'

Katya stood up and walked around the room. She suddenly saw Max as a small boy, sitting before her in class, pencil in hand, waiting to take dictation.

'Socquet de la Tour went home soon after that. Some of the officers stayed behind for a last drink, while I was waiting for my driver. I listened to their conversation. They thought that if the Japanese campaign against Chiang Kai-shek went well, they would immediately thereafter turn their attention to the Soviets.'

'But not this year?' asked Max.

'They mentioned 1938. They talked of Japan's having one strategy and two enemies.'

'I know what that means. Moscow must get ready for war in '38 or '39. The non-aggression pact won't be worth the paper it's printed on. It is a grand deception.'

With that Max leapt to his feet, unable to contain himself further, bade farewell to Katya and shot out of the room. She heard his feet clattering down the stairs. He did not even wait for the lift.

She smiled to herself. Bait taken.

Chapter 44

The more Max wrote up his report to Moscow, the more he recognised the value of what Katya had told him. He would say to Stalin that he need not fear a Japanese attack this year . . . no, better not say that, because Stalin wasn't afraid of anything! To suggest otherwise was to risk the Gulag or worse.

Better just tell him that there was no risk of a Japanese attack in 1937, because they wanted to defeat Chiang Kai-shek first. If anything, the Japanese feared a Soviet assault while they were dealing with the Chinese. The Japanese foreign minister would soon approach Comrade Stalin with a proposal for a mutual non-aggression pact. Except that the pact was doomed to the briefest of lives. Once the Chinese were defeated, Japan would turn on the Soviet Union in 1938 or 1939. The Japanese 'one strategy for two enemies' was built on the blackest treachery.

Max typed the report at the Trade Office. Once he had finished and was content for it to be sent, the text was encrypted and despatched by wireless to Moscow.

The reaction of his NKVD colleagues was typically sour and fearful. Nobody liked to express a firm opinion to Moscow.

'You're taking a risk with that report of yours,' said one of them. 'You'd better be right about the Japanese. Otherwise, it will be the Lubyanka and a bullet in the back of the head for all of us.'

Or a medal and promotion, thought Max. What really upset his colleagues was the thought that he might have stolen a march on them.

The report once sent, Max was immediately faced by the *Shanghai Times'* looming deadline. He had to come up with an expurgated, yet expanded, version of his top-secret report. He could not avoid mentioning the non-aggression pact. That was the headline, after all. It would immediately establish his reputation as one of Shanghai's top columnists. Was he clever enough to be able to do this without Moscow accusing him of treason – of revealing state secrets intended for Stalin's eyes only?

After much tearing of sheets of paper out of his typewriter and throwing them in a ball across the room, Max settled on a paragraph:

Shanghai is an international city of rumours, which blow in on the summer breeze rippling the waters of the Wangpoo River. Some are extinguished as soon as uttered. Others gather strength with every day that passes. Among the latter, blowing now at gale force, are insistent reports that our city will once again be the focus of hostilities between the Republic of China and the Empire of Japan. Behind the noise of the oncoming storm, a lesser sound can also be detected – a discreet crescendo of whispers that the god of war will invite the god of diplomacy to be his companion. To what end? I hear you ask. To ensure, so I am told by reliable sources of high authority, that the vortex of war does not suck in neighbouring powers such as the USSR, either by accident or design. To avoid any such risk, your correspondent has even heard talk of a mutual non-aggression pact between the Russians and the Japanese being taken out of the diplomatic toolbox and dusted down.

Max read the paragraph several times. It was a bit mannered, a bit arch even. It did not say in so many words that there was a Japanese plan for a non-aggression pact with Russia. But those who followed these things would immediately understand and the word would get around. Moscow, which had liked the idea of his becoming a journalist, could hardly reproach him for writing about interesting rumours.

*

Alan Broadwick was delighted with his new columnist's first offering.

Al, as he was called, read it twice in silence, standing in his pokey office which reeked of tobacco smoke. He assumed that Max was talking about a Japanese initiative with the Russians, though it might be the other way round. It did not matter. It was a scoop either way.

'Max, I am minded to put this on the front page. The stuff about a non-aggression pact is ... interesting.' This was praise indeed from someone usually so taciturn and undemonstrative. 'Who is your source?'

'It was given to me by someone of the utmost reliability, who heard it fall from the lips of an impeccable Japanese source.'

'Max, I don't usually publish anything unless I know exactly where it comes from.'

'Al, you know I can't tell you more.'

Max held his breath. He did not want to be faced with a choice between having Al spike his piece or revealing Aiko's name or, worse still, Katya's.

'What if it's propaganda, a false trail? I can't have the *Times* being made a fool of.'

'Then I would tell you the source and you could unmask him in the paper, if you wished. That in itself would be an interesting story.'

Broadwick lit a Senior Service. He inhaled deeply. The paper desperately needed a boost. If circulation did not pick up, he would be back at the bank asking for a loan. He was not sure that he would get one this time. Cigarette between yellow-stained fingers, he looked up at Max and grunted. Then he said, 'Fair enough, Max. I suppose you won't tell me the intermediary either?'

'My lips are forever sealed,' Max replied with a smile of relief.

'Hm, must be someone close to you,' said Broadwick with a mildly amused light in his eyes. 'It's not one of your girls at the brothel, is it? Who's been servicing a Jap general?'

'Permit me to use a phrase that I have just learned from an English comedy film – you are not so green as you are cabbage-looking.'

Max immediately regretted his rashness. He had given Broadwick a clue. That was his vanity speaking. For an instant Broadwick looked quizzically at Max. Then he exploded with laughter, something he had not done for months.

'I haven't heard that since I was a child in Liverpool. And I have to come to China and meet a Russian to hear it again! I think I may have come close to guessing your source,' Broadwick said, as he rang for a messenger.

Within half a minute there was a knock at the door and a grubby English teenage boy in shorts and a Fair Isle sweater came into the room.

'Harry,' said Broadwick, 'take this to Cho. Top speed. Don't give it to anyone but Cho. I'd better put it in an envelope. Off you go. Chop, chop.'

'Yessir, Mr Broadwick, sir.'

As the boy raced out of the door, clutching the envelope to his breast, Broadwick turned to Max and said, 'Seriously, though, you exceeded my expectations. Well done, Max.'

A surge of emotion passed through Max's mutilated face. Broadwick's praise had disarmed him. It made him feel pathetically grateful. Max suddenly realised that he was on the verge of weeping. It was a terrible weakness, which he just could not overcome. He never used to be like this. The bomb had wrecked his face and was still playing havoc with his emotions.

Max pulled himself together and replied, 'Thank you. I appreciate that.'

They smiled at each other and shook hands.

*

Just after dawn Katya picked up the newspaper from the kiosk on the street corner. Goodness, Max was on the front page! Her pulse began to race as she read his column. She was standing on the pavement outside her apartment block, hunched over the paper, oblivious to the waking world around her. Not a mention of her or the dinner. She felt dizzy with relief. Her legs were shaking. She returned upstairs to her flat and downed a glass of vodka.

A little later, Major Seko called Captain Abe. They were both standing in their respective office doorways at the Japanese consulate general. Seko threw him a copy of the latest *Shanghai Times*. He had a broad grin. 'Read the front page. Our Russian countess is worth her weight in gold.'

Fifteen minutes later, an unencrypted message went from the consulate general to certain headquarters in Tokyo and Harbin. It was short. It said, 'Mission accomplished.'

Meanwhile, Richard Sorge, a prominent German journalist, working for the *Frankfurter Zeitung* in Tokyo, who was also a Russian intelligence agent, took a phone call from a friend in Shanghai, just as he was making mid-morning coffee. He listened intently as the friend read him Max's column.

'Who is The Thunderer?' he asked.

'Al won't say,' said the voice from Shanghai. 'Why don't you come down and use your silken powers of persuasion?'

'I might do just that. I haven't been to Shanghai for a while.'

'I'll book you into the Metropole.'

'No, don't do that. I'd much prefer the French Concession. See if you can get me into the *Club Militaire*. Mention the name of Major Crédence.'

'Next weekend?'

'Yes, next weekend.'

No sooner had Sorge put down the phone than it rang again. It appeared to be from his head office in Frankfurt, but he knew that it was not. The voice, which spoke with a Russian accent, said to him in German, 'Get over to Shanghai. There's a big story there. Our friends will be expecting you.'

All roads lead to Shanghai, thought Sorge.

Broadwick did not have a moment's peace all morning. He took telephone calls from military attachés, diplomats, a businessman or two and fellow journalists. The questions were the same. Who was The Thunderer? Who was the source? Broadwick was opaque in reply. This only stoked the flames of speculation.

Just before lunch a call came in from the Generalissimo's military assistant, a colonel with good American English from a childhood spent in San Francisco.

'So, Al, you think it's war between us and the Japs? Who is this Thunderer?'

'You know I can't tell you. But I can guarantee he knows what he's talking about. He has the right contacts at the right level.'

'Any of these Japanese, by any chance?'

'Yes, but don't ask me who.'

'I won't. Sounds like Aiko, though. Drink sometime, Al?'

'Anytime. Regards to the Generalissimo. Time for an interview before we go to war?'

'Sure. Why not? I'll talk to him. I owe you.'

Chapter 45

These were turbulent, violent times in China. Katya, ever mindful of what had happened to her family in the Russian Revolution, was beset by the dark fear that once again they would find themselves destitute. More and more the fear broke surface in her sleep.

Her fear found its obsessive focus in documents. She had an old Tsarist passport – no longer valid, of course, but at least they attested to her identity. She had temporary Chinese papers, which she had been renewing every other year. Then she had special, secret Japanese papers, mainly for protection from marauding Japanese troops and overzealous Japanese officials. These last she kept behind a brick in the unused chimney of her apartment.

By contrast, Gulya had almost nothing. She still kept the *laissez-passer* that the Japanese had given her in Harbin, though it was long out of date. But that was it, apart from a letter of support from the Victoria Trading Company.

It was Monty who pointed out to Gulya that she was officially stateless. Gulya then asked her mother: shouldn't they go to the Soviet consulate to get a new passport? 'After all, we are still Russian,' she added.

'The only way to get a Soviet passport is to go back to the USSR. But they would arrest us as enemies of the people and send us to a labour camp.'

Gulya was thoroughly alarmed. 'But what about the special protection we had in Harbin, thanks to the Japanese?'

Katya took her time to reply and weighed her words very carefully.

'That was all down to the late Mr Amae and the language lessons I used to give him and his family. What a tragedy his death was! The documents we have would help if the Japanese were to invade Shanghai. But it doesn't alter the fact that we are stateless.'

'So, what's the answer, Mama? Should I ask Monty?'

'Monty can do little to help. The English have turned their backs on us Russians. They abandoned the Tsar and his family to their fate. There's only one way.'

'What *do* you mean, Mama?'

'Marriage,' said Katya. 'If, say, one were to marry an Englishman or a Frenchman. Sometimes Je Jin suggests it for me, so that I am better protected.'

Katya fell silent and a distant look came into her eyes. She gazed out of the window at the setting sun. Her eyes glistened with tears. Suddenly she spoke, with a startling vehemence. 'I told him that the thought of sharing a bed with another man disgusted me. General Socquet de la Tour will, so I am told, propose to me as soon as he has buried his wife, who is apparently on her deathbed in France. He's not a bad chap, but physically I can't think of anything worse. I told Je Jin that. He laughed. I said it was no joke.'

Je Jin would still come to Katya most nights. She never knew whether she was awake or dreaming. He looked so real. He would stand at the foot of her bed. They would talk. Sometimes she would reach out to touch him, but then he would fade immediately from view.

'But maybe Je Jin is right,' Gulya replied. 'For the sake of a French passport and a secure life in France, couldn't you just close your eyes and think of something else?'

'For me that's no great prize,' she replied. 'My soul will always be Russian. One of these days, God willing, I will return to Mother Russia, if only in a coffin.'

'It's not the same for me, Mama,' replied Gulya, 'because I can't remember anything about Russia. I don't have anything against Russians. I gave away my virginity to a Russian. But to be honest, I'd rather marry a Frenchman or an Englishman – or even an American.'

'It sounds like you have someone in mind.'

'Actually, I have.'

*

His name was Olivier Marnier and he worked for M. Smet, managing director of the Compagnie Tonkinoise de Commerce, based in Hanoi, in French Indochina. The CTC was keen to expand trade with China and had just signed a contract with the Victoria Trading Company. Gulya had met Olivier when Monty held a champagne reception to celebrate the deal.

Katya learned from Gulya that Olivier Marnier came from solid bourgeois stock, the son of veterinary surgeons from Amiens in northern France. They had grand ambitions for their only son, which he consistently disappointed with his resistance to schooling and inability to avoid getting into scrapes. It was thanks to M. Smet, an old family friend who, according to gossip, was his mother's lover, that Olivier was offered a position with the CTC. His parents had been relieved to get their wayward son off their hands.

Olivier was not really good-looking, but he was not unattractive. He was no intellectual, but he was not stupid. He was mad about sport, loved a practical joke and was an excellent dancer. And he had already proposed to Gulya.

With Monty's agreement, M. Smet had left Olivier behind in Shanghai to oversee the contract and look after the CTC's interests. He was given a little flat in the company building and a posting for six months. Olivier was near the end of the first period when he went down on one knee in the garden of the French Officers' Club and asked for Gulya's hand.

As she and her mother went through the pros and cons of marriage to Olivier, it became clear to Katya that Gulya would accept. Privately, she felt her daughter could have done better, but she kept that thought to herself. Under the circumstances, he would do.

Chapter 46

The following evening, Olivier took Gulya to her favourite place, Le Perroquet Bleu, where she accepted his proposal of marriage. The night passed in a blur of wild dancing, lobster, truffles, kisses, peach sorbets and champagne. Olivier, delirious with happiness, made plans for their future life in Hanoi in an almost unstoppable monologue, before dropping Gulya back at Sue's flat, where she fell instantly asleep, with Toby the dog for company. Just before dawn, she was woken by a noise. Thinking it one of Toby's explosive farts, she tried to go back to sleep, but it was nothing of the kind. It was a Chinese mortar aimed at advancing Japanese marines.

*

Katya, who was awake already, worrying whether she had given Gulya the right marital advice, immediately recognised mortar and rifle fire. She had heard them too often in Harbin.

*

Ever the light sleeper, Max woke up with a start. 'Damn! What was that? Don't tell me they've started. I'll have to rewrite my column.'

*

Richard Sorge, smoking opium with two Chinese prostitutes in his room at the French Officers' Club, heard the mortar shell and saw its flash across the sky. Then there was the rattle of rifle fire. He sighed and reached for the more uninhibited of the two girls.

*

Major Seko, shaken awake by his frightened wife, was shouting down the phone to Captain Abe, 'What the hell is going on?'

*

General Aiko was awoken by a call from his military secretary. 'Sir, there seems to have been an exchange of fire between our forces and the Chinese on the northern perimeter of the International Settlement.'

'To be expected. Is it the marines on our side?'

'I think so, sir. First reports say it was a detachment of marines from one of our warships tied up on the Wangpoo. I'll get that confirmed.'

'No need. Put me through to the admiral.'

*

Monty Carleton-Sinclair, wide awake after the explosion, peered out of his bedroom window towards the sound of rifle fire in the north. He could just see a plume of smoke rising vertically in the early dawn's still air. That was too close for comfort, he thought.

*

General Aiko summoned his military secretary.

'I have just spoken to the admiral. He tells me that a detachment of marines, no more than a platoon, was sent discreetly to probe Chinese defences on the northern perimeter. The marines were soon spotted by the Chinese, who fired a mortar. The platoon responded with a single volley and withdrew. No casualties. We have told the Chinese it was a mistake by an overzealous officer, who will be reprimanded. The incident is officially closed.'

'The Chinese reaction shows them to have been on the highest alert, sir,' said the military secretary.

'Quite so,' said Aiko. 'It will be the devil's own job to catch them by surprise when the moment comes. That alone is a useful thing to have learned.'

*

Generalissimo Chiang Kai-shek listened to his military assistant's report over breakfast.

'Speak to me in English, Colonel Jimmy. I need to practise,' said the Generalissimo in English. He and Madame Chiang called him Colonel Jimmy because when speaking English he sounded just like the American film actor James Stewart. 'You don't mind us calling you Colonel Jimmy, do you, Colonel Jimmy?'

'Thank you, sir, I am honoured,' said the colonel, inordinately proud of any resemblance to the great star. 'Despite the apology, it was obviously a probing mission by the Japanese.'

'Casualties? Prisoners?'

'None. The shell flew way over the Japanese. They hit some flowerpots and a horse trough.'

'Tell the world the Japanese fired first in an attack of unbridled aggression. That will infuriate them. At least they will know that we are well prepared. Their attack can't be long coming. We must discover the date.'

'Well, sir, there might just be a way. You remember that anonymous article in the *Shanghai Times* I showed you last week? The one that said the Kwantung Army's objective is definitely us and not the Russians? I tried to find out from the editor the identity of the author. He wouldn't say, of course. But he didn't deny it when I suggested the source was Aiko. So, it must be somebody who's been talking to Aiko.'

'But that, Colonel, takes us no further forward if this editor won't speak. What's his name?'

'Al – Alan – Broadwick. I think there may be a way of getting him to speak, sir. He wants an interview with you. You should give him one in return for his telling us the name of the columnist and the identity of the source.'

The Generalissimo thought for a moment. He and his wife, a public figure in her own right, were good at manipulating the press.

'Good idea, Colonel. Fix it up. I need to get a few messages out to the English-speaking world anyway – otherwise the Japanese will pin the blame for the war on us when it comes.'

'I'll tell Broadwick if he doesn't play ball, you will give the interview to the *New York Times*.'

'Play ball?'

'Cooperate, sir.'

*

A couple of days later, Major Seko asked to see Katya.

He had been caught on the hop by the incident on the northern edge of the International Settlement. The navy never talked to the *Kempeitai*, which it regarded as a bunch of lower-class thugs. The Chinese were making a terrific fuss in the newspapers and on the radio, laying the blame for the incident at Japan's door. Aiko and his people, terrified of saying the wrong thing, were doing nothing to counter the Chinese version of events. Nor was the navy, which did not like soiling its hands on anything as common as public relations.

But something had to be done or, when war did break out, Japan would be automatically blamed. An order had arrived from General Tojo himself demanding immediate action. That was another way of saying that if Seko did not deliver, he faced professional oblivion.

'Countess, we have a problem. You will be aware of the incident the other night,' Seko announced after the briefest of greetings. He looked pale and strained, a sheen of perspiration covering his forehead. Even Captain Abe, usually more urbane, looked anxious.

'Indeed, I am. We are being told that it's all the fault of overzealous Japanese soldiers.'

'That's precisely the problem. It is the opposite of the truth. To be quite frank, Countess, our military and naval commanders have been derelict in their duty. They should have put out long ago an official communiqué with the facts of the incident.'

'Well, Major, to be equally frank, they need to hurry. The Chinese version is close to becoming the received truth. You are widely seen as the aggressors, testing Chinese defences before you start an all-out war,' Katya replied, taking pleasure in piling discomfort on the two Japanese officers.

'That perception,' said Seko, 'must change. But because the navy and army cannot agree on a version of events, we're going to have to take matters into our own hands – and fast.'

'We?'

'Yes, Countess, you and I and your son-in-law.'

'How so, Major?'

'Let me explain.' Seko pointed to a beige folder at his elbow with vertical red stripes on the cover. 'I have here a full account of what happened last Sunday night. It is based on interviews that we ourselves have conducted with the commanding officer and members of the marine platoon. Captain Abe has kindly provided a translation into English.'

Major Seko pushed the folder across the table towards her.

'What do you want me to do with it?' she asked, though she knew most of the answer already.

'We want your brother-in-law to put our version into the *Shanghai Times* in his Thunderer column. Thanks to his first article, it will be read by almost everyone who speaks English. He is the man of . . . '
Seko looked to Abe for help.

'Scoops,' said Abe, taking pleasure in his pronunciation of the word, rolling it around his mouth like a good claret.

'Yes, scoops,' said Seko in staccato imitation. He continued in Japanese, 'The story would have to be presented cleverly, as if from a highly placed and trustworthy source known personally to the author.'

'Of course. It also has the merit of being true,' Katya answered drily. 'I think you can rely on my son-in-law to know how to do this.' This provoked vigorous nodding from the two officers.

'I am going to General Socquet de la Tour's dinner on Saturday,' Katya continued. 'Because of the incident, Aiko has been invited. It will give me perfect cover to brief Max.'

'Brief?' said Seko. 'No, Countess, we want you to give him the paper.' He pointed at the folder with red stripes. 'The article must appear tomorrow or the day after. I am afraid my orders give me no latitude. You must give him the paper today.'

Tension entered the plain little office like a physical presence. Seko had started to sweat again. Abe was inspecting his fingernails, which were a fine example of the manicurist's craft.

'But how on earth would I be able to explain that I had got my hands on such a paper? Max would immediately suspect that I had an, er, unusual relationship with the Japanese.'

'We have thought of that. You could say that it was given to you by a member of Aiko's staff, with whom you are already familiar. Or that it was a member of Socquet de la Tour's staff, who had got it from the Japanese. Or a Japanese diplomat, to whom you are giving English lessons. None of these explanations should arouse Lebedev's suspicions.'

'All right. I will do as you say,' said Katya. 'I will arrange to meet Max tonight. Give me two copies of the paper. You never know where a second copy could come in useful.' She had decided to give the paper to Chiang Kai-shek's people as well.

She took her leave of Seko and Abe and went straight home, where she sat down and thought for a while. Then she telephoned Svyet. Max answered. She invited the two of them for a drink at six o'clock. Max would join them but Svyet could not, which, thought Katya, was all for the best.

'So, Katya, how is life?' asked Max, as soon as they had settled down with their glasses of Chablis.

'Very good, Max, though I am almost overwhelmed by my schedule of classes. It's getting too much.'

'Perhaps you should drop some of those Japanese.'

'I think not, Max. They pay upfront and are excellent pupils. I cannot say that for all the others. But that is what I wanted to talk to you about – the Japanese, or, rather, one Japanese in particular.'

Max's one eye shone forth with its searchlight brilliance. He leaned forward slightly.

'One of my pupils is a Japanese diplomat called Watanabe. He is quite senior, a counsellor, I believe. He was the first to employ me and we have become, not exactly friends, but reasonably comfortable with each other. My lesson with him lasts ninety minutes, half an hour longer than with everyone else.'

'I hope he pays,' Max interjected.

'He does, handsomely. During the first hour I teach him in the usual way. Mr Watanabe is an excellent pupil and learns fast. The extra thirty minutes are, at his request, devoted to unstructured conversation between us. He chooses the topic and off we go. This morning it was the incident between the Chinese garrison and the Japanese marines.'

His single eye was now shining like a cut diamond.

'Go on, Katya,' said Max, 'why the incident?'

'Well, why not? Everyone is talking about it. What's more, Mr Watanabe was bursting to tell me something. It turned out he was enraged by the version of the incident that has taken public hold, heaping all the blame on Japan. He gave me a document in English, which purports to be the true version. According to this, the Chinese fired first without warning.'

'Why would he give this to you, his language teacher?'

'My very question, Max. His reply was that he had learned of my good relations with the consulate in Harbin and that I was someone in whom his people had confidence. I was well connected in Shanghai's international circles. He mentioned General Socquet de la Tour.'

At this Max nodded and murmured, 'Go on, Katya.'

'So, would I, please, pass round this document to my friends in high places? You can't imagine his agitation. The consulate, he said, would publish the document as an official communiqué, but probably not till next week. Max, he almost shouted in frustration.'

'How very interesting,' said Max. His hand was starting to shake. 'Do you have the document?'

'I certainly do. At first I thought of giving it to General Socquet de la Tour – I probably will, in any case – but then I thought of you. Would you be interested in it for your column?'

Katya was almost ashamed of her brazen *fausse naiveté*.

'I certainly would,' said Max, barely able to contain himself.

Katya rummaged in her large bag and pulled out a white foolscap envelope and handed it to Max. He read the document three times. He drained his half-full glass of wine in a single, audible gulp, then he turned to Katya and asked, 'Do I have your authority, Katya, to put this document – with verbatim quotes – in my column next week?'

'Yes, of course. But, Max, you must surely act faster. I am not a journalist, but if you want another scoop, shouldn't you get it out before the Japanese plan to issue the official communiqué?'

Max half turned from her and gazed silently at the setting sun. His first scoop about the non-aggression pact had caused a stir in the circles in which he liked to mix. To follow up with another sensational exclusive – now that would be something. It would seal The Thunderer's reputation.

The Thunderer! He wished he had not agreed to write under that wretched pseudonym. He could not claim any of the kudos and glory for himself. He would have to find a subtle way of letting it be known that he was The Thunderer.

'Well, Max?' Katya asked. She was starting to get a little anxious at his prolonged silence. Max suddenly snapped out of his trance. He slapped his forehead histrionically.

'You're right, Katya. I am getting old. I'll talk to Al tonight. I doubt we could get it into print before the day after tomorrow.'

'That would be just before my next dinner with Socquet. It will give us all something to talk about.'

'May I use your phone?'

'Of course, Max.'

Chapter 47

'We'll put out an extra edition tomorrow afternoon,' said Al Broadwick. His journalist's enthusiasm for a good story broke through the foggy resonance of the phone. The line was always poor, beset by clicks, echoes and changes in volume. I wonder who's eavesdropping, thought Max. It could be anyone or everyone – Chinese, Japanese, British, French and us. Perhaps the Americans, too.

Another thought came to him. Before he devised a clever way of disclosing The Thunderer's identity, one or more of these intelligence services might do it for him and drop his name into the public domain. He would have to prepare for that. Who would do it?

Al's voice broke into his thoughts.

'Max, are you still there? We'll run it as your Thunderer column and as a front-page splash. See you in fifteen minutes at the office. Well done, Max!'

Max put down Katya's telephone, suffused by a euphoric sense of satisfaction at Al's praise. He returned to Katya's drawing room. He drained the last tiny drop of his Chablis, pecked her on the forehead and rapidly made for the front door.

'Sorry, Katya, must dash. The editor thinks we have a very strong story. I am in your debt yet again.'

'So, it will appear on Friday morning?'

'*Naoborot*, on the contrary, tomorrow afternoon in a special edition. Bye!'

Katya waited until, through her open windows, the distinctive sound of Max's Buick faded into the distance. Then she walked into the hall and dialled a number.

'Is that Lieutenant Combloux?' she asked in French. 'This is the Comtesse Polkonina.'

There followed a brief conversation. Fifteen minutes later the lieutenant was ringing Katya's doorbell. He entered her apartment, declined the offer of a glass of wine and took possession of a second white foolscap envelope.

'I have been in such a quandary since the Japanese diplomat gave me this document. But, then I thought of you and the General. You would know what to do with it,' said Katya with an expression of earnest innocence.

'Comtesse, I am sure you have done the right thing.'

'It is not, of course, for me to say, but my instincts tell me the Chinese should be warned. The Japanese may give it to the press, to that *Shanghai Times*, which caused such a stir last week.'

'Personally, Comtesse, I share your instincts and I would wager that the general will be of the same view.'

'I do hope so, Lieutenant. Please give the general my best wishes and tell him that I much look forward to Saturday's dinner.'

Katya then touched the lieutenant's sleeve and, looking him pleadingly in the eyes, said, 'I can rely on your complete discretion as to the provenance of the document that I have just given you?'

'You have my word as a French officer, Comtesse.'

The lieutenant bowed, brushed his lips once more over Katya's hand and took his leave.

That, she thought, had carried out Major Seko's command to the letter. Yet, provided Lieutenant Combloux gave the Japanese document with all despatch to the general, and the general did not dilly-dally in passing it to the Generalissimo, she would also have honoured her higher allegiance to Je Jin and China.

She smiled to herself. 'Well, that wasn't so difficult, was it?' Then a shiver passed through her. Was she getting perhaps a little too attuned to this life of duplicity and deceit?

*

Katya could not have expected more from Lieutenant Combloux. Within the hour he had secured Socquet de la Tour's authority to pass the document to the Chinese. He despatched it by motorcycle courier to Colonel Jimmy with a short covering note that the document might appear somewhere in the press at any moment. Perhaps the *Shanghai Times* again.

The colonel and the Generalissimo discussed the document over breakfast.

'This is a little awkward,' said the Generalissimo, 'as it happens to be true. The *Shanghai Times* has it, eh?'

'Possibly. Probably. But, sir, we can't change our story about who fired first,' exclaimed Colonel Jimmy.

'No, of course not, Colonel. I think we should tell the world that Japan's exaggerated outrage shows they have a guilty conscience. Anyway, who fired first is not the main question. We should be asking what a platoon of Japanese marines was doing creeping around unannounced on Chinese sovereign soil.'

'If I may say so, sir, that is a powerful riposte which would be even more powerful if you yourself delivered it. May I suggest the following? Now is the moment to approach the editor of the *Shanghai Times* and grant his request for an interview, as we have already discussed. In return we should demand that he give us his sources and the identity of The Thunderer.'

They fell silent as they drank their coffee. Then the colonel said, 'There is one other thing to consider, sir. Your interview will raise the temperature with the Japanese. It is already dangerously hot. It will bring war nearer.'

'I have thought of that,' said the Generalissimo. 'But we are ready, aren't we, Colonel Jimmy Stewart?'

'Yes, Generalissimo, we are.'

*

As Lieutenant Combloux was clattering down Katya's stairs two at a time, Max, but half a mile away, was bent over his typewriter, turning the Japanese document into a column for the *Shanghai Times*. He had already sent a summary of the document, with a brief covering note, to headquarters in Moscow.

> *The Japanese authorities, incensed that they have taken the blame for the recent incident on Wengshe Road, will strike back in the next few days with an official communiqué, repudiating the Chinese accusation that it was the Japanese troops who fired first. I am informed by reliable sources of high authority that the Japanese communiqué will contain detailed witness statements to the effect that it was a Chinese mortar shell that provoked the exchange of fire. The question that observers are asking is who will divert these two angry parties from their collision course.*

Max handed in his column to Broadwick as the sky was lightening in the east. By four o'clock that afternoon, the special edition hit the streets, kiosks, hotels, clubs and diplomatic missions of Shanghai. It sold out within the hour.

*

Monty Carleton-Sinclair read the special edition with his usual afternoon cup of tea. It filled him with foreboding. Neither side showed any interest in trying to calm things down. He had already been contemplating closing the business and moving operations to Hong Kong. He would be mad not to do it now.

*

Captain Abe knocked on Major Seko's office door and walked in without waiting for a reply. He had a newspaper in his hand.

'She's done it again,' he said as he dropped it on Seko's desk.

The major glanced at the front page of the *Shanghai Times*. Then he seized it hungrily. When he had finished reading, he looked up at Abe.

'Send it, Captain, without delay to Tojo.'

'She has saved us, hasn't she, Major?'

'She is worth her weight in gold. From now on we must use her sparingly. Otherwise, the Russians will smell a rat and Lebedev will realise he's being used.'

Chapter 48

Richard Sorge's fixer in Shanghai had managed to get him a suite in the Marengo Wing of the French Officers' Club. The Club was more discreet than a hotel. And in the wing, which had its own entrance through the garden, he could bring in prostitutes or smoke opium, provided this was done prudently and quietly.

Having conferred upon himself the rank of colonel, Sorge offered a Belgian passport at the Club's reception desk. He passed off his lightly guttural accent as Flemish. He would not have got a room had he admitted to German nationality.

Sorge had been a journalist all his adult life. At an early age he had become bitter at the lack of recognition and money that his many talents, as he saw them, deserved. He had been an easy target for recruitment by the Soviet military intelligence service, the GRU, who had flattered him and paid him generously. He had gone on to play his part well. After a decade spying on the Nazis, the GRU had sent him to Tokyo to find out Japan's plans for war against the Soviet Union. He had the impeccable cover of bureau chief for the most prestigious of all German newspapers, the *Frankfurter Zeitung*.

It suited him to be well away from Moscow. He was able to indulge his taste for debauchery without fear of being denounced.

Sorge fancied himself the spymaster of the Asian world. There was nobody in the byzantine structure of Soviet intelligence, still less among its western rivals, to match his sources in the Japanese military and among those who had the ear of the Emperor.

Richard Sorge – spy, libertine, fearless rider of motorcycles – was unrivalled in his sphere. Or so he thought, until the message from Moscow arrived.

Sorge knew that there was an intense rivalry between the NKVD and the GRU. It had reached such a pitch that there had been mutual denunciations in Moscow, leading to executions and labour camps. But, out in East Asia, he had never had to bother about the NKVD. He knew they had their agents spread across the region. He had always assumed that this was because of the huge number of Russian exiles on whom the NKVD liked to keep tabs.

It came, then, as a rude shock to be told that someone else, probably NKVD, was reporting to the Kremlin on Sino-Japanese tensions and the threat Japan presented to the Soviet Union. The shock was all the ruder for the high quality of these reports.

Sorge was under GRU orders to help identify the NKVD source. He would have done so anyway and, if possible, eliminated him.

It was like a detective story. He had some clues. His rival was clearly someone with good connections to the Kwantung Army. The mystery agent's report to Moscow had, most interestingly, been immediately followed by a column in the local paper. The author of the column had hidden his identity behind a pen name, The Thunderer. So had the NKVD agent, his report signed off with a code name.

Very soon after he arrived in Shanghai, the Wengshe Road incident took place. It had been immediately followed by another Thunderer column – in a special edition. It too had been preceded by a report sent to NKVD headquarters in Moscow, under cover of the same code name.

They were clearly written by the same person. The style was identical. It was most unlikely the author was a native of Japan. But nor did his somewhat stilted style suggest a native familiarity with the English language.

What if The Thunderer and the NKVD agent were one and the same? That could make him a Russian. If he were, who was he working for? *Cui bono?* It looked like Japan, but the evidence was not conclusive.

Sorge decided to seek help from his man in Tokyo, a Filipino male prostitute who had a small and exclusive clientele in the upper reaches of the government and armed services.

Sorge's man reported that he had stumbled on something that appeared to have originated with the *Kempeitai*. It was a mention of one Maxim Konstantinovich Lebedev, a professor of philology at Shanghai University, whom the *Kempeitai* had identified as a long-standing NKVD officer. A brief biography was attached. Linked to his name was someone the *Kempeitai* called 'the Russian countess'. There was no explanation of their relationship.

This was interesting, thought Sorge. If Lebedev had been correctly identified, he must be a deep-cover agent. He was not on his list of NKVD officers holed up in the Soviet consulate. Sorge looked at the biography again. Maxim 'Max' Konstantinovich Lebedev, former Tsarist officer, seriously injured in the Great War, a hero of the civil war, then recruited by the NKVD, a commissar here, a commissar there, etc. etc. A double agent? Surely not. He was one of those Robespierres of the Russian Revolution, a sea-green incorruptible. But you never knew.

Then there was the so-called Russian countess. He would have to look into her, though Russian emigrants in China claiming membership of the old aristocracy were two a penny.

The first signs of a migraine warned him that he needed to get out of his suite. The sun was up and trying to break through the shutters. It was going to be another boiling day. His room was fetid with tobacco smoke. He needed fresh air.

After a shower, he put on one of his striped seersucker suits, stuck an ancient black leather helmet on his head and donned a pair of goggles. He went down to the Club's garden, where a Chinese attendant pulled out his motorcycle, a battered English BSA he had hired from the Club. Sorge roared out of the Club's back gate.

At perilously high speed he weaved his way through the traffic to the Shanghai Club in the International Settlement, where journalists liked to congregate. If there were intelligence to be had about Lebedev, there was no better place to start the search.

Sorge felt reinvigorated. The headache was in retreat. Speed, like sex, was the great cure-all. He got off his motorbike, left it with a doorman and, tugging off his goggles and cap, ran up the steps towards the high revolving door of the Shanghai Club. At the top he almost collided with Al Broadwick, who was coming out. As experienced Asia hands, they knew each other quite well. They embraced, genuinely pleased to see each other.

'Well, I'll be damned, if it isn't Dick Sorge! Why didn't you tell me you were coming? You are here, I take it, for the war. Trouble follows you like a faithful hound.'

Broadwick was slurring his words. Despite the early hour, he was hopelessly drunk.

'Al, I have never seen you look better. That's what success does for a man,' Sorge exclaimed, trusting to his talent for flattery. 'All eastern Asia is talking about you and the stories you've been breaking. Sure, I hope to be here for the war, whenever it comes. But right now, Al, old man, I want to know who The Thunderer is and how he gets his stories.'

Al Broadwick beamed. He held on to Sorge's arm for fear of falling down the steps.

'So would everyone, Dick, so would everyone. But it's top, top, top secret.' He put his finger to his lips.

'Come on, Al, give me a break. A small clue. Don't forget how I helped you on the Nanking story last year.'

'True, true.' Al Broadwick's eyes were bloodshot and unfocused. He tried to look at Sorge. He was swaying on his feet.

'Let's have dinner here Wednesday night after I've put the paper to bed,' he cried, as he staggered down the steps on the arm of the doorman, who propelled him into a taxi. 'Eight o'clock, Dick, my old friend.'

'Just like old times, Al. I'll be here.'

*

Sorge's dinner with Broadwick, two nights later, was an interesting and amiable occasion, full of reminiscence and discussion of the situation in East Asia. But every time Sorge tried to get him to reveal the identity of The Thunderer, Broadwick deflected him or changed the subject.

Towards the end of dinner, as they were each on their third glass of Armagnac, and Broadwick well in his cups, Sorge saw him looking across the room with an expression of surprise and alarm.

'I'll be damned, speak of the devil,' said Broadwick under his breath.

Sorge heard him. He turned in his chair to see an apparition approaching their table. It was dressed in an exaggerated English fashion – double-breasted blazer, cravat, cream trousers, correspondent shoes. It had only one arm. But what caught the eye was its ravaged face, with a single eye blazing forth, the other covered by a silver eye patch.

'Evening, Al. Who's your friend?' said the apparition easily, clapping Broadwick on the back.

Sorge rose to his feet in greeting. It had addressed Broadwick in impeccable English, though there was a trace of an accent, which he could not immediately identify.

'Max, let me introduce you to Dick Sorge, Tokyo bureau chief for the *Frankfurter Zeitung*. Dick and I go back to the stone age. Dick, meet Maxim Konstantinovich Lebedev, philology professor extraordinaire. Max is Shanghai's man-about-town. You see him here, you see him there, at all the posh parties. Max, get a chair.'

'What brings you to Shanghai, Dick?' Max asked affably, pulling another chair to the table and sitting down.

'War,' replied Sorge. 'Everything I hear in Tokyo says China and Japan will be at each other's throats before the summer is out.'

'In my view,' said Max, 'the war has already started. You heard about the shooting incident here the other week? Some people think it was the opening salvo.'

'They may well be right. I actually heard the firing. It happened just after I arrived.'

'How's the family, Max?' asked Broadwick, who wanted to change the subject.

'They're all fine, though Svyet – that's my wife – finds the heat very trying. On the other hand, Katya – that's Svyet's mother – is like a perpetual motion machine. Her energy is phenomenal. She's making an obscene amount of money with her language classes. She does eight, ten hours a day. She's got half the Japanese consulate on her books,' Max replied.

'I take it, Professor Lebedev . . . '

'Call me Max, Dick.'

'I take it, Max, that you and your family are Russian?'

'That's right. We are all refugees from the Revolution, like thousands of others in this town.'

'Shanghai is crawling with them,' Broadwick interjected. 'But Max's mother-in-law, the countess, bestrides them like a colossus.'

'It would be an honour to meet her, perhaps interview her,' said Sorge. 'She must have led an interesting life.'

'We'll have you round to the apartment sometime, Dick. Give me your card.'

'Let's have another nightcap,' said Broadwick, looking round for a waiter.

'No, Al, no. I have to get up early tomorrow because of you. You are a hard taskmaster,' said Max, wagging his finger at Broadwick and rising from the table. 'Good night, gentlemen. A pleasure to meet you, Dick. I'll be in touch.'

'Astonishing fellow,' said Broadwick, after Max was out of earshot.

'Why did he call you a hard taskmaster?' asked Sorge.

'Because he writes the odd piece for me,' answered Broadwick, his brain addled by Armagnac.

Chapter 49

On Monday afternoon Gulya arrived at Katya's flat bearing the news that the Victoria Trading Company's Shanghai office was closing immediately, and she was to be transferred to Hong Kong.

'I hadn't imagined the Victoria closing down. When word gets around that Mr M is shutting up shop for fear of war, that's going to disturb the entire foreign community and panic some people. Shanghai without the Victoria Trading Company is well-nigh unthinkable!'

'It's you I'm worried about,' said Gulya. 'If it's too dangerous to stay here, where will you go? Mr M said this morning that during the last war parts of Shanghai were completely flattened and even the French and international quarters were damaged. I'll have to postpone my wedding and tell Mr M I can't come with him. Mama, I can't leave you and Yu Yan alone!'

'Don't talk such utter nonsense. You will do no such thing. I will be perfectly capable of looking after myself and Yu Yan.' Katya heard the note of irritation in her voice, masking how deeply Gulya's words had moved her.

Gulya reached out, taking her hand. 'But how, Mama? Who will protect you? And what about Yu Yan?'

Gulya was getting worked up. Katya thought for a moment. 'Come for a walk with me in the park, Gulya, I need some air to clear my head.'

As Gulya drew breath to protest, Katya glared and put her finger to her lips, then led the way to the front door. Sensing another objection, she spun on her heel in the door frame, again put her finger to her lips and, with her other hand, seized her daughter by the arm, hard enough to hurt.

When they reached the park, Katya looked around her and then spoke.

'Gulya, there are things I need to tell you. You will find some of them hard to believe. But they connect directly to the decision that Yu Yan and I have to take, about leaving or staying in Shanghai when the war comes. I did not want to talk about this upstairs because it is very possible that somebody may be listening to our conversations.'

It had been Lieutenant Combloux who had warned her, after finding a bug in General Socquet de la Tour's office.

Gulya's face was a mask of bafflement and concern.

'Yes, I know this must sound outlandish. But Shanghai is a place of spies – Chinese, Japanese, Russian, French . . . and heaven knows who else.'

'But Mama! You are not a spy. That's absurd!'

Once again Katya looked around.

'Gulya, it is a world into which I have been drawn,' she continued. 'It is not what I would have wanted. It is not without risk. But it has given us protection against all the dangers that have beset us over the years. And it will almost certainly protect Yu Yan and me if we choose to live out the coming war in Shanghai.'

They bought cold tea from a passing vendor and sat down on a park bench in the shade of a large elm tree.

'Now, Gulya, it is time to tell you everything.'

It took a good hour. Most of the time they were seated on the bench. Then, when they were joined by a mother and her noisy young child, they walked around the park. Gulya occasionally asked a question, but for the most part just let Katya talk.

When she was finished, they sat again on a bench, facing the large fountain in the centre of the park.

Katya said, 'I am exhausted, Gulya. You know what I feel like?'

Gulya knew.

'A cigarette. Me, too. Shall I get a couple from the kiosk?'

'Yes, yes. See if it has the strong Russian ones – *papirossy*.'

She returned with two *papirossy*. They almost caught fire as they lit them, the smell was overpowering, and as they inhaled both Katya and Gulya began to cough uncontrollably, which made them laugh. And with the laughter came a great release of tension.

'A glass of vodka would go very well with this cigarette,' said Katya.

Gulya got up again without a word, went over to the kiosk and bought two cardboard cups of so-called Siberian vodka. It was probably made in China or Mongolia. They knocked them back fast in the Russian style and got two more. They continued to draw on their *papirossy*. A French couple walking past gave them dirty looks.

'That's better,' said Katya. 'I feel as if I have been in the confessional for the last hour.'

'Except that I am not your priest but have become your partner in crime, so to say.'

'Well, Gulya, what did you think of my confession? Will you grant me forgiveness?'

Listening to Katya's tale, Gulya had gone through an entire sweep of emotions – shock, anger, anxiety, fear, astonishment and, finally and overwhelmingly, admiration and love. What a woman! What courage! If only I could be the half the woman she is, thought Gulya.

'*Molodyets!*' Gulya exclaimed, a word that conveys congratulations and admiration.

Katya turned to her daughter, tears streaming down her face. 'Dearest Gulya, that makes it all worthwhile. I don't know what I will do without you.'

'Well, Mama,' said Gulya, giving her a great hug, 'what do we do about Max?'

Max was now the pressing issue. Was he friend or foe? What was he doing in their family? Had Svyet married a monster?

'If your father were here, he would say that we have to kill him before he kills us. I may be wrong, but I don't think the Max of 1937 is the Lebedev of twenty years ago. The effort of coming to terms with his disfigurement has – I am looking for the right word – blunted the cruelty and ruthlessness of his character so valued by the Bolsheviks. I have, maybe against my better judgement, started to pity him.'

'Perhaps we should confront him.'

'Yes, but not quite yet, or at least not directly.'

They sat in silence for a while.

Then Katya said, 'But we will have to discuss with Svyet and Max the Victoria's decision to shut down. Should they not start thinking about finding refuge somewhere? I don't know. Let's go home. But remember, Gulya, be careful what you say.'

Chapter 50

Broadwick knew that he had been indiscreet at the dinner with Sorge. So had poor Max without realising it. But, really, did it matter? Who read German newspapers in Shanghai? What if The Thunderer's identity did begin to emerge? He knew that, deep in his heart, Max would love that.

So, when Colonel Jimmy came on the line the following day to offer an interview with the Generalissimo, Broadwick did not need much persuading to meet the colonel's price and reveal The Thunderer's identity. His scoops had given a real boost to the *Shanghai Times'* circulation and renown. An interview with the Generalissimo would be a very large cherry on the cake. It would finally remove the spectre of having to go to the bank, begging bowl in hand.

'All right, Colonel, I surrender, but only share this with the Generalissimo and no one else.'

Broadwick, taking a deep breath, began to feel unexpectedly nervous.

'The Thunderer is a Russian, called Max Lebedev. He's a professor of philology at the university. You could hardly miss him. Half his face was burned off in a German bombing raid.

'He's quite a character. He wears an eye patch. He's fluent in English. He's married to a Russian. He mixes with a high-powered, cosmopolitan crowd. He has a slight whiff about him like many Russian refugees.'

'What do you mean?' asked the colonel.

'Well, does he hunt with the hounds or run with the hares, if you get my meaning?'

'You mean he's spying for someone.'

'Possibly. Just a whiff.'

'That usually means someone in Moscow. Who's his Japanese source?'

'I don't know, Colonel, I really don't.'

'You are going to have to try harder, Al, if you want the Generalissimo.'

'Let me put it this way. I'm pretty sure he's not talking directly to the Japs. There's an intermediary, someone he knows well.'

'Have a guess, Al.'

Unable to resist the colonel's remorseless pressure, Broadwick went on.

'I thought at first it was a tart in a brothel. Max is a frequent visitor to whorehouses.'

Damn, I have just made a mistake, thought Broadwick.

'How do you know, Al?' asked the colonel.

'To be frank, I quite like them myself.'

The colonel decided not to twist the knife with Broadwick's well-known proclivity for young boys.

'Something Max said – I can't recall what exactly – made me think it was a family member,' continued Broadwick. 'And then, using my reporter's bloodhound instincts, I thought of his mother-in-law, the Countess Polkonina. She attends those dinners given by that old fool of a French general, Socquet de la Tour. In fact, she has taken on the role of official hostess, with the general's wife away sick in France.'

Where, thought Colonel Jimmy, had he heard of the countess before? 'Go on, Al. You are doing better. This is starting to get mildly interesting.'

'That's about it, Colonel. The rest is guesswork. I think the countess picks up stuff at the French general's dinners and passes it to her son-in-law for his column. I know that General Aiko was at one of them with her. They were seen talking to each other for quite a long time, in German of all things. But, beware, I may be putting two and two together to make five.'

'Understood, Al, but it's worth looking into. There's maybe more to this.'

The colonel prepared to bring the conversation to an end. He guessed that he had squeezed Broadwick pretty well dry. He needed to report to the Generalissimo as quickly as possible.

'You haven't forgotten the interview, have you, Colonel?' said Broadwick, sensing that Colonel Jimmy wanted to get off the line.

'You have been very helpful, Al. You have earned your interview! I'll call you. Promise.' Broadwick heard the click of the receiver being placed in its cradle. He worried that the colonel would not keep his word.

As soon as Broadwick had mentioned the French general's dinners, the colonel remembered where he had heard of the Russian countess. It had been from the Generalissimo himself. He had come back from one of these events and remarked on the interesting conversation he had had with her. This was most unusual for the Generalissimo, who could not abide small talk with foreign women. She was, he had said, reputed to have been Je Jin's lover in Harbin. When he had referred to Je Jin as a bandit, the Russian countess had defended him with the ardour and emotion of a lover. The Generalissimo had concluded that she had great sympathy for China and a hatred of Japan.

In which case, thought Colonel Jimmy, why did she have these privileged connections to the Japanese? She could, of course, have been play-acting with the Generalissimo. But he was not someone easily deceived. Then the colonel thought of something else. He had been sent that tip the other day that the Japanese would publicly claim Chinese troops had fired the first shot at Wenshe Road. It had come from the French. But they in turn had said that they had got it from a highly reliable source, who was not French.

Might that not be this countess? It would be good to find out. He would check with the Generalissimo and, if he agreed, put a watch on her straightaway.

The Generalissimo agreed.

Three days later the surveillance team said that a Chinese girl was living with the countess, at least part of the time. Further investigation revealed that the girl was Je Jin's daughter.

'Hm,' grunted the Generalissimo, when Colonel Jimmy told him the news, 'she's one of us. But, then, what kind of game is she playing with the Japanese?'

*

The big social event of that fateful week was the American consul's grand reception to celebrate the Fourth of July. It was held in the ballroom of one of Shanghai's largest hotels in the International Settlement. A gigantic Stars and Stripes flag stretched across the entire wall at one end of the room. A corner of it was covered in scorch marks. The consul thought this gave a suitably dramatic effect to represent the defeat of British troops in the War of Independence. In reality the flag had been rescued from a burning storeroom, hit by a bomb in the 1932 war.

Le tout Shanghai was invited. Despite its size the room was so packed with guests that they and the waiters found it difficult to move. Great fans turned as fast as they could on the ceiling. There was a stifling potpourri of odours emanating from multiple perfumes and powders, all struggling to suppress the natural bodily smells aroused by the heat.

The three Polkonins were present, together with Max. After careful thought, he had decided that these were the best surroundings in which to reveal that he was The Thunderer. There was camouflage in numbers. He had settled on the *Frankfurter Zeitung* correspondent, Dick Sorge – his new best friend – to be the recipient of his disclosure.

The Polkonins and Max Lebedev had arrived as a single group. But soon Max moved into the crowd in search of Sorge. Yu Yan had stayed at home with a good book.

*

Max and Dick Sorge had found each other, as if by accident, in a group of journalists. The journalists were discussing the likelihood of war. Then the group broke up, as happens at cocktail parties, leaving Max and Sorge alone together.

Sorge made his opening gambit.

'When's your next column, Max?' he asked in English.

Without thinking, Max replied, 'Next Wednesday.'

No sooner were the words out of his mouth than it hit Max. He had been tricked into blurting out his revelation by the oldest ploy in the book. He had, of course, intended to tell Sorge, but at his own pace. He was embarrassed to have been caught so easily. Then he was alarmed. Sorge must have known already that he was The Thunderer. How the devil? His scars and ruined skin could not conceal his discomfort.

'Don't worry, Max, your secret is safe with me,' said Sorge with an ironic, predatory light in his eye. 'It was your editor who accidentally let the cat out of the bag. You did, too, for that matter. You should both drink less.'

He continued, 'If I may say so, as one journalist to another, I have found your columns remarkable for their acuity and style. But I have been struck even more by the . . . unusual . . . sources that you must have inside the Japanese machine. I mean, I am based in Tokyo and I cannot rival your access.'

Sorge's praise fully restored Max's composure, as was intended.

'To be honest with you, Dick, it is not I who has the contacts, it is an intermediary to whom I am very close and who knows what I am looking for.'

'Like, say, a family member?'

The crowd pushed and jostled around them. Max had the strange feeling that the two of them were quite isolated, impervious to the surrounding hubbub, alone together in a bubble of Sorge's creation. There was something hypnotic about Sorge's face so close to his own.

'Yes, a family member.'

I have done it again, thought Max. He had never been like this in the old days – so easy to outmanoeuvre.

'Well,' said Sorge, reaching into an inside pocket for his GRU badge, 'it's not your wife, who doesn't get around enough; and it's not your sister-in-law, who is too young; that leaves your mother-in-law, the countess. Elementary, my dear Lebedev!'

Sorge laughed out loud, then grinned triumphantly at Max.

The two of them were very close to each other. The GRU badge with its shield was in the palm of Sorge's right hand, visible to Max, but hidden from the throng. Sorge glanced down with slow deliberation at his hand. Max's eyes followed.

'Let's go for a stroll in the garden, Max. It would be good to get some fresh air.'

Max did not demur. A chill, close to fear, had taken hold of him. Was that a Soviet badge? His one eye was not quite good enough to be absolutely sure.

He began to smell danger, something he had not experienced for a very long time. It awoke old instincts and reflexes, some of which had lain dormant since that morning of fire and destruction twenty years before in Lemberg.

They pushed their way to the garden doors. Max heard Svyet call, 'Where are you going, Max? Take me home, please.'

He turned to see her red face, shiny with perspiration, distorted in exasperation. He felt revulsion rise in his gorge.

'Back in five minutes, my darling,' he shouted above the noise.

Once in the garden, Sorge said to Max, 'Let's walk calmly around the path, like two old philosophers discussing the condition of mankind.'

'And why, Dick, should we be anything but calm?' asked Max. He wished he had his revolver with him. He rarely carried it now because it spoiled the line of his blazer.

'Listen, Max, I'm not here to do you harm. Far from it. I find the competition between the GRU and the NKVD absurd. We all serve the Union of Soviet Socialist Republics.'

'No one can disagree with that,' replied Max warily. 'But what do you want from me? Who are you?'

'Richard Sorge is my real name. I am a German who has transferred his loyalties to the Soviet Union. I hold the rank of colonel in the GRU. I am your superior officer, albeit in a different service.'

Sorge paused to let this sink in.

'Go on,' said Max, his mind racing.

'I am based in Tokyo. Journalism is my cover. Officially, I am here to establish your loyalties. Unofficially, I am here to give you a warning, as one brother officer to another.'

'What on earth . . . ?'

'I have heard on my network that you are suspected by your own people, the NKVD, of spying for Japan and that you will soon be either summoned to Moscow or liquidated here. I would not return to your office in the Soviet consulate if I were you.'

Sorge thought Max's one eye would fly from its socket, such was the shock and horror that it expressed. But the moment did not last long. With a superhuman effort, Max brought his feelings under control.

'So what is it that I am supposed to do?'

'Disappear,' came the reply.

'This is ridiculous,' said Max. 'I am wholly innocent. I have, by great good fortune, discovered things about Japanese plans, thanks to the connections of my mother-in-law. As a result, I have been able to give timely warnings to Moscow. They should be giving me medals, not threatening me.'

'Max, Max, that is not how it works. I don't have to tell you. Under Comrade Stalin, guilt and innocence have no objective meaning. Having good intelligence on the enemy can be proof of treachery to suspicious minds.'

'And if I disappear, as you put it, that will simply confirm their suspicions.'

'Face facts, Max. It is either that or death, possibly for your wife as well,' Sorge pressed on. 'Who, by the way, is your mother-in-law working for?'

'She's not working for anyone,' replied Max, irritation reigniting his spirit. 'She finds out things from the Japanese because she gives English lessons to their senior diplomats and families. She once had an interesting conversation with General Aiko at a diplomatic dinner. She has been helping me with my columns, that is all. Journalism is part of my cover, too, in case you have forgotten.'

That, thought Sorge, has the ring of truth. It was always absurd to think that the unglamorous Russian countess could be a latter-day Mata Hari.

'Does your mother-in-law know you are an NKVD officer?'

'Absolutely not. Nor does my wife.'

'What does the countess think of the Soviet Union?'

'She is Russian to the depths of her soul.'

'That was not my question.'

'That is my answer.'

'Very well, Max. I must return to the party. There are others I have to talk to.'

They completed the circuit of the garden.

'Look, Max, I can do no more than warn you. I will report to my headquarters that I can find no evidence of your spying for Japan. But that won't cut much ice, given the atmosphere of mistrust that reigns in Moscow. It might even throw suspicion on me. Death or flight – that is your choice. I'd say you have thirty-six, forty-eight hours at best.'

'Let them do their worst, Dick, I'm not leaving Shanghai. You are bluffing, though heaven knows why.'

'As the Lord is my witness, this is no bluff. I could not be more serious.'

As he spoke, Sorge gripped Max by the upper arm. Then they both turned as if to go back to the ballroom. Sorge moved swiftly. Max hesitated behind him. Then he spun on his heel and, almost running, headed for the garden exit.

Sorge, once through the ballroom doors, turned to speak to Max.

But he was nowhere to be seen.

*

Max took a taxi to his and Svyet's apartment. He unlocked the door to their storeroom – only he had the key – and, from behind a pile of boxes, took out a large leather suitcase. It contained clothing for all seasons, toiletries, a gun, ammunition and a quantity of US dollars and gold coins. It was heavy. It had been packed, ready for a swift departure, ever since he came to Shanghai. Svyet knew nothing of its contents.

Max relocked the storeroom. He changed rapidly into an anonymous grey suit, put on dark glasses and, despite the heat, donned a trilby pulled low over the eyes. With suitcase in hand, he returned to the taxi, which was waiting downstairs. He ordered the driver to take him to the station. There he waited for the overnight train to Hong Kong, which left in two hours.

Chapter 51

Despite the heat and the crush, Katya was thoroughly enjoying herself at the American party. She kept running into interesting people. It gave her an opportunity to have long chats with Monty Carleton-Sinclair and Gulya's *fiancé*, Olivier Marnier.

After talking to Monty, she felt a presence at her side. She turned to see a smiling Captain Abe, dressed in the smart summer uniform of a naval officer. He greeted her warmly.

'I did not know you were in the navy,' she said.

'Oh, yes,' said Abe, 'that is why I am allowed to go to receptions of this kind and wear my naval uniform. I am on secondment to the *Kempeitai* for two years, because they need an English interpreter.'

'It really suits you, Captain. You look very handsome.' Abe clicked his heels and bowed. Katya could have sworn he blushed a little.

'I enjoy wearing it. I cannot wait to return to what the English call the senior service. The navy was always my vocation, as it was for my father.'

'He must be very proud of you.'

'Unfortunately, he fell at the Battle of Tsushima against the Russians, one of the few Japanese casualties.'

'Oh, I am sorry,' she said, distressed at having opened an old wound.

'You were not to know and, besides, I bear Russia no grudge – though I fear that one of these days, quite soon, we will go to war again.'

The captain had discreetly manoeuvred Katya close to a wall. She had not resisted. They were well shielded from eavesdroppers.

'Which reminds me, Countess. Major Seko would like you to call at the consulate tomorrow on an urgent matter.'

'What might that be?' she asked.

Abe thought for a moment. He looked around him and moved nearer to Katya. He was so close it was almost unseemly. He spoke, *sotto voce*, in her ear.

'There is going to be another incident between us and the Chinese, this time near Pekin. It will be three days from now. It will trigger a war. Can you, please, express surprise, Countess, when the major tells you? And, in the meantime, don't breathe a word to anyone.'

'You mean 7 July? Will Shanghai be attacked?'

'Yes and yes. We want you to come in to collect papers that will protect you and your household from any misunderstandings with the Japanese army, if you choose to stay in Shanghai.'

'Eleven o'clock?'

'Perfect. I repeat: please treat what I have told you with the very greatest discretion. The major would shoot me – literally – if he knew I had been so indiscreet.'

*

Now that is very interesting, thought Colonel Jimmy. Thanks to his height he had been able to observe over the heads of the guests Katya's conversation with Captain Abe. The Japanese was dressed as a naval officer, but wasn't he *Kempeitai*? Their conversation had lasted a good fifteen minutes. It had clearly been between two people who were well acquainted. What was the countess doing with a *Kempeitai* officer? Perhaps the Generalissimo had misjudged her loyalties. He had better find out.

While Colonel Jimmy contemplated Katya, she was thinking hard what to do with the information she had just been given by Captain Abe. She stood alone in the crowd, her brow creased in concentration. Je Jin came to her in her quandary, as he so often did. 'Give it to the Chinese, and fast, my love.' An irritating Russian couple loomed before her, seeking to start a conversation. To their shock and anger she turned her back on them to engage in conversation with a tall Chinese army officer.

'Good evening, Countess. My name is Colonel Lee,' said Colonel

Jimmy in his flawless English. 'You may remember me from that dinner of General Socquet de la Tour's where General Chiang Kai-shek was guest of honour. I am the Generalissimo's aide-de-camp. He has asked me to convey to you his best wishes.'

'That is very kind of him,' Katya replied, wondering just a little why General Chiang Kai-shek's aide-de-camp should seek her out. 'Please tell him that it was a great honour to be seated beside him.'

'I will certainly do that,' said Colonel Jimmy. He decided to plough straight ahead. 'Forgive my bluntness, but who was that Japanese naval officer I saw you talking to just now?'

Katya looked into the garden. She had seen Max go outside earlier with someone she did not recognise. Now the garden was empty again.

'Let's continue this conversation in the garden,' Katya replied. 'I am finding the heat and the crush a little too much.'

'But, of course, Countess.'

It was now dusk. The fading light gave the little garden an intimacy in which confidences could be safely exchanged. They walked halfway round the oblong path before she spoke. Colonel Jimmy had the good sense not to press her before she was ready.

'That was Captain Abe, a naval officer on secondment to the *Kempeitai*. He is based at the Japanese consulate. I have got to know him quite well since arriving in Shanghai.'

'Because of the language lessons you give to Japanese officials at the consulate?'

'That is part of the story.' She paused. She had to assume that the Chinese already knew a good deal about her.

They started their second circuit of the garden. Je Jin's exhortation was ringing in her head.

'He has just told me that Japan will provoke an incident outside Pekin on 7 July, three days from now. It will mark the opening of general hostilities between Japan and China, including an assault on Shanghai before the summer is out.'

'Captain Abe told you that? But he doesn't have the seniority. And why you?' Colonel Jimmy asked in astonishment.

'It's a long story. Abe works for a Major Seko, who has summoned me to his office tomorrow. Apparently, I will be told officially what Abe just told me, rather indiscreetly. As far as I can tell, the major has a direct line to General Tojo's staff, perhaps to the general himself.'

'What exactly is your relationship with the Japanese, Countess?'

They stood facing each other under a cherry tree. This moment had to come, thought Katya. The sky was a deep mauve. There were shooting stars everywhere, a common occurrence at this time of year.

'It all started in Harbin many years ago with my giving language lessons to the Japanese consul and his family. As refugees, we were very short of money. I had to get work where I could find it. In due course I became a full-time translator for the consulate and *Kempeitai*. Though I recoil at the expression, to all intents and purposes I turned into a double agent, ostensibly helping the Japanese, but passing everything to the Chinese – firstly to Je Jin, then, after his death, to his followers and now to you.'

She paused. Colonel Jimmy was stunned. Katya continued.

'I am, I think, trusted to a high degree by the Japanese. They say that they will give me tomorrow, as they gave me in Harbin, papers to protect me, my Chinese ward and my family from harassment by the Japanese military when and if they occupy Shanghai.'

'Astonishing. Extraordinary,' said Colonel Jimmy almost to himself, as he stared at Katya as if she were the eighth wonder of the world.

'Speak to Lieutenant Combloux on General Socquet de la Tour's staff if you have any doubts,' Katya continued. 'It was he who tipped you off about the Wenshe Road incident. He got the tip from me. I got it from Seko. He got it from Tojo.'

'And I suppose it was you who gave your son-in-law the information which appeared under the Thunderer byline in the *Shanghai Times*.'

'Your supposition, Colonel, is correct.'

Colonel Jimmy slapped his thigh and grinned. The Generalissimo would love this. So would Madame Chiang.

'Well, I'll be doggone!' he exclaimed. He took Katya by the hand and, somewhat to her astonishment, squeezed it hard.

'Rest assured, Countess, that I will convey this information to the Generalissimo tonight. He and the Republic of China will be forever in your debt. I don't care what the Japanese offer you, but you will always enjoy the Generalissimo's personal protection.'

What on earth is doggone, wondered Katya, as Colonel Jimmy sped from the room.

*

She suddenly felt exhausted. It was near ten o'clock and the party was finally thinning out. She had been on her feet for a good three hours. She went in search of her daughters. Svyet had gone home. Max had disappeared. Just as she spotted Gulya and Olivier she was intercepted by the tall and rather distinguished-looking European man.

'Good evening, Countess,' he said in German. 'My name is Richard Sorge and I am the Tokyo bureau chief of the *Frankfurter Zeitung*. It is a pleasure and an honour to meet someone of such distinction in Shanghai society.'

'Good evening, Herr Sorge,' Katya replied in German. 'I am likewise honoured.'

She was actually rather taken aback by his oily smile and the obsequious hyperbole of his words. There was also something unfocused about his eyes. Overall, the impression he created was not terribly pleasant.

Since his conversation in the garden with Max, Sorge had drunk several whiskies and smoked a pipe of opium in one of the club's storerooms. He had then tried to have sex with one of the Russian serving girls. She had been perfectly willing for five American dollars, but he found himself unable to perform, an increasingly common occurrence of late.

'I just wanted to tell you, Countess, that your son-in-law, Maxim Konstantinovich, has done me the great honour this evening of revealing that he is The Thunderer, thus solving one of the journalistic mysteries of our times. I believe that I am the first to know. He also suggested that you were the source of his scoops. Tell me more, Countess, I beg of you!' said Sorge in tones of mock pleading.

Katya now found Sorge's manner loathsome, but in reply she was courtesy itself.

'My dear Herr Sorge, there is nothing to tell. I pick up all sorts of gossip because of the life I lead in Shanghai. I find the Japanese to be both boastful and indiscreet. Of course, I gave Max their juiciest morsels for his new column. But here's the funny thing about you journalists. The last thing Max wanted people to know was that his scoops came, not from his professional prowess, but from his mother-in-law. Would you? So, he decided to create a mystery.'

Sorge laughed out loud. It was actually quite funny. And the countess was no fool. She had got the Japanese exactly right. It was absurd to think she worked for them.

'*Touché!* By the way, we had quite a long conversation. He is an interesting man.'

'I know. I saw the two of you in the garden. You were outside for ages. What did you talk about?'

'Well, Countess, you know what happens when you get two journalists together . . . '

Sorge felt his head starting to swim. This always happened when he mixed opium and alcohol. He must get a grip. What was it he wanted to tell her? Or was it to ask her?

'Max told me quite a lot about his early life. About the Russian Civil War and how he defended Samara against Kolchak. It must have been tough.'

'It certainly was, Herr Sorge. But, you will forgive me if I take my leave. I have to go home and rest my aching feet.'

Sorge smiled benignly at her, all focus leaving his eyes. He swayed on his feet.

'Of course, of course,' he said almost to himself.

*

Max hid, with his case, in one of the first-class waiting-room lavatories until it was time to board the train to Hong Kong. He shut himself in his compartment, opening it only to the ticket collector and a customs official. From Hong Kong station, he went straight to the P&O shipping office, where he bought a berth on a freighter leaving that same night for Manila and bribed the booking clerk to give a false destination if asked.

Just after midnight, with the sky more purple than black and the dying moon peering through a few thin clouds, he stood on the tiny balcony of his modest cabin, glass of whisky in hand, as the freighter picked up speed in the South China Sea. He watched the lights of Hong Kong and the China coast recede into the distance.

Max felt an almost unimaginable sense of relief. He was shot of the NKVD, the GRU, the Shanghai University philology department, his tiresome wife, Al Broadwick, Andrey Polkonin and the ridiculous pretence of his life in Shanghai. This had been brewing for a long, long time. He had wanted out for months, maybe years. He should be grateful to Dick Sorge, whoever he really was.

He would miss only Katya and Gulya. He was not quite sure why. In their company he felt truly Russian, and at ease, while his hatred for Andrey Polkonin had shrivelled to nothing. He even imagined that one day they might even have some sort of reconciliation.

Max poured himself another whisky. He reflected on his life's trajectory. He had lost his devotion to the Tsar because of the cursed German Tsarina. But, what in God's name had led him to believe the Bolsheviks were the true embodiment of Mother Russia? He thought of the cruelties and killings that he had carried out in their name. He shuddered. There must be a special place in hell for someone like him. He fingered the crucifix on the chain around his neck and crossed himself. Maxim Konstantinovich Lebedev, the Soviet commissar who had burned the Yaroslavl monks alive!

Because of his disfigurement, Max could not be confident that he had not been spotted fleeing China. Though he had used two false passports for his journey so far, and would use a third in the Philippines, there was no avoiding a photo of his ruined face. He did not want to spend the rest of his life looking over his shoulder for fear of a Soviet assassin in silent pursuit. In Manila he hoped that he could truly disappear until it was time to re-emerge with a new face, a new identity and yet another passport. God willing, he would find refuge in Europe, in France or Switzerland.

That, anyway, was his plan. For the umpteenth time he checked the address of the clinic just outside Manila.

Chapter 52

Just before dawn Katya was awoken by the telephone. It was Svyet telling her in a quavering voice that Max had not been home all night.

'I wouldn't worry, darling. Men do that. It's something you have to get used to. He will turn up sometime today. He will beg your forgiveness. You should be slow to give it.'

'But, Mama, he has never done this before.'

'There's always a first time. Stop worrying. Ring me later when he gets back.'

*

Katya arrived promptly at eleven o'clock at the Japanese consulate to keep her rendezvous with Major Seko and Captain Abe.

Major Seko confirmed that there would be a military incident on 7 July near Pekin that would provoke a war between Japan and China. It would lead soon after to hostilities in Shanghai itself. If the 1932 war was anything to go by, there would be heavy fighting and damage to buildings, with many casualties. It was not the Imperial government's intention, but the French Concession and the International Settlement might get caught up in the conflict.

He would be grateful if she would keep the information to herself for thirty-six hours, though he suspected that French and British intelligence had already got wind of what was about to happen.

Personally, Seko added, he would leave Shanghai until the war was over. But, if Katya was determined to stay, he had papers that should give her and her family protection.

'In this envelope, Countess, you will find documents with the Imperial seal that put you, your daughters and your Chinese ward under the protection of the Empire of Japan. But I must tell you that this protection cannot be extended to your older daughter's husband, Maxim Konstantinovich Lebedev.'

'I am not surprised,' replied Katya.

Seko, still clutching the envelope, paused, changed tack and asked, 'By the way, are you aware of Lebedev's present whereabouts?'

'My older daughter told me this morning that he had been out all night after the American Independence Day party but he should be home by now.'

'I am afraid that is not the case. He is not even in Shanghai. Our agents have reported seeing him board a train to Hong Kong last night. Why, Countess, would he do that?'

Katya felt a miasma of suspicion enter the room. It was always the way when Seko did not know something which he suspected she did. She must tread very carefully. She had to avoid doing anything to cause him to retract his offer of protection. He still held the envelope of documents tightly in his hand.

'I did not know that Max had left Shanghai. It will come as a terrible shock to my daughter. But it fits with something that happened to me last night.'

'What is that?' asked Seko.

'Do you know Richard Sorge, Major, Tokyo bureau chief of the *Frankfurter Zeitung*?' said Katya, reading ostentatiously from Sorge's business card.

'No. Do you, Abe?'

'Not personally. But I know he is the correspondent of a German newspaper in Tokyo.'

'Why do you ask?' said Seko, frowning.

'I met him for the first time last night at the American party. Earlier in the evening I saw him and Max go into the hotel garden and have what looked like a long and earnest conversation. After a while he came back into the reception, and I saw Max leave by the garden gate. I found that very odd, since my daughter was desperate for him to take her home.'

She had the two Japanese officers' absolute attention.

'Just as I was leaving the reception,' she continued, 'Sorge introduced himself to me. At first sight he was polite and charming. He proceeded to tell me that Max had revealed to him that he was The Thunderer and I his source. He said this with a certain . . . how can I put it? . . . menace behind his smile. I told him there was nothing unnatural in a mother-in-law helping her son-in-law with high-quality gossip in his second career as a journalist. I mentioned my contacts with General Aiko. He seemed to accept this, because he immediately moved on to say how much he had enjoyed his conversation with Max.'

Katya paused. The room was utterly still except for the swishing of the ceiling fan. Seko and Abe, in those horrible khaki uniforms, which were not quite khaki, were like statues on the other side of the table, their eyes fixed on her face.

'Now, this for me is the interesting part, Major. It may help answer your question. According to Sorge, Max revealed that in the Russian Civil War he had taken part in the capture of Samara from the White Army. That means he must have been a Bolshevik. You and I know that this is true. But nobody else does in Shanghai, because Max has always passed himself off here as a former Tsarist officer, who fought with the Whites. So, the question is, would why Max confide in Sorge in this way unless he knew Sorge was also a Soviet intelligence officer? It is a question which has been teasing me ever since.'

Seko and Abe spoke to each other in Japanese.

'Why do you think Sorge would have made such a mistake with you?' Seko finally asked through Abe.

'I realised that there was something odd about Sorge. At first, I thought he was drunk. His eyes were unfocused and he sometimes lost the thread of what he was saying. But by the end of our conversation he had lost control of his faculties. He must have been under the influence of more than alcohol.'

Seko picked up the phone and spoke into the receiver.

'We must wait a few minutes,' he said to Katya.

The three of them sat in silence. The atmosphere had eased.

Soon a uniformed orderly knocked and entered the room on Seko's barked command. The orderly placed a thin file before him and, saluting smartly, withdrew from the room.

Seko read the file quickly, closed it and started speaking for Abe to interpret.

'We have some information here on this Sorge from a European informant.' Seko pointed at the file. 'He has been to Shanghai before. He likes to stay at the French Officers' Club. He is a journalist of good repute, but . . . ' Seko referred again to the file, 'in his personal habits is dissolute and debauched. He frequents prostitutes, he is addicted to opium and he likes to drink. He drives a motorbike at dangerous speeds.'

Seko closed the file with a slapping sound.

'That is entirely consistent with your account. But there is not a whisper on the file of his having Soviet sympathies.'

Katya now felt herself on firm enough ground to venture a question.

'You tell me that Max is on his way to Hong Kong. He hasn't been seen since his conversation with Sorge. What could Sorge have said that led Max to take immediate flight – if that indeed is what happened?'

Seko and Abe discussed in Japanese how to answer Katya.

'We cannot be sure,' said Seko, leaning forward and resting his forearms on his desk. 'But your son-in-law's behaviour is typical of some Soviet agents we have observed. They are recalled to Moscow. They fear execution. They go into hiding. They never return. Perhaps Sorge came to Shanghai to order your son-in-law to go back. It is something to be investigated.'

Seko lit a cigarette and pushed the envelope across the desk to Katya. She took it and put it in her bag. They all rose to their feet.

'Countess, we will have to suspend our meetings until the end of the war. We will also be evacuating most of the consulate staff and their families. That will, I am afraid, put an end to your language lessons. One day, if God permits, normal life will resume.'

But they knew that they would never meet again.

*

The day after the meeting, a Japanese army courier arrived at Katya's front door. He spoke no English. But, having produced from a satchel a single piece of paper, he managed to convey to her that she should read it while he held it in his hand. There were two sentences typed in English, one confirming Max's arrival in Hong Kong and the other his booking a passage to Portsmouth in England on the P&O liner *Strathnaver*.

Chapter 53

Monty gave a little farewell party the evening before the Victoria Trading Company decamped to Hong Kong. It was a modest, subdued occasion. Despite the champagne and Gulya's excitement about the new life awaiting her with Olivier, there was a certain melancholy in the air. Monty had also invited Katya, Svyet and Yu Yan. This was more than simple *politesse* on his part. He was developing a weakness for Katya, which he hoped she might reciprocate.

'It's a bittersweet moment, isn't it,' Sue said to Gulya. 'I hope Toby won't be too much of a handful for your mother and Yu Yan.'

'You needn't worry. Yu Yan and Toby are like brother and sister,' she replied.

Monty made a little speech, with a brief coda at the end plainly directed at Katya.

'Don't forget that if life in Shanghai gets too difficult, a comfortable berth awaits you in Hong Kong.'

'Or come to Hanoi!' said Olivier exuberantly. His clumsy intervention was clearly not welcome to Monty.

Katya, Yu Yan and even Svyet thanked him warmly. But if he had hoped for a peck on the cheek from Katya, he was disappointed. She shook Monty by the hand as she had been brought up to do. She did not want to do anything to encourage him.

Then it was time for a last family meal, at the Russian restaurant where they had lunched with Max on their arrival in Shanghai the previous year. Olivier understood that this was no place for him. He made his excuses and stayed behind with Monty.

But it was less a last family meal than a much-needed council of war, which was why Katya had decided to have it in a restaurant rather than in her apartment. She was sure that she was surrounded by eavesdropping devices at home.

There was a real sense of urgency in the air. The previous week there had been a clash between Chinese and Japanese troops at the Marco Polo Bridge outside Pekin. It was only a matter of time, Monty had said, before war reached Shanghai.

Katya, Gulya, Svyet and Yu Yan took a discreet table at the back of the restaurant. They ordered quickly and got down to business.

Max's disappearance was, of course, at the top of the agenda. It was the talk of the town – anything to avoid the disagreeable topic of war. Some said he had killed himself, no longer able to tolerate his disfigurement. Others thought he had run off with someone's wife, though nobody could work out whose. Prayers for his safe return were offered in the Russian Orthodox church. There were reports of sightings in Shanghai, Pekin and Harbin.

Al Broadwick made a story of it in the *Shanghai Times* under the headline 'Where Is Our Columnist?'. This was in a very large font. Underneath it, in smaller letters, were the words: 'Maxim Konstantinovich Lebedev Disappears'. Broadwick speculated that because of the sensational nature of his revelations, poor Lebedev was even now floating face down in the Wangpoo, a victim of either Chinese or Japanese assassins. This prompted a furious response from each side and the cancellation of Broadwick's interview with the Generalissimo. But the circulation of the *Shanghai Times* went up and up, aided by Svyet, who emerged from her purdah and gave an exclusive interview to Al himself. He noted that she was surprisingly unemotional.

'One of my pupils at the Japanese consulate – a well-connected senior diplomat – told me that he thought Max had gone to Hong Kong,' said Katya carefully.

This prompted a blank stare from Svyet.

'I don't think anyone has a clue where he is,' she replied in a surprisingly matter-of-fact tone.

Katya had wondered whether, in the light of *l'affaire* Max, she should be as frank with Svyet about her own activities as she had been with Gulya. But the estrangement between them in Harbin had been so deep it felt beyond repair, and she simply didn't trust Svyet not to betray her in some way.

So she found herself in a quandary over dinner. She had decided not to tell Svyet that her husband had been a Bolshevik, an officer in the NKVD and a sworn enemy of her father. But, without telling her these things, how could she explain why she thought Max had gone and why he was not coming back?

To her surprise Svyet already had her own answer.

'It was a horrible shock at first and I couldn't stop crying. But I can't say he didn't warn me. Remembering that has calmed me down and made me less anxious.'

'What do you mean?' asked Katya.

'Just before we married, Max told me that he was doing some work for Mother Russia that could lead him to disappear one day, to escape his enemies. If that were to happen, I should be patient, get on with my life and wait for him to contact me.'

'What kind of work?'

'I don't know. Something secret. He didn't want to tell me and I didn't want to know. It explained his rushing around town and his exhausting social life that went far beyond the demands of the philology faculty. But I didn't mind if it helped our Russia survive in this horrible world. I agree with you. Max won't return to Shanghai. But I know we will be reunited one day in our beloved homeland.'

'But surely not while the Bolsheviks are in power?'

'Who knows? If that is what Max wants, I will follow him.'

'But that would mean he was a Bolshevik, too. Never forget, Svyetlana, that it was the Bolsheviks who destroyed our family and our Russia!' Katya exclaimed indignantly.

'I know, Mama, but the world moves on. There was a lot wrong with the *ancien régime*. You can't make an omelette without breaking eggs. Wasn't it Napoleon who said that?'

Svyet's calm acceptance of Max's disappearance was on its own enough to have taken the wind out of Katya's sails. But now she was suggesting, cool as you like, that he had been working for the Soviet Union.

'Are you telling me, Svyetlana, that all along you knew Max was a Soviet agent?'

'He might well have been. But so what? We are all Russians.'

'Russians and Soviets are not the same thing, Svyetlana.'

'If you mean the Russians of Harbin and Shanghai, you are of course right, Mama. They are frozen in the past, never stop talking about the old days, smell of moth balls and have no interest in this astonishingly brave new world that Stalin is building in the USSR. That is where the future lies and one of these days I want to be part of it.'

Katya was lost for words. She looked at Svyet in dismay and bewilderment. She truly did not know or understand her older daughter.

Gulya became angry. 'If you feel like that, Svyet, what's keeping you in Shanghai, now that Max has left you in the lurch? How brave of him to abandon you to the tender mercies of the Japanese army, which, don't forget, Mama and I survived by the skin of our teeth in Harbin. If I were you, I'd get my ticket to Moscow or Vladivostok or wherever before it's too late,' she said, her voice dripping with sarcasm.

'I am not going anywhere, Gulya, until I have heard from Max – who has not abandoned me, you silly little fool!'

Svyet spat out the words, her face red and furious. Yu Yan, who had not yet said a word, looked down at the table, desperately uncomfortable. Yu Yan did not drink alcohol and hated confrontation. As tempers had frayed around the table, fuelled by the wine, she had taken repeated nervous sips from her glass of water.

Katya regained her composure. She would wait until she was in bed with a cup of tea to think through what it all meant. Right now she knew that she had to restore order at the table or there was a risk of Svyet storming out.

'That's quite enough, girls. Svyet, will you serve the fish, Gulya, please pour some more wine. Then I want to say something.'

The routine duties of the table drew some of the tension out of the air. Svyet's face returned to its normal colour and Gulya made an effort to contain her irritation.

'Let me get straight to the point,' Katya continued. 'War is coming to Shanghai soon and everybody tells me that it will be very unpleasant, even in the foreign quarters. Gulya's employer, Mr Carleton-Sinclair, suggested the other day that Yu Yan and I wait out the war in Hong Kong. He kindly offered us accommodation. But I cannot face starting life again in another city, though the English are pleasant enough. So I have no intention of leaving. And nor, I think, does Yu Yan.'

'That's right. I'm not leaving. I cannot interrupt my studies,' said Yu Yan, in a low, flat voice, still distressed by the family tensions that had boiled over before her.

Gulya said, 'Mr M has a soft spot for you, Mama. Haven't you noticed? I know you don't want to encourage him, but his offer of sanctuary in Hong Kong is not to be lightly dismissed.'

'I just don't want to lead him on,' Katya retorted. 'Besides, Je Jin has told Yu Yan and me to stay and has promised to protect us.'

Katya saw Svyet raise her eyebrows and look to the ceiling at the mention of Je Jin.

'I know you think this mere superstition, Svyet, but it's real enough to us. You may be more impressed by General Socquet de la Tour's offer of refuge inside the French garrison compound should things start to get difficult.'

'Not really,' Svyet replied gracelessly. 'That won't be much use if the Japanese threaten to attack the French. I wouldn't put any trust in the French. That's what Max always used to say, anyway.'

'Then perhaps this will meet your exacting standards, Svyet,' said Katya, her voice heavy with sarcasm. 'I have managed to acquire papers, which put you, Yu Yan and me under the personal protection, respectively, of the Emperor of Japan and General Chiang Kai-shek. The Japanese documents include a notice with the Imperial seal to pin on the front door. These papers are supposed to keep us safe at home and allow us to move freely around town.'

Katya took an envelope out of her handbag.

'Gulya, you won't need them now that you will soon be married to a Frenchman, but I have copies for Svyet, Yu Yan and myself.'

She handed the envelope to Svyet, who undid the flap and started to inspect the documents one by one.

'How on earth did you get these, Mama?' asked Svyet, at last showing some interest. 'And from both sides? Max would have been impressed by these and would have wanted a set for himself. He dislikes the Japanese and they dislike him. Somebody told him that, because of his poor face, he looked to the Japanese like a devil.'

'And to the Chinese, too,' said Yu Yan.

'Well, thanks to the French general, who you were so quick to dismiss, Svyet, I have been fortunate to meet people who can provide papers like these. In Harbin we were saved from violation and death by documents given us by the Japanese consul, to whom I happened to teach Russian.'

With that the table fell silent. Everyone suddenly felt terribly tired.

The meal was, in any case, almost over. The fish had been a wonder, followed by large helpings of vanilla ice cream with figs. The waiter brought coffee and small glasses of plum brandy. Svyet pulled out a pack of Russian *papirossy* and, except for Yu Yan, they each had one.

There were tensions only just beneath the surface. But, as they smoked their cigarettes, drank their coffee and plum brandy and sat back in the elegiac glow of candlelight, the three Polkonin women were as much at peace as they had ever been.

EPILOGUE
Spring, 1966

The rain beat hard on the train window. Behind it everything was daubed in shades of grey – sky, mountains, lake. The red roofs of houses and farm buildings provided occasional flashes of colour. The little stations passed in flares of electric light lasting only a second or two, long enough to see their reflection in pools of water on the platforms.

Gulya, alone on the afternoon express from Geneva to Montreux, tried to take refuge in a volume of poems by Anna Akhmatova, her idol. But the pull of the drab scene was more powerful. She let the book fall into her lap, rested her cheek on the cold glass of the window and stared out.

*

Six weeks earlier she had received a large, stiff invitation card, heavily embossed in ornately cursive script, topped with the Imperial Russian coat-of-arms in three-dimensional gold. It had been sent to her London address, where she had been living with her second husband since the mid-sixties.

The invitation was to the opening of an exhibition of Russian paintings from before the 1917 revolution at one of those posh galleries which lie in the angle between Jermyn Street and St James's. The invitation was in the name of one Count Mikhail Tolstoy. Gulya had never heard of him, though she was herself from the Tolstoy family. But they were a large clan, infiltrated by all kinds of imposters laying claim to the Tolstoy name.

As she passed through the front door of the elegant Zephyr Gallery a few hours later, she was approached from her left by a waiter with a tray of glasses of champagne and to her right by a dark, squat individual, who, with a deep bow, identified himself as Count Mikhail Tolstoy. A look of discomfort began to supplant his oily smile when she revealed that she, too, was a Tolstoy.

She took a glass of champagne, sipped it and asked, 'To which branch of the family do you belong? Are you from the Volga region or St Petersburg?'

She had already concluded that if he was a Tolstoy she was a Dutchman.

'Dear Madame Pallois,' replied the dubious count in heavily accented English that to her ear betrayed a Greek or Caucasian origin. 'We are from Estonia. I am afraid that I don't even speak Russian.'

She wondered whether he or his forebears had ever stepped foot in Estonia.

The count ploughed on regardless.

'But I have things that may be of interest to someone like yourself. In the room next door there are two walls which are – in my humble opinion – of special attraction. They are portraits from around the turn of the century of men and women of the old nobility. Pray, come with me.'

Trailing a strong scent of patchouli cologne, he led Gulya into a smaller room at the back of the gallery where there was an elderly couple whispering to each other in Russian.

Eight portraits hung on the walls, of surprising quality, a couple of Serovs among them. Gulya pointed this out to the count.

'Yes,' he replied proudly, 'they are the jewels in our crown. As is this. We don't know who he is. But look at the light in his eyes. Unfortunately, it is unsigned and the seller could not apparently recall the artist's name. We think it's by a pupil of Serov or even of Repin.'

It was a full-length portrait of a youngish man with dark, close-cropped hair in military dress uniform. His coat was dark blue, with gold epaulettes, collar and other military accoutrements. A sword hung from his waist. He held a cap in his right hand. The face was not exactly handsome, but it was strong, full of character. His big, luminous eyes held you in their gaze. He looked as if he was about to step out of the canvas, the very picture of determination and resolve.

Gulya stood transfixed. She went up close to the portrait and examined it in detail. Then stood back again. Her heart began to beat faster.

It was her father.

In real life she had, of course, never seen him as a young man. But there was no doubt. The artist had captured perfectly his eyes and the distinctive shape of his mouth and nose.

'You like him?' asked the count, looking at her curiously.

She did not answer directly. She felt out of breath, as if she had been running.

'How is he listed in your catalogue?'

'Portrait of An Unknown Russian Imperial Officer.'

The count, tired of waiting for a reply, went off to attend to the old couple.

They did not need much help. Like many émigrés of their generation, they were too impoverished to buy anything. Soon the count was back at Gulya's side.

'Where did you find him?' she asked.

'In Switzerland, Madame Pallois.'

'Yes, but where?'

'That, as they say, is a trade secret. My source deals exclusively with me, an arrangement which is conditional on my total discretion as to his identity. You see, he goes in and out of the Soviet Union in his search for artworks from this period. But not before a number of palms are greased with Swiss francs or American dollars. This is . . . how can I put it? . . . a sensitive, a delicate business. None of those involved on either side of this so-called Iron Curtain wish to attract publicity.'

'But were I to purchase this portrait, you might be a little more forthcoming with information?'

'I might be. What would you wish to know?'

'The dealer's name and address. You see, the man in the painting is my father. I have not seen him for more than thirty years.'

'Goodness me! Are you sure it's him?'

'I have no doubt.'

'What's his name?'

'Andrey Andreyevich Polkonin.'

She gave the count an extremely potted history of the family.

'Fascinating! Extraordinary! That explains your strange reaction to the portrait. You looked as if you had seen a ghost. I presume you wish to buy the painting.'

The count's eyes were lit with the hope of a payment over the odds for a family heirloom. Gulya guessed as much and quickly said, 'I can give you three hundred pounds. It's no good trying to barter. That's all the money I have.'

'There's always more money if you squeeze hard enough. With all my expenses and overheads I cannot afford to take less than five hundred pounds. I'm confident that I'll be able to make even more than that for such a gem.'

'Then so be it. There is nothing more to be said. I must take my leave,' she countered haughtily. She walked towards the exit.

Then, just as she was about to swallow her pride, turn on her heel and reopen negotiations, she heard: 'Madame Pallois!'

The count was approaching her at a trot.

'Four hundred pounds,' he said.

'Three hundred is the best I can do,' she retorted firmly, turning to walk away.

'All right, all right,' he retorted, his face a pantomime mask of weary resignation.

He did not want a cheque, but took the five ten-pound notes she had on her as a deposit.

She returned early the following morning with the balance. The painting had already been wrapped professionally.

'Only one thing remains,' she said. 'The name of your Swiss dealer.'

'He is not Swiss. He is partly Greek, like me. My Greek grandmother.

She was raped by a Captain Igor Tolstoy when the Russian army was fighting the Turks in Bulgaria. Strange to relate, she then proceeded to live with him happily ever after on his Baltic estate. My mother was the product of their union. She married the Russian steward of the estate. I inherited all her Greek features. But I think I can justifiably claim to be a member of the Tolstoy family, even if there is a little embroidery in my use of the title.'

'I think you can,' she replied. Now the deal was done, her irritation was replaced by guilt at her earlier disdain for this curious man who, just like her, had struggled to survive in a harsh world.

'Thank you, Madame Pallois,' said the count, holding her hand in both of his.

'The dealer's name is Georgiou Sokratis. He lives in the little town of Vevey, not far from Montreux, at the north-eastern end of Lac Léman. He has a shop called Sokratis et Fils at number 17, Avenue des Alpes. It is very dingy from the outside, but is something of an Aladdin's cave within. From what I remember, he obtained your painting locally. That is all I can tell you, Madame Pallois.'

'Would you mind telling this Mr Sokratis that I will be in touch? By all means say that I am searching for my father and may come to Vevey.' A thought occurred to her. 'You might wish to add that I still have family in Moscow. They could be of assistance to him in making contact with what is left of the old nobility.'

The count's eyes lit up. 'That would be helpful to me also.'

Counterfeit or not, he had a certain roguish charm.

*

Within the month, Gulya had exchanged letters with Mr Sokratis. Then she visited the Zephyr Gallery, where the count had promised to arrange a telephone call with him.

The count booked a call through the international operator. The count and Mr Sokratis shouted at each other in Greek at breakneck speed. Suddenly they stopped. The count passed her the telephone.

Mr Sokratis greeted her in very loud Russian. Then he switched to

English, still bellowing as if he were shouting to London from the top of the Matterhorn. Would she care to come to his office in four days' time? He was sorry to make this a little rushed, but he would be leaving for Moscow shortly thereafter.

'That sounds perfect, Mr Sokratis. Where would you suggest I stay?'

'You could stay at the Grand Hôtel du Lac. It is one of those slightly faded Edwardian hotels much loved by the English. It is on the lake with splendid views. It has comfortable rooms and an excellent kitchen. Shall I make a reservation for you?'

'Yes, please. Say, for three nights.' Then, unable to contain her impatience: 'Forgive me, Mr Sokratis, but did you buy the portrait from my father, General Andrey Andreyevich Polkonin?'

'That's what I was going to say. No, I did not. I must be frank. I cannot guarantee to be able to help you find your father. The invoice is in the name of another Russian, a Mr Lebedev. It was he who came to see me about the painting. He is my only link to it.'

She felt the hairs rise on the back of her neck. A vision from the past flashed before her eyes – of Max in his absurd English dandy's outfit, with colour-coordinated eye patch, standing on the steps of the Shanghai Club.

'What did he look like?'

'He bore no resemblance to the young officer in the painting. I remember him quite well. He was unusual. It was very hard at first to tell his age. He had an odd, smooth, plastic complexion. He kept one arm inside his jacket all the time, like Napoleon. At first, I would have said he was middle-aged. But his voice and movements were those of an elderly man.'

'What about his eyes?'

'Ah, yes. It took me a while to spot it, so well had it been made, but one of his eyes was glass. The left one, I think.'

'Extraordinary. You see, there was a time when Maxim Konstantinovich was my father's mortal enemy.'

'I know,' said Mr Sokratis.

'We shall have much to talk about, Mr Sokratis.'

She handed the telephone back to the count, who bellowed a Greek farewell and put down the receiver.

*

The rain had eased as her train pulled into Montreux. It was dusk. A shaft of light from the setting sun emerged briefly from the low grey clouds to fall upon the steep slopes behind the town. In the other direction, across the lake, the mountains were vanishing into the darkening gloom.

A porter carried Guyla's suitcase to the taxi rank, where she quickly found a driver to take her to the Grand Hôtel du Lac in Vevey. Once she had registered, an elegant Italian gentleman in a morning coat led the way to her room.

He introduced himself as the general manager, Signor Rossi. He explained that she was to be lodged in the Imperial Suite, so called because the Emperor Napoleon III and Empress Eugénie had once stayed there. This had been at the express request of Signor Sokratis.

'Mr Sokratis is well known to you?'

'Signora Pallois, he is well known throughout Vevey. Indeed, in Montreux as well.'

*

Next morning, Gulya awoke with the dawn. The rain clouds had disappeared, revealing a sweeping view across the lake towards Saint-Gingolph and the mountains behind. The sky was a clear, pale blue in the early light. It promised a beautiful day.

The young man at reception told her that she could walk to Mr Sokratis' office in ten minutes. It would take another ten to walk to the adjoining commune of La-Tour-de-Peilz where, according to her mother, her father might be.

Armed with the hotel's map, she stepped out into the morning sun. The water sparkled in the brilliant sunlight. The steam ferry to Lausanne, with its tall, thin funnel, chugged past. It was all very peaceful, but it couldn't counter her growing unease at the possibility of meeting her father.

Before long she came to a sign announcing that she had entered La-Tour-de-Peilz, and realised with a shock that she was only a few metres from the street where Andrey had once lived – or perhaps lived still. Butterflies took hold of her stomach.

Number 14 rue du Chateau was a narrow three-storey brick building, with a small wrought-iron balcony on the first and second floors. There were three doorbells. None bore the name Polkonin. Just as she was about to try her luck with one of the bells, the front door opened and a woman asked in French if she could help.

'Yes, please, if you don't mind. I am looking for a Colonel Polkonin. I was told that he might be living at this address.'

The woman looked her up and down, unsmilingly. She was probably in her late fifties. Her grey hair was severely pulled back into a bun. Her face was tired but not unattractive, and Gulya sensed a good figure hidden beneath her drab clothes. She must have been quite a beauty in her day.

She held a feather duster in one hand, which she tapped impatiently against the other, as if she were about to strike Gulya.

'I can see the likeness. You must be his daughter,' she said abruptly.

'Is Colonel Polkonin here?'

'No. Andrey's long gone – and good riddance. When you find him, will you please tell him that he still owes me forty francs' rent.'

An instinct made Gulya immediately reach into her bag, from which she pulled two twenty-franc notes, offering them to the woman.

'I am afraid my father was never very good at managing money.'

'Well, nothing has changed.'

She took the notes quickly, as if they might disappear, and remained on the doorstep.

'How did he come to lodge with you?'

She did not answer immediately. For a few moments she gazed abstractedly over Gulya's right shoulder. Then she began to speak. 'From time to time I take in lodgers sent by the Red Cross. One day the Red Cross sent me Colonel Polkonin. They said that he was a Russian aristocrat who had lost everything in the Revolution, including his family. At first I thought he was ideal. He was cultured and his manners were impeccable.'

She paused and looked at the ground, turning her head slowly from side to side. It was clear what she was thinking – *more fool me*.

'Please go on,' said Gulya gently.

'A friendship developed between us. He would take me to tea every Friday at the Grand Hôtel du Lac. In the evenings, we would have supper together, talk about art, literature, world events. He was so knowledgeable. I thought it was truly a relationship made in heaven. But it was nothing of the sort. It was made in hell!'

Her last words sprang from the deepest well of bitterness.

Gulya put it as delicately as she could. 'Did my father take advantage of you?'

The bamboo handle of the duster snapped in her hands.

'Yes, I gave myself to him – though at his age it did not add up to much,' she said, with dismissive contempt. 'All was going swimmingly. Then the money from the Red Cross stopped coming in. Andrey promised to get a job. He said he would have no difficulty obtaining a position with the *Tribune de Genève* as a writer on international affairs. I don't think he ever did, or even tried. Occasionally, he would give me some cash. He had led me to believe that we would be married! Then I found a letter inside his trouser pocket. It was from another woman. It was filled with intimate endearments and talk of their future together. I confronted him with his betrayal. Andrey went up to his room without saying a word. Then he came downstairs, carrying his suitcase. He looked at me and said coolly, "I have clearly outlived my welcome. It is time for me to go." Then he walked out of the front door. That was two years ago. I have no idea where he is living and I do not want to know.'

She sobbed piteously for a few moments. Then she pulled herself together, blowing her nose loudly into a handkerchief.

'I am told that if you want to see him, you should ask at the Russian church in Vevey. That is why you will never find me in that part of town.'

*

Gulya's entrance into Mr Sokratis' dingy shop was announced by a loud bell attached by string to the door. After the bright sunlight outdoors, she could barely see a thing. Then at the back of the room she spotted a shape of great height and bulk standing behind a desk.

'Madame Pallois, I presume. Good morning, or should I say afternoon,' the shape rumbled in Russian. 'I am Sokratis. Call me Georgy.'

'And I am Olga Pallois.'

'Welcome to Vevey. I hope you have settled in comfortably at the Grand Hôtel du Lac. I told that scoundrel Rossi I would be after him if he did not give you one of their finest suites.' Georgy Sokratis let out a low rumbling laugh.

As they moved to shake hands, Gulya saw before her a vast hulk of a man, in a dark blue pin-stripe suit, the stripes too broad to be entirely in good taste. Atop this colossus was a huge, hairless head. The face was fleshy, with a large, straight nose, full lips, dark eyes and a jutting chin. He might still have been in his forties, but his bulk made him look ten years older.

'May I offer you a glass of champagne?' he asked while assessing her. 'It is after noon.'

His detached, appraising gaze turned into a charming smile and twinkling eyes. He moved with surprising grace and speed to a small refrigerator hidden behind a Second Empire china nude and extracted a bottle of Roederer and two glasses.

They drank a toast to finding Andrey and got down to business.

Georgy recounted how Max Lebedev had come to the shop one day with Andrey's portrait wrapped in a blanket. Georgy liked the portrait a great deal. He agreed that it could be a Serov or a Repin. Max had been quite frank. The painting belonged to a friend who needed money. It was not easy to survive in Switzerland as a destitute septuagenarian refugee. They had haggled a bit, but it was not long before they settled on a price. Max had borrowed Georgy's phone and had spoken briefly to someone in Russian. Then he had signed the bill of sale.

'That, I assume, was my father,' Gulya interjected.

'Quite,' Georgy replied. 'I even asked – on a hunch and at the risk of seeming overly inquisitive – whom he had called and whether it might be the young officer in the portrait. Max had confirmed this without hesitation, explaining that his friend was ashamed to have to sell the portrait because of his straitened financial circumstances.'

'You must, Georgy, have an address with the bill of sale.'

'I do. But neither your father nor Max lives there, as I have just found out. After you and I had spoken, I decided to drop by to give Max the good news that the portrait had been sold in London to, of all people, Colonel Polkonin's daughter. But he had gone.'

'Surely he left a forwarding address?'

'Apparently not. His landlady said he was perfectly polite and always paid the rent on time. But he didn't like to talk, especially about his past. All she knew was that he was a Russian, who was one of the Red Cross refugees. Occasionally, another elderly Russian, who walked with a stick, would come round for tea. Max had once introduced him as his oldest friend.'

'How bizarre!' Gulya interrupted. 'If that really was my father, they were once sworn enemies. Max was a Red and my father a White.'

Georgy's face was alive with interest, his dark eyes shining.

'I think I can explain that, too,' he said. 'You see, Max found out – heaven knows how – that I was looking for him. He paid me a call last night.'

'Did you get him to say where he was living?'

'I did. He was perfectly straightforward about it. He and your father share a caretaker's cottage at the Russian church in rue des Communaux. You'll see. It's tiny. But they don't have to pay anything. In return they look after the church and open it up when the Archdeacon holds a service. Anyway, over a bottle of Scotch in my shop I got Max to talk some more. It was fascinating.'

'So, my father is definitely alive.'

'Most definitely.'

*

At the Grand Hôtel du Lac, Signor Rossi led them to a table on the tree-shaded terrace with uninterrupted views over the lake, where they lunched on a platter of cold lobster and grilled fish – *féra*, caught in the lake that very morning – with an excellent Saint-Véran.

Eventually, after Georgy had ordered raspberry soufflé and another bottle of Saint-Véran, Gulya decided to open the batting, as the English say.

'Tell me, Georgy, what did Max have to say under the influence of your Scotch?'

'Max more or less said the same thing as you. He and your father had first met as enemies on opposite sides of the Russian Civil War. There had been some incident in Ukraine when they were saved from shooting each other by a German air raid. But the raid had cost Max an arm and had horribly disfigured his face. For years he blamed your father; he made it his life's work to hunt him down and take revenge. But your father had always eluded him.

'Time passed. Max rose rapidly in the ranks of the NKVD. But in the 1930s his luck ran out. He fell victim to the murderous infighting inside the NKVD. He was lucky not to have been shot. Instead, he was banished to Shanghai, a notorious listening post for the world's spies. His brief – to find out whether the Japs intended attacking the Soviet Union through China – was an important one. Stalin himself took a personal interest. Yet it was still exile. It was the start of his rapid disillusionment with the Soviet system.

'Then he received a warning that he was suspected by Moscow of being a Japanese spy. According to his informant, he risked assassination or kidnap to the Soviet Union. So, without telling a soul, Max fled Shanghai.'

'Where on earth did he go? Hong Kong?' asked Gulya.

'Yes, but only to catch a boat to Manila. He feared he would be too easy to find in Hong Kong. Manila, he said, was a place where you could go to ground, especially if you had money, as he did. He had the damage to his face repaired at a clinic, where a shady Hungarian doctor specialised in changing the looks of those who needed to disappear.

'He told me he liked the Philippines. He might have settled there. But then, as in Shanghai, the Japanese came calling. Once again he had to leave in a hurry. And, eventually, he wangled his way into the safety of Switzerland. By then he felt secure enough to resume being Max Lebedev again.'

Georgy paused to take a long draw on his cigar.

'Sometime in 1948 Max was sitting on his bed in the Red Cross hostel in Gstaad, when your father walked in. They were introduced by the hostel manager. It was their first encounter since the railway station in Lvov. There was a moment's hesitation on each side. They shook hands hesitantly. Then they burst out laughing and fell into each other's arms. Their laughter became hysterical and then turned into mighty, soul-wrenching sobs. Max said that they had clung to each other like two sailors adrift in the ocean. By all accounts they have been the best of friends ever since. Now they lodge together, with Max looking after your father, who can barely walk.'

'How and when did my father get out of China?'

'Max didn't say. But I imagine it wasn't that difficult in the chaos of revolution.

'And that, dear Olga,' he declaimed like a Shakespearean actor of the old school, 'is the story of how Max Lebedev came to live with your father in an *izba* in the grounds of the Russian Orthodox Church of St Barbara.'

She smiled to herself, thinking of those two old men, all hatred spent.

'Fate plays such a strange hand, don't you think, Georgy? Capricious, often cruel, setting ambushes for us all. My mother often says that our family should have suffered a violent end several times over.'

Gulya paused, thinking of Granny Alissa. After Alissa returned to St Petersburg from Harbin, she was never heard from again. Eventually, they discovered that, not as they had thought, she had been taken off her train at the Soviet frontier and detained by the NKVD, then sent to a labour camp in the far north-east, one of the harshest. Already frail, she wouldn't have survived for long. Gulya thought, too, of poor

Olivier, her first husband, who had died heroically in 1945 defending the French flag at Hué in French Indochina. Gulya had been pregnant with their daughter.

'Yet, thanks to fate, I and all those I love most have survived,' she continued. 'In the end fate has been our great protector. Is there some divine pattern to all this?'

'Dear Olga, if there is one, I am damned if I can see it.'

It was now Georgy's turn to look at his watch.

'Rossi! *La dolorosa, per favore!* I will take you to the church, if I may, and then leave you to it.'

Georgy made to haul his great bulk from the chair, when Gulya said, 'Hold on, Georgy, it doesn't matter if we're a few minutes late. There's a loose end.'

Georgy fell back into his chair.

'Svyetlana. Svyet. My sister. Max's wife. Did Max have anything to say about her? You see, it was while they were together at the American consul's Fourth of July party in 1937 that he disappeared into thin air.'

'That's a detail Max didn't mention,' said Georgy.

'She never saw him or heard from him again. For her it is a great mystery, which haunts her to this day. Is there anything you know that I can tell her?'

'She now lives in Moscow?'

'Yes. Svyet rebuilt her life there and married a professor of linguistics. My mother is there as well. Immediately after Mao's takeover, life in China became intolerable. Like my father, they had to leave.'

'I hope it was not a case of out of the frying pan into the fire.'

'Probably! Things were very tough while Stalin lived. They were treated with great suspicion, like most returning exiles. At one point my mother and sister thought they would be interned. But then Stalin died and under Khruschev life has become more tolerable. My sister has a flourishing career as a writer and journalist. My mother leads a peaceful life as a part-time librarian.'

'Have you been to Moscow to see them?'

'Every year for the last three years and I am going again later this year, this time with my husband and little daughter, Katya. But we are digressing.'

'Yes, we are. But I think I have the answer. It was the last of Max's nuggets, courtesy of Johnnie Walker. I must warn you – it may not be something you would want to pass on to your sister.'

'That's for me to judge. Go on, Georgy.'

He was unexpectedly hesitant, searching for words.

'Max told me that he had met your sister quite by chance at Shanghai University, where he worked his cover. She let slip who her father was. Max could barely believe his luck. He set out to seduce and marry her in the sure belief that she would lead him to your father. He had, he confessed, no other feelings for her – indeed, he found her rather irritating. But then his disenchantment with his superiors and the Soviet system grew to such a point that it not only extinguished his Leninist faith but also his lust for revenge against your father. That in turn removed all motive for staying with Svyet. Her presence increasingly grated on him. You see, according to Max, he fled not only to be rid of the KGB, but also to be rid of his wife, your sister. That, actually, was the greater relief to him.'

'Poor Svyet. Yes, I remember their relationship deteriorating before my eyes. But, of course, I didn't know why. Sometimes, though, I think my mother had an inkling.'

Georgy lit a cigar and drained an espresso. He was basking in the beauty of the day. But at the mention of Katya, he sat bolt upright.

'Now you are talking, dear Olga. If there is mystery anywhere in the Polkonin saga, it lies above all with your mother. This is something I did not want to broach with you until we had got to know each other better – until, to be frank, we had built a certain level of trust between us. But you have, as it were, forced it out into the open.'

'Georgy, you are speaking in riddles. Explain yourself.'

Georgy thought for a moment. He reached across the table and put his massive right hand, like a bear's paw, over Gulya's.

'My grandmother used to say that there was no fool like an old fool. I am an old fool. Wine and a beautiful woman have always been my undoing. I talk too much. I become indiscreet. I show off. I am pitiful.'

'Georgy, will you please tell me what on earth you are talking about.'

Georgy was genuinely in turmoil. He kept looking at her, then at the table, then back. Then, all of a sudden, he became perfectly still.

'I beg you, dear Olga, for your utmost discretion. Not a word must be said of what I am about to tell you to anyone, above all not to your sister, not to your mother, not to any relatives and friends in the Soviet Union. It is not a matter of life and death, or at least I don't think it is. But if the *vlasti* were to learn that I had told you these things, that would be the end of my business in Russia.'

'Who do you mean by the *vlasti*?'

'Shall we just say the powers that be in Moscow?'

There was a pause while he hesitated on the edge of his high diving board of revelations. Then he took the plunge.

'You see, *ma chère* Olga, I have been buying and selling works of art on behalf of Soviet clients for many years now, even in the Stalinist period. Do not imagine that this has been possible without an oiling of the wheels. Sometimes this has involved a gift here, a gift there, a bribe here, a bribe there. But more and more, to preserve my Russian business, I have allowed myself to become ensnared in a spider's web spun by the *vlasti*.'

'Come clean, Georgy, what is it they require of you? Are you a spy?'

'I am not, dear Olga. I pay for the privilege of being allowed to trade in *objets d'art* from Russia in the coin of information. I am a vacuum cleaner that sucks up high-grade gossip as and when I find it on my travels. I keep an eye on the Russian community in Switzerland, particularly around here. Geneva and Montreux are good listening posts, as good as Shanghai used to be. I pay Rossi for scraps of information on the guests at the Grand Hôtel du Lac.'

'You are the very definition of a spy, Georgy! But where does my mother fit into all this? You have found out something about her, haven't you?'

Georgy was now perspiring.

'After Tolstoy – who incidentally plays a similar role in London to mine here – told me about the portrait and your search for your father, I mentioned this to someone of authority in Moscow. He looked in the archives and found a fat file from the 1930s on your mother.'

'Goodness!' Gulya exclaimed.

'There is nothing to worry about,' said Georgy, shaking his head. 'On the contrary. The *vlasti* have an unusually favourable view of her. I did not get much in the way of detail because we were talking on the phone. But, apparently, at great risk to her life, she informed against the Japanese while working for them. This went on for years, in Harbin and in Shanghai. The astonishing thing is that she may have been working on her own account.'

'I know she had a very great friend in the Chinese resistance to the Japanese invasion of Manchuria,' Gulya said carefully. 'She also had some kind of pull with the Japanese authorities, because she saved the both of us from violation and murder when the Japanese army marched into Harbin.'

'All that is in her file. There are one or two in Moscow who would even say – I know, it sounds fantastical – that the Soviet victory over the Japs at Khalkhin Gol in '39 was ultimately hers. When she and your sister arrived in the Soviet Union from China in '51, they were indeed destined for the labour camps of Norilsk, like almost all the returnees. But someone at the highest level stepped in and spared them.'

'Who stepped in?'

Georgy opened his palms and shrugged his shoulders.

'Who knows? I don't. Let's go.'

They drove to the Russian church in the rue des Communaux.

'I got the hotel to phone ahead and say we – you – were coming. We don't want the old boys fainting from shock.'

The church was large and white, unmistakably Russian with a gold onion dome on top. The gates were open.

A tall, bearded figure emerged from the church, dressed in a long black religious tunic, buttoned from top to bottom.

'That's the Archdeacon Sergei. He is quite young and active in the Russian community.'

'Is he an eavesdropper, too?' Gulya asked on an impulse.

'Don't ask, don't tell,' replied Georgy, a light smile playing on his lips. 'Let me introduce you.'

The Archdeacon greeted them in Russian. Close up he looked to be in his thirties, well built, with ruddy cheeks above the dark, black hairs of his beard. He exuded energy and restlessness.

Archdeacon Sergei grasped her hand and shook it vigorously. He smiled broadly, his large white teeth a striking contrast with the blackness of his beard.

'Welcome, welcome, Madame Pallois. I am very confident that in a few moments you and your father will be reunited in this, God's house. Let us go in. When your eyes get used to the gloom, you will see two figures seated in the front row, with their backs to you. One, with a stick, is your father and the other, with one arm, is his companion, Maxim Konstantinovich Lebedev.'

She walked up the steps and pushed open the church door. Her nerves were shot. The interior was as gloomy as Archdeacon Sergei had said it would be, but she could dimly discern the two silhouettes sitting in the front row.

As she approached them and her footsteps became audible, the talking stopped. One of the men got slowly to his feet and turned.

His face was like an alabaster mask in the shadowy light. If you had dressed him in priestly clothes and got him to stand still, he could have taken his place with the plaster saints, whose statues adorned the interior of the church. It was unmistakably Maxim Konstantinovich.

He stretched out his one arm towards her,

'Gulya, Gulya, more beautiful than ever,' he cried. 'Look how your daughter has blossomed over the years, Andrey.'

She had walked round the end of their pew and was now standing in front of Andrey. Compared with Max, many more years had passed since they had last seen each other. He had lost nearly all his hair. His body was shrivelled, his face wizened. If he were her father, he was a hunched, diminished version.

Then the sun emerged from behind a cloud and shone its light through the stained-glass windows onto the little group of three. It cast a clear, yellowy brightness on the old man's face. She could see the eyes looking at her: judging, critical, slightly irritable, slightly impatient, the can't-you-do-better-than-this-Gulya look which she had endured in childhood, before Katya expelled him from the family.

'Hello, Papa.'

'As usual, Gulya, you are late.'

AFTERWORD
By Catherine Meyer

My mother was 100 years old when she died in Paris in 2017. From the day she was born in Petrograd, on the eve of the Russian Revolution, she found herself caught in a succession of revolutions, civil wars, invasions, massacres and conflicts. Her life story is one of courage and fortitude – a determination to survive.

My mother was only a baby when her family was forced to escape from the Bolsheviks. Their perilous journey across Siberia was overshadowed by the fear of capture and execution, but they managed finally to arrive in Harbin, Manchuria, in 1920.

China proved to be as dangerous as Russia as their fate was now determined by the alternating dominance of Russia, China and Japan. Caught in the middle of the power struggle between the warlords, the Chinese civil war, the Japanese invasions and their brutal massacres, my mother lived in constant fear of attack and often in poverty. When the Japanese invaded and occupied Manchuria, she was forced to move to Peking, to Shanghai, then as Japan entered WWII, to Hanoi, Hué and finally Saigon, where at last she found love and security.

In 2015, a French historian published a book on my family's epic history. Mother was not entirely happy with it. She adored Christopher and persistently nagged him to write her story in English. When Christopher retired, he decided to take on the task. As he did so, he began to transform her story into a novel, introducing fictitious characters and imaginary episodes into the narrative. By the time he had finished he had written more than 200,000 words.

It has been a daunting task to edit Christopher's manuscript. Removing passages that were characteristic of his personality – funny, sometimes sardonic, always discerning and even, on occasions, rather surprisingly, fond of animals – nearly broke my heart. Particularly, when I see Christopher sitting on the terrace of our Megève flat, still tweaking his manuscript, on the very afternoon he died on 28 July 2022. He could not let go of it. *Survivors* had become part of him. It was a work of love that he was never to see published.

I hope that you will understand why I wanted to publish this book. I hope that you enjoyed reading it as much as I did.

Printed in Great Britain
by Amazon